Sweet and Tender Hooligan

IAN PATTISON was born in Glasgow. He lives and works there. This is his second novel for Picador.

Also by Ian Pattison

A Stranger Here Myself
Being the life story and revelations of
Mister Rab C. Nesbitt of Govan

IAN PATTISON

Sweet and Tender Hooligan

PICADOR

First published 2003 by Picador
an imprint of Pan Macmillan Ltd
Pan Macmillan, 20 New Wharf Road, London N1 9RR
Basingstoke and Oxford
Associated companies throughout the world
www.panmacmillan.com

ISBN 0 330 41199 3

1 3 5 7 9 8 6 4 2

A CIP catalogue record for this book is available from
the British Library.

Typeset by SetSystems Ltd, Saffron Walden, Essex
Printed and bound in Great Britain by
Mackays of Chatham plc, Chatham, Kent

To Andrea

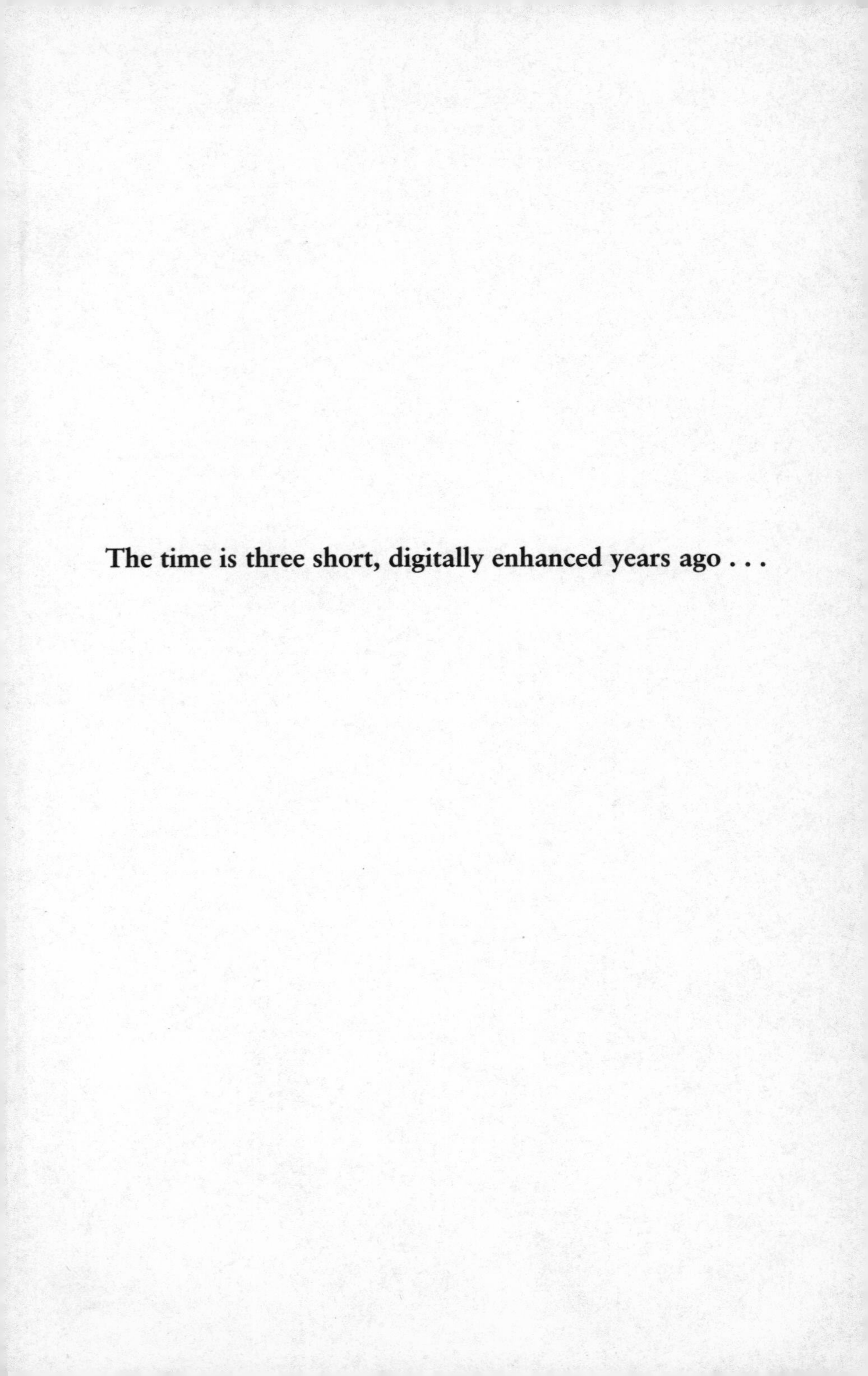

The time is three short, digitally enhanced years ago . . .

Chapter One

I had liked the Krays. They were always prepared to give youth a chance. I had played a trial for them, back in the late sixties. By then, they knew the great team they'd built up had peaked and while they were on the lookout for new blood, my name had come up. I travelled down on the overnight bus and did a spot of violence for them in south Kent. I acquitted myself well, I recall, and was complimented on my performance, which I thought a nice touch. There were handshakes all round and I returned to Glasgow to await what I thought would be the offer of a contract and the beginning of a glittering career of mayhem. As the whole world knows, they were arrested soon afterwards and the rest is, well, infamy. Naturally, I was gutted. My stab at the big time had gone. For a long while afterwards I couldn't even look at a hammer without a lump springing to my throat. Older now, I realize everything in life is timing. You keep going though, don't you? You pick yourself up. And after all, what else was I to do? We're talking about my only gift.

I'd never wanted to be a gangster. Not the Scottish kind anyway. Who wants to fight twenty battles a week in your good suit then die in a hostel with nothing in your pocket but your balls. I had always craved life with as little unnecessary fuss as possible. I was renowned for the economy of my style. I'd single out my victim, step up behind him and bludgeon him six to twelve times with a weighty implement. Which is how I acquired my nickname, the Surgeon. I didn't go in for that square go, Queensbury rules malarkey, in a fair fight I might easily lose, then I'd have to lug some hideous debilitating wound around with me from that moment to my grave. I once watched two Shropshire lads hold a rival down, shove a boning knife up his arse and twist. I had nightmares for weeks. I always knew violence hurt like fuck, which is why I approached it in the way I did, with extreme fear and a need to get it over with quickly. A bit like this funeral I was on my way to attend – my mother's, as it happened.

I travelled by aeroplane, of course. I used to travel business class, when I was working, but as I'm semi-retired I sat in economy with the plebs, with my knees scrunched up and fighting for the armrest like everyone else. I enjoyed decent health, except for a back complaint that gave me a nagging, ongoing form of gyp. That was why, whenever I travelled on a plane, I never put my document bag up on the overhead locker, I shoved it behind me, like a cushion, to keep me straight. People told me it was a stress-related ailment. But that was only because they knew what I did and made assumptions. When I said, 'Fair enough, if it's a stress-related ailment, why don't I have a heart attack instead?' they tended to grow more reticent with their medical opinions. The thing was, in this case, I think they may have been right. I hadn't been up north in over five years and there'd been a reason for that; I'd been waiting for the right moment for a change in my emotional climate. Well lately I'd felt a lightness return to my battered old soul and a spring to my faltering step, both of which dovetailed nicely with my mother dropping dead from a fatal stroke. In short, I was taking it as an encouraging sign.

*

I lived in West London, in Bayswater. I'd a little basement flat, big enough for one person with maybe the occasional long-weekend stopover, but that was it, otherwise I was solo. I'd shut my front door, walk up the steps and three minutes later I'd be in Hyde Park. You could lose yourself in Hyde Park. I liked that. Which was all the more reason for my feeling a bit fluttery about having to make this trip to Glasgow. I nearly called it a duty trip, but it was more than that. If all went well, I'd have achieved a laudable double whammy; I'd have buried the Cuntess and restored myself to my former hooligan pomp. All in all, there was a good deal to be nervous about and, as I considered the possibilities, the clenching ache in my lower back seemed the least of my concerns. Not for the first time, it occured to me I'd made a poor career choice all those years ago.

*

I'd had a normal upbringing, so normal it sounded sinister when I talked about it. My father died when I was nine, and again about five years later, but no one told him, so he still sits around the public park with Ruth Rendell on his lap, smiling at passers-by. Like most, and excuse me, I do use the term blushingly, gangsters, I have a father complex. People assume we have a mother complex because we're all supposed to be kind to our dear old mums, but when did you ever hear the Krays talk about their dear old dad? People talk about what they're comfortable with, they keep schtum about the rest. Anyway, I never used to have this father complex, at least not until he turned into my mother, but I'll come to that. To begin at the beginning, he once borrowed money from the wrong people. In those days, as now, there were right wrong people from whom to borrow in times of desperation and there were wrong wrong people.

The right wrong people would cut you some slack, as they say nowadays, indulge your lowly punter status with a spot of latitude before reluctantly reaching for the big stick with the nails through it. They saw themselves as keen-jawed career criminals with bigger fish to fry. They didn't want their valuable time eaten up with kicking the shit out of some whimpering factory hand for twenty quid he didn't have. They were rational. If they hurt him, he couldn't work, if he couldn't work, he couldn't repay, so nobody got anywhere. Basically, it was in their best interests as sensible thugs to smile sympathetically and put it on the interest. That way a twenty-pound debt soon turned to forty, then sixty, and before he knew it, the whimperer was carrying a debt-burden it would need Bono making a waiver appeal to the United Nations to tackle. So it was important to know the calibre of cunt from whom you were borrowing. To borrow from the wrong wrong people meant an enraged pummelling on default, with no exceptions, followed by a heavier beating for every subsequent offence. This *modus operandi* was a symptom of insecurity on the part of the wrong wrong people. These were actually sensitive souls, bone-headed clumpers who lived in fear of being sniggered at by the more intelligent and culturally advanced right wrong people, so they compensated themselves by hobbling home with stubbed toes and bloodied chinos. Perversely, my father borrowed wrongly by borrowing from the right wrong people, he should have borrowed from the wrong wrong people and got it all over with a near-death beating or two. My father had a capacity for absorbing pain. After all, he married my mother.

Until my father borrowed fifty from Billy Waugh, we didn't even know a bad person, at least not knowingly. Our horizons were limited. If we lifted our heads, all we saw were other people with limited horizons. Good people, or if not good then ordinary, wave upon wave of these ordinary good cunts, as far as the eye could see. My eye anyway; because I'm talking in an intended singular here. I had a patch over one eye, the right eye, to correct a squint, until I was ten. Billy Waugh took it off. What I'm saying is, my family was ordinary up till then, up until the day we borrowed that fifty. After that, we were dipped in shit by the heels, Nothing was the same again. So why did my father borrow the fifty? If I told you it was for the greater glory of his wife, the Cuntess, would you be surprised, even at this stage? Fucking fifty.

There's no question my mother was a good-looking woman. Even I knew that, and I speak as a healthy young Scot who was revolted by the idea of human emotion. I picture her with a towel around her hair, wearing my father's coat for a dressing gown and peeling dead skin from her heels with the blade from his Gillette. If my father had been a butcher or a cobbler we'd still have gone without meat or shoes if it meant he had to steal. The fact that he worked in a cardboard box factory meant the lack of perks was less dramatic or regrettable.

My father was honest as the day was long, and by fuck was it a long day. He rose at six, and left at six thirty. In the half hour between rising and leaving he crept around our tiny flat with the stealth of a housebreaker, his presence no more than a faint rustle in the air, or the odd creak of a floorboard as he washed, dressed himself and made ready to face whatever challenge the world of cardboard would throw at him that day.

How do I picture him? The thing is, I don't. I can't see him anywhere. Perhaps that's because he's at my side, lackey like, steadying my mental camera. I've a copy of their wedding picture in a Waitrose bag. One day, or never, I'll assemble the ingredients of a stable domestic life again and dot a few nostalgic mementoes around my living space but, if truth be told, I haven't the peace of mind for that, for years now everything's felt, well, temporary. Now and then, after a few too many red wines I'll rustle the bag and stare into the faces of these two dangerous nincompoops, my mother and father, the Prick and the Cuntess. There they stand, in Burton's suit and Littlewoods' dress, aspiring to look a million dollars but achieving about four and eightpence.

My mother liked to go out and my father liked to stay in. My mother married my father for security, hers, of course, not his. He took her on the rebound, otherwise he'd never have had a sniff, so hell mend him. Women always gravitate towards a boring cunt after a let down; they need to wipe their feet on somebody before skipping off again with some other preening bastard just like the one who shat on them before. When I say my mother liked to go out, it paints a false instant picture. She wasn't one of those cackling peroxide yahoos with lipstick on her teeth, but a rather quiet, intense woman, possessed of some unspecified yearning, the only outlet for which was noisy pubs on Friday nights.

*

I prefered to fly British Airways, rather than British Midland. In the old days, I preferred Midland, the slobber was about the same but Midland clinched the deal with the hot towel. Trash like me responded to those little touches of puerile pampering. Midland were concentrating their favours on business-class passengers, which no longer included me. Being with the dogs in the cheap seats meant you didn't even get the hot towel, let alone hot slobber, the stewardess just came bowling down the aisle chucking these cling-wrapped cheese rolls at you. On long haul, you could catch glimpses of the posh cunts through the curtain of Club class, all wolfing down the tasty treats and gulping back the miniatures as they tapped on laptops and daydreamed about pole dancers. I couldn't use a laptop in a public place. And I'd sooner do a Highland fling than stand in a departure lounge braying into a mobile phone. So I travelled with Airways, for the hot slobber and the residue of past glories when I'd Red Star my tools ahead and have them greet me at the airport.

The fact was, there were a number of persons I wasn't at all keen on meeting. These persons, it was fair to say, were persons who entertained reasons, real or imagined, to bear me a grudge. The upshot of these grudges was that I was fearful of being pummelled, or murdered. A pummelling I could just about accommodate. I enjoyed, as I said, reasonable health and, provided I went down in a crouch and protected my weak back against a wall and covered my head with my arms, I was confident I could survive even an exuberant assault. A murder I was less sure about; though I have been left for dead on at least one occasion and survived not to tell the tale. Call me a traditionalist, but my area of endeavour still demanded a code of silence and any person who knew when to stop gibbering was worthy, in my world, of at least a vestigial respect. So I'd always maintained a dignified schtum concerning the events of my life.

Let me qualify that slightly; I'd blabbed the lot in a book I once wrote. It was called, embarrassingly, *They Call Me the Surgeon*, and it peaked at number nineteen in the spring bestseller lists between Alan Titchmarsh going up and Sophie Grigson coming down, before tumbling, ignominiously, into the 'all at two pounds' bin at Bargain Books. Perhaps you've seen it. I'm pictured on the front cover in my midnight blue violence suit, holding two hatchets criss-crossed over my chest. This was my idea, one I'd reconstructed from James Dean in that crucifixion pose with the rifle. Of course it's done to death now, what with Chopper Read and Vinnie Jones, but to be fair, maybe they just borrowed from the source, as I did. I'd wanted hammers for artistic purity, but the publishers were persuasive, arguing that this might confuse the casual browser into assuming we were yet another DIY manual. So hatchets it was. I'd made a timely fifty grand out of that book and it changed my life in ways I was still struggling to come to terms with.

I said I'd been left for dead once, call it twice if you count how I felt when Felice walked out. Felice. You didn't meet bints called that in my circles, books did that, books and the imagined allure of mayhem. Up till then, being Scottish, I'd only met Isobels and Sandras. And of course, Brenda, my ex-wife. The book gave me a calling card to the exotic world of Feliceness and for a while I was, pardon my English, entranced. The trouble was, during the period of monkish discipline under which I'd written the book, I'd failed to take into account that people might one day, well, read it. And while I'm not stating it's bullshit, I will admit there is excrement and that some of it is, yes, bovine. The fact was, I'd found it hard to write about my experience nakedly, in the first person, which is a drawback in an autobiography. But once I had the idea for the front cover it liberated me, I knew who I was supposed to be and that's the 'I' I wrote up to, if that makes any sense.

Anyway, the upshot was, I was on this plane to Glasgow for this fucking funeral and I was worried shitless because it was the first time I'd been back since the book came out and even the people I knew were not averse to picking up a yarn once in a while. So what, Albert? you may say. So what if they'd read your book and taken issue with your robust salty style, or interpretation of events. 'Fair enough', I'd say to you, fair enough, if we were talking a verbal savaging from Mark Lawson on the *Late Review*; 'Fine', I'd say, 'fine, here's my bare chest, lash it with vitriol.' The trouble was, literary criticism in my circles took on a different form, it was more, how shall I say, visceral. The fact was, if I ran into the wrong people I could expect recrimination, even if I had changed the names to protect the guilty. Unfortunately, I'd written the book at the wrong time, needy, as I've said, of the money.

Generally, these books are written by venerable elder statesmen, at the arse end of distinguished careers in mayhem. People who once tried to saw each other's legs off, now sitting playing dominoes together, or augmenting their pensions by bussing tourists round the quaint old East End sites of carnage past. The trouble was, my peers aren't yet these august gentlemen, they're more, so to speak, June and July, middle-aged and fearful, blindly stabbing, kicking and gouging to stay up with, let alone ahead of, the ever younger pack. The last thing they wanted was some poncy anglophile like me churning up the sediment of the recent past before it had even had a chance to settle. If it was lonely at the top, it was fucking seething at the middle.

All these thoughts were coursing through my restless mind as I nursed my warm lemonade and dug stringy ham from a molar with a plastic toothpick. Why didn't these bastards give us our dinner like in the old days? Why was there one law for the rich and another for the envious? And why had I drawn attention to myself by writing that fucking book? Oh yes, and in amongst all that I was thinking about my mother, and grieving and that. Old cunt.

*

I was an only child. They'd intended having more but plans changed as relations deteriorated and mother discovered other distractions in life. When I was about eight there was a brief flicker of hope when my father spotted a man putting his arm around her outside a pub and decided to remonstrate. I was with my father, I recall, and as it was late at night by an eight-year-old's standards, I can only assume he'd gone there out of suspicion. We stood outside waiting, I remember, and my father gave me Toffos. When my mother appeared with her group of friends, I made to run towards her but my father held me back. That's when this swaying bear in a suit appeared and put his arm around her waist, and pulled her in towards him. To be fair to my mother, she didn't do anything to encourage him, but to be fair to my father, she didn't do anything to discourage him either. I saw my father steel himself and walk towards the group. He was in his shirtsleeves which made him look desperate in the drizzly night. I called for him to come back. When he wouldn't, I ran towards him and pulled his arm like a brake as hard as I could. When he gripped me round the wrist and wrenched me off, I realized I was a mere adjunct to the proceedings, with no role to play other than that of a poignant child. The group of women froze and stopped laughing when they saw my father coming towards them. They looked embarrassed and, if recollection serves, expectantly thrilled. My mother didn't look embarrassed, I noticed, she stood serenely, cradling her handbag in her arms.

My father wasn't looking at my mother, he was glaring at the bear. So really, my mother could afford the luxury of serenity, to stand back and await the outcome of events while she was fought over, like a small country or a Lonsdale Belt. The bear unwrapped his arm from my mother's waist, smiled, and ran his hand through his hair, like a man who was open and tactile, and not at all scheming or sleazy. In another age, or another town, this affectation might have worked, but not in Glasgow, and not then, when wives were not for touching, except by the gracious approval of a husband. I watched my father fight hesitation before he confronted the bear. They stood face to face. The bear was taller than my father, who, I noticed, was still wearing his carpet slippers in addition to being in shirtsleeves. A few words were spoken, then shouted, as my father worked up a head of steam. These blusterings proved ineffectual and the bear smiled on, leaving my father with little alternative but to up the stakes and push him. The bear pushed my father back. Then he struck my father hard, on the side of his face, which made a hollow, splatting noise as the hardness of knuckle hit flaccid cheek and cheek hit teeth, making them crunch. My father was on the ground, rolling with the bear, while the women stood watching avidly, shouting, for show, 'Oh my God,' and 'Get the polis.'

Like most fights, it was an ugly, ungainly affair, all glimpses of sad white Scottish calf, of grunting noises and ripping seams. A one-punch knock down can look sexy, to men and women alike, but the gouging of nostrils, or those sudden Ken Dodd squalls of hair, of blood and snot on torn shirt fronts, these leave both participants diminished, not enhanced, in the eyes of their fellows and, more importantly, women. No, fights are an affront to human dignity. Unless you win. And my father didn't win. He tired quickly and the bear rained down blows and kicks as my father sat, bemused, on the damp pavement, trying to cover his head. Finally, the bear was wrested from my father by a couple of barmen and the threat of the polis.

It's an unsettling thing for a child to watch his father bested in battle. My father staggered to his feet and turned to face my mother. For her sake, I thought, not his, she took his arm and walked him quickly away, up the street. Myself I was not so sanguine. My mother called me, but I shook my head and followed a good distance behind them. I could see my father's shirt tail hanging out, but he was saved from the shame of its flapping, in the evening breeze, by his braces which trailed, ripped and dangling, behind him. He had damaged a slipper and, limping, bore it by the tongue, so that the sole boyoygned up and down, jauntily indifferent to his humiliation. My mother walked behind him in her good going-out coat, her dark hair up in an elegant beehive, her legs shapely above the click clack of shiny stilettos. Though my father paid a heavy price for those legs, they still walked wherever they wanted. 'Are you all right?' my mother called to me. I nodded to shut her up. But I wasn't all right. My world had been undermined, and it was a good hour before I felt well enough to finish the Toffos.

Up and down Britain, councils were tearing down old slums and putting up new ones in breezeblock nirvanas like Dagenham and Linwood. Houses for workers, the car would save the world. The car was to the sixties what the computer chip would be to the nineties, Microsoft on wheels. Trash labour would deliver an economic miracle in exchange for an inside toilet and easy payment terms on a Hillman Imp. For a while, it worked. Scottish trash started buying new furniture, instead of hand-me-downs from relatives, and taking holidays in exotic locations like Morecambe and Whitley Bay. Spain would come later, for now the English were as strange and colourful to us as the Maya Indians to the Conquistadors. Those increases in living standards arrived with more than one price ticket. Self-awareness was delivered with the three-piece suite and with it competition. Trash was pitted against trash in the war to own the deepest carpets, the easiest easy chair, the tallest tallboy, the longest Long John sideboard. Everybody's father worked overtime, two nights and a Sunday, to buy matchwood foam-filled junk that their wives would grow tired of and discard, often before the last HP payment had been made. Everybody's father, except mine that is.

Somehow, in the middle of an economic boom when everything, including cardboard, came wrapped in cardboard, my father's firm conspired to go bust. He found a job as a shipyard labourer instead. Except that there weren't any shipyards in Linwood. So he bought an ancient moped to take himself to work, an ailing black thing with indicator lights the size of elephants ears that stuck out from either side of a cracked windshield, and what with higher rents, repair bills for this puttering monstrosity and the lower wages, the boom became, like swinging London, something else we'd read about but never for ourselves experienced.

Until we moved to Linwood, I'd never felt anything other than equal to any friends I'd made. After we moved, it wasn't the same. We had holes in the furniture, holes in the carpets, we even had holes in the fucking lawn because the Prick couldn't afford enough grass seed to make a proper job of it. On top of that, there was this ludicrous joke moped sitting under a plastic tablecloth near the bins, but not too near in case the bin men felt compassionate and took it away. I made new friends easily enough but, from then on, I kept them at arm's length, never inviting them in. I knew they'd talk about my place the way I'd heard them talk about other people's, competitive snobbery having filtered down to pubescent level.

The estate was barely finished when we moved in. There was a big plot of waste ground across the street, with tall weeds and thistles, the odd scabby bush and a muddy stream skirting the edge. Though the stream was rat infested I didn't care, I'd never seen so much open space, I could've written Dvorak's New World Symphony, but luckily he'd already done it, saving me the trouble. Of the kids at school, practically all had fathers who worked in the car plant, or else some factory supplying related parts. This was the first generation of trash to know the luxury of having money left over come pay day, all, of course, except us. Generally I was able to disguise our shabbiness from friends but every so often a challenge would arise and the great beast poverty would escape from the cellar to cast its shaming shadow over my desperately compartmentalized little life. So one Christmas, when I asked for a bike and received a fucking Biggles book, I stole my first car. It was Boxing Night, I remember, and the world was indoors watching Roy Castle or Harry Secombe, or some other of that legion of tedious cunts who sang duets and made trumpets out of kitchen sinks to astound us all with their horrible virtuosity.

Actually, I say 'stole' but I had no idea how to drive, let alone hot-wire the thing, so I ended up smashing the side panel, climbing in and releasing the handbrake. It was a Ford Consul, I recall, and parked on a gentle gradient, so I was able to coast sedately down to the end of the avenue, and come to a jolting halt in the middle of a newly planted municipal flower bed. Not much of a joyride, admittedly, but the act of theft elated me and I had an astounding wank, among my first, lying across the passenger seat, before fear set in and I ran off through the back gardens towards home.

*

The trouble is, when you have three wounded animals under the same roof, all bellowing for different things, that's when the tensions start. All father wanted was a quiet life, with maybe a little workshop where he could put on his hair shirt and build a shrine to my mother on his Saturdays off. A woman doesn't want all that pedestal malarkey though, she knows, deep down, how crap she is and to have some gormless dick doing the vacuuming and being sensitive to her ludicrous needs is, for her, a measure of his piss-poor judgement rather than an esteemed token of his undying love. My mother wanted the good life. She knew it existed, she'd seen it in the the *Power Game* on telly. No amount of quilted Valentine cards or cups of hot sweet tea were about to provide a viable substitute. Sensing this, my father played his last card. He got her pregnant.

At first, my mother was horrified, then thrilled as she

considered the attention, then she went back to horrified again when she thought of being lumbered with one more hideous little fucker like me. The first I knew of this pregnancy was when I was conscripted into helping my father create a path in the newly grassed scrap of garden which, as ground-floor householders, was our own exclusive domain.

'We need it wide,' my father said.

'Fair enough,' I said, 'how wide?'

He gave me a look. 'Wide enough to accommodate a pram.'

I mulled this information over. 'Am I getting a brother then?'

My father sunk his skinny shovel into the brown and white limy clay. 'Or a sister,' he said. 'Girls are people too.'

We dug all day, knocking our incompetent pans in, building this fucking garden path. At the end of it, we were filthy and I was knackered but I remember feeling close to my father following our joint struggle, even at one point calling him 'Da' instead of the usual, well, nothing. As soon as we went back indoors the closeness evaporated and by the time I went to bed, my father and mother were rowing.

I couldn't make out the full discordant symphony through the wall, just the tones their voices struck, my mother's shrill and unpredictable, hurtling around the scale of possibility like a tone-deaf clarinettist, with my father's dull monotone, providing its hesitant bass-line accompaniment, often overpowered but always returning, shaky but insistent, to carry the unwanted weight of their small mad tune. The following day, without speech, or closeness, I helped my father fill in the garden path. When finally we'd done it, he said, 'We'll grass it over.' When I asked him why, he said, 'Your mother knows best.' I think it was at that moment I first began to despise him. Well, you would, wouldn't you? Plainly, what my mother needed was a good slap in the mouth. Having been shat upon in one big previous relationship, she was determined now to pass on the abuse, to become the shitter rather than the shitee. In those days, there was no therapy, only speech therapy and in any case you can therrup some people till you're blue in the face, as my father had done, but it makes no difference. In some marriages, direct action is the best policy and a good, deserved, whack in the kisser can save ten years of whiny counselling. Nowadays this viewpoint is so unfashionable it teeters on cutting edge and I'm gratified that our more enlightened feminists have embraced its pragmatic charm. The upshot was, my mother disappeared, then reappeared and lay in bed, moping, for a couple of days. Finally she got up, slapped on some generous coats of Yardley and stepped out, once more, to face the world. The matter of the wee brother, or sister, was never referred to again and the only visible scar on their relationship was the open contempt with which my mother now, publicly, treated my father. He ceased to have any name, as far as either of us were concerned and became instead, 'he' or 'that'. Indoors, she took to addressing him by his surname. Bit by bit, I felt my sympathies lean towards my mother. Through her eyes, I saw this tepid, unreasonably reasonable, bloodless wretch absorb insult and injury in craven and culpable silence. He worked, he went for walks, he dug his patch of scabby garden and he took abuse. Maybe his submissiveness gave him a thrill, perhaps this was his strength dressed in the clothes of weakness, fuck knows. What I did know was that something had to give.

*

It happened, inevitably, on a Sunday. *Two-Way Family Favourites* was playing on the radio, clothes were drying by the choking fire and a pan of Brussels sprouts was steaming up the windows. As usual, they were bickering, which, combined with the cloying, overpowering drone of Cliff Michelmore and Jean Metcalfe with their BFPO this and 'love to all in Pontefract' that, the sooty stink of the fire and the fetid warmth of the sprout pan and well, the long and the short of it is, I decided on a spot of remedial action.

Just like with the car theft incident, I didn't stop to think about the consequences. I got up suddenly and did it. At school, I was regarded as unremarkable, even borderline thick. I blamed my first school for this, it took them years to work out I could hardly see the blackboard, let alone read it. Maybe it was my fault, maybe I should have spoken up but believe it or not, I didn't realize I couldn't see. I was like those Aboriginal natives who, when Captain Cook sailed up, couldn't see his boat in the water. Never having clocked a boat that big before, they didn't have a visual vocabulary for dealing with the concept. I was like that. I didn't know that every other bastard could see and I couldn't. I knew something was wrong but couldn't quite work out what, so, being Scottish, I blamed myself. I felt guilt, therefore I was guilty and this was God, or some other middle-class fucker in a tweed suit, punishing me for my crimes. The guilt over being half blind made me secretive and pulled me even further apart from the other kids. By the time the school nurse rumbled me and they stuck a pair of specs and a squint corrector on my face, the damage was done and I was way behind the average. So I'd go home and watch the nightly psychodrama that took place over the kitchen table.

I recall, once, my mother, half scattered with frustration and boredom, breaking eggs over my old man's head while he sat mournfully, with hands clasped, being reasonable. For myself, discovering this talent for standing up, brushing myself down, then toddling off to do something criminal, turned out to be my saving grace. It gave me a foundation of security where before there had only been God and family. Instructed by the indifference of the outside world and the madness of my domestic world, I retaliated with acts of mad indifference.

Anyway, I recalled the whining of the Cuntess and the edgy drone of the Prick as I stood up and headed for the kitchen. I'd no firm plot in mind, other than to find a spot of quiet. The sprout pan was boiling over and the spuds were soggy from over-cooking. A guff of fatty mince hung in the air. I turned off the gas taps, thinking to rescue our Sunday dinner, then thought about the hideous ritual of sitting down, eating it, and turned them back on again. Only I didn't bother to light up the gas. Instead, I headed for the door. Outside, the air was cool and damp and I walked across the waste ground to the ratty stream and sat down by its banks. I pulled apart a flattened Smedleys garden peas carton and lay down. The way I saw it, they had a fifty–fifty chance of survival. If they stopped growling and yapping at each other and behaved like civilized human cunts, they'd notice, quite quickly, the stink of gas seeping into the living room. If, on the other hand, they continued to behave like two wasps in a jar, then fuck them, what's a couple less gurning halfwits to the world?

Wearied by my weighty, Solomon-like deliberations, I shut my good eye. A moment later I opened it again as a heavy crumping sound and a shattering of glass filled the air. I jumped up and ran along the bank of the ratty stream to where I knew I could achieve an unobstructed view of the rear, kitchen end, of the flat. The blast had blown out the windows, a cupboard door, a radio and a laundry basket. I watched my mother stagger out followed by my father. They reeled around the back garden before the Cuntess, sensing humiliation, began gathering up the shabby underwear and socks that spattered the area. Neighbours appeared and began leaping about, comforting and dabbing, making cups of tea and doing prelim investigations. I watched from a little hillock of half bricks, feeling oddly detached from the dramatic human mime I'd set in motion. A police car and two fire engines arrived minutes later and maybe a dozen assorted uniforms and raincoats began milling about. I realized my detachment would soon be put to the test and, judging that it was better to be seen than not, I made my way down from my private box, through the wings of the close, and out into the heart of Act Two, to speak my lines.

They couldn't prove anything. Though the police had established I'd walked out of the house minutes before the explosion, and though they could see from the position of the dials on the buckled cooker top that the taps had been turned on, they were unable to point a finger at me and say, 'You, you little fucker.' They took my parents to hospital for sedation, then they drove me to the police station in Johnstone, three miles away, for questioning. I was given tea and a Jacob's Club biscuit first, so I'd think they were my pals. But before I'd even bitten the chocolate off from the round the edges, they were stoving in with leading questions: had I done this sort of thing before? Did I like school? Who did I dislike less, my mother or father? Instinctively, I adopted the mental position that I was entirely innocent and knew even less about the incident than they did themselves. The questions about ill feeling I was able to deflect into biting ricochets that knocked chunks from the unexamined monolith that was my parents' marriage. No, I loved them both equally, when they had time for me, when they weren't too busy fighting, Officer. No, I'd gone into the kitchen for a damp cloth, I'd seen yolk on the carpet from where my mother had gone berserk with the standard-sized farm fresh. Why, was that important, Officer? They couldn't decide whether I was a sly little cunt, or whether my mother, in one of her manic, I-hate-my-life moments, had turned on the taps herself, hoping to take half the street with her and go out with a bang. Had the damage been worse, the investigations, no doubt, would have been more lengthy. When the gas board confirmed there was no serious damage to the mains supply and that all that was required were some new windows, a cooker, and a new pair of eyebrows for my father, the matter was allowed, conditionally, to rest.

My father found life without eyebrows a difficult

journey. Pending their reinstatement, he took to pencilling in a couple of smudged approximations using the contents of my mother's make-up bag. I suspect I was not alone in noticing that, even after the first shoots of new life had restored a visible fuzz to the jutting crags of his forehead, he continued with the practice. Truly, life was a ludicrous game of chance. If he hadn't gone to the kitchen for his Swan Vestas, he wouldn't have struck the match that blew off his eyebrows and planted the seed that would later reach its full hideous bloom as Cindy. Very probably, he'd be dead, my mother too, and I'd be in a children's' home, trying to look appealing so I could be adopted by a nice couple with a shaggable teenaged daughter. The incident awoke my father's dormant tastes and marked me in the annals of authority as a potential star in the firmament of the deranged. As for my mother, she continued to sit by the window, watching and waiting for the stranger who would one day, surely, come to change her life.

*

Once a fortnight, for the next year, I attended a clinic for apprentice weirdoes in, appropriately enough, Paisley. Like all forms of psychiatric help I've ever encountered, it was completely useless and, if anything, counterproductive. Until then, as far as the school playground was concerned, I was 'a wee queerie,' or, less charitably, 'a lippy little squinty-eyed fucker.' Now though, thanks to the joint endorsement of the state education and health departments, my forehead bore the stamp of classified calamity and my status changed from tolerated maverick to I-don't-want-you-playing-with-him-and-that's-final official leper. In the eyes of the others, fellow pupils and teachers alike, my every action became charged with the dark resonance of psychosis, a situation some teachers did not help, eager as they were, from the platform of the classroom floor, to use my fate as a terrible warning to others who might wish to stray from the one true path of righteous boredom.

The psycho sessions themselves were dreary and humiliating. I was given tests meant to gauge my adaptive and communicative capabilities. These consisted of one-to-one, 'Hello, my name is Gus, I'm from Barrhead and I'm keen on reading and arson' embarrassment sessions. None of us had any faith in them but, being kids, we allowed the big people with the obey-me voices and the pokers up the arse to yank us around and play their demeaning games. I had no friends. Bonded by mutual isolation, we'd see our wretchedness reflected in each other's eyes and do the decent thing and look away. I say no friends. Not quite true. The most grotesque session, and the one I personally dreaded, took place in a small gym room. It was called Movement and Expression, though it could just as easily have been called Make a Cunt of Yourself in Public. A fat old bag with a size twenty arse on a size eight stool banged out some kiddy tunes on a dead piano. We were instructed to become different creatures, according to the mood of the music. Then this gaunt, long-haired bint in crimplene ski pants would come in, and shout out commands like, 'And now the mighty elephant,' or 'Can this be the slithering snake?' And we'd all have to clump about, all us little fire-starters and car thieves, turning ourselves into bounding gazelles and that, in this gym at the arse-end of Paisley.

It was while I was being a graceful sea bird hovering over the warm Pacific that I first noticed Cissie. I was charging about in my squeaky plimsolls, banging into the wall bars, when I saw this vision of genuine grace. While the rest of us caromed around, she'd improvized this elegant slow-motion action, arresting the moment, arms light and lithe as streamers in the breeze, feet marking pit-a-pat time, giving her an ethereal air that excited my world-weary, half-dead, nine-year-old heart. Fuck me, I remember thinking, I've never seen that before. Knocking a few lumbering albatrosses aside, I negotiated a new flight path, next to her. She turned her head, her neck plumage turning suddenly crimson, and fluttered away. I didn't give up and flew alongside her for a bit.

'Go away,' she said.

'Can I speak to you later?' I asked. She ignored me, caught an updraft and headed for the safety of the Azores, over by the vaulting horse. It wasn't a 'no', so I assumed it must be a 'yes' and turned myself into a helicopter to celebrate, shredding a few gasping cormorants and lesser-bellied snipes with the ingenious invisible rotary blade on my head.

I waited for Cissie outside, I don't know why, I wasn't after her body. At nine, I had hard-ons for Archie's girlfriend Betty or Patricia Driscoll from *Picture Book*, but not skinny girls with flat chests and knees more knobbly than my own. There was just something about her. It wasn't her name, that's for sure. Sissy

Spacek could get away with it, because she was American and therefore fictional, but being called Cissie in Scotland, and certainly then, a time when the wearing of brown shoes could lead to public unrest and a stern warning from the police, was just asking for trouble, it was just, well, sissy.

'It's short for Cecilia,' Cissie told me as I walked her up the street towards Burton's corner at Paisley's Cross, where she was meeting her mother. If truth be told, I knew exactly what it was about her. Aside from her eye-catching grace, she also had, like me, an eye-catching eye. Cissie had a patch over one eye, the left eye, so that if I walked on the inside of the pavement we made, between us, one good, fully functioning set of eyes. How could we help but feel bonded? Maybe her name too, Cissie, chiming with sis, sister. I never had a sister. Or a brother. Or a fucking bike, come to that. So right off the bat, I had this thing for Cissie. A hunger, that's what it was. We walked along Love Street, past the St Mirren ground, and I stopped to tie my lace, hoping to slow down the pace and string out my time with her.

I winkled out that she came from Foxbar, an estate over the back of the town, by the hills. She mentioned being peckish, so I excused myself and returned with crisps, an act of chivalry that condemned me to a three-mile walk home, being now minus bus fare. I tore open the packet and thrust it at her. 'What flavour?' she asked. I was taken aback. Men never asked finicky questions like that, all that mattered was they were free. 'Dog shite,' I said, which teased out a first, reluctant smile. Cheese and onion had just come out. I indicated the alluring green and yellow flashes on the packet. 'Don't think so,' she said. This pissed me off, so I started to pull back. Being a woman, this made her come forward.

'So where are you from?' she asked, finally deigning to ask me about myself.

I told her Linwood, then got down to the nitty-gritty. 'What are you in for then?'

She looked at me warily. 'You first,' she said. When I told her I'd blown up the family seat, she feigned being appalled. Again, this irritated me. When she asked me, 'What with?' I told her with a fucking chemistry set, what else? She looked peeved but I could see she was becoming less hoity-toity. 'What about you?' I asked. She gave me a hesitating look, for show, to pretend she was judging my capacity for discretion. Really, she was as keen to serve up the shit soufflé as I was. 'I took rat poison from the garden shed and put it into my mother's soup pot.' This confession provoked a respectful silence during which we caught each other's good eye and thrilled inwardly.

'What happened to your ma and da?'

'They got sick,' said Cissie, simply. And we risked our first titter. Near the Cross, we separated, Cissie having spotted her mother and become agitated.

In those days, only the mixed gender pairing of brother and sister was permitted to walk the streets, hatless and brazen, without fear of interrogation or derision. We respected this taboo for our own purposes; already we were being secretive, which, in Scotland, is an open declaration of love. As she waited to cross at the traffic lights, she called back to me. 'What's your name?' I told her Blaney. 'No, your first name.' I told her Albert. I could see her turn it over in her mind, like it was a dead rat and she had a stick. 'I prefer Blaney,' she said. 'Me too,' I said. I watched her cross the street and saw her disappear among the sullen bundles of adults in dull, damp gabardine coats, then reappear by her waiting mother, a zipper-mouthed woman with an ugly perm and no shopping bag. Then I turned with a singing heart toward the Linwood Road. Curious how the mind works, in such passionate absolutes. That's something you lose, if you've any sense, as you grow older.

*

'Coffee, sir?' I looked up. She was about thirty, blonde hair in a ponytail, good cheekbones. 'Aileen', her British Airways badge said. To see her hands, I said 'Yes, please.' No wedding ring. I gave her my warm smile, the one that said 'confident but not arrogant successful professional who is definitely not on the pull', hoping she didn't notice my Apex fare at the ticket scan. Not that it mattered, she blanked me anyway. And I started to feel nervous about the trip.

Like I've said, everything in my game was subject to the whim of timing. Suppose I met an associate from days of yore, who, let's say for argument's sake, was missing a thumb, or lung, which I'd separated him from at some previous juncture. Well, ordinarily, you'd expect revenge to be at the top of his list of priorities for the rest of his natural life, wouldn't you? But that wasn't how it worked. How it worked was that after a safe passage of time, if he'd been otherwise successful in business, marriage and general fornication, and this had induced in him a sense of well-being, then chances were he'd not only forgive me, but he'd very likely hail me as a friend, like we were old golf chums and not cunts who, not so long ago, were trying to deep fry each other's faces. That's because people grow lonelier as they get older, and experiences feel less rewarding and intense with age, so that even an act of cuntitude like removing a thumb, or lung, without the owner's consent, becomes a gleaming link with the golden days when we were all young, straight-backed and had cocks you didn't need to jab with a cattle prod to make them stand to attention. So he'd hug you and there'd be a glass of passable sherry. But if, on the other hand, this hypothetical associate hadn't enjoyed a rewarding career since our last encounter, if, say, he'd suffered penury, or the misery of a happy marriage, or a jail sentence that'd robbed him of his top earning years, then I'd better watch out, because very likely he'd have done a good deal of brooding in the interim, and would be on the lookout for someone to blame for making him piss down his own leg; thoughts of revenge would be much to the fore.

So you see, I've always found it prudent to enquire after the health of my ex-associates when I've found myself visiting an old stomping ground. That's why, on arrival in Glasgow, I took a taxi to the Marriott and, after preparing myself a relaxing hot chocolate and having a lie down for my back, I made a couple of phone calls.

I rang Claw Hammill on his mobile. Claw knew me from early hooligan days and, being an alcoholic, was seldom out of circulation round the pubs. Knowing his state of health, I allowed the phone more rings than I would for any other living being. Claw had arthritis in his hands, hence his jovial nickname. Waiting for him to uncurl his digits gave me time to assume the appropriate note of jolly nebbiness. Finally, he answered, and I announced myself.

'Claw,' I said, 'it's me, Albert Blaney.'

Claw said, 'Albert? Fuck me.'

And off we go. Yes, we agreed. It'd been a long time and for fuck's sake what a surprise, and dear me, what an awful shame about your mother, a smashing wumman. I reminded Claw that she was an old cunt and we laughed and started to relax. I asked him out for a drink and it was my turn to be surprised.

'Thanks, but no thanks, Albert, I'm dry now, like East Kilbride.' I asked him since when. 'Since I got the triple bypass,' he said. 'Scared the shit right out of me.'

He asked if I remember wee Craigie Wemyss and I told him, 'Yes, wee Craigie, fit as a very fit thing, lifted weights religiously, all through jail, how's he doing?'

'Quadruple bypass,' said Claw.

Not wee Craigie. I was taken aback but steamed on with the obligatory banter. 'Triple not good enough for him, eh? Flash bastard.'

Claw told me about his new woman, Sandra or Shandee or some fucking thing, I couldn't tell through his croaky monotone as he gibbered on about her saintly qualities and how she'd pulled him back from the brink and how he's a changed cunt, putting up his own saloon doors in the kitchen.

I was flicking through the free *Daily Express* I picked up when boarding the plane. There was a picture on an inside page of Prince Charles pulling an 'ouch' face and a story about his bad back. I empathized with Charlie, him being the same age as me. I could remember from his teens the cherry brandy incident at Gordonstoun. Him taking a wigging from his private detective. I'd never had a private detective, only shared, municipal ones.

Claw didn't volunteer anything on the people who concerned me and I'd no choice but to ask him outright. I'm making out here that I was Mr Prudent Professional Criminal, never known to make a foolish move, but was I fuck. The truth was, I was just scared. Over the last five years, what with my nerves and a couple of bad career calls, then more lately Felice, I'd lost a bit of confidence. Unfortunately, Felice had a humanizing effect that made it difficult for me to earn a living. I couldn't stroll about, in my line of work, considering people's feelings, being sensitive to their needs and wants, it wasn't on. It was unethical, in a psycho, to have ethics. All that benign maturity crap was all right when you were seventy, when the only thing liable to creep up behind you was your prostate gland. But the thing was, many of my peers were still bustling businessmen, actively downloading old grudges onto the laptop of psychosis, so I was obliged to step lightly, if at all, which is why I wanted to avail myself of the latest up-to-the-minute data. So why was I asking this lying bastard, Claw? And how did I know he was lying? Well it wasn't rocket science. He was telling me he was in his house, not in the pub. But how many people do you know with a fruit machine in their living room? Stupid cunt. Anyway, I hit him with some names, giving my enquiries a mellow, nostalgic air that didn't sit well with either of us, me or him. It was embarrassing to both of us, and a bit incongruous, as if Mad Frankie Fraser was suddenly doing an ad for Werther's Originals, so I dropped it. Let's face it, nobody has friends in business. And since business is life to most of us, that means we don't have friends, full stop.

I asked him straight out about Darko. And Calum. And the two Grady brothers, Peter and Paul. I was hoping he'd say something miraculous like, 'You mean you haven't heard? They were on their way to a violence seminar when their minibus sailed over a cliff. Yes, they all plummeted to their deaths, singing, "I love to go a-wandering." ' But he didn't.

'Fine, all fine,' he told me.

I took a deep breath but I couldn't disguise my nervous laugh. 'Do they ever ask about me?'

Claw knew what I meant. I had aspirations when I last lived up here. I aspired to have them again, once I'd buried the Cuntess.

Five years ago I took a breakdown and walked, or rather staggered, out of a quarter share of the imperial empire of Paisley. I laid claim to all I surveyed, south from Simpson's Bar all the way to the old racecourse. This was a sentimental attachment in some ways, as my old childhood lunacy clinic was situated nearby. From the old racecourse, my ranch extended west to a rusting banana slide in Ferguslie Park and north to some of the worst council housing for miles, in other words prime grazing land. Now I wanted it back. Admittedly, some of this grazing land belonged to Calum, but I'd been cosying up to Peter and Paul at the time and when Darko, who had an understanding with Calum, was laid up in the Nuffield being fitted with a plastic kneecap, I saw my chance and pounced. Calum was raging but he couldn't move without Darko's army for fear of Peter and Paul joining forces with me and the three of us wiping him out. I set up a base camp in a run-down sweetie shop near the Watermill Hotel and set about consolidating my extended interests. I wanted to do this quickly. I knew that once Darko had thrown away his aluminium walking stick he'd want to prove his sprightliness by running about chopping and stabbing. I felt sure there'd be a battle ahead and braced myself accordingly. The older guys I set to work on the traditional Scottish heavy industries, policing pubs, easy loans, blackmailing the odd poof councillor, that sort of bread and butter stuff. As a sweetener to business, I undercut Calum's previous pricing structure. To enable me to do this, I had to encourage prompt settlement of accounts. I put in place some incentives to ensure this occurred. Some damage to property and a spot of blood-letting early doors, served both as a warning and an aide-memoire to tardy customers. The young boys I let run the drugs. Young boys like running drugs, doling out franchises, locating esoteric pharmaceutical plants in remote Scottish islands, there's a kudos to that, akin to rummaging around second-hand record shops, looking for rare grunge. Personally, I'm a conservative, I regard all drugs post cocaine as inferior. So I'd have felt ridiculous running about in a white Beamer, with a baseball cap on back to front, looking like John Swinney on a youth vote blitz; let's face it, Puff Albert I'm not. Nevertheless I kept a hands on approach, even though I held the reins lightly.

*

People often had a problem when it came to my involvement with drugs. I'd sat at Chiswick dinner parties with

Felice, amusing my hosts with wry tales of thuggery and casual violence, yet they'd turn po-faced at the mention of the D word. Or, more specifically, the E or the H word, Ecstasy or heroin. The middle classes are very selective about their alphabet when it comes to drugs, I've noticed. The C word, cocaine, they're comfortable with, well how couldn't they be, usually it was me who was bringing the C word around, in lieu of a bottle of Beaune. But you try them with anything past C and you'll receive a very testy response. It was all, 'How could you, Albert? How could you deal in death to innocent kiddies and wretched junkies? Have you no morals?' This always tickled me. Many of these people had Hogarth prints on their walls, but to my mind, most of them should've been in their own print. The answer is yes, of course, I have morals. But like everyone else's, they're personal and arbitrary. For example, if you were walking down the street in front of me and I saw you drop a tenner, I'd almost certainly pick it up and run after you to give it back. Equally, if you were walking in front of me and I saw you drop a small brown bag containing a ten-pound wrap, I'd give you that back too. Even if you were as gaunt as Yorrick's skull and had more track marks than Clapham Junction, I'd figure, that's your right, this is a democracy and you're free to enslave yourself to drugs if that's your wish. Therefore, by extension, I was more than happy to provide drugs to those who wanted them, even if I suspected they would likely die as a result of these and similar transactions. As far as I can see, morals have more to do with contemporary fashion than they do with any so-called classical human values. Let's face it, it's not so long ago the British Empire was quite happy to fight the Opium wars, and how far down the alphabet is O?

There are probably thousands of middle-class Mrs Hogarths of Chiswick who've been brought up, sustained, educated and finessed on the legacies of great Uncle Toke and his contribution to British Trade and Industry. Ah yes, Albert, I hear you say. A cunning tactical move. You're historicizing the present in order to distance yourself from responsibility, but what about the kiddies, Albert? The poor urchins with their trusting little faces and their pathetic nicked car radios, held pleadingly up for you to swap for life-giving shit? All right, I'll tell you. I had a policy about brats. The under ten policy. No deal under ten-pound, no sale to anyone under ten. I kept that in place for a while, but I had to junk it, know why? The drink industry was undercutting me. In every public park and scrap of waste ground, alkies as young as eight and nine were rolling about, tanked up on Tennent's Super and Buckfast Tonic Wine. There are thousands more alcoholics than there are junkies, yet I've never yet seen any monk lead from Buckfast Abbey in cuffs with a blanket over his tonsure, being spat on by a jeering crowd of Mrs Hogarths, off to stand trial at the high court. Those cunts are holy, yet they're in exactly the same business as me. No, don't talk to me about morals. I mean, I was a fucking criminal, it was my job to be evil, what's their excuse?

*

As I talked to Claw, things flashed back to me. Like how, pending Darko's rehab, Calum contented himself by sending round a coffin, empty but for a human shite. On

Valentine's Day, it was a private joke for public consumption, the symbolism of which wasn't lost on me.

'Aye,' said Claw, 'every bastard's fine, I see them all from time to time. Except Darko. I don't know where he's keeping himself.' Claw gave it Burl Ives, sunny afternoon lazing on the porch intonation but what he was telling me was the structure of the present allegiances, that the kaleidoscope had taken yet another of its periodic shakes and Darko was, at the moment, the odd man out, spoiling the pretty pattern. Of course it could all change tomorrow, or never, or maybe it had changed already. The only thing was that Claw wasn't daft enough to be seen having a drink with me.

The key, as usual, was Peter and Paul. 'And the boys,' I said, 'how are the boys? Did you ever give them my number?' After a moment, he said 'Aye.' That was a stupid question, because now Claw knew the boys weren't in touch with me and if he was pally with Calum, or Darko, he could give them the lie of the land and they'd be encouraged to know that, in the event of either, or both, of them choosing to stab me in the giblets while I sat at the funeral giving it 'Nearer my God to thee,' then Peter and Paul were unlikely to be distraught. Claw asked me where I was staying. I lied and told him I was still on the move. Great things for liars, mobile phones. It'll be sad day when videophones take off and all of us duplicitous bastards have to start lugging stage sets behind us in a truck.

'Are you coming to the funeral?' I asked Claw.

'I will if I can,' he said, a non-committal answer that told me fuck all. 'I was very fond of your mother, Albert.'

'Lying cunt,' I said, and we laughed, freely, again.

'Ta-ta, Claw,' I said.

'Ta-ta, Albert,' said Claw. 'Keep in touch.'

I rang off and had a rummage in the minibar. The Toblerone looked inviting, but I didn't want to move it in any way, shape or form, thereby incurring a charge. In the old days you could have a miniature and a Toblerone easily, provided you were diligent in the matter of tidying up the bottle and carton and could make them appear unsullied.

I had a bath, then I sat in my shower cap, staring into the minibar, pondering the problem of how to eat a bar of chocolate without touching it. Defeated, I lay on my bed and listened to the traffic rumbling up and down the M8. Before I came up, I promised myself that, if I wasn't murdered, I'd take a couple of days out from business to look up old haunts, a thing I've intended to do for years but never done. There was something about the death of a relative, even it it was only a mother, that has you reaching back into your own past, touching it, so to speak, to remind yourself where you've come from and, more importantly, that you're still alive and breathing. 'This time tomorrow,' I told myself, 'it'll be all over.' Then I could begin.

*

The Cuntess never settled in Linwood. She missed her Friday nights out and felt goaded by the neighbours, with their big car-factory wages, buying clothes and filling up their flats with furniture from Hardy's and Clydesdale and even, on occasion, the mighty House of Fraser. She had holes in her stockings, holes in her carpets and therefore holes in her soul. Sometimes she'd look at me and I'd know, right off the bat, what she was thinking. Ugly little houseblowing fucker, it's him that's holding me back. The Prick hoped, I'm sure, that by bunging her a few kids she'd eventually have all that guff about fulfilment and material comfort knocked out of her, then they could settle down to a life of quiet misery and be happy. What he failed to recognize was that the Cuntess, by having the abortion, had paddled her first strokes down the River of No Return.

I don't recall how the subject of the semi-detached in Ralston came up. I do recall it being discussed, however, in strained and heated terms on more than one occasion. I had pressing matters of my own to attend to, being an idealistic young arsonist who was madly in love with a child poisoner. Of course our flames of love were fuelled by the petrol of imagination, given that we seldom saw each other. When we did, our secret intimacy made us both feel awkward yet gleeful, and we made do with shy smiles and signalled jokes until the therapy class was over, when, as usual, I'd walk Cissie to Paisley Cross to meet her mother.

Sometimes, of an empty evening, a state of intoxicated despair would come over me and, as if tantalized by her very existence, I'd walk past Linwood through Ferguslie then into the woods and through the fields towards the grey magical streets of Foxbar where I knew, somewhere, she lived and breathed. At times, overcome, I'd pause among the trees to dedicate a wank to her deliciousness or occasionally, less overcome, a shite. In the stark prison cell of my tormented life, it gladdened my heart to know that she was alive and, apparently, loved me. As the Cuntess raved her Ralston rants and the Prick sighed at the kitchen table and as the temper tears rolled and the sauce bottle clattered, I'd fumble in the dark cave of my being for the Cissie lifeline that would haul me back, blinking, into the blazing light.

I had yet to learn, of course, that all love is conditional, the condition being that a better offer may come along at any time. So it was that one day, abruptly, I was not loved by Cissie.

I turned up, as usual, for the session. I lavished at her feet, as usual, an exquisite selection of adoring looks, duck walks and pulled-faces for her delight but noticed, strangely, that they were not received with the usual pleasure. Afterwards, I learned how so. Waiting for Cissie, on our usual discreet corner, I observed her emerging from the building with another man, a fresh-faced and handsome young bed-wetter called Leonard. They stood together while Leonard's father, smiling, held open the door of his large Rover car and, still smiling, motioned the two lovebirds to climb in. It was a sad and bitter betrayal and I was to suffer pangs of abandonment for a solid week and a half.

In the second half of the week, when the tortuous subject of Ralston again re-surfaced at the kitchen table, I decided to listen. In Ralston, situated equidistantly on the Glasgow and Paisley boundaries, a man and more importantly a woman could, it seemed, be happy. New Dream Homes for trash with aspirations were available and might be reserved for a modest cash deposit. Once again my heart sank as the Cuntess cranked up her arguments to ramming speed. This time, however, the Prick was to thwart her momentum with a brave new tactic: surrender.

‘I went to see a man today,’ he said, dabbing a doorstop of Sunblest into his tomato soup. ‘A man who knows people.’ The Cuntess stopped ranting and blinked. I could see the questions tumbling in a heap down the narrow staircase of her mind. ‘What man? What’s his name?’ The Prick, giddy with empowerment, continued nibbling his bread. ‘You mean the name of the man,’ he said, ‘or the man who knows the man?’

‘The man,’ my mother said. ‘The name of the man.’

‘Billy,’ said my father. ‘Billy Waugh. He’ll lend us fifty for the deposit.’

And that, as they say, is how it all began.

Chapter Two

I slept badly at the hotel that first night back. In the function suite, a convention of dentists in kilts twisted half the night away to Abba hits. They didn't stop yakking in their rooms till gone three. I thought about ringing down but I didn't want to make a fuss, which was odd since normally, in my day job, I wouldn't think twice about braining one of the fuckers. Let them enjoy themselves, I decided. Poor cunts, tomorrow they'd be back to gazing at furry tongues while halitosis breath steamed up their specs.

I showered, shaved, then put on my funeral suit, ready. The do at the crematorium didn't kick off till half two but I hadn't brought up much kit and I didn't want to put yesterday's sweaty shirt back on. I was fastidious about personal hygiene; it was something I caught off my father. It used to drive Felice crazy, the way I'd want to wash a shirt through after only wearing it a couple of hours, but you know what London's like, take a Tube across town and you feel like you've been stoking a boiler for forty minutes. All her clothes needed to be dry-cleaned but she resented the inconvenience and expense so would douse herself in extra scent to cover any odour that was less than exquisite. She wouldn't put it like that, of course, she'd say she was 'giving the rose an extra touch of dew.' That sort of cavalier approach is foreign to your average working class sow. A scumette, like Brenda my ex-wife, wouldn't step across the door without a good descaling. For a night out you'd practically have to prise the scrubbing brush off her or she'd have skin like raw mince.

I took a taxi from the hotel up the motorway to Paisley with the intention of having a brief, reflective wander about. Due to meanness, I ordered a minicab and was punished with acrylic zebra-skin seat covers and the obligatory lank-haired, grunting ex-con at the wheel. We drove in silence till we hit the motorway but I could see him sizing me up in the rear view with his beady little crim eyes, trying to puzzle out where he knew me from and whether it was worth the risk of starting up a jaw to find out. Evidently, he decided it was because he said, 'I tell you what, pal, I know your face.'

I said, 'Oh yes?'

Then it dawned on him. 'Are you Albert Blaney?'

I told him, yes.

'The Surgeon?'

'Yes,' I said. 'Aye.' I don't know why I added the 'aye', it's just that 'yes' can sound poncy to Scottish ears.

'That was a helluva book, mate,' he said. I thanked him. 'I didn't read it myself,' he continued, 'but one of the boys picked it up in Bargain Books and had a wee rummage through it, two quid though, what daft fucker would pay two quid for a book, though, eh?'

I suggested there were plenty of daft fuckers around. I might have added that some of them drove minicabs.

'Well they'd be fucking stung, because apparently it

was down to a fucking pound the following week, no luck, eh, Albert? Ha ha.'

He kept needling. He'd assumed, obviously, that I'd renounced my former life in favour of becoming a remaindered author and was now a soft touch. He was already looking forward to regurgitating our encounter when he got back to base, leaning on the Klix machine, slurping a Bovril and telling them how that Albert Blaney was in his car, how he was past it now with a soft belly and a bad back, and how he took the piss in such a masterfully subtle way that silly old Albert couldn't take offence. Albert Blaney? Albert fucking Tatlock more like, ha ha.

I ignored him and asked to be dropped at the abbey.

'The abbey? Christ sake, how long you been away, Albert? All fucking one way now, pal, bit changed from your day, do my fucking best for you though, you being a fucking local boy made bad, eh? Fucking abbey, dream on, need to be behind the abbey now, mate.'

I told him all right, behind the abbey would be fine.

'Fucking need to be, no choice, fucking abbey, you're kidding.'

He was pissing me off and I hadn't come back to be pissed off, I wanted reflection, a quiet wallow in cherished nostalgia before the big kick off, I'd forgotten that up here it's considered pretentious to have anything as personal as an inner life.

'This'll do fine,' I told him, as we headed along Back Sneddon Street. He grunted and kept driving, pulling up, for spite, about a hundred yards further along.

'Eight fifty to you, Albert,' he said, half turning to lean on the back of his seat.

I wanted to damage him but, having no tools, resisted the urge. I gave him a note. 'Give me a receipt for ten,' I said, 'and keep the change.'

He raked about under the dash for a pen then, laboriously, wrote out the receipt. 'There you go, Albert.' No sign of a thank you. I took the receipt and was folding it into my wallet when he said, 'Don't take this the wrong way, but you don't look very fucking hard to me.' Then he drove off.

The drizzle had stopped and the sun shone thinly, like a rundown torch beam, through the grey curtain of cloud. I felt unsettled and vulnerable and had to fight a sudden impulse to weep. I turned the corner and, for old time's sake, walked into Arthur's pub. Only it wasn't called Arthur's any more, the frontage was tarted up and it was calling itself Fingal O'Flaherty's. I bought a pint of Murphy's and sank the first half in a gulp. Drink never tastes better than during the day, but it must come laced with Rohypnol because I'm usually out on my feet a couple of hours later. So I just stuck to the one and sat there in the corner, looking at all the hanging harps and shillelaghs and wondering when it was every second pub stopped being German and turned Irish and whatever happened to Bier Kellers?

*

Arthur's held sentimental memories for me as it was where I'd first met Brenda, and also where the old ex-army pistol had been purchased for one of my first murders. That's the sort of statement that can bring a thrill to a *Daily Mail* reader's stomach, unless, like me, you know the kind of calamities that lay behind it. As

I've kept saying, there's a lot of bollocks talked about gangsters these days, most of which is down to gangsters themselves and their arse-licking media associates, all of whom are keen to perpetuate the usual myths for their own financial and egotistical ends. As a result of this media manipulation, a great many members of the general public imagine that all gangsters are like the Krays. Now whatever shortcomings the Krays may have exhibited as human beings, no one can say they didn't fill their suits well. Which was more than could be said for many of us. Most gangsters in suits looked more like farmers going to the Saturday dance than Harvey Keitel on his way to bail out Samuel L. Jackson and John Travolta. In my experience, there was no glamour in taking a human life, though there was, on occasion, a deep sense of satisfaction. But sexiness? Forget it.

Take the task I bought the pistol for, a complete mess, but not untypical. I'd been despatched along with two colleagues to dunt this chap for crimes of lippiness and default against a venerable gentleman. We picked him up at Kinning Park outside the Old Toll Bar and took him to a derelict flat at the arse-end of Erskine. For glamour, I had decided to shoot him. Only no one had a gun. So I instigated a whip round and Donny Kite, I think it was, Donny, was despatched around the pubs to procure some sort of pistol. Only he was gone fucking hours. Meantime, we've got this large chap tied to a chair. For a time his attention, naturally enough, was taken up with fear and panic and that, but after a while the poor cunt was getting bored and whiney, waiting around to die. So we untied his bonds and took it in turns to play pocket draughts with him until Donny got back which, finally, he did. 'Look,' he said, 'I've got a pistol.' And so he had. Only what a decrepit object it was. It was this ancient effort with a slack hinge on the breach and these coloured elastic bands holding it together. 'Don't be fooled by appearances,' said Donny. 'It's reliable.' So I took his word for it, but when I went to shoot into the chap's head, it jammed. It was only when I opened the gun up, I realized it had got the wrong-sized bullets. Not only that, it had cost the fucking earth and Donny had the cheek to ask me for the excess. So we were having a right set to about Donny's budget overspend and this victim chap was in the chair thinking, Fuck me, it's a wonder anybody gets murdered these days, if they're all as incompetent as these silly fuckers. After a vigorous discussion, we ended up carrying the chap downstairs, covered in a fireside rug, still sitting in his chair. We drove him to a railway bridge, having decided to chuck him under a train. After a couple of tense fags, we finally heard a train coming. Trouble was, by the time we were able to hoist the chap up, we'd missed our moment with the engine and he ended up in a truckful of slag, heading for Stranraer. He was DOA, luckily, we discovered from the papers, which saved a lot of embarrassment all round. Anyway, after that I'd thought, Fuck glamour, I'm back to hitting people over the head with weighty objects, it's safer. And from that day forward, the cranial pummel was my favoured method of despatch.

*

There's a Chinese proverb I'm rather fond of which goes, 'If you sit by the river long enough, the body of your enemy will one day float by.' So it was that the door opened and a stooped runty figure entered, dressed in a V-neck T-shirt and a blue linen suit that was creased in all the wrong places. He stepped up to the bar and ordered a voddy and Red Bull. I took out my mobile and tapped in a number. I pressed the green button and waited a long time. Finally, Claw Hammill's voice said, 'Albert? What you up to?' I invited him out for a drink, but he reminded me he was dry and that anyway, he was out with Shandee, shopping in Debenham's.

'In that case you won't need this,' I told Claw, appearing beside him and lifting his voddy off the counter. To be fair to him, he did have the decency to look cuntish.

'Hello Albert,' he said.

'Hello, Claw,' I said and I put his glass back down on the counter and slid his Red Bull towards him.

'I didn't expect to see you today, Albert,' he said. 'I assumed you'd be busy with grieving and the wreaths and shit.'

'Yes,' I told him, 'I've arranged a floral tribute. I'm having "Good Riddance" spelt out in pink gardenias inside her hearse.' Having established the desired tone, I invited him to join me at the corner table.

'Cancer, was it?' said Claw, fumbling in his pocket for his fags.

I corrected him, 'Stroke,' I said. 'She'd been on pills for years.' He asks me how I found out. I told him I'd had a message from Billy Waugh.

'In person?'

'Not exactly,' I said. 'He faxed me the deaths column

from the *Evening Times* with a felt tip round the bit about the funeral arrangements.

'Still close then?' said Claw, taking out a packet of Navy Cut. 'You've got to look after your mother, Albert,' he said. 'If I've learned one thing, it's that a mother is the greatest friend a man ever has.'

It irritated me, watching him trying to tear the cellophane off, so I put us both out of our misery by taking a couple and lighting them up. I watched him watching me do it.

'Your hands are shaking, Albert,' he said. 'You been having trouble with your nerves?'

I found myself nodding, 'Yes,' I said, 'matter of fact I've been through a bit of a rough patch, Claw.'

I was taken aback to hear what my mouth had just said. It was the tone of his enquiry that had wrong-footed me. It had been a long time since anyone had asked me a personal question, he had quite caught me on the hop. Claw gave me a moment of sympathetic eye contact to see whether I wanted to run with it. Instinctively, I looked away and he took the hint. We pulled our mental visors down and resumed our allotted roles of psychotic ruffian and treacherous shufflebutt.

'You were saying you hadn't seen much of Darko,' I reminded him. 'How's his plastic knee been holding up?'

He gave me a little raise of the eyebrows while he changed gear. 'I wouldn't know, Albert,' he said, 'being as how I haven't seen much of him. But I'm given to understand, in general terms, that they can be right gyp-giving fuckers, these plastic knees.'

I nodded, sympathetically. 'And Calum?'

Claw shrugged. 'How should I know, Calum's knees

are a mystery to me. Now ask me something else, for fuck's sake.'

I leaned in closer to him. He smelled of sweat, fresh but pungent, a fearful sweat, the kind you find trickling down your sides, cold and unpleasant, when you're very tense and haven't even realized your breathing has turned all shallow. It was the kind I could also pong from myself as I reached into my jacket to suggest the presence of a weapon, imaginary, at this stage, but Claw wasn't to know that.

'Look here, Claw,' I said, 'there's no need to turn smart, I only asked you a fucking question.'

'Settle down, Albert,' he said, 'just relax, there's no need to get heavy, Jesus Christ.'

I remained calm. 'I'm not getting heavy,' I said, 'I'm only reminding people of the possibility of heaviness should they try to take the piss.' I marvelled at how far I'd dropped down the Premiership Fear League when a gnarled runt like Claw Hammill felt he could give my balls a free squeeze. 'They think I've lost it,' I found myself saying.

Claw poked the statement with a stick, decided it was harmless and said, 'I wouldn't go that far, Albert.' I asked him how far he would go. He looked at me. 'Honestly?' he asked.

I nodded. Claw settled into his chair, relishing the prospect of nailing my faults to the door of the safe house called Attribution. 'Calum thinks you've lost it, Darko thinks you never had it and Peter and Paul, well.'

I was all ears. 'Well what?'

Claw tried on an ill-fitting, caring smile and shrugged again, inviting me to cajole him into repeating the obviously tasty insult. I wasn't about to fall into his trap. Then I thought, Fuck it, I can't help it. I needed to know. 'You can tell me, Claw,' I said. 'Well what?'

Claw did an impression of a man having words pulled from his throat like teeth. 'Well the boys,' he began, 'and this is not me, Albert, you know that, I've always had the highest admiration for your ability, but the boys think you've turned into, what was it again, a mushy southern poof.'

I blinked and leaned back in my chair. 'A poof, you say?'

Claw nodded. 'From the south,' he said. 'And mushy. If you ask me, I think it was the book that done it, Albert.'

I became defensive. 'What about the book?'

Claw fidgeted in his chair. He knew he was about to say a bad thing and I watched his momentary struggle between the gloating thrill of temptation and the dull rewards of discretion. No contest.

'Well apparently, Calum's the worst. Whenever your name comes up, he calls you a lying prick. He says you made up half of it and stole the rest from other people. He says . . .' he paused, for decorum.

'It's okay,' I said, 'go on.'

'He says you're nothing but a circus act.'

I felt my face flush. Claw gave a little cough to hide the relish in his voice. 'You're sure about this?' I asked.

'Oh aye,' he said, 'you should see him on a roll at parties. He does this impression . . . I seen him at it a couple of months back. I told him to pack it in. Albert wouldn't like that, I said, but what could I do? I was just a voice in the Paisley wilderness.' He turned his head away, like a man who's said too much. 'I've said too much,' he said. I sat silently for a moment, letting it sink in.

I felt mortified, the way anybody would who'd lost the respect of esteemed or semi-esteemed fellow cunts. Yes, Albert, you may point out, the loss of respect from one's peers is a terrible thing, but think yourself lucky, after all, if they're all chuckling at you with merry disdain, surely they'd now be of less of a mind to pummel or dunt you about the person? And in any other trade or industry, I'd be inclined to concur with your hypothesis. But not in my business.

My peers and I, we were at the unpleasant end of the crime spectrum, the end where people may be chopped and blasted or, as it happened once, served their own testicles on a tennis court. Weakness in a rival did not eliminate that rival as a possible threat, No, weakness in a rival allowed his peers to fuck his wound. There was no subtle, psychological subtext that could dress this up, it was just a simple God-given opportunity to kill you, feed you down the mincer and, take your stuff. House, clothes, car, wife, Everything Must Go. So you see, you daren't show weakness or you were already dinner.

In our trade there was no retirement, either you stole away to a distant land and forged a new existence or else, if you couldn't be arsed with that, you spent your twilight years looking over your shoulder on the bowling green, scared to bend too far over the jack in case some cold-eyed assassin in a white sun hat clumped you over the nut with a bag of woods. There was no doubt about it, to remain at home meant being *vigilant for the rest of your natural life*. Obviously I'd opted for option one, distant land scenario, not because I loved munching jellied eels as I whizzed around on the London Eye but because it was easier to remain alive when you were forgotten. To be forgotten was to be, effectively, dead already. The main problem with option two, eternal vigilance scenario, was that if you were permanently in people's faces, they were more apt to recall your evil deeds of the past. What could happen, and there were many recorded instances of this happening, was that you could be strolling round Asda, casually pricing cherry tomatoes or, like Big Rudge Deakin, standing outside Rumbelow's on a Saturday afternoon, trying to catch the Celtic score, when suddenly you were the unlucky recipient of a bayonet in the spleen. And why? All because somebody from a time long ago clocked your greying hair and paunchy belly and remembered he had a grievance. For fuck sake, even Billy Waugh had been shot, firebombed and stabbed with a hatpin and he was the king of Scottish hooliganary.

Having let all this sink in, I turned to Claw. 'Look here, Claw,' I said, employing an Anglicization of speech I'd grown quite fond of, 'Let's stop pissing about. What I want to know is, am I on the wanted list or aren't I?'

Claw didn't reply. He rose, suddenly. 'Sorry, Albert,' he said, 'if you're going to spoil a pleasant conversation with all these ugly direct questions, then I—'

I gripped him by one of his horny mitts as he tried to leave, and he winced and pulled an 'Ow-I'm-an-invalid' face.

'Sit down,' I said. I indicated an authentic old Irish bar milking stool and made him park his bony little bum on it. In the old days he'd have had the good grace to shit himself, but now he just gave me a look of tetchy indignation. I'd lost it up here and no mistake.

'I don't know anything, Albert,' he said shrugging. I felt myself losing patience. 'But if you're inviting me to speculate . . .' He let it hang in the air. I nodded.

'I won't quote you on anything,' I said.

'Just opinion?'

'Just opinion,' I said, 'you're just an innocent bystander in this, I respect that.' I was reassuring him but to tell the truth, I was quaking more than Claw was. What he stood to lose was purely financial, the withdrawal of a small, well-paying, fetch-and-carry tasks, for me there was a heavier price.

Claw let his shoulders down a few inches and gave a nervous cough. 'Okay,' he said. 'Well let me tell you, Albert, you pissed off a lot of people up here, you really did. You ran around like you owned the place, undercutting colleagues, putting noses out of joint, taking over business that wasn't yours to take.'

'Only Calum's,' I protested.

'Oh, really?' he said. 'You mean you never nudged over into Darkoland?'

I stopped protesting. He went on.

'You and that stupid little team of yours. They would've run through walls for you. Most of them looked like they already had. You were a mad cunt, Albert, and I mean that in a complimentary sense. But it's just as well you got out, because harsh words were being spoken. People were about to come together to protect their interests.'

'What people?'

'Fill in your own blanks. You were a loose missile. You know what happens to that kind of person.'

'No, I don't,' I said, 'tell me.'

This was bravado on my part and he saw through it. 'I don't have to tell you, Albert. You know. That's why you got out when you did. You weren't that fucking mad.' His little eyes were dodging about in his head, as if trying to escape. He knew he'd given me a hard slap of reality and that I didn't necessarily love him for it.

He tried a few verbal curtsies. 'Don't get me wrong, I respected you for that. In fact we all did, we all respected your decision to get out.' He stopped speaking. I thanked him for his respect. 'No problem, Albert. I mean that.'

It was his turn to squeeze my hand. I nodded, like a man who was truly touched. 'I know you do,' I said. But did I fuck. I realized quite well the nature of the problem I had. Sure, they respected my decision to get out, but here was the rub. They also despised me for doing it. Why? Because my success had been founded on madness, of being mentally beyond the pale. By getting out, I'd shown that I was sane and therefore human. Implicit in this was my demonstration that, like every other privet-trimming, Volvo-washing, dope-dealing extortionist fucker, I knew the meaning of fear. I was Iron Mike after Buster Douglas had given him that shot to the chin. I was fallible. I was the Surgeon with the shaky hand. Therefore, as I've said, I was now vulnerable to being killed and eaten. The simple question I now required an answer to was: which of them, if any, now wished to dine on my corpse?

Claw asked me a question which hinted at an answer.

'Did you ever insult Darko's wife?' he said. 'Last time I saw him, he mentioned an insult.'

'I've never even seen his poxy wife, let alone insult the bag,' I said as a reflex action. In fact I recalled I had insulted her, ugly old bun. For my last year up here, I'd been pissed and crazy, not giving a fuck what I'd said to anyone, male or female. Insult his wife. It made you laugh. Darko was a bad-tempered fucker who once bored a hole in a debtor's head with a brace and bit, then sent him home to his loved ones on a bread board with a bunch of tulips sticking out the hole in the skull. But let me politely suggest that his peroxide tart kept her hooked beak out the vol-au-vents when she sneezed and fuck me, the next thing you know he was running around, snorting righteous indignation, smacking cheeks with kid gloves and playing the affronted gentleman. Cunt.

So as you can imagine, I was laughing, but I was also shitting myself, because I knew what Darko was like. Basically, what it came down to was this: if he wanted to kill me, then this afternoon, he'd know where to find me; at the funeral.

Now neither Darko nor any of the others were particularly close to my mother, sure they were on nodding terms through their acqaintenceship with Billy Waugh, but since Billy, from all accounts, had for some years dispensed with my mother's services and consigned her to a granny flat in his basement, it was unlikely they would turn up for the express purpose of saying their fond farewells. In other words, if any of them were there, then it was not unlikely they were there for me. Remembering this ancient insult could be Darko's way of stoking his fire, charging himself up with a God's-on-my-side adrenalin fix so he could cloak his real desire, which was to kill me for pleasure and profit. I didn't know how loaded he thought I was but, if I thought it'd make any difference, I'd email him to point out he was now dealing with a struggling criminal who travelled Apex and stole Toblerones from hotel minibars, but as I've said, it wouldn't make things any better and would probably make them worse as it would look like I was panicking. And I'd still end up a corpse, only then I'd be a pathetic corpse. Like Liberace I intended going to my grave without ever having shown the public my true face. After all, I wasn't just any cunt, I was 'the Surgeon,' ice in his veins and all that bollocks. As Claw needlessly reminded me, 'You've made a lot of enemies, Albert. That book. Big mistake.'

'Not my last mistake, I hope.' I finished my drink and stood up. The Pogues came on, singing about Poor Paddy who's working on the Railroad. I shouted over it to Claw, saying I'd walk him as far as the taxi rank at Gilmour Street Station if he liked. He looked a bit dubious, so I said 'Tell you what, Claw, you get off, I've things to do anyway.' I was finding the music oppressive. Claw looked relieved and got off his mark. When he'd gone, I walked to the toilet, entered a cubicle and slumped down on the seat like a boxer after a hard round. Normally I liked music in pubs, it made me feel jubilant. But not today. The long and short of it was, I just didn't know if I'd got the nerve any more.

*

Paisley used to be a nice town, a respectable town, famous for boring but worthy things like the abbey and the cotton mill. Then life changed. It changed in your town, as it changed in everybody's town, as it certainly changed in this town. The trouble was, people like me sprung up. I didn't even realize I was part of the problem till I read the stories in the tabloids. I just thought I wanted a house in Potterhill with a garage and gravel path, and was prepared to kill, thieve or extort to get it.

As far as Brenda and I were concerned, this aspiration was the summit of achievement. On our fifth anniversary I had a Brookfield firm deliver a lorry-load of granite chippings. Brenda was so ecstatic she took my cock out on the spot, perched her bum on the hostess trolley and sucked till it glowed in the dark. Whatever happened to that hostess trolley? Whatever happened to that hostess? The answer was, she was living in a two-apartment tenement flat in Silk Street with an out-of-work painter and decorator. Maybe she still had that trolley. I didn't know, most of the time I was off mine and wasn't disposed to worry about anyone else's. One morning I arrived back from an all night biff and batter session to find she'd cleared the house. I didn't care. I moved the guys in and we designated the kitchen as a war cabinet room and the box bedroom as an arsenal. We also had a thriving pharmacy in the pantry, which shows I was the sort of general to whom caution was not a watchword. Within days I'd cleared the chest freezer of garden peas and chicken croquettes and locked up a gambler called Aiden Franks for persistent non-payment of interest. When we looked in four days later, you could've stuck a broom handle up his arse and licked him like an ice lolly, so long as you liked ugly flavour. He had a number of tattoos and we had to be careful of recognition, so we arranged to have him crisped at a bent crematorium, near Darvel. Poor Aidan, I was always blowing hot and cold with him.

I know I'm making this sound like the *Bumper Fun Book for Naughty Boys and Girls*, but in my saner moments I knew I was rocking on the rails and that a head-on crash was coming, which was why I jumped clear of the runaway train and took off down to London. Didn't make any difference, the crash still came, though not in the way I'd expected. Anyway, I'm getting ahead of myself, it's just that the past comes back to you in sharp, jabbing fragments as you walk around, a stranger in your own skin, smelling old smells and seeing old sights, which leave you blushing at sudden recollections and groaning out loud, like a loony, in the street.

*

The town hall clock told me there was an hour to go and I got this fluttering in my chest as my heart shat itself. Did I need a weapon? Yes or no? I pondered this question for the umpteenth time, debating the pros and cons of being metalled up or not. In my experience, violence begot violence, it raised the stakes a hundredfold. If you knew, or sensed, that the other chap had something on him, self-preservation stepped to the fore and reason receded. Your foe was free to batter away with equanimity since, by bringing a weapon, you'd indicated that violence was included on the menu. On this occasion, however, I chose to ignore my own advice and decided to take a pummeller to the party since, historically speaking, restraint had always been an underused tool in the Paisley problem-solving department.

I was in Causeyside Street, coming out of H. Baxter Limited, Ironmongers, an old haunt of mine, when a strange thing happened. I'd just bought a nice butcher's cleaver, a popular tool with my particular class of surgeon, when, out of the corner of my eye, I spotted a woman about to push a pram across the street. I scrunched up my bleary old peepers for a better look. Could it be? Fuck me up the funnel if it wasn't Brenda. I remained looking, knowing I should glance away in order to avoid any possible confrontation, it was just that I couldn't bring myself to do so, I was too drawn. She clocked me, of course, women always being alert to any form of attention, and she faked a double take. She'd had the opportunity to blank me but the fact that she hadn't told me something had changed since the last time, five years earlier, we'd looked into each other's faces. Remembering that occasion I recalled snarling (hers) and a bleeding ear (mine.)

Six months after that, her broken heart superglued by pride, she had shacked up defiantly with this wispy wallflower of a painter and decorating article, the one I've mentioned before, called Stuart. And together, as far as I was aware, to the juncture here described, they had remained. Was she happy? Who knew? I don't think people are ever happy, I think they just end up giving up the struggle for perfect love and stay put, through exhaustion.

Anyway, she went, 'Well hello, for heaven's sake,'

and extended a friendly hand. I smiled and shook it. The last time I'd seen that hand, it had been trying to separate my right ear from my head.

'Hello, Brenda,' I said. 'My, you've been busy.' I indicated the sprog in the pram and she laughed lightly.

'Oh, he's not mine' she said. 'I wish.' Her hand had flown up instinctively to fiddle with the locket at her neck, I noticed. 'He's called Stuart,' she said, 'after his granddad. Quite a thought, isn't it?'

'For him maybe,' I said, 'not for me. How about you?'

'What about me?'

'What's it like being a grandma?' I'll say this, credit to her, she didn't miss a beat.

'I don't know,' she said, 'why don't you ask Cindy, your father?'

We looked at each other, thin smile to thin smile. 'That'll be the formalities over with then, is it?' I said.

'Looks like it,' she said. 'You up for the funeral?' I told her I was. 'I liked your mother,' she said, 'she lived life to the hilt.'

I glanced at the snoozing sprog in the pram then back at Brenda. 'Same as you, eh?'

'I get by,' she said.

'Yes,' I said, 'you look like somebody who gets by.' I don't know why I was nipping at her, it was just something I couldn't help doing. Perhaps it had something to do with the hard-on I now had or the strange, familiar smell of her perfume. Here we stood, chatting more or less politely, on the pavement like two people who had never bought their first home together or fucked each other using handcuffs and blindfolds.

She pushed a hank of dark hair behind her ear. 'You know,' she said, 'hating your mother was always one of your least endearing traits.'

I shrugged 'She made it easy for me,' I said.

'Then why come up for her funeral?'

'I'm writing another book,' I said. 'I thought it might give me inspiration.'

She adopted a vague, faraway tone. 'Yes,' she said, 'I'd heard you'd come out with a book.'

Come out with, I liked that. As if I had just vomited it up onto the page. Which, who knows, maybe I had. 'I glanced through it once myself,' she said. I bet you did, I thought, I bet you glanced through it with a lawyer at one elbow, a private detective at the other and a jeweller's monocle in your eye. Then she said something that pricked up my ears. 'Stuart's pal did Darko Lyall's living room this weekend. Your name came up.' I felt my heart give that same little flutter. 'Oh yes?' I said.

'Yes,' said Brenda, 'he didn't know there was any connection with me, but this is a small town . . .'

'I've noticed,' I said.

'And I'd be careful if I were you. Stuart's pal heard him talking on the phone to Calum. It was the day after your mother died. Stuart's pal said it sounded like they'd a big score to settle.'

'I see,' I said. 'He say anything about Peter and Paul?'

She looked surprised. 'Peter and Paul? Haven't you heard?'

'Heard what?'

'Peter and Paul are in the IT business. They did three months in Barlinnie for tax offences and when they got out they started up a company, PrisonArt.com. They handle every big name artist at present in captivity. There's rumours of a big money bid for Jimmy Boyle.'

I felt the ground shift under my feet as another of the old certainties crumbled. 'You mean they've got out of the hooligan racket?'

'Maybe,' she said. 'If you believe the Scottish papers, that is. There was a bit of a rumpus in the *Sun* over them wanting to sell concrete handprints of top mass murderers, you know like they do with movie stars, but it turned out to be a wind up.'

'It's not like the Gradys to chase the limelight,' I said.

'Naked is the best disguise,' said Brenda.

'Thanks for the tip,' I said. She blushed a bit, or maybe that's just what I chose to think. She pushed that unruly hunk of hair back behind her ear again. 'I'd have phoned to let you know,' she said, 'but I didn't have your number.'

I reminded her that phones and us had an unfortunate history. She'd thumped me with one as I'd slept one night, an onyx repro antique effort with a Bakelite receiver, a four-stitch misdemeanour. 'It was the nearest thing that came to hand,' she said, 'think yourself lucky we weren't in the kitchen.' I acknowledged my good fortune. 'Take another tip for future reference,' she said. 'Next time your tart gives you a blow job, it's best to wipe the lipstick off your cock before going home to your wife.'

I nodded. 'When I see Stuart,' I said, 'I'll pass that on.'

The sprog started to whimper as it woke up.

'There's no need,' she said, 'Stuart never gives me a

minute's worry.' She rocked the pushchair like a real bona fide mother.

I put a hand on the rail and helped her.

'What about you,' I said, 'do you ever give him anything to worry about?' She looked away. She wet a dummy and stuck it in the sprog's mouth. 'You'd have to ask him that,' she said.

I told her I would. 'Where is he?' I asked.

'Saudi,' she said, 'six-month industrial contract.' She extended her hand again. 'Well cheerio then,' she said. I held her hand, then leaned in and kissed her on both cheeks, London fashion, for badness. 'Cheerio then, Brenda,' I said, 'maybe we'll bump into each other again.'

She took an old electricity bill from her bag, tore off a scrap and scribbled a number. 'Here,' she said. The green man was flashing. She released the brake on the pushchair and hurried across. Her figure was still trim and her arse pert. I felt a sudden spasm of shame over the slight paunch that was hanging over my belt.

*

I took a minicab to the back end of the crematorium and paid off the driver. When he was out of sight, I walked down somebody's garden path, into the back and climbed over the stone wall, down into the graveyard. The crematorium block stood a couple of hundred yards up ahead, half hidden by trees and large, ornate sculpted headstones. To the right I could see wrought-iron gates and the straight, pock-marked road along which the hearse and cortège would drive. A minister was standing outside the building, leaning on the small brick wall, Bible in hand, fag in the other, having a swift drag between disposals. I made my way through the long unkempt grass and toppled headstones towards a big, dank mausoleum structure, probably the tomb of a local alderman or maybe some failed tobacco baron who couldn't hack it in Glasgow. I positioned myself so that I could see the driveway without attracting undue attention. Anyone spotting me from this distance would take me for a meditative cunt, mourning some distant loss as I ambled reflectively among the headstones. Standing among the discarded needles and chip papers it occurred to me I'd been here before. I even dredged up, from somewhere, the name carved into the smooth stone plaque built into the mausoleum I was standing by. Archibald Nathan Ferguson FRCS. I said it over to myself then checked on the plaque to see if I was right. It hit me that this is where I'd dodged off to, the week following the hideous revelation of Cissie's defection into other arms. With an afternoon to kill, I'd ambled around the town then too. Boredom had lead to morbidity and I'd enjoyed a hearty outdoor wank under the grimy sandstone eaves of Archibald's last resting place. At the time I'd no idea what FRCS stood for but now, thanks to the instilled benefits of a spasmodic comprehensive school education, I felt humbled to know he'd been a surgeon, just like myself. Though it was unlikely I could match him in the technical department, one area in which I did feel I could comfortably compete was pain, I had grown used to its give and take. Though, if truth be told, I still preferred to give.

A light drizzle started and I stepped backwards, onto

a mulch of last year's dead leaves and fag ends. To the right, through a crater in the stone lattice window of the mausoleum, I could see the minister step back onto the portico, take out a hanky and wipe drizzle from the lenses of his gold-rimmed specs. Like me, he had time to kill. In my experience, that's one of the main differences between ordinary civilians and criminals, the handling of boredom.

Most of the time, even feared criminals lead the same lives and have the same fretful worries as everyone else: they grumble about the phone bill, they watch *Holby City*, they support Charlton, but when it comes to the black holes of boredom that punctuate everyday life, the difference is marked; they can't handle it. Many would sooner take the gee-up of some hare-brained dotty snatch plan than slouch on the Parker Knoll for weeks on end between jobs, listening to the rain pattering off the dormer window. In these cases, boredom is the policeman's friend. Intelligent criminals will often take silly chances, moving outside their accepted area of expertise, rather than endure one more evening of Carol Vorderman and her *Better* fucking *Homes*.

The town hall clock struck something, distantly, I couldn't hear what above the rumble of the traffic. I took out my mobile and tapped one, two, three. I hated dialling the time. I couldn't stand that failed Shakespearean actor cunt who did it. 'Good hello, kind sir, my name is Arnos Grove, permit me to furnish you with the hour. At the third stroke, the time sponsored by Accurist will be . . .' Anyway, thirty-five minutes to go, not a mourner in sight and I was starting to turn twitchy. I felt for the edge of the new cleaver sticking out from my waistband but the touch didn't bring reassurance, only dread, because, tell the truth, I was scared stiff of having to use it. It was five years since I waved tools in earnest and I was concerned about my lack of match fitness. On top of that, I was well aware that technology had moved on in the interim. It was all very well me leaping out the shrubbery clutching a fierce kitchen utensil but if they were all standing there holding rapid-fire automatic weapons, I'd look a right lemon, wouldn't I? They'd bury me where I fell and carve donkey's ears on my tombstone, my reputation would be thoroughly shredded. I took deep breaths to compose myself, feeling in dire need of a pee.

I was cascading into a corner when I took a sudden flash of *déjà vu* and looked up. I scraped my nails over a thick film of grime and moss, and there it was, etched into the stone, the message I'd carved out with my mother's potato peeler all those years ago. *Albert B loves Cissie C.* I was so choked up, it was all I could do to piss straight, let alone run amok with a cleaver. Standing there four decades down the track with my bad back and my Marks and Sparks suit, I felt like fucking Methuselah. About a fortnight after I carved this, we'd moved to Ralston. If I turned and craned my head I could see the Ralston Road. Why had we moved there? It was no place for poor trash like us. Billy Waugh made it happen, so all hail to King William, Friend of the Poor. Though I doubted if my father would agree.

*

We were moved in by a Barrhead firm, whose name I don't recall, possibly Robbing Bastard and Sons, because they swiped, in the process, two large cardboard boxes containing my American comics and my mother's china ornaments. Our accusations were met with indignation, which turned to outright scorn when they realized my father was unwilling to engage them on the matter. They drove off, leaving the entirety of our possessions, but for beds, in a loose heap on the living-room floor, like a badly stacking bonfire. I committed their faces to memory and to the list of Those Who Must Be Slain when I reached the magical age of homicidal capability, which I'd judged to be around, oh, eighteen.

Over the next months, the talk was of furnishings and the finer things in life, like central heating and blankets that didn't come with sleeves. Curtains were purchased, from the mighty House of Fraser and, though ready made, they were also lined, allowing my mother to demonstrate their double-sided luxury to the world with cunning folds and an artful use of tie backs. For the first week she'd open them like a mayoress performing a civic duty, pausing as if for applause, while I lurked in the corner by the standard lamp, eating bread and sugar. A three-piece suite arrived, which I was ordered to treat with care and reverence, like it was a disabled relative or a policeman. A new double bed appeared, with velvet headrest, and lino for the bathroom floor, which the Prick, while laying, managed to stick his foot through, thereby causing the Cuntess much anguish and chagrin. Occasionally, the dread spectre of money would loom up but the Cuntess would quash all doubt by promising to find part-time work, maybe at Gailbraiths, where they were 'always' looking for counter assistants. The gap between intention and achievement seemed non-existent to her and she treated discussions about employment like they were work itself and therefore subject to reward in the shape of clothes and soft furnishings. The Prick found himself ground into the lino under the heel of my mother's social aspirations. One Saturday morning over breakfast, I watched as she removed his *Daily Mirror* from his hand while he ate and replaced it with a copy of the posher *Glasgow Herald*. Plainly, a reckoning lay ahead. But how far ahead? And what form would it take? As usual, the answer wasn't long in coming.

I'd been enrolled at the local high school and didn't like it. I resented the loss of my privileged status as psychotic school freak and knew it would require the odd unusual action to impress my new classmates and restore myself to my former pinnacle. I also knew that school wasn't worth a fuck to a young man of my invisible talents and that, consequently, I had little to lose by behaving badly. Whether I had anything to gain by such behaviour was a factor in the equation I hadn't stopped to consider. Anyway, the upshot was, I went in for a spot of civil disobedience. This took the usual form of lip, backchat and general non co-operation. When requested to do homework, I'd question its relevance to everyday life. If required to display manual dexterity, say by creating some rickety toothbrush holder in woodwork, I'd make a deliberate arse of it, or else just down tools. These offences were punishable by the then traditional means of belting and when I'd refuse to present my hands in the accustomed fashion for punishment, the system was thrown into confusion. Nowadays, rebelliousness in schools is of epidemic proportions but back then the heavy hand of educational authority still commanded respect and wasn't for pissing on.

By the time of my third refusal to accept corporal punishment I'd achieved my heart's desire and was regarded as a man of consequence around the playground. Since my celebrity was founded on defiance of authority, and posed no threat to my peers, indeed was often a form of blissful disruption to some dreary lesson, I achieved for the first time in my life a measure of popularity. In the playground, guys took to hanging around with me, the odd girl too, a few even cultivating a milder form of my belligerence in the classroom, which irritated rather than flattered me, since I felt myself alone to be the one True God of Truculence. By accident, I had acquired the makings of a small and motley mixed-sex gang. This sort of celebrity, however, carried a price ticket.

In order to maintain my position as leader, I pushed myself, and the school, to an inevitable conclusion. Following several unhappy meetings between my parents, the headmaster and a representative of the local education authority, I was duly expelled. Two more schools and two further, rapid expulsions came and went. My past life as an apprentice arsonist was, inevitably, dragged up, which meant that each time I entered a room, I'd find my reputation had arrived before me. Not that I was worried. I had no concerns for my well-being, moral or otherwise. I didn't think of myself as a bad person, I just couldn't see the point of being good. Looking back, I should perhaps have stayed onside, it would have made my early life easier and at least I'd have kept some friends. As it was, what with constant chopping and changing and the ongoing friction between the Prick and the Cuntess, I retired into myself and stayed there. It was as if my life was both eventful yet, at the same time, deadly dull. Anyhow, one day, as I say, all of that changed.

I'd been sent for an interview at a remedial school, two bus rides away in Giffnock. There'd been some gibberish about special tuition and a psychologist called Mrs Elgin had recommended me for acceptance. I'd found this perplexing, as I thought I'd given all the appropriate responses to avoid such an outcome. After the interview I headed home. I remember turning into our street and seeing yet another delivery van parked outside our door. No surprises there. I could see my mother in animated discussion with two porters who appeared to be carrying a glazed mahogany sideboard into the house. This struck me as odd, as we already had one just like it, identical in fact. Mother started shouting stuff and that's when it dawned on me, they weren't there to deliver, they were there to collect. That side-board, a dining table and chairs, a pouffe, in Regency stripe with corded tassels, they all went. My mother was making lunges at the front door, with her sleeves rolled up and her eyes all red and puffy, trying to stop them. When she saw me, she made a grab for the pouffe and screamed for me to help. I shuffled a bit, irked and embarrassed. I wasn't about to make a cunt of myself over some fucking footstool. I could see eyes behind curtains and sense hot telephones on hallway tables. 'Let them have it,' I said, 'it's all crap anyway.' She glared at me like I was mad, gave me a slap on the jaw and resumed the struggle over this fucking pouffe. The touching thing was, I could quite understand why she was making such a big fight over it, true it was lightweight and liftable, but that wasn't the main reason. The real reason was the tassels, they'd given our home that piquant touch of shitey elegance that was so dear to my mother's heart.

That evening, at tea, my father was surprised to find the table gone. He sat, plate on lap, in silence, while the Cuntess howled against the imperial Lords of Furniture and how the public had to be protected against heartless bastards who expected payment in return for goods and services. The Prick said nothing, it seemed all he could do to lift his fork to his mouth, so it came as a surprise when he sort of gulped suddenly, let the plate drop from his lap and lurched round to vomit down the side of the chair. He sat with his head in his hands, moaning, while the Cuntess frisked into the kitchen for cloths and disinfectant. Though I was eating, I couldn't resist a look at the trail of vomit that ended in a spatter on the plum-coloured Axminster. Curiously liquid it was, and beige in colour, as if it came from the belly of a man who hadn't eaten much lately.

As it turned out, my father had good reason for the recent diminution of his appetite. He sat there, looking wretched and useless, while the Cuntess got down to it with the Dettol and the Marigolds. When she'd finished, he offered her one of his fags, a Senior Service, a rare occurrence. What was more, she took it, an even rarer occurrence and an acknowledgement of the gravity of the situation. I watched while my father took a first steady puff, before exposing the contents of his troubled mind.

'I met Billy Waugh,' he mumbled, and picked a tobacco fibre off his tongue.

'Who?' asked my mother.

'The bloke I borrowed the fifty from. I owe him.'

My mother frowned. 'I know we do,' she said, 'but so what, we're paying him back, aren't we?'

My father didn't answer. Revelation dawned.

'Oh, my God,' said my mother, covering her mouth. 'How many weeks?'

'Four,' he said, 'it'll be five on Friday.' My father looked up. 'He's a gangster, Jessie, you know that, don't you?' My mother composed herself. She remembered my presence. 'Albert,' she said, 'away to your room.'

I stood up. 'How long before you get the kicking?' I asked.

My father shook his head, like a man who was out of his depth and frightened. 'I don't know,' he said, 'I've stalled them all I can.'

'Kicking?' said my mother. 'Jesus, that's all we need, you not being able to work.' She slumped forwards, placing her head in her hands, while my father tried to reassure her it wouldn't come to that.

'What will it come to then?' I asked.

'I thought you were told to hop it,' said my mother sharply. I shifted cheeks on my chair as a sop to upward trajectory.

She looked appealingly at my father. 'What'll we do, Jackie?' I was startled. It was the first time in years I'd heard her use his first name.

'I'll speak to him again,' he said. 'If I do a Saturday morning, I can make the payments, it's not the payments, but the interest, I can make the payments, but that damned interest . . .' He let his voice trail off.

In his hopeless, sluggish silence, I watched my mother's mind working furiously, darting this way and that, scratching like a ferret in a box for an escape. Finally, it came to her. She stubbed out her cigarette and sat upright in her chair, arching her back. 'Don't you speak to him,' she said.

'I've got to speak to him,' said my father.

'No, you don't,' said my mother. She let her voice settle. 'I'll speak to him.'

My father blinked. I waited for him to dismiss the notion out of hand but he didn't 'You'll speak to him?' he said. His tone was one of bemusement but I recognized the coward's seam of slyness.

'Yes,' said my mother, picking a stray dark hair from her stocking, 'I'll speak to Billy Waugh.' She looked up at my father and smiled. She seemed serene. 'Where would I find him?' she asked.

I noticed that my father was breathing hard, his vomity shirtfront rising and falling, rapidly. 'I'll take you there,' he said, 'I'll take you to where you can find him.'

And that's how my mother first met Billy Waugh.

Chapter Three

I was standing under the stinking, dripping, eaves of this tomb, thinking these thoughts when it occured to me that things had started happening: mourners were arriving in private cars and limos; I'd even missed the hearse pulling up and only snapped out of my reverie in time to catch the tail end of the coffin, borne by the usual dodgy-looking professional body handlers, disappearing into the chapel service area. Old bints with slosh-on tans and shiny black outfits were bowling in, alongside men with thicker waistlines than my own, tough old men, with lined faces and cropped hair, who clearly wanted to stand and jaw but who were tugged on invisible rope by their desiccated wives towards the gloomy organ music. Naturally, I was watching with keen interest for anyone I knew, or who knew her. The trouble was, after she took up with Billy, he controlled her, cut her off from her old friends, the ones she'd liked to go drinking with on Friday nights, association with him had catapulted her out of the poor trash category straight into the rich trash criminal culture. She was, as they say, a tart in a gilded cage. Without any way out, or back. And she did try to get back later on, as it happened.

In addition to the chief suspects, I was keeping an eye open for Billy. For the last three years, he'd been rumoured to be a semi-invalid, with talk of lungs and hearts and breathlessness and what have you, and though I thought there was some truth in that, I suspected it was just the usual party games to get the Revenue off his back and to lure his rivals into a false sense of security in preparation for a massive assault on their interests. The dogs in the street knew he'd have to do this before Mick, his son and heir, was handed the reins of the business. Mick being less than robust mentally, it was generally viewed that what he'd need to inherit would be a nicely fearful, pacified landscape, which would at least buy him a couple of years grace while he grew into the Big Chair. If this didn't ensue, so the argument went, then, after Billy retired, his rivals would rub their hands with glee and start snapping away at Mick's new domain like piranhas, until one day he'd wake up to find himself standing in the street in his underwear, clutching a box of Coco Pops. If, on the other hand, Billy could orchestrate a timely, large-scale offensive, it would send the message that even though he might be considering retirement, he'd nevertheless left his beloved spunk on the Big Chair, so maintained an active interest in all aspects of Mick's welfare. Of course, no cunt believed that Mick would ever grow into the Big Chair, except Billy, and then perhaps only because he had to. So, to all appearances, he'd boxed himself into a corner. Though it might all have been so different.

*

You see, it could have been me. Let me put that another way. It could never have been me. But it should have been. Billy had an eye for me once. It was him that fixed up for me to play that trial with the Krays. He didn't send Mick, because he knew Mick would have fucked it all up, playing the big I Am, refusing to pay his gambling debts, opening his big, broken-toothed yap, all of that. Oh yes, I was the apple of Billy's cock, once. So why didn't I climb onto the Big Chair? Easy, I wasn't family, was I? At least not blood family, not like Mick. In fact I hadn't seen Billy for ten years, not since that day at Duck Bay Marina, when he told me I had prospects and should be patient.

'Patience,' I said. 'Fuck me, Billy, I'm forty-one now.' That's when I told him to stick his job up his funnel. This was both unwise and ungrateful and forks went down heavily over the prawn cocktail, I can tell you. To this day, I think the thing that saved me was his relationship with the Cuntess. She'd long been Mrs Billy Mark 2 by then and even though she was on the way out, it would still have been unseemly, in Billy's eyes, to go chopping up his own extended family. In addition, there was no question that I'd be in line for an influential position someday, come the Coronation. The trouble was, I'd touched the Big Chair, and been close enough to feel the warmth of Billy's arse on it, I didn't want his poxy influential position, I wanted to be the new him, the cunt. And that was never going to happen, not unless Mick choked on a Smartie, or abdicated for the South of France with the Springburn equivalent of Mrs Simpson. Other than that, I was doomed to a life of frustration.

So I made the remark about the funnel and the job. Luckily, Billy didn't have me killed. Instead he gave me dispensation to continue making a living. The catch was, I'd no longer be permitted to earn it in Glasgow. Which was why I moved over the city boundary into Paisley, land of opportunity.

*

Thinking about Billy made me look about for him, all the keener. It was well known that Billy rarely stepped outside his own Glasgow neighbourhood, let alone into the next town, so the fact that he'd honoured my mother's wishes and was having her crisped in her home town, showed that there had remained between them, at least, a vestigial respect. More selfishly, the terse fax that Billy had his minion send me, suggested that underneath his unforgiving exterior, he still observed the old decorums. I might not have been family to him but I was to her. I made up my mind that if I saw Billy, I'd risk putting in a public appearance, reasoning that since he'd extended me an invitation to attend, however grumpily, I'd now be his guest and could move about in the cover of his protective wing. That's of course, provided he showed. If he didn't show, if the rumours had been true, that he and my mother had hated the sight of each other, then I couldn't hover about here indefinitely, waiting for some adversary to leap off a granite cherub and stick a bayonet into my tripes. Come what may, I decided to lurk around till the service was over, then push off, out of harm's way.

A female figure with a blonde Doris Day bob, had taken up a stance by the gates. She wore black evening gloves, carried a white handbag and looked generally, like a bit of a lost soul. She had a self-conscious way of flicking her hair back from her cheek that looked, oddly, both diffident yet stagy. I watched her, watching a shiny limo pull up, and was intrigued by the way she stepped back into the shadow of the trees, to be half hidden by the pillar of the big iron gate. Three arseholes in quilted black bomber jackets got out and did a lot of silly we-are-professional-our-steely-gaze-never-leaves-the-crowd-type amateur bodyguard acting. They were the kind of big rough boys that, up until a couple of years ago, people would employ as doormen. Their presence here was some kind of statement. I found myself wondering what sort of tasteless oaf was making it.

So when one of the bomber jackets, the one wearing a black Kangol hat, waved the chauffeur away and held open the passenger door, I was interested to see who'd step out.

An ageing man appeared. He had a fierce, craggy face that looked like it should be carved on an Ancient Greek's war shield. He stood up with slight difficulty and stretched his back. He wore white shirt, black tie, dark blue suit and, on his feet, a pair of tartan slippers. He didn't even bother to look about. Why should he, he'd seen it all. As I've said, he'd been shot, firebombed and stabbed with a hatpin. Against my will, and despite my disappointment at his low-rent entourage, I was thrilled to see Billy again.

He stood, calm as you like, while two of the rough boys replaced his slippers with a pair of patent leather black slip-ons. That done, he made his way over the loose chippings on the path up towards the chapel. I noticed squares of white sock showing through his shoes, where he had holes cut to accommodate his bunions. One of the Jackets, one with faded red hair, offered Billy a stick and he looked at it like he'd been invited to hold a dog turd. This gratified me. It told me that the entourage wasn't Billy's but had only been supplied, like a rented suit, for the occasion. As the Jacket stepped back, I noticed the Doris Day blonde sidestep briskly, to avoid being trodden on. People were making for the chapel, but not her, she clung to the shadows. Once into his stride, Billy moved purposefully, nodding this way and that to well-wishers and star-fuckers, all eager to pump to the hand of the greatest living Hard Cunt in Caledonia.

It was supposed to be a quiet, family gathering, but I recognized a couple of retired footballers, a cable game-show host and an ex-weather girl wearing please-look-at-me-I'm-grieving black Ray Ban's. A couple of press snappers mingled with cameras unobtrusively poised, clicking away whenever two mildly famous cunts chatted together or rubbed their faces in any gesture that might loosely be construed as tearful. The sight of lots of people lowered my defences a bit and I began to acquire a spot of shaky confidence. For some reason, you don't believe you can be stiffed if there are handshakes and cheesy grins and feathered hats all about you, it seems incongruous. So I found myself creeping out of the shrubbery and making my tentative way through the long, unkempt grass towards the chapel building. If anyone was after me, they'd be unlikely to do anything here, I reasoned, not with Billy present in his funeral suit, it would be downright disrespectful.

On balance, it looked the percentage shot to me to find a spot on the pews, with everyone else, and warble my way through the hymn sheet. Nevertheless, I'd sit at the back and keep the cleaver handle peeking out, ready in my waistband just in case.

So it was, to the sound of her favourite song, 'Secret Love', that I saw my mother cremated. I won't pretend a thousand memories flashed by, but I can say I was in a state approaching turmoil by the end of it, her being, old cunt or not, the only proper mother I've ever had. I sat tight on my pew, on the aisle, back arched for posture and comfort, while the Collar made his eulogy. 'Jess was a wonderful wife and mother,' he said, 'a tower of strength to all who knew her, and bore her illness with fortitude and courage.' Discuss. It was all bollocks, for a start, no cunt ever called her Jess in her life. I hate that stuff, you know they're just reading off the same script, with the names changed, they ran through half an hour ago, when they crisped the last old bag. Billy was seated at the front and I watched the back of his head for signs of emotion. Not a flicker. When it was all over the Collar thanked us for coming. I swung my knees in to let the rest of my row out first. I wanted Billy to see me. There'd be a buffet afterwards and if he invited me, I would go. If he didn't, I wouldn't impose myself, it was up to him, all I could do was place myself in his eyeline and let him decide.

I watched him stand up, accepting help he didn't need with good grace, since it was more to do with being the centre of attention this time rather than infirmity, and make his way up the aisle. The fucking great meat cleaver was cutting into my leg. I had a sudden panic that if one of Billy's people were to clock it, my motives might be misconstrued and I could find myself in a bit of a pickle.

On the other hand, it was the only insurance policy I had. After a brief swither, I opted for discretion and crouched down, pulling out the cleaver and pushing it under the red velvet cushion on the seat next to me. I felt quite naked without it, and with this thought occupying my mind I almost had a heart attack when a big shovel of a hand slapped down onto my shoulder.

In fact, I must have actually jumped, because Mick Waugh's beefy, boozer face looked extra gleeful as it said, 'Fuck me, Albert, I better get a cleaner, there's a puddle under your seat.'

I straightened up, offering him my hand to shake. 'Hello, Mick,' I said.

'Hello Albert,' he said. He didn't shake my hand, but instead hugged me, one of those vomity gangster-flick affectations that have no place in Paisley.

'I didn't realize you were here,' I said.

'You weren't supposed to,' he said laughing, 'I was on the door, making sure there were no gatecrashers. Have you said hello to Billy yet?'

I shook my head. 'I'm waiting to pay my respects,' I said.

Mick gripped me by the elbow 'You don't have to wait, Albert, you know that.' He turned and called Billy. 'Da,' he said, 'look who's here.'

Billy looked into my face. He stepped up to me. He was still big close up, and kingly. 'Well, well, well,' he said, 'you made it then?' He offered me his hand. I shook it.

'Yes, Billy,' I said, 'I felt I had to come.'

'Good boy,' he said in a loud voice. He remained

gripping my hand. He wanted the gesture to be seen. And so did I, believe me, so did I. I always had this feeling around Billy that, no matter how old I got, or how much I had achieved, I was still naïve and coltish next to him, like an impetuous schoolboy.

It was as if I'd never had a team of my own, or a jail sentence, or a divorce, or any of the other manly afflictions that are supposed to temper character. Next to him, I was this partial creature, scuttling around under the shadow that he cast. But I suppose a lot of people felt like that about Billy. And credit to myself, I hid it well.

When he'd finished shaking, he let my hand drop. 'There's a purvey up at the Hilton,' he said, 'are you coming?'

I affected a diffident shrug. 'Am I invited?' I asked.

He showed me his short stumpy teeth. 'Don't talk like a wumman,' he said, 'you'll come in my motor.' I made a mental note to lend him my copy of *Modern Man Reconstructed*. He turned to Mick. 'Mick,' he said, 'Albert's coming with us.'

'Is there room?' asked Mick.

'There is if you get out and follow in the second car,' said Billy.

'Right, Da,' said Mick. He wasn't smiling. Neither was I, but I knew I would be later, when I'd time to look back and savour it. We walked outside together, side by side.

'She was quite a gal,' said Billy.

We were standing on the chippings waiting for our car. 'Yes,' I agreed, 'she wore the trousers in our house.'

Billy gave me a quizzical look. He took a deep breath

and threw his arm around my shoulders. 'Let's go,' he said. So we went.

*

It was good to find myself among enemies again, it made me feel wanted. In the bar of the Hilton, following the ham tea, we all bought rounds at exorbitant prices, pretending not to notice, for we were criminals and money was supposed to be no object. In no time at all, I'd run out of cash and was reduced to flashing the plastic. This brought a gloating snicker from Mick and the first signs that the drink was beginning to loosen inhibitions. Luckily, most of the others were in the same financial boat as myself so his jibes fell on resentful ears. When I pointed out to Mick that, unlike him, most crims in the room were freelance while he was featherbedded, working for the criminal equivalent of Microsoft, Scotland Limited, I felt, for the first time, a spot of warmth head in my direction. Even Billy, who prided himself in his lack of humour, managed an approving grunt. 'Same old Albert,' somebody said and I raised my glass. Just for a second, I believed it too, that I was Mr Cheeky Hooligan Chappie and that the last five years hadn't happened. I began to wonder if I'd found my way home.

Mick tapped on his glass for silence and Billy got to his feet and made a final speech, thanking everyone for coming and wishing them a safe journey home, a polite way of saying, fuck off, me and my mates want a gutful. He and Billy stood at the door, bidding farewell to Glasgow's more tedious or henpecked gangsters, kissing their clapped-out wives goodbye and promising the men they'd be in touch if anything suitable turned up.

People still wanted to work for Billy, his name was a brand that cut deep into the market place and, in these uncertain times, was still a guarantee of satisfaction and a job well done. That was the reverential version. To anyone under forty, of course, Billy was a fucking neanderthal from the tenement swamps, long overdue his walk into the sunset, and whose continued dominance was an affront to progressive on-message Scottish thugs everywhere. The new wave wanted a gangster they could identify with, with a plastic septum and a website, someone who didn't tuck in his shirts, who chummed up with Ray Winstone and could walk into the Corinthian without looking like he'd come to fix the boiler. They resented the old-school chiv elitism of the Barlinnie Special Unit with its taint of privilege. What they wanted, of course, was the middle-class Britflick image of gangsters, not the thing itself. It also went without saying that the subtext to all this was, can we be kings now? And one day, sure enough, one of these gel-headed, Tommy-shirted piranhas would seize the Big Chair and perhaps blossom into majesty but, for now, no one could say which of them, or when. Between that generation and Billy's stood me and mine, and if any one of my lot wanted ever to sit on the Big Chair, we'd have to make our move soon, or feel for ever thwarted. And in the meantime, we were all stuck with Billy: with his keg heavy and his reading specs, his Dickie Valentine records and his square-sliced sausage; Billy, who three years earlier had arranged the mincing of a colleague's love rival in exchange for six tickets to *Riverdance*. I was tickled when I heard this tale, not from Billy, of course, but from Mick, with his size-twelve mouth on his size-eight face. Billy rarely yielded details of any incident, past or present, that might link him, directly, to an outcome.

We moved on. We were in the lounge bar of the Variety in Sauchiehall Street, ties and tongues loosened, we sat drinking with the assurance of men who were at one with the pride code. Normally, I didn't like drinking in a group of men, I like the odd woman around, for frisson, but I felt the need of friends and, in their absence, as I've said, enemies do. Up at the bar, getting a round in, I felt hands squeezing me round the neck.

'I recognize them hands,' I said without turning, 'firm yet sensitive, they're Danny Wooler's hands.'

He gave me a big smile while his eyes narrowed, as always. 'I'm impressed,' he said.

'You shouldn't be Dan,' I told him, 'I could see you in the mirror.' I started to load drinks up onto a tray.

'I've got to ask you something, Albert,' he said. Oh yes, I thought, here it comes. 'That fucking book,' he said.

I looked surprised. 'Which fucking book's that, Dan?' I said. 'The fucking book I wrote or the one I'm writing now?'

He took a whisky off the tray, uninvited, and sipped it, swaying. 'The last one,' he said. 'What's it called, *They Call Me the Fucking Tree Surgeon*, that one.'

I invited him to tell me what about it, knowing he would anyway.

'That pissed a few folk off, that thing did,' he said. 'We never knew Robert De Fucking Niro came from Linwood, Albert.'

I tried shrugging. 'It was just a laugh, Dan,' I said. 'they wanted guns and violence, glamour and that, you know.'

He let his smile soften but his little eyes carried a glint. 'You named names, Albert.' I assured him I hadn't named names. He sensed me trying to wangle a side step and moved in front of me. 'Not directly, no,' he agreed, 'but get a grip, any cunt could tell from the way you told it, who was who and who did what to who.' It was fucking treachery, Albert, you surgeon cunt, you know that, don't you?'

I challenged him on his findings, asking who, exactly, had been arrested as a result of my luminous prose style.

'Nobody,' he admitted, 'yet. But thanks to you the polis know where to look.' He put the glass to his lips but didn't drink. 'And worse than that,' he said, 'we know where to look too. A lot of folk like things in compartments, Albert, they feel safer that way. You knocked down the walls, you cunt, you raided the treasure chest, and what's more you didn't even have the decency to tidy up after you.'

I stood and took it, though the irony of being lectured on decency by a man who employed twelve-year-old holes the way McDonald's hires counter hands wasn't lost on me. The way he was going on, you'd think we were fucking mafia, jealously guarding our ancient traditions while observing this strict code of secrecy, which was bollocks. Anyway, the point was, the subject of my perceived treachery had been broached and I knew that Dan, the walking bile duct, was pissed enough to say to my face what others were only bitching about with each other. Scratch the surface and I was not a popular fellow. Best not scratch the surface then, I reasoned.

We'd joined three tables together and I sat there, smiling till my jaws ached, listening to these tedious, self-glorifying cunts buffing up their war stories and hoping to pass them down into folklore. They were like a bunch of reps at the regional conference swapping unit sales boasts. I felt the benefit of the drink drain out of me and the longer I sat there the more sober I became. I'd forgotten how corrosive and jagged west of Scotland voices are and I found myself listening, fascinated and repulsed, by the staccato barks and brayings that passed for human speech. It was like one of Felice's dinner parties in reverse, where this time they were dancing bears and I was Mr Sensitive-Hyphen-Cunt, from Bayswater. Mind you, some of the content was quite entertaining, once you'd accustomed your ear and if you hadn't heard it before. Tommy Chung, the Chinese, told a nice restaurant story; how he'd done in a rival with a cleaver and had to keep bunging this CID guy to keep schtum. Eventually, Tommy got so fed up with greasing him, he'd shut down the restaurant and had relatives say he'd bolted to Liverpool. Six months later he re-opened across the street with a shaven head, thick specs and a Fu Manchu moustache, claiming to be his own elder brother from Stockport. It worked, according to Tommy, because 'One inscrutable Oriental cunt looks much the same as another to the average mason.' What larks, eh, Pip? Alex Howie was prevailed upon to tell his crazy rebel tale. Alex, always a hot head, was in Barlinnie and decided to go on hunger strike and dirty protest following a withdrawal of privileges. Unfortunately, he'd overlooked the fact that these were two mutually exclusive forms of dissent. The other cons had got to hear of Alex's plight and two days later, on his birthday, had arranged a special gift. A tray covered in a shiny wrapping paper was left outside his door and when he opened it, there was a platter of shite with a big birthday candle and a card saying 'From all your friends on A wing.'

You'll appreciate I'm giving you the pick of the crop here, the others being less piquant or well-turned examples of the hooligan raconteur's art.

Billy listened politely to all this and expressed amusement in the appropriate places but I noticed him taking discreet glances at his watch. At ten o'clock, on the button, he rose and said his goodbyes. Mick, with his big red face and his black tie trailing out of his pocket, looked disappointed, even trying to chivvy Billy into changing his mind. A chilly prolonged smile dissuaded him and reluctantly Mick stood and he too made his apologies. Everyone felt obliged to make a token show of breaking up the party but Billy, to his credit, was insistent they all stay and even put a chunk behind the bar to ensure a lively last hour. I stood up myself and, on the pretext of heading for a piss, walked with them to the door.

'Quite a day, Billy?' I said.

'Yes,' he agreed, 'I wonder what your mother would have made of it, probably she'd have wanted more fuss and palaver.'

Mick threw what he hoped was a consoling arm around his father's shoulders. 'Fuck it,' he said, 'funerals are for the living not the dead.'

Not for the first time today, I noticed that Mick had grown to be tone deaf where his father was concerned, constantly hitting bum notes that I could see grated on his old man. Billy turned to me. 'He means well, Albert,' he said, 'but unfortunately my son is a blithering cunt.'

I didn't know what to say, I couldn't exactly smile agreement or guffaw or that. I glanced at Mick. He was attempting to grin like it was meant as a good-natured tease, to be followed by a buddy punch and a fatherly hug, but was it fuck. Mick had the eyes of a stricken man and I almost felt sorry for him even though he was, to be fair, a blithering cunt. I shrugged and tried to strike a suitably philosophical note. 'I don't know what she'd have wanted, Billy,' I said, 'though a mink-lined coffin would've been a start. It strikes me she didn't know herself what she wanted, I think that was her main trouble.'

Billy wasn't having any. 'Oh no,' he said, 'she knew all right. For a long time I thought it was me she wanted, but it wasn't. The world thinks I was King Cunt to Jessie, but it was me that couldn't please her, not the other way round.' He looked at me in the face as he said that, which disconcerted me. I'd heard the tales of how he'd thumped her about, the dark glasses on dull days, the pashmina scarf hiding stitches, yet seeing him stand there, with his big dry monstrous eyes wide with emotion, I didn't feel anger. How could I? Because the thing about Billy was, you only had to look at him to know what you were getting. And my mother had looked at him. And liked what she'd seen.

'Where are you staying, Albert?' Billy asked. I told him the Marriott. 'Get your coat,' he said, 'we'll walk back.' I wasn't ready to sit in my room watching *Question Time*. I'd sooner have headed up Sammy Dow's and had a nightcap on my own, but I didn't want to blow out Billy, we were still, after all, roughly speaking, family.

*

Billy liked to walk, he explained, as we sauntered along Sauchiehall Street, even though he had didn't find it easy any more. 'It's age,' he said, 'and I'm not pretending but appearances are deceptive. I mean I'd lose to the fucking Queen Mother in a hundred metre sprint but from the ankles up I'm fit as fuck.' Mick and I nodded, dutifully. 'You've come a long way, Albert, since you were a boy,' Billy continued. I told him I hoped I still had a long way to go. This seemed to interest him. He turned to Mick. 'Did you hear that, Mick?' he said. 'He says he's still got a long way to go.' They both looked at me and laughed. I felt a bit isolated and tried a spot of grovelling to warm the atmosphere. 'I'd never have got anywhere without you giving me a leg up, Billy,' I said.

We stopped in the doorway of the kiltmakers shop for a breather. 'What you talking about?' he said. 'You talking about that wee message you did for the Krays out south Kent way?' I nodded, surprised he'd remembered. 'That was a favour to Joe Chisnall, you remember Joe?' I asked if he meant Young Joe or Old Joe. 'Old Joe,' he said.

'God rest him,' I said, like I was a warm human being.

'Yes, it's Young Joe now,' he said, 'and soon it'll not be Old Billy, it'll be this young cunt here.' Mick grinned, pleased to be a plain cunt, minus the former adjective.

He turned back to me. 'Whereas you were always ambitious,' said Billy, 'you always fancied London, didn't you, Albert?' I told him yes, I'd always fancied London. I told him I'd enjoyed my sally to south Kent with the Twins and had felt at home in the East End and had been, in all, saddened when my trial period hadn't been extended. When I added the bit about the unfortunate timing of events, Billy said, 'Fucking bollocks.'

I said, 'Pardon.'

Billy continued. 'You bang on about this unfortunate timing thing with south Kent and the Twins and what inconsiderate cunts they were for getting arrested but you don't mention Essex, do you?'

'Essex?' I said.

'Yes,' said Billy. 'The Braintree incident. You don't mention that as a fucking factor in your blighted career, do you?' I felt uncomfortable. Mick was gawping in the window at the kilts, probably looking up his relatives in the McArsehole Clan. Billy slipped off his shoe and wiggled his toes. 'That incident caused me a lot of fucking bother, Albert, and yet I don't recall as much as an apology out of you over that.'

I was taken aback. 'I'm sure I did, Billy,' I said. 'I believe I did apologize.'

Mick looked round from the window. 'Is there such a thing as a Hunting Waugh tartan?' he asked.

Billy gave me another of his full-frontal glares. 'You were always too free with your temper,' he said. 'You've got to be careful who you stab when you're a guest in someone else's home, or else you've a full-scale diplomatic incident on your hands.'

I told Billy the circumstances had demanded that I

prove myself. It hadn't been a question of going down there to shake hands and swap pennants. But even all these years later, he wasn't for listening.

'You went down there as an ambassador, you cunt. I gave you my special blessing. But did you give even the mildest of fucks about that, no you didn't.' He was shouting now. I stood, looking suitably chastened. 'To this day, that Desmond Elkins incident lives on,' continued Billy, 'I tell you, Albert, you done a bad thing there. If it hadn't been for your mother, I'd have left you down in London for the wolves.'

'God rest her,' said Mick, behind him.

Billy wasn't simmering down. 'I tell you something, Albert, you're still a fucking boy at the game. You think you're smart, but the only difference between you and him is he knows he's fucking stupid, in't that right, Cunt?' He gripped Mick by the chops and shook.

'Don't start, Da,' said Mick, wiping his face, 'don't spoil the night.'

Billy looked from me to Mick and back again. 'Don't spoil the night?' He poked Mick in the chest with his shoe. 'I've just buried a wife, you dud. I've got her fucking false teeth in one pocket and her wedding ring in the other, you callous fucking whoreson.' He started to beat Mick about the head with the shoe, like Mick was a big kid. But Mick wasn't a kid, he was a dangerous cunt and he didn't like being humiliated in front of me.

To spare him, and me, I turned away and started looking at the fucking kilts too. Maybe I'd find my tartan, Clan Valium. Billy was loud and gruff and drawing disapproval from the restaurant set and the crowds pouring out from the King's Theatre, round the back in

Bath Street. The lights changed and I saw a police car veer in, the wrong way, round the corner. I thought it was about to book a white van that was illegally parked further down, but when they swerved past that, up onto the pavement, I moseyed along the wall to the furniture shop next door. I was hoping that, in the event of Billy and Mick being huckled, I might pass myself off as Mr Innocent Bystander.

Two cops got out, an older one and a young one, and did the slow walk round the motor bit. Billy and the older cop started sharing a few words, and when I heard a bit of chuckling, I knew the temperature had cooled. When the older cop pulled out a notebook, I wondered what was going on. Billy wrote something and called to me.

'Albert,' he said, 'come here.' I approached, smiling benignly. Billy showed me the old cop's notebook. I read, 'To Jason, with all good wishes, Billy Waugh.'

'Jason's the officer's nephew,' explained Billy. 'Go on, Albert,' he said, 'you next.'

I took a biro from Billy. I looked dumbly at the policeman. 'Can you sign it from the Surgeon?' he said. 'Jason'll be well chuffed.' I obliged.

'Where you headed?' asked Billy. The policeman told him Baillieston. 'Can you drop us off at Springburn? Would you mind?' The policeman said it would be a pleasure and Billy and Mick climbed in. I watched as the two cops struggled to contain their thrilled smirks. Scotland's top hooligan duo in the back of their car, life would be all downhill from here. 'What about you, Albert?' asked Billy, winding down the window. 'I'm okay,' I said. 'I'll walk.'

'Suit yourself,' said Billy and shut the window. Then he opened it again. 'When you going back, Albert?' I told him I didn't know, maybe a few days. He couldn't resist asking, 'You got business?' I shrugged and said nothing. 'Do yourself a favour,' he said, 'get back to London. It suits you.'

I stole a look at the dashboard clock before the car squealed, in a florid arc, to join the traffic flow up to Rose Street. Five to eleven. Fuck it. *Question Time* and a hot chocolate sachet it was then. What the hell, I thought, it would be nice to stand under the shower, washing the pub smoke out of my hair, then have a little stretch out on the bed to rest my back. I'd think about dear old mum and all those joyous family times we had. Okay, so even allowing for sarcasm, why then did I find myself turning away from the direction of the hotel? Why was I heading, along West George Street, past Blythswood Square, and looking down the hill towards Anderston bus station? Easy. Because that's where the holes hung out. But I wasn't looking for any old hole. I was drawn by the singular attractions of a very striking and vivacious professional lady.

Looking back, I should've been more careful. But what with the drink and the imagined security of darkness and the fact that I'd just said cheerio to a couple of the most ferocious cunts in the Strathclyde region, I'd allowed myself to become unguarded. Consequently, my fearometer, which normally resides in my sphincter, wasn't functioning with its usual vigilant aplomb. I'd caught sight of the lady in question, standing at her usual isolated beat, well away from the other girls, at the NCP entrance. She'd changed from the demure dark two-piece

I'd last seen her in at the cemetery gates and was now done up in a lime green miniskirt with three-quarter length leather coat, held open for effect. The blonde wig was still in its Doris Day bob and she carried the same leather shoulder bag. She wasn't one of the smack herd across the street, you could tell that at a glance, and didn't seem to need their acceptance or approval. From a distance, my distance, this gave her isolation an alien quality, which was resolute yet faintly ludicrous. Did I say faintly? Make that slap-your-thighs-and-pitch-forward-howling-for-mercy hilarious. Mind you, my perceptions were admittedly tainted, given that I knew her history.

Seeing the holes smoking made me want one and I leaned against the wall, halfway down the slope of Douglas Street, and lit up. I still don't know why I let my guard down so much, maybe some obscure Queensbury rules part of my psyche thought that no foe would be so unsporting as to attack a rival on the day of his mother's funeral. In actual fact, that's the best time to do it, because rivals have their guard down and tend to lean against walls, smoking fags. At any rate, I barely noticed the squeal of brakes and the slamming doors of the white van till the fuckers were upon me, flaying into me with what I hoped were sticks and bats. The first hit thumped me on the side of the skull and, as my hand shot instinctively up to shield my head, the next caught me on the wrist bone, causing me to cry out. I couldn't see a single thing, just a blur of unspecified things beating down on me. I dropped onto one knee and someone started pulling my hair, trying to lift my head to make it a clearer target. There was a lot of swearing, they were calling me every cunt under the sun and I tried to fight back but it was hopeless. I grabbed a leg and pulled its trouser and some cunt hopped about cursing till he toppled over, hitting his head. I could make out the padded sheen of a bomber jacket and a hand grabbing a black Kangol hat off the pavement. They didn't appear to want to stop and I could hear groans of surprise and pain coming from my mouth as my brain tried to wrestle with what was happening to the body around it. When I heard myself saying, 'Oh my God, oh my God,' I knew I was approaching a point of no return.

Dimly aware of the need to protect my back, I crawled on my hands and knees towards the wall. The blows were beating the breath out of my body and I was gasping and wheezing for air, and flailing about in a panic. I had a notion in my mind to get away from this hill. There was a cobbled lane only yards away where the holes took their outdoor fucks and I knew if they yanked me out of sight down there, I'd be a dead person very quickly.

I needed Bothwell Street below, with its traffic and its watching holes and its CCTV. So I did the only thing, given my predicament, it seemed possible for me to do; I wrapped my arms around my head and I rolled, or rather, forced myself to approximate that action; because it's not fucking easy making like a roll of lino when your knees and ears are slamming off the pavement and cunts with table legs are battering at your ankles. I speculated they were hitting me with wood and not cleavers, because obviously, had it been the latter, I wouldn't have had any senses left to speculate with. So I fucking rolled and kept rolling, while the cunts kept leaping sideways, and in front, trying to stop me, but what with me having the momentum and them facing uphill, they couldn't, as the saying goes, achieve a proper purchase. They'd leap over me, panting and swearing, then elbow their way back into the pummelling pack, to thrash away like a bunch of old Indian women beating clothes.

Even when I hit the flat I kept rolling, and it was only the squeal of brakes and the shriek of voices that told me I was out in the middle of the street. The next thing I knew there was this piercing whistle and some fucker cutting loose with a pepper spray that choked my nose and eyes, and I have to report that blood and pepper taste better served up as sirloin than in phlegmy sickening gulps washed down from behind your own adenoids. The beating had stopped and I was lying, peacefully, looking up at the twinkling stars. Gruff Glasgow voices were crowding over me but, feeling as poorly as I did, I absolved myself from the responsibility of getting my arse off the middle of the street to allow the traffic past. Let somebody else do it, I thought, cometh the hour, cometh the man. Or woman. A pair of short-skirted legs were kneeling before me. I could see pantied crotch and didn't want to. Doris Day was reaching into her white shoulder bag for a Handy Andy. She began to dab my face. Somebody, a taxi driver I think, asked if she wanted to take me to the Royal Infirmary. 'Just help me get him off the street,' said Doris. I was sitting on the marble step of an office building, next door to the Admiral pub. From the jukebox I could hear Cher asking if I believed in life after love. The blonde was leaning in close and gazing, with a concerned expression, into my eyes. I blinked to let her know I was just stunned and hadn't croaked. A faint smile of reassurance flitted across her ancient, badly made-up face. The powder lay on her skin like the dust on Miss Haversham's curtains. Below her bobbing Adam's apple, I could discern a shaving rash. It occurred to me if the apple was bobbing, she must be speaking.

'You all right?' she asked. When I didn't answer, she shook me gently by the shoulder.

'Yes,' I said, 'I'm all right.' Then, out of politeness, I added, 'Thanks, Da.' And that's the last I remember.

Chapter Four

The complacent stupidity of the average Scottish heavy can be breathtaking. No wonder we haven't produced a genuine, top-flight, world-class evil cunt since the sixties. True, we did throw up Denis Nilsen, a workmanlike and diligent enough serial killer but, in the big league, he was a squad player rather than a star turn. I mean, how can anybody murder twelve people and still be boring? Des managed it somehow. Yet Nilsen, at least, was dedicated to his craft. Nowadays, the young talent values style over substance, it's all fun'n'guns and the Sean-Penn sneer. They're mesmerized by their own imagined reflection.

How else can you explain a recent incident, in which two hired hands from a council estate not five miles from Glasgow were delegated to snuff an enemy when the following occurred; they were sitting about the house watching *Trisha* and thinking, It's rotten being an assassin, we haven't had any assassinating work for yonks, I wish an employer would gamble on youth and give us somebody to kill, when the phone went, and it was a job. Naturally, they were overjoyed, they were two of Paisley's most promising young psychos. It was a chance to put themselves in the shop window. They were given the name of the target, where he lived and his place of work. It was also mentioned, in the course of extraneous detail that, oh, by the way, he plays goal for an amateur football team up Renfrew of a Saturday morning. They'd put the phone down giving it, 'Oh, thank you for this chance, gaffer, we mean to grab it with both hands.' Then they set about plotting the dastardly deed.

Now I ask you, put yourself in their shoes, how would you tackle this task? If you were to shrug and answer, 'I dunno, Albert, I'm just a decent, ordinary citizen to whom murder is abhorrent, but since you ask, maybe I'd wait until dark, ring his doorbell, then blast him on his Scooby Doo doormat and run away,' then that would be a worthy response. In fact, if that was your call, you'd make better murderers than they did and, like as not, you don't even murder. What you probably wouldn't do is this; you probably wouldn't think to yourself, as these two up-and-coming young regional superstars did: question – under what circumstances would we be most likely to kill this person and escape undetected? Answer – I know, why don't we wait till he's playing a football match with twenty-one other on-field witnesses and at least as many watching spectators and do it then? Brilliant. Oh yes, and let's make sure we blend skilfully into the crowd by standing behind his goalmouth wearing balaclavas, long coats and partially hidden shotguns. Great. Then when we've done him, we'll make a highly professional getaway in our own car and, in a further devilish twist, we won't even bother to change the number plates. As I say, you probably wouldn't do it that way, being sane, and that's why they're currently shuffling around the exercise yard at Barlinnie, fretting about the golden chance that slipped away, while you're now considering a new career in contract killing.

You probably wouldn't believe me, or maybe you would, if I added that they shot the wrong goalkeeper. The one they wanted was sitting at home, watching *On the Ball* and nursing a dose of flu. I mention this because it sprung into my mind as I was lying in a ward at the Royal, trying to piece together how I'd got there. Feeling pain, I asked myself if I was hungover. It reminded me of the run-up towards the end with Felice, when I would be out boozing and tomming around and doing the walk of shame in last night's suit along Holland Park Avenue at six in the morning. But I wasn't hungover, or, if I was, it was the least of my problems because my limbs shrieked and my shoulders burned and I could sense a large plaster across a throbbing ache on my cheekbone. Bit by bit it dawned on me I was in hospital and that I'd been done over.

My first panicky thought was for my back, so I arched it, with some trepidation, to see if I still could. When there seemed to be no more discomfort than usual from that quarter I began to calm down and assess events. Naturally, I wondered who'd done me and how I'd ended up in here.

Then I remembered my father in that hellish foxy lady get up. Oh fuck, I thought. I felt humiliated and furious just picturing the stupid old cunt. Of course, some may say, 'But Albert, are you sure that's all you felt? Didn't you also feel threatened and confused, that somehow your father's orientation was placing your own sexuality under attack?' No, I fucking didn't. I'd spent years, after my mother left, getting used to him parading about in dodgy get ups. No, the only insecurity it caused me was purely professional, that he could undermine, by association, my hard-won reputation as Mr Cold-Eyed Ruthless Monster. Try as I might, and yes, maybe I should have tried harder, I never got use to calling my father Cindy.

After my mother left, there was yet another reason why I could never take a friend home, assuming I could even find a friend, which usually I couldn't, because by then I'd stopped going to school and where else do you meet the cunts? I mean, to be fair, would you take a mate back, in sixties Scotland, and bear in mind the sixties didn't reach Glasgow till the eighties, if you thought there was a fair chance he'd bump into your old man in the kitchen, wearing slingbacks and a halter neck and peeling potatoes? I suspect not.

I grew angry as I lay there, thinking about how this pathetic secret had burdened my life. I resented that it was still happening now, when I was fifty plus, at a transitional stage in my career, yet here was this grotesque relic still tottering about trying to turn tricks and threatening to blow holes in my carefully cultivated image. A tart for a mother I could tolerate, but not for a father too. He was my Achilles high heel.

I asked a nurse for a rundown of my condition. Apart from a hairline fracture of the cheek and some heavy bruising, I'd got off lighter than I might have done. They'd pumped me up with Volterol when I started gibbering, in a panic, about my back, but I'd no recollection of that, it must have been a mild delirium.

The trolley came round with the newspapers and I bought a *Daily Express*. On page eight there was a picture of the funeral. Billy and Mick were snapped talking to me. A bit underneath read, 'looking frail, alleged underworld boss Billy Waugh leans on son Michael for support'. There was a close-up insert picture of a pair of hands displaying a cleaver. The byline read 'Horror find among the pews'. I had to laugh, even though I didn't feel like doing so. To tell the truth, I was ready to kill some cunt and I was starting to have a fair idea of who that cunt should be. As I've said, it's surprising how slovenly the work of some of these big-name Scottish heavies can be. Having mulled over the events, I had made a fair assessment of who was most likely responsible for the warning pummelling I had sustained. I was pretty sure it was a warning otherwise I'd be speaking to you now via an upturned glass on a Ouija board. Also, I was pretty sure the warning meant, 'Our thoughts are with you at this sad time. Now fuck off home and don't come back.' I just needed Cindy to confirm a couple of details and I'd be satisfied.

Needless to say, I hoped he'd have the decorum not to visit me wearing his working clothes and when he turned up in an anorak, looking reassuringly dreary, I could have kissed him out of relief. He pulled a chair from a stack in the corner of the ward, positioned it at a prim 'vous' distance near the end of my bed and perched his little bum daintily down. 'Hello, Da,' I said. 'Have a grape.'

His wary little eyes flitted about. 'You haven't got any grapes,' he said.

I nodded. 'No further questions, M'Lud,' I said.

He looked sheepish. 'I nearly didn't come myself,' he blustered, 'let alone bring grapes.'

His hands were all fidgety and his fingernails bore traces of varnish, which annoyed me. The stupid fucker had been a full-scale no-holds-barred bint for decades now, you'd think he'd have mastered the basic cleansing practices.

'I don't know why you came up for the funeral,' he said, 'you treated your mother like shit, like shit on the end of your shoe.' Before he could start playing all his usual cards, I thought I'd trump him early, so we could have a normal conversation.

'Possibly, Father,' I said. 'If so, I was only following the example she set with you.' He saw my searing sarcasm and raised me an inscrutable smile. Again this irritated me, as it was a card he didn't have in his hand to play. As far as I was concerned, no cunt could be more scrutable than my old man. Anyway, he started to elaborate in his fake smug way, trying to convince me, and possibly himself that, far from being an obvious, long term, arse-in-the-air, submissive cuckold, he had in fact been playing some wise and superior long game all along.

'You just don't get it, do you?' he said. 'I knew I could never control your mother, that's why I gave her plenty of rope. I knew it was my best strategy.' His use of the term 'strategy' tilted my mood over into the sardonic. It was like Julius Francis after the Tyson fight, claiming his strategy had been to get knocked out.

'Let me clear this up for you, Cindy,' I said. 'You

lost. She left you. Billy Waugh took her away. You had no say in the matter. You were shafted.' I hadn't really intended to crunch him, but the jovial staccato-type sentence structures I'd embarked upon had quite carried me away and had demanded a firm conclusion. His bum cheeks fidgeted in the chair. 'Let's talk about something else,' I said. 'I was hoping you could fill me in on the details of what happened last night, what with you being in the area like.'

He raised a restrained eyebrow. 'I'm often in the area,' he said, 'I'm not ashamed of how I live my life. The question is, what were you doing there? Eh, son? What were you looking for? And more to the point, did you find it?' I said nothing. He had Royal Flushed me in the short sentence routine, no question about it. I gave a sort of lame fuck-it smile.

'It was a funny sort of day all round,' I said. 'I hadn't expected to see you at the service.'

He became interested in one of his fingernails and began scratching at a bit of varnish. He mumbled one of those funeral platitudes about paying his respects. It's always people who've never had any respect who are the most lavish when it comes to dispensing it.

'I know you still loved her,' I said.

I was surprised to hear myself say the love word; I put it down to the kicking having unhinged my emotions. I tried to be manly and leave the 'l' word alone to steam and quiver there in the raw, but then I funked it and covered my tracks. 'Whatever the fuck loves means,' I said.

My father didn't answer. He picked up the love word,

folded it carefully and put it in a drawer somewhere in his heart. 'What is it you want to know about last night?' he asked.

I questioned him and he filled in the blanks. Yes, it was a van, a white transit. No, there were only four of them, including the driver; they'd got out and started booting me in the stomach to try to stop me rolling down the hill. I thanked the Prick for his timely use of the pepper spray and whistle. My father explained that, as a transvestite whore, these were essential items of everyday survival. Expressing a polite interest in his professional activities I enquired if there was much demand for seventy-year-old male Doris Days in Glasgow or, indeed, anywhere else on the planet. Not even my father could muster sufficient self-delusion to convince himself, let alone a sceptical other like myself, that his services might be regularly called upon.

'It gets me out of the house,' he said, 'and of course, I enjoy the craic with the other girls.'

I tried again, this time being gentle with him, for he had been gentle with me over my abuse of the love word. 'No you don't,' I said, 'you work the other side of the street, I know you do, I saw you. I never saw them other holes so much as look at you, or you them.'

He eyed me, thinking about whether to do perky-pensioner acting but seemed daunted by the effort and instead let his shoulders settle into a resigned sag. 'I know that,' he said, 'but fuck it, Albert, the frocks is all I have.' He looked up at me, voice tetchy with grudging confession. 'I need the buzz,' he said, 'it's like you with your bloody . . . mayhem.' He gave me a defiant, pleading look that reminded me, weirdly, of my mother. It made me wonder if the old fucker had been practising that look for badness. If so, it had worked and we stumbled together into a little crater of fellow feeling, the Prick and I. He confirmed the bomber jackets and the black hat that had fallen off when I'd gripped a leg.

By and large, he supported my theory that the slovenly, self-important arseholes who'd worked me over were the same ones who'd provided Billy's guard of honour at the funeral. All I had to do was find out who they worked for in order to establish which of my several enemies had borne the grudge. Why the fuck they hadn't just taken off their jackets before laying into me, I don't know. As I've said, the bone-headed stupidity of the Scottish criminal establishment shames us all. Small wonder the Mafia set up home on Sicily, and not Bute.

Sensing an end to our chinwag, my father sought to stretch the conversation. He took out the love word again and unfolded it. 'Where are you staying?' he asked. I told him. 'You can stop with me if you like,' he said, a bit tentatively. 'The company would be nice.' Not for me it won't, I thought. I thanked him and explained I'd be heading back to London in a couple of days. He gave me another of his inscrutable looks, then shook his head like a great seer who'd just opened for business. 'Don't take me for a mug,' he said. He stood up, stretching his creaky septuagenarian back which, I ruefully observed, was slightly less creaky than my own. 'I know you, Albert,' he said. 'The good bits and the bad. When all's said and done, you're still my son.' He picked up his chair, dutifully, and replaced it on the stack.

'Da,' I shouted after him, 'I'll call you.'

He nodded and left. I don't know why I said I'd call

him. I don't even know why I called him Da. Maybe underneath it all, I was feeling a bit of a lost soul myself. On the other hand, I reflected, that's when I'd often done my best work.

*

I rested up at the Marriott for a couple of nights while I steeled myself for my next move. I told myself the beating was a useful thing, I should regard it as a punishing training session. Naturally, this was bullshit, as no matter how beneficial to my mental and spiritual condition, I certainly wouldn't be putting myself in line for any similar workouts. Doings, like hangovers, take longer to recover from, the older you get.

As I reflected on the incident, I decided it was both a compliment and an insult that I'd been pummelled and not shot. It was a distinction that tended to break along age lines, with your hardened pummellers unwilling, on grounds of taste and personal prestige, to lay into some portly hooligan of advancing years, preferring instead to despatch him humanely with one through the ear. You could see their point, those mismatches had an unsavoury bullying air about them that could tarnish rather than enhance a reputation, a bit like when one of those WBA prospects tanned the arse off a fifty-year-old Larry Holmes. On the other hand, it was usually the case that those portly gentlemen were powerful figures and if you attacked one, well, you'd better make sure you killed him or woe is you when he got back from his Bournemouth rest cure. In other words, while the form of assault I'd been accorded flattered me that I was still a vibrant and vivacious physical threat, it also told me that I was no longer regarded as a mythical beast of the criminal jungle, who had to be despatched with a stake through the heart, lest he wreak terrible revenge for the indignities he had suffered.

This assessment of my capabilities peeved me, yet at the same time suited my purposes. Let the cunts underestimate me, I thought, that way I could go about my business diligently and unnoticed.

To work off some tension, I buzzed the hotel desk and complained about the chocolate and miniature Glenfiddich I could see charged to my account on the telly billing facility. A member of the service staff came up, rummaged about in the minibar and sort of hovered, looking unconvinced. I swayed him with my vehemence, however, pointing out that though the said items may indeed have been moved, they had nonetheless been returned unsullied to their former habitat and that consequently any form of billing was at best, unfair, at worst, unlawful. I hinted at powerful friends in local government. In actual fact what happened was that I'd succumbed to temptation during my recuperation, after consuming said items, and had replaced the Toblerone and Glenfiddich from the offy around the corner, a cunning tactic that resulted in an over-all saving of roughly two pound fifty. As a gesture of goodwill from the hotel, my modest bar bill was restarted from scratch. As a gesture of goodwill from me, I gave them my funeral suit to clean. It's not the principle with me, it's the money.

I walked into town and bought myself a brand-new set of kit. Nothing flashy, I'm only comfortable with labels that were labels before labels were labels, if you know what I mean. For instance, I'll wear Jaegar, or Grenson, but not Burberry. Thomas Burberry was too sneakily self-conscious, if you ask me, in the craven way he reinvented his brand for today, so that now, in my eyes, he's as tainted as the rest. So fuck Burberry, basically. But where, I cry out in the night, is Rael Brook? In my heart I still pine for Rael Brook shirts, a man's shirt, not a showman's shirt. Anyway, I walked back to the hotel, a mere fifteen-minute clump, had a shower, then stuck on my new kit to invigorate myself. The trick with new clothes is to wear everything new, that way nothing stands out as awkwardly spanking or shabbily old, despite the fact that it's all awkwardly spanking. Nobody thinks, Look at that twat in his new shirt, instead they go, 'Fuck me, that cunt gleams from head to toe, he must be minted.'

I felt guilty about the money I'd spent and, in an irrational attempt at economy, I took a train from Central Station to Paisley Gilmour Street. I had to stop behaving like I was on holiday and instead realize I was a small businessman trying to prise open his former niche in the market. I tried every pub in Paisley High Street, looking for Claw Hammill. I could, of course, have rung him on his mobile, but I didn't want him giving me the hipsway, or gauging anything untoward, in advance, from my tone of voice. I'd toyed with the idea of ringing Mick, inviting him out for a drink and saying casually, 'By the way, who was that team of useless, mouth-breathing fuckers who were snoking around Billy the other day at the funeral?' But as I've said, I didn't know the structure of the present allegiances and was anxious nobody should be tipped off and go on red alert. Also, if Billy, through Mick, caught wind and disapproved of my intentions, then I'd have no choice but to obey or be skinned and eaten.

Much better I ascertained the information from someone I could trust, that treacherous cunt Claw for instance.

Instinctively, I hung around McGinley's, which stands next door to Clore, the bookie, and sure enough, he appeared, wearing the same suit and T-shirt and waving a twenty at the bar staff. I did my previous trick of ringing him on his mobile, to see how he responded. He didn't look pleased to hear my voice and turned his head down, as he made towards the door. Being a psychic cunt, I was already there, blocking his path. I invited him to accompany me to the toilet. He protested that he didn't need the toilet.

'But you have to,' I said, 'there's no where else handy for kicking the fuck out of you.'

He pulled a shocked What's-it-all-about-Albert? face. I steered him into a corner and said it was largely all about the doing I'd been furnished with. I pointed out the ugly welts and bruises on my formerly pristine profile. He asked if we could sit down.

'Okay,' I told him, 'but I'm putting a clock on it, because I'm going to pummel you.'

He looked a bit perplexed. 'Is that negotiable, Albert?'

I reminded him he was a slimy pus bag, that he had sat and drank with me only days previously, knowing full well I was due to take a hiding, yet hadn't even had the courtesy to tip me the wink. 'If only you'd tipped me the fucking wink,' I said. He protested that he'd had no wink to tip and I found myself gripping his elbow. My teeth were clenched and bits of spit were hitting him as I spoke.

'You lying cunt,' I said. 'How can you fucking sit there, doing shocked acting, when you know you hung me out to dry?' I gave him an evil stare. 'No,' I said, 'you've got it coming.'

He sort of fell slack inside his suit and the tension drained out of him, leaving resignation. 'I know I should have said, Albert, but I was scared to get involved. I didn't want to risk a hammering. I can't take the batterings the way I used to, I'm getting old.' He shrugged and looked about in a startled way, having caught himself, to his astonishment, telling the truth. 'If I'd told you, they'd have pummelled me,' he said, 'because I didn't, you'll do it.' He gave a little whine as he looked at me. 'No offence, Albert,' he said, 'but all things considered, I'd sooner take my chances with you than the bunch of them, nothing personal, but I hope you understand.'

I did. How could I not understand his point of view? It was practically my own. If I'd been a better human being, I might've hugged Claw on the spot, given him an understanding pat on the shoulder, than sat down by a roaring amplifier, while we shared a malt and spoke about the old days. Luckily, however, and I speak as a businessman, I was a cunt and not a human being, so I took him by one of his gnarled misshapen hands and squeezed.

'Maybe that wasn't such a wise choice,' I said.

When I saw little tears glisten at the corners of his eyes, I let go and told him to head for the bogs, where I planned to continue the reprimand. Claw took two steps forward, turned, and whizzed out the door like a man who'd borrowed Linford Christie's legs, giving me no time to react. I ran outside, in time to see him jooking round the corner and running pell-mell down Storrie Street. I jooked after him, though I use the term 'jooked' in a qualified sense, relative to my age and condition. And for that matter, his. As I dodged, inelegantly, round little old ladies with their shopping bags and stone grey macs, I wondered if Claw could feel his tits wobble up and down the way I could mine.

I didn't make any serious attempt to catch him, knowing that if I just stayed in touch, he would, as a long-term forty-a-day man, eventually run out of puff. As it happened, this came to pass almost immediately, and when he pulled up gasping, hands on knees, I was so close I almost buggered the cunt. I let him stop wheezing but kept myself goal side to prevent any more electrifying runs down the wing. I was steaming like a horse and most aggrieved. I wasn't in the mood for any jokes, which was possibly why he made one.

'Isn't this the bit, Albert, where you say to me – "you're a big man but you're out of condition, with me it's a full time job?"' He was smiling. He didn't see the short butcher's boning knife, but I let him feel its hint on his abdomen as I leaned in. From hot and puce, he went cold and white in an instant. It's difficult to stab a man who's just made a comical remark, and I put the blade pack in my pocket.

'By rights, you should be dead,' I told him.

'I know,' he said. His smile was frozen on his face, like it was a good luck charm he was afraid to lose.

'Look,' I said, pointing across the street, 'there's a

nice tea room. Why don't we have a soda scone and a friendly chat, what'd you say?'

He said yes, having no choice, so we went in.

*

'Calum,' said Claw. 'It's his security firm. But I didn't tell you that.'

I spread a bit of butter on my scone and tried to resist the little pot of strawberry jam. 'What's he want with a security firm?'

Claw took a drag at a roll up. He wasn't a great one for afternoon tea. 'It's cover for drugs,' he said, 'the nice stuff, the Ibiza pish, his blokes sell on the doors of the clubs, but the bulk of it, the jellies and that, the leg rot, that stuff goes to the gangrene armies round the estates.'

I was puzzled. I asked him what happened to Calum's Cabs, the previous business he'd used as a cover for drugs.

'Oh, he sold that,' said Claw. 'It was a nightmare, cunts kept ordering taxis, it was driving him demented. He was working like fuck, making up wage slips, filling in VAT forms, poor bastard's supposed to be a drug baron, he's worrying about how to get early morning cleaning firms up to the airport, fuck that. He ended up selling it to Darko, which was a bad move if you ask me.'

I asked him why it was a bad move.

'Because Darko's got his drivers dealing,' he said. 'Never mind a cover, the cunt's got a full-blown delivery service Pizza Hut would envy. He's moved out of the town centre, away from prying eyes, but it's still too in your face. All right if you're in the South Bronx, Albert, but we're only fucking Paisley, get a grip.'

I told him I still didn't follow why Darko buying the taxi firm was a bad move for Calum. In other circumstances, Claw might have risked looking at me like I was a chap who was slow on the uptake. On this occasion, he just paused, nodded, and continued, as patiently as he could.

'Put it this way, Albert, it suits the punters fine. They buy from the cab driver in the quiet convenience of his clapped-out Sierra. By the time they hit the clubs, Calum's bears are scratching their heads, wondering why no fucker's buying their stuff. I mean it can't last because it's too blatant, but meantime Darko's cleaning up and Calum's standing with his thumb up his arse, looking like the cunt that sold the Beatles. That's why Calum wanted to hammer you, Albert, to show the world, or Paisley at least, that he still had the magic dust.'

A little blob of butter dropped from my knife onto the plastic tablecloth. The cloth had glamorous place names, done like passport stamps, all over it. Acapulco, Monte Carlo, Athens, that sort of thing. They're always stingy with butter in these gaffs, expecting one sachet of butter to suffice for both halves of the scone. I dabbed the blob with a paper napkin off Cannes. As casually as I could, I asked if Darko was now undercutting Calum.

Claw looked shocked. 'No, no,' he said, 'there's a gentleman's agreement with prices, it's a cartel after all, Albert. Sure, there might be a bit of bumping and boring but no cunt's prepared to rock the boat to that extent. Peter and Paul wouldn't take kindly.'

I thought I'd better rewind, out of harm's way, but Claw beat me to it.

'That's why Calum coughed up the guard of honour at the funeral. It sucked Billy's cock, making him look like fucking Napoleon and at the same time it gave Calum access to you. No cunt knows where you're staying, Albert. Where are you staying?'

'The YMCA.' I said. 'So are you saying Billy wouldn't give a fuck if he knew Calum had pummelled my body?'

Claw gave his approximation of a kindly smile. 'How can you be sure Billy didn't know anyhow? Maybe he just didn't want to be about when it happened. Calum wants you on the next plane back to London. You two've got a history, don't forget.' He dragged an ashtray close, covering Capri and Sorrento. 'So has his wee scare tactic worked?' he asked. I didn't answer. I had a quarter of a scone left and no butter. I screwed the lid off the little pot of jam and spread it on, thickly. Claw watched me. 'I knew you couldn't pass it up,' he said.

'What?' I said.

'The jam,' he said, 'that sweet tooth'll be the death of you.'

I shrugged and took a bite, a small bite, to display my iron will power. 'No chance,' I said. 'There's life in the old Surgeon yet.'

Claw gave me a wary look to check the irony meter. He risked a snicker. 'The fucking Surgeon,' he said, 'I ask you, Albert.'

I laughed back. 'I know, fucking pathetic, isn't it. Still,' I said, 'it pays the rent.' I finished my tea and pushed my empty cup back over Barcelona, the city that never sleeps. A waitress with a crimped perm and a club foot put the bill down on a saucer. 'Could you pay now,' she said, 'only it's halfday closing.'

We walked out into the early summer Paisley gloom. It was raining. 'No wonder cunts round here want drugs,' said Claw. I nodded but I wasn't listening. I'd decided to take a look in H. Baxter the ironmongers on my way back to the hotel, provided he was the sort of free spirit that opened all day Wednesday. They had a long-bladed steak knife that matched my short ebony-handled boning knife and I decided I'd be requiring the pair. Claw made to say goodbye, but I insisted on walking him as far as the old Burton's corner at the Cross. On the way back up the slope I'd chased him down earlier, we talked some more.

*

It occurs to me I may have painted for the unsuspecting tourist, a tainted and, somewhat lurid pen portrait of Paisley. May I take this opportunity to reassure you, the traveller, that the town is, in the main, soothingly dull, duller possibly than the last town you visited, or indeed, the one to which you will next journey. Paisley is a sturdy fusion of the dead and the commonplace. It boasts, at its tidy heart, a twelfth-century abbey that nestles close to a twentieth-century shopping mall, the finest, some say, in West Renfrewshire. A feature of the mall is its smooth and even thoroughfare that provides quick and easy access to Gilmour Street Station and therefore places far away. Further items of interest include the civic museum and art gallery, which is situated, remarkably, between two churches. So wave goodbye to that fruitless, wandering about, looking-for-somewhere-to-pray malarkey. Above the art gallery on Oakshaw Street, you'll find Coats Observatory (Tues–Sat 10 a.m. – 5 p.m. Free). Wherein, has been stored astronomical and meteorological data since 1884. A more recent feature is the town's thriving drug and violence trade, which has superseded the more traditional cloth and weaving industries that once made Paisley such a byword for tedium. To sum up then, Paisley offers something for every visitor, easily accommodating, as it does, the familiar schizophrenia of repressed Victorian stuffiness together with the latest fashionable advances in organized crime, substance abuse and casual barbarity. Yes, Paisley can truly lay claim to being the most ordinary town in Britain.

I'm being sarcastic, as I expect you recognize. What I'm saying is, Paisley used to be a nice little town, like anywhere else. Now it's a nice little town, with the underbelly of a hellhole, like anywhere else. As I've said it may be people like me were to blame for that, and I for one would agree. All I can tell you is, I didn't feel like the cause, I felt like the effect. I was the symptom, not the disease. All right, Albert, if you're a symptom, just what is the disease, go ahead, tell us, we're parents and citizens, we'd love to know. But I can't tell you. I've no more idea than you have about the nature of the disease. All I can tell you is, if I was the disease, I was not in charge. I was a worker ant. Take my work away from me, and I didn't know who I was. I suppose what I'm saying is, I'm a product of the old-school values that made this country great, just like you, even though I may also be the hideous, blinkered self-centred cunt that's doing it in, just like you. Fuck knows, we do what we do, victim and perpetrator.

*

I was thinking such thoughts as I lay in my hotel-room bed, admiring the ebony-handled knives I've told you about, the ones I'd bought from Baxter's. There was something satisfying about steel utility objects, like knives and tools and that, which made me regret, in some unspecified way, that I'd never employed myself with learning their intended function, instead of just hitting and sticking people in the guts with them, a gift which, let's face it, was well within the aptitudenal range of even the least dextrous individual. Nevertheless, uncomplicated and repetitive though it was, my trade had been good to me, offering me a lifestyle well beyond the reach of most people from my background. Hurting people had been for me the key that'd opened the door to a world of literature, music, fine wine and top-quality minge. Consequently, I honoured my craft and was protective of it.

But Albert, you may ask, didn't the collision of those two alien worlds, the worlds of books and fragrant ladies and that, didn't that world chafe against the world you knew, which was a threadbare world, of gashed settees and dried vomit, of moonlit kickings outside boozers, a world in short, of cunts, engaged in acts of cuntitude, didn't that collision fuck with your nut?

Well, to tell the truth, it did. I didn't think so at first. I had revelled in the contrast early on. In fact, before my first black tie charity function with Felice, well nigh our first date, I'd stolen away to perpetrate an act of violence against a lippy pub landlord who wouldn't pay his debts. I invited him out back into his bin yard and gave him a few taps with a hammer. An hour later, I was sipping Chardonnay with a tableful of elegant cunts, laughing politely and tugging up my cummerbund to hide the snot and brains on my shirt front. Did I have a conscience? No, Your Honour, I did not. I was more worried about the right way to tear my bread roll than what I'd done to that poor fucker's head. Did Felice know? Yes she did. Did she approve? No she didn't. Crucially, she didn't see the pictures. I think she imagined colourful cockney bar-room-brawl-type antics rather than the aftermath of weeping mothers and damaged sons left drooling in wheelchairs. In truth, her interpretation of events was one I was eager to encourage. For that reason, I kept my toolbox well tucked away and if ever I bumped into associates while in her company, say up the Groucho, or in the Atlantic Bar, I'd either tip them the wink or, if I couldn't, simply swerve her dainty arse out the door to safer pastures. Fucking women. They all like the poppy, every last one of them, but how did they think a cunt like me was going to get it? Selling futures on the stock exchange? I went out with a PA briefly, whose father was a brain surgeon. I bet I put a lot of work his way, but what thanks did I get? Anyway, there was tension with Felice and no mistake. On top of that, like my old man with his prostitution, I liked the buzz.

But I'm getting ahead of myself. I was describing lying on my bed, toying with my knives, all right, fondling my knives, for the amateur psychologists among you, and the long and short of it was, I'd bought them for a purpose.

*

I'll say one good thing about Paisley, at least it wasn't Clydebank. People from Clydebank probably went to Paisley for holidays. Once you'd escaped from Scotland and moved among straight-limbed cunts who'd more than three teeth, who spent more on a year's school fees than most of us mutton pie eaters left when we croaked, it was certainly a shock to the system to come back. Nevertheless, those were my mountains and that was my glen and blood was thicker than water, especially when it was clogged with temazepam. Clydebank was the temazepam capital of Europe. The drug came in tablet form, but it was still imported there in its banned capsule form in many millions. Druggies pierced the green and yellow rugby-ball shapes and used the jelly-like substance to eke out their heroin. The effect of this cocktail could be, and often was, lethal. On the plus side, it was a great hit apparently, and could stretch a ten-pound deal so that it did the job of a thirty-pound deal. If the choked vein blew a crater in your leg or opened up a foot-long meat ravine in your arse, well, that was the risk you ran, and anyway, it'd happen to someone else, not you, wouldn't it? Users loved temazepam and capsules were off the street as quickly as they were on it, hence my interest. I'd done a raging trade myself until 1995 when, by an unfortunate configuration of circumstances, legislation banned the capsules and my own position within the criminal fraternity became similarly untenable. Now capsules were back, and so was I. A capsule cost, what, two pence to manufacture in Switzerland and Holland? Even allowing for the accrued costs of diverting loads, laundering them through crooked haulage companies, and delivering them down the docks for discreet distribution, capsules could be sold on the street for a gross profit of around a hundred times the original outlay. As a get-rich-quick scheme, temazepam was second only to the London property market and a preferable way of doing business since there wasn't the added pressure of pretending to be honest. And the risks? Well, the previous year the Glasgow police had grabbed 74,000 illicit capsules, less than 5 per cent of the market, so you'd have to be unlucky to the point of divine persecution to be pulled.

Nevertheless, I cloaked myself in my customary caution as I hung around in the damp night gloom, waiting for something to happen. The thing I wanted to happen was a specific thing, involving another party paying for drugs, taking receipt of them, then me relieving the party of their purchases at an opportune moment. I was aware that a lot hinged on the outcome of this enterprise and I knew I was hyper because I couldn't feel the customary discomfort from my lower back that arose whenever I crouched down at an awkward angle, say to pick up a sock from the bathroom floor or, as in this case, to position myself near the white transit van that was marked outside a warehouse, near the end of the cobbled lane, where Claw Hammill told me it would be. Though we were not too far from the main road, there appeared to be no on-site security nor the curse of CCTV, which explained the choice of venue. I stood in the shadows opposite the warehouse and awaited developments. I'd brought both knives in a green M&S carrier bag as well as a good-sized Black and Decker hammer I'd procured as a last-minute impulse buy. Right now, I was feeling like a machine gun might've made a better investment. I'm aware that for occasions like these, crim to crim, I'd be justified carrying a gun. With no innocent civilians liable to be hurt, a judge would be less likely to be punitive. The trouble was, carrying a gun became a bad habit, like driving to the corner shop, and you ended up taking it everywhere. Then it was only a matter of time before something went awry and you found yourself with an eight-year sentence when you might only have received four.

That was the reasonable explanation. The other one was that I'd have felt foolish carrying a gun. To me, it was a young man's affectation, it would be like arriving for work on a skateboard. I abhored this sad trend prevalent among young hooligans of getting all pistolled up to go screw a sweet shop, it was pathetic. No, I'd stick to the old ways, the country ways, if it's all the same to you, young sir.

So I slid the long steak knife out of the bag and I watched as the two lumpen arseholes in bomber jackets, one, pleasingly, still wearing the black Kangol hat he had on the night they duffed me up, loaded oblong cardboard boxes labelled 'self-assembly pack' into the back of the transit. I assumed the pay off had already taken place as there was not another soul to be seen, the importers, quite sensibly in my view, having dissociated themselves at the earliest opportunity from this vulnerable part of the distribution process. So there was nothing but these two fucking numpties, probably on six quid an hour plus bonus, shifting two hundred grand plus worth of finest jellies. My betting was the transit wasn't even registered in Calum's name, but instead one of theirs and here were the poor loyal exploited cunts about to get it in the neck. And, as it turned out, to the left of the spine. I'd been aiming for the kidneys but couldn't remember which side was them and which the liver, so I ended up jabbing vaguely, in a left-of-centre direction.

To be stabbed in the neck is a most disagreeable cunt of an injury as there's no fat, just small intricate muscles, tendons, and glands and that. Not forgetting, of course, the jugular. I was hoping he'd go down with a soft 'ooh', or something, but he didn't, he got a bit shouty and his ski hat fell off, and he began flailing about, shocked, as the blood pumped out, and he started calling out 'Mammy,' the way men do. He lay on his side at the back end of the van making the sort of sounds he probably hadn't made since infant school. This satisfied me, so I scuttled round the side of the van, between van and wall, daring his mate to come ahead.

In fact, I believe that's what I was growling, 'Come ahead, you cunt,' But he didn't come ahead, as I'd hoped he wouldn't, and instead looked quite ill. All the same, I wasn't to know if he mightn't be pistolled up or whatever, young people being what they are, so when he reached for his jacket, I sprang forward instantly and gave his head a little tap with the hammer. It made a sort of 'poom' noise and he slumped against the van in shock, calling out, 'Oh no, oh no.' He was worried about how injured he was and he put his hand to his head then inspected it, crying in a sort of girning way, as he looked for bits of skull, silver threepenny bits or whatever in his bloodied palm.

To tell the truth, I was concerned myself, as I didn't want him seriously injured, I wanted him fit enough to drive the van so we could fuck off out of here, back to Paisley and wherever Calum had his lock-up. I allowed him a moment to throw up, then I asked, 'What were you going for in your pocket?' He held out his wallet, which, I hadn't noticed, he had clutched for comfort in his other hand. I took it and opened it, for show, to make myself look like Mr Big Bad Cunt. There were a couple of tens, three fives and a Scottish single, the sort of denominations most crooks in suits wouldn't even sully the line of their Hugo Boss jackets with. 'You're in the wrong game, mate,' I told him. 'You should work for Burger King, you'd get meals and a free uniform.' I chucked the wallet back at him. He fumbled the catch and it landed between us. He was scared to pick it up in case I hit him again with the hammer.

'Go ahead,' I said.

'You'll hit me,' he said.

'No, I won't,' I said, 'trust me.'

He picked up his wallet and put it in his back pocket. 'If you don't want money,' he said, 'what do you want? We've nothing here but flat-packs.'

I gave him a little laugh. 'Now don't be silly,' I said, 'we've been getting along fine so far.' Kangol was lying on an arm, looking up. The limb was twisted and I wondered if he'd broken it. If so, it wasn't the most pressing of his troubles. His face was very white and he was bleeding a big syrupy puddle all around his head.

Luckily, owing to the camber of the lane, the rivulets were heading for the drain, rather than the van tyres which might, in the event of calamity, have created some unfortunate forensic inconvenience to all concerned.

'Don't mess with him, Davie,' Kangol said, 'it's Albert Blaney, the fucking Surgeon.' He let out a moan. Davie gave me a wary once over and I could see recognition dawn behind his eyes. Kangol made an impressive back-of-the-throat rasping, not unlike Roy Orbison on 'Pretty Woman'.

'By the way, you cunt,' he gasped, dying. 'Your fucking book was shite.' Okay, fair enough, as Lit. Crit. went it wasn't Tom Paulin, but it had a raw bravado, which I found piquant, and as soon as he'd said it, I knew one day I would write it down. I prodded Davie with the steak knife and together we loaded Kangol's carcass into the back of the transit. 'It's pity about all this mess,' I said, indicating the sticky cobblestones. 'It would be nice if we could get rid of it. You don't keep a small pan and brush in the van, do you?'

Davie said that no, he didn't keep a small pan and brush in the van. Or a J-cloth, my kingdom for a J-cloth. He shook his bloodied head. 'Forget it,' I said, 'we'll just have to hope the rain cleans it up during the night.' I gave Davie another little jab and made him climb into the driver's seat. I got in beside him and slid the door shut. The acrylic leopard-skin seat cover was still warm from Kangol's arse and smelled of his sweat. Though not for those reasons, I wanted rid of his carcass, pronto. Davie's hands were shaking on the wheel and the van lurched forwards when he tried to start the engine. 'Take it out of first,' I told him. I let him sit with the engine idling for a moment while he composed himself. I took out a packet of Trebors. 'Would you like a mint?' He shook his head. He didn't look well. 'If you vomit in this van,' I said, 'I'll crown you proper this time.' This prospect helped concentrate his mind. 'I'm all right, Albert,' he said, 'where to?'

'Nowhere,' I said. I looked at him. 'Why did you just call me Albert?' I asked.

'Because that's your name, isn't it?' he said, not unreasonably.

I wasn't satisfied. I knew what he was trying to do. 'I know what you're trying to do,' I said. 'You're trying to strike up a relationship with me, aren't you? You think if we're on first name terms, it'll make it harder for me to do you in, don't you?'

He blinked a bit but didn't answer. I went on. 'Well you've been watching too many hijack dramas on the telly, Davie. Unless of course, there's another reason. Unless maybe you're a cop.' I let him, for effect, see my hand tighten on the handle of the long steak knife. I knew the poor cunt wasn't a cop, cops tend not to have knitting-needle tattoos on the backs of their hands, but I was keen to let him know I knew he was an intelligent cunt. The stunt he'd done with the wallet had alerted me and now the name game he was trying had confirmed my impression. 'Are you a cop, Davie?' I asked.

He shook his head. 'You know I'm not a cop,' he said. 'Fucking Frank Serpico couldn't go undercover in Paisley, every cunt knows every other cunt and their granny.'

I was satisfied. 'Okay,' I said, 'let's go.'

He hesitated. 'Where to?'

'That's better,' I said. 'Take the Expressway to Partick, then right at the roundabout before the Exhibition Centre.' He asked what for. 'We've something to drop off,' I said, all ironic and gangstery. 'And by the way.'

'What?'

'You can call me Albert,' I said. And we drove off.

I had him drive down the riverfront to a point near the old ferry landing. I remembered it being a not inconvenient spot from which to dispose of an unwanted carcass. Trouble was, there was now a Daewoo showroom right there on the cobbles, which I hadn't bargained for, and as a consequence every available guttering that wasn't hanging loose had a CCTV camera bolted to it. I tell you fellow countrymen, our nation is headed in a sinister direction. Andy Warhol had it wrong. In the future, everyone will be anonymous for fifteen minutes. Anyway, we couldn't risk a suspicious stop so I had David drive a big arc, without slowing, back onto the roundabout and westbound again, towards the Clyde Tunnel. That way, if any bright junior plod had occasion to view the endless hours of footage, all he'd see was an unmarked van that had appeared to take a wrong turning and fucked, innocently, off. The thing was, everywhere you looked, there were fucking cameras pointing up your exhaust pipe, and if you happened to be cruising along the public highway, as I was, steak knifed up, carrying a fresh-hewn corpse, and a couple of hundred grand worth of nasty drugs, you didn't half feel discomfited.

My practised mask of cold-eyed psychosis was starting to slip as I contemplated the twenty-year sentence the evening's catalogue of crime would demand were I stopped.

'Where to now?' Davie asked.

I could tell that, in a perverse gallows way, the cunt was enjoying my uncertainty.

'I don't know,' I said limply, 'this place has all changed.'

He allowed my ineptitude to hang in the air where we could both see it before offering his solution.

'I know a place,' he said. 'It's a place where they wouldn't think to look and even if they did they'd stick it in the bottom drawer as a last resort.'

I considered, for a nanosecond, my list of alternative options. 'Okay,' I said.

And that was how we came to bury Kangol, whose real name was Gary, by the way, Gary Moss, not that either of us give a fuck, you or I, about that.

Ten minutes drive away, off the Paisley Road, we parked the van up a farmer's track and got out.

'What's that stink?' I asked Davie.

'You'll see,' he said, 'put this over your nose.' He gave me an oily rag from the van and we both tied them on, like B-picture desperadoes.

We carried Gary Moss about a hundred yards up the track, then negotiated him over a barbed-wire fence, which wasn't easy, and across a field, dodging rabbit holes as we went. At the end of the field lay one of those big, circular, chemically treated sewage plant efforts, and that's where we dropped the cunt in. Davie went to chuck in his Kangol hat after him but I stopped him and kept it, to assist with my evil plan. The stink was fucking awful, as Davie had warned it would be, and though we kept the rags on, it was one of those stenches you seemed to taste, as if the air was thick with matter.

On the plus side though, there were no cameras, well, let's face it, who's going to break in and steal shite, even in Paisley?

We leapt back as we dropped him in case he sloshed us. Then we both crept forwards and peeked in, each wary of the other because, let me assure you, I would not like to drown in a vat of human shite. To my relief, and doubtless to Davie's, since he would've been delegated the task of climbing down and pushing him under, Kangol Moss had sunk without apparent trace. Our little spot of grisly bonding out of the way, Davie stood, looking all wretched over what we'd done.

'Was he a pal of yours?' I asked him, speaking through my rag.

Davie shrugged. 'Hardly knew him. He lived up Feegie. Liked a line. You couldn't see him but he was coked up. That's why he was here, putting in the overtime, it wasn't even his turn to fetch and carry. His mother'll be in some state.'

I told Davie I didn't want to hear that. I don't like to think about weeping mothers and bereaved cunts when I'm busy, it's out of context and clouds the issue. 'I'm a human cunt too,' I said, 'I've got feelings of my own.' Davie apologized. I made a mental note to cut down my swearing; I always swore a lot when I came back to Scotland for some reason. In point of fact, I think I was irritable. I was confused about whether or not to kill Davie and I think the extra swearing was about me stoking myself up to do another murder. After all, this was a lovely tranquil setting in which to club some cunt to death and escape undetected. I knew this but Davie knew it better.

'What happens now, Albert?' he asked.

I was swithering and still hadn't pulled out a weapon. The basic question was whether this individual, much as I liked him, and I did like him I'd decided, would prove a greater hindrance to my aspirations, dead or alive. If that was the question, I concluded, there could only be one answer. Plainly, he would have to go. I pulled out the big steak knife, stepping in front of him as I did so, placing his back to the shit pit and cutting off his avenue of flight. I was thinking about where to stick him, I don't care what anybody says, it's definitely more difficult to take a life in cold blood; in the heat of fury you don't stop to think about tedious details like avoiding belt buckles and where exactly the heart is located – is it, as folklore has it, situated to the left or does it, as I seem to recall from a TV documentary, occupy a more central position behind its protective rib cage? No, as I've said, when the adrenalin's pumping, you tend to just chop away, willy nilly and well, if he dies, he dies. For his own convenience, I made him put his hands behind his back. 'Otherwise,' I said, 'you'll only cut your fingers trying to fend off the blade.' Which was true. Nobody can resist trying to grapple at a sharp blade with their soft hands, it always happens.

'Don't do me in,' said Davie. 'I'm better use to you alive, I can help you, honest.'

I explained how I'd already thought about that and concluded to the contrary. 'You can kneel down, if you like,' I said, which luckily, he did. He doubtless took this to be some twisted killing ritual I perpetrated on all my hapless victims but I was just worried that the young cunt would run away, he was a lithe young fucker in his runty way, and I doubt if the old Surgeon, for all his fabled gifts, could include cross-country running among them.

He started to cry.

'Don't cry,' I told him, 'you're better than that.' And he was. As I say, I liked the lad, he'd shown potential.

I'd just invited him to thrust back his head to bare his throat when he started gurgling out some hoarse last message or other.

'What is it?' I asked. I let him relax his head while he repeated it. In point of fact, it was lucky for Davie I did, because he then said the one thing that arrested my attention sufficiently to grant him a reprieve.

'It's true,' he said, 'my big cousin worked for you, wee John Mackie, in the old days, what, about six years ago. Gen up, Mr Blaney, I swear to God.' And he did, he swore to God, so I believed him. He made a crossing motion over his chest like he was twelve years old which, to be fair, he must have been when Wee John started working for me. I was a bit stumped by this information, not knowing now whether to enquire after wee John's health or slit his young cousin's throat. I chose the former and held fast, as they say, my trusty blade.

'Wee John went to Australia,' Davie explained, 'to make a fresh start in a new country.' I asked how he was doing. 'He isn't,' said Davie, 'he was shot by a Serb at an all-night garage after some argument about a frozen pizza.' I was sorry to hear that. Wee John had been my most trusted lieutenant back then, a fiddling fucker to be sure, but never enough to be greedy, or to take the piss. I could do with knowing someone like Wee John. Which is when it occurred to me that Davie was like Wee John.

'Look here, Davie,' I said, sheathing my blade in its M&S bag scabbard, 'what would you do to go on living?'

He pleaded that he would do anything. Still kneeling, he grasped my hand. I told him to pack it in, as it felt oddly disgusting. 'Just because I'm a psycho doesn't mean I'm a poof,' I told him. That's the vanity of youth for you, they think every cunt with sagging tits must fancy them. I put the bag in the inside pocket of my coat.

'Well look,' I said, 'I liked wee John and fuck knows why but I like you.' Davie seized this opportunity to get up off his knees. 'I'm going to go and do a wee message now,' I told him, 'and I want you to help me.'

He gave me a grateful look. 'What sort of wee message?'

I didn't spell it out for him. I didn't want him getting all trepidatious on me. 'The thing is, after we've done it, you'll be working for me and not Calum. Do you understand?'

He nodded. 'But Calum'll kill me,' he said. Maybe he wasn't so bright after all.

*

We rattled through the pockmarked streets of Barrhead, with its bargain shops and fortified off-licences, up the spine road into the no-man's-land of scrubby open country that marks the separation of retreating poor from the creeping rich. I hadn't been up that way in years, not since the old days, when Calum, Darko and I, heady with coke and off to a barbie at Peter Grady's, had stopped to piss. On Darko's arm was Annie Frew, Paisley's state-registered wild child, and while Calum and

I were shaking our pegs, Darko was having a line snorted off his hard-on by a giggling Annie. 'You should've brung your extension,' shouted Calum, 'you couldn't pack enough on that thing to give her a decent sneeze.' Darko laughed, I remembered, but it wasn't a thing I'd have said. Later, after cocktails, he had to be restrained from lodging Calum's nose between the grill bars of the barbie. It was all so much simpler then.

I asked Davie whether he'd seen anything of Darko.

'That mad bastard,' he said, then corrected himself. 'Sorry, I mean that as a compliment, is he a friend of yours?'

I said I knew him.

'That's one guy I wouldn't like to get the wrong side of,' said Davie, 'normally people grow mellower as they get older, don't they?'

'Yes,' I agreed, 'normally. Though it's not an absolute rule, trust me.'

He blushed a bit, which tickled me. All in all, the more I weighed it up, the more satisfied I was I'd made the correct decision in selecting Calum. Taking him out, as they say, meant I'd be back in the game again. I'd grab another share of all the good stuff that was on the magic table, the stuff that waits for anybody with hands strong enough and greedy mouth big enough to climb up the tablecloth. I slapped Davie on the knee. 'Foot down, Davie son,' I said, with glee.

Calum lived in a fifties villa, halfway up a hill, just outside Kilmacolm. His living room looked directly onto a small river and he had furtively sawn down a couple of spruce trees to enhance the natural wonders of the vista and to up the SP several grand should he ever decide to sell. A narrow gravel track slipped off the spine road toward the large farmhouse-type kitchen at the back, and that was the track we were headed towards.

There had been a Significant Other in Calum's life, one of those standard-issue retired model types with platinum hair, deflated arse and wobbly jawline who set out hoping to sleep their way to the top but usually end up stuck around the lower middle. She had even managed a wedding ring but according to Davie that was all over now and, at the present time, she was busily engaged trying to cut herself a divorce deal.

'What's he doing for a poke then?' I asked.

'Why, you volunteering?' said Davie.

Life's a strange and interesting condition, isn't it, one minute a cunt's on his knees pleading for succour, the next he's ripping the piss like you're his decrepit uncle.

'No,' I said, a bit coldly, to put him in his place, 'what I'm asking, is whether he's on his jack?'

He nodded, duly scolded, taking the point. 'He's been seeing a lot of Danny Wooler, you know Danny Wooler?'

I said I did, I knew Danny Wooler.

'Well then,' he said, 'form your own conclusions but as far as I know, it's just tarts,' he said. 'They're not in business or anything.' I asked him if Wooler was likely to be in the house. 'Nah,' he said, 'that's worlds colliding, isn't it? Calum wouldn't want a treacherous cunt like him know where he collects his drugs from and when he has them dropped off and that.' He thought for a moment then the penny dropped. 'Which kind of begs the question, how did you know, Albert?'

I told him how I knew. 'A little bird told me,' I said.

I pictured the little bird. It had a stained V-necked T-shirt and arthritic claws.

Davie treated me to his disarming grin as he pushed the envelope. 'And how did the little bird know?'

'Easy,' I said, 'Danny Wooler told him.' Which, of course, was sheer mischief. So far as I was aware, Claw didn't even know Wooler, let alone share trade secrets with him over a cappuccino. Claw was a scuffler that's all, and occasionally a good laugh, so people allowed him into their company and he heard things, simple as that. Much better I protect him and if I could do that while raising a nice question mark over a tit like Wooler than bully for clever old Albert, thought I.

We were parked arse first, up the gravel path, just out of sight of the spine road. If Calum looked out of his kitchen window, all he'd see would be Davie's face in the wing mirror with maybe a hint of a certain black Kangol hat that I happened to be wearing. 'What happens now?' Davie asked.

'Do what you normally do,' I told him. I was looking at myself in this Kangol hat. It didn't look appropriate, I noticed. Well, the hat did, but with me in it the effect was less gangsta rapper than a middle-aged cancer victim on a chemo day. Davie gave two long toots of the horn. 'He'll peek out of the window,' he explained, 'then he'll step out and open the lock-up.' He pointed to a prefabricated structure I hadn't noticed, painted dull green and so well concealed it almost melted into the slope of the hill. Sure enough the kitchen curtains twitched, net curtains too which, tense though I was, gave me a little tickle of amusement.

'You're quite clear about what's going to happen

here, aren't you, Davie?' I said. Davie nodded. 'Good,' I said, 'then out you get.' As Davie slid his door open, I opened mine too, synchronized door opening, so it would sound like just one.

As Davie stepped down I heard Calum's voice call out, 'Took your fucking time, what happened?'

I heard the jingle of keys as I slipped, unsighted, round the offside of the van. Davie was saying sorry, that he'd come the Clyde Tunnel route and not the Erskine Bridge route, which had been a mistake, he was explaining at masterfully tedious length, since two of the lanes were closed, which had created one hell of a tailback like you wouldn't believe. I could almost hear Calum's eyes rattle in his head with boredom as I slid the big steak knife out of the bag and gripped the hammer. A hollow rending sound told me Davie had opened the rear door at the driver's side, like I'd told him to. Give him his due, he was still gibbering on about M8's and A77's – when you asked this kid to do something, he was thorough. Calum was giving it tetchy, 'Aye, ayes,' like a man who's heard all he wants to know, and when I heard him ask, 'Where's Gary, is he not with you?' I took it as my cue to speak.

'Gary's not here, unfortunately, he's feeling shite. But I'm here,' I said, stepping out at last to make my entrance, 'Coco the fucking Clown, remember?'

'Albert,' he said.

'Calum,' I said. I was slightly startled to see he'd grown a goatee. However, this didn't put me off my stroke as I brained him with the hammer. As he toppled back against the van, I was gratified to notice his gut was bigger than mine, though he'd tried to disguise it by wearing his shirt out. I leant in with the steak knife, sunk it, twisted and stepped back. His legs folded and he lurched forward onto his hands and knees. Disappointingly, he didn't have the bald spot on his crown that I had on mine. I watched as he crawled about in odd little circles, like a dog preparing to bed down for the night. I gave him another little tap with the hammer and he looked up.

'Albert,' he said, 'you twisted cunt.' His head started to loll and he made it look up at Davie. 'You in with this bampot?' he said. Davie didn't know what to say and shrugged. He mumbled something I couldn't hear and pointed, for effect, at the blooded mark on his own head, congealed now and dull burgundy, like some ancient royal seal. He wasn't sure where his loyalties lay and was covering his tracks in case Calum didn't die or I fucked off or took a sudden heart attack or something. 'I'll tell you what, kid,' said Calum, trying to rise, 'you're an ungrateful little cunt.' He pawed about his pockets, clumsily, looking for something. 'Young cunt,' he kept muttering.

'Do something, Albert,' said Davie. 'He carries a gun now.' I stepped forward and gave Calum a hearty tap on the head as a diversion. This drew his hands up, enabling me to deliver an unencumbered downward thrust with the steak knife into his chest. He shuddered and fell, face down, onto his gravel path. I crouched over him and gave a few more meaty taps until I was fairly sure he must be deceased. There was no rattle, no fine words, unless you count 'Young cunt', and I straightened myself up and rubbed my aching back.

'Well,' I said, 'that'll be that then.'

Davie drew his hands down his face. I asked him if he wanted to pop indoors for a glass of water but he shook his head. 'Let's get rid of him then,' I said. 'We can stick him in the lock-up.' Davie squatted down to take Calum's arms. 'No,' I said, 'on second thoughts . . .' Davie looked up at me.

'This is a showcase job,' I explained, 'what's the use of slaying the local giant if no cunt gets to hear about it? This needs to be a statement.'

David let go of Calum's arms. 'Who to?' he asked.

'To the other giants in the area,' I said. 'They need to know there's a giant slayer on the loose.'

Davie shrugged, at a loss. 'Uh huh,' he said, 'where then?'

I looked about. Hills, trees, river, road. Not much of a canvas on which to paint an unforgettable Blaney masterpiece. In Calum's front garden, a couple of rooks were thrashing their beaks and squawking, fighting over a dead field mouse. 'Go sit in the van,' I told Davie, 'toot if you see anybody slowing down.' He asked me what I was going to do. 'Just sit in the van,' I repeated, quietly.

*

So it was that the following morning, at the airport, I was able to pick up the midday edition of the *Evening Times* and read with satisfaction 'Kilmacolm Horror Find. Head on hoe in garden'. There was a picture of a policeman standing guard outside Calum's house and a mobile incident unit. Under the picture a byline read: 'Shady Life of Local Businessman. See pages four and five.'

I bought a small latte at the Costa Coffee shop while

I waited. Yes, it had been an eventful first foray back to fair Caledonia: I'd buried a mother, committed a double murder, stolen a shitload of nasty drugs and delivered a 'Guess Who's Back' wake-up call to my former colleagues in the hooligan fraternity. And done it all on an Apex fare. Next time I came back up, I might travel Business Class to celebrate. As a sign I'd once read on a tube train had put it, 'The unconsidered life is not worth living'. I'd told Davie to mind the stuff and we'd lie low for a bit, then I'd come back up again and we'd go to work. I picked up my briefcase and holdall and headed for the departure gate. At the last moment, I veered off, on an impulse, and doubled back into John Menzies. For old times' sake I bought a packet of Toffos. I wanted the taste of the past in my mouth.

Chapter Five

I didn't know how long 'for a bit' would entail. Well, how long is a piece of intestine? Until, I vaguely hoped, 'Garden Horror Murder' had shrunk from pages four and five and come to rest as a filler paragraph under 'No new leads in head case'. I'd been reassured by the utterances of the Paisley Constabulary who'd admitted that the murder bore 'all the hallmarks of a gangland slaying'. While I appreciated the use of the term 'hallmarks', implying as it did, a certain professional respect, I knew that the cops hadn't intended this as any standing ovation for my performance so much as a spot of verbal Valium to the public and others. This sort of terminology got the papers and telly off their backs in case they started licking their lips and implying that some indiscriminate psycho was bounding around topping innocent rose pruners. So long as it was clearly implied that this was a trade matter, the thermostat of public opinion, which is to say the tabloids, could be lowered to a comfortable collective temperature. Which was of course, a very far cry from saying a blind eye was being turned.

The police, like the media, score most of their successes from the same source, namely, some cunt with a grievance picks up the phone. Since the only two cunts in a position of privileged insight in this instance were Claw and Davie, I felt reasonably secure that my heinous acts would pass unpunished. Claw was unlikely to shop me since it was he himself who had furnished me with the crucial information regarding Calum's drug collection and distribution runs. If the perception were to spread that he was no longer a useful and loveable dodgy character but instead simply unreliable, then concerns would be voiced over what other sensitive data was in Claw's keep and he would undoubtedly be despatched, as a prudent measure, to an early and expeditious grave. Davie, too, had plenty to lose, being implicated in both head tappings, but I hoped and felt that he was a young man of some moral fibre and as long as his nerve held out and he didn't turn out to be fucking Raskolnikov or some other tediously self-loathing fuckwit then we might well be home free.

So I lay low, in my Bayswater basement, and worked diligently at shrinking my waist size, pending my return to Caledonia and my ain folk. I don't expect you'll ever come across the Double Murder Diet in the health section of the *Daily Mail*, but I thoroughly recommend the taking of human life as a prelude to any act of nutritional discipline: as an exercise of will, murder is unsurpassed and gives a handy boost to the esteem at a vulnerable time, thereby providing a kick start to the solitary and daunting enterprise of weight adjustment. Additionally, I found that pondering the consequences of my actions and plotting my future course offered a welcome, if temporary, reprieve, from brooding thoughts of Felice. Dead cunts, you've controlled, live ones present more of a challenge, walking about smiling and that, as they tend to do, on the arms of other men.

Being a bint she liked a bit of reaction so she still

hung about at the usual places, a cocktail at the Halcyon, a coffee at Tootsies, just drifting into my eyeline from time to time to let me know she was still around. But I never called or gave as much as a hello. She'd crossed the line, you see, she'd gone against every grain and fucked another guy, this developer cunt. Even though it was a revenge fuck, and one which my mind could see was justified, my body felt differently. My emotions told me there was no way back. I have great respect for morals, you see, probably because I've got so few. So all in all, there was this cleft stick scenario with Felice. I still wanted her, but I refused to have her, even though my instincts told me the opportunity to do so would arise again.

In the circumstances, I'd decided to play a long-game strategy with her, on the basis that it appeared win–win. I reasoned she couldn't be totally happy with Mr Bricks and Mortar or she wouldn't keep wafting in and out of our once favoured places. I mean it was just not ex's etiquette, was it?

Admittedly, she could be just a twisted cuntess who liked a spot of drama, but if that was the case then she had worse psychological problems than me, and I was a practising psychopath, so I'd be better off without her anyway, see what I'm saying? But all things being equal, they'd likely split up at some point and I'd then have to ask myself whether what she was offering was something I couldn't live without and, if the answer was yes, offer some kind of olive branch. The sooner this happened the more susceptible I'd be. On the other hand, the longer time went on the stronger I'd become and the less in thrall to her big brown eyes and small tight quim. So

I'd sit in Tootsies, watching her fork polenta into her gob and doing that touchy feely 'we're so right together' pish and I'd keep my own counsel. I'd glory in my own restraint, in my steady hand as I lit a fag, or spooned my coffee, and I'd console myself that with each draw or sip, time was passing and that strength through distance was returning to my heart. Of course when I'd get home, I'd feel like shit and sit in my armchair, watching the racing, but everything in life is front, isn't it?

No doubt the more literal minded among you will be puzzled by these revelations and be thinking, Well Albert, these lovebirds seem indeed to be causing you some psychic turbulence, so why don't you just do what you normally do and tap him, or her, or both? Surely this is well within your capabilities? And yes, it was true, the act in itself would have caused me little grief, at least as far as he was concerned. But eliminating him would only drive her further away from me, as well as taking a terrible risk at a sensitive time. Let's face it, if Felice found her boyfriend taken unexpectedly dead one morning with matter leaking out of a crater where his brain used to be, I could expect to feel a hand on my collar before I'd time to pull on my coat. No, women are like cats, they'll only come back when they're ready, and I had to be ready for her being ready. If and when that day came, would I welcome her over the threshold or slam the door in her alluring middle-class chops, I was fucked if I knew.

As I've said, when I first moved to London, I knew no cunt. Just distant crim acquaintances in far-flung housing estates in places like Stratford and Basildon and that. Having jack shit for a social life at least gave me the discipline I needed to write the book. Given the state of my nerves at the time, it was also, I suppose, a form of therapy. Because I was solo, I wrote more revealingly than I ought to have done, but sometimes you think fuck-it, I could be dead tomorrow, what's the point in being some coy old granny? I wrote it up in longhand, in block letters, and when I'd finished, I didn't even read it over, I was too scared, in case it was shit. I sent the manuscript to this publishing house I got out of the Yellow Pages, up Bloomsbury way.

Because of their location, I thought they'd have a reverence for literature, which was why I favoured them, but in the event it proved a bum steer. They didn't so much reject it as eject it, with this terse note saying they didn't publish 'this sort of thing'. I wrote them back an equally terse thank you note, on Andrex toilet paper, saying I hoped this would come in handy for when they had the poker removed from their arse. Through ignorance, I hadn't realized they published poets and cunts, old grunter feminists with Pre-Raphaelite tresses, them sorts, so it wasn't really their fault, the onus was on me to target my efforts more diligently. Once I did this, I received a more favourable response and within a year I was a briefly celebrated author, signing copies in the shopping malls of Orpington and Penge.

This, as I've already intimated, is how I met Felice. She produced, on an occasional basis, this arts programme on Radio Four and one day I was a studio guest. I'd clocked her as I was shown in through the production office to the big square interview table with the headphone sets laid out, and I remember thinking, Aye, aye. Being as how I was the last cunt on, I could legitimately dawdle over pulling on my coat at the end and she'd stepped out from behind her big window to give me a personal thank you. She didn't have to do this, she could just have said lovely things down the mic from the sealed security of the technical area, but because she didn't, I drew the faint hint that I might be in, so I asked if she fancied a cup of tea. Turned out she'd gone to art school and taught ceramics to a mate of mine at the Barlinnie Special Unit before moving onto freelance art design, then radio, so, unlike the Bloomsbury cunts, 'this sort of thing' held an ongoing interest for Felice. Right from the off, as we chatted politely, I was all aflutter to be at her, which was a thing that rarely happened with me, surprisingly enough, what with me being this alleged rough cunt.

Part of the attraction, of course, was her middle classness, muck like me, we're suckers for any sort of refined quim, I don't know why, like I've said, one quim tastes and smells much like any other in my experience. It's magical thinking, I suppose, we fancy this comparative poshness will somehow rub off, we'll remove our cock after a session and it'll somehow be buffed and manicured and we'll stroll off with it over our arm like a rolled umbrella and go and sip chocolate at a chocolate house. All in all, Felice presented an educated erudite brunette package and I was smitten enough to ring her up at her office sometime the next day and invite her out for a drink. Luckily or unluckily, my opinion still varies on a day-to-day basis, she said yes. And that was how we came to be involved.

*

A couple of days after the 'Horror Find' headline, I put in a call to Davie about, naturally enough, Calum's head. I'd been mulling the matter over and had decided it would be better if we got all the lurid publicity over in one go, so I had him ring Pitt Street station in Glasgow and report, anonymously, the missing body of Gary Moss and where it could be found. I also told him to give the van a good clean and park it in Springburn, on a certain corner not fifty yards from Billy Waugh's front door. This was a spot of calculated mischief on my part. Now Billy's name would be dragged into things and even if he was quickly eliminated the suspicion would still remain that he was somehow involved. Especially, of course, now that he'd raised his profile unnecessarily by having a guard of honour at the Cuntess's funeral. Naturally, Billy wouldn't be pleased by this attempt at guilt by association but with any luck he'd blame it on Mick, thinking he was up to some clumsy scam, and give him a fatherly, blithering cunt backhander.

I was keen to plant the notion that Glasgow scumballs were involved in these terrible deeds rather than decent, honest-to-goodness local lads. It would bring the Glasgow police into play and disarm the local press who would stop painting their inflammatory pen pictures of this horrible unknown demon who was stalking the quaint homely streets of Godfearing Paisley. Tests on Gary Moss's body should reveal that he was a regular coke user, which would suit my purposes since, coke being expensive and him being unemployed, it would lead the polis to the conclusion that he was a dealer or crim, or hopefully, when they perused his CV, both.

Naturally, there was the chance that a check of

Moss's associates would lead to Davie but he'd shown a cool head when I'd stood over him, hammer in hand, thus it seemed a safe bet he'd remain suitably composed when confronted by a Glasgow or Paisley detective, each of whom would be eager to palm the matter over to the other. There's no doubt I was laying a heavy load on Davie's slender shoulders but he had a vested interest in everything proceeding nicely thank you, since he had several thousand illegal temazepam capsules sitting in his allotment hut, not a half a mile away from Paisley Police Headquarters. If anything went wrong, then the polis now had a buck and somewhere convenient for it to stop and young Davie would likely be humping a hole in his cell mattress for anything up to fifteen years. I decided that if Davie came through unscathed I would reward him by naming him my first lieutenant. What he had in his favour was that he looked like a gormless prick – a rare and undervalued gift amongst hooligans as most can't resist drawing attention to themselves by sprouting over-inflated 'I've been to nick' muscle cladding and covering it with 'I also deal drugs' Versace gaudy glitz. Young Davie wore a windcheater and had a permanent coldsore. Handsome.

Three weeks after the last sighted newspaper report – 'Head case: Police Still Upbeat' – and having received no unwelcome knocks to the door, I packed my trolley suitcase and took the Piccadilly Line to Heathrow. Despite my habitual caution, I was feeling chirpily confident and felt troubled by it. I couldn't help remembering a spot of Roman history I'd read whereby victorious generals returning home to receive their tribute would employ the services of a wise counsel to whisper in their ear, 'Remember you are mortal, you are mortal.' Of course for all the notice some of the dozy fuckers took they might as well have been saying, 'Remember, you're a Womble.' But I, the putative Emperor Albert, didn't want to fall victim to any bout of over-confidence. Let's face it, in my line of business, you can only do that once. I was my own wise counsel those days so, on a superstitious whim, I got out at Acton Town and headed back, the way I'd come to Kings Cross.

Once on board the Glasgow train, I made for the buffet car and stood with a tepid beer in my hand, trying to read the paper. In the *Daily Mail* was a picture of a barely remembered telly bird in half a dress and spangled knickers at the premiere of a British gangster film called, appropriately enough in her case, *Snatch*. The director looked like a Grenadier Guardsman and had one of those fashionable gang-fight scars on his jawline that looked like he had acquired it not so much in Harlesden as in Harley Street. Still, he was humping Madonna now, so he should care. Beery Jock and Yorkshire business types bumped around me in the car, talking sales units and sharing private jokes in public voices. Tetchy, rankled and edged with spite, I felt more like my old self again and made my way back down the carriage to join the harassed, lactating bint with two small brats who'd decided to become my travelling companions. Which was more mad, I asked myself, obeying that wise voice in my head or ignoring it? Hearing the fucker in the first place, I supposed.

I took a B&B in Renfrew Road, just inside the Paisley boundary. I knew I would be up for a while and wanted to keep my expenses down till I was earning. What is it with these couples that run B&Bs? Every cunting thing was done in floral: walls, pelmets, bedspreads, chair covers, but the killer was, it was all different floral, no cunt matched, so you woke-up of a morning thinking you were in the exotic fucking plants section of the botanical gardens. Honest, I needed a fucking machete to hack my way through to the toilet bowl, and even then there was quilted roses on the seat cover. Luckily, of course, being me, I had a machete.

I negotiated a rate that included evening meal but this was foolish since I couldn't even eat the breakfast. This was due to the husband, the bloke who served it. He was one of those cloying, cheerful old cunts who won't just let his guests sit in misery to chew but instead wants to create a family atmosphere. I've seen families, I don't like the atmosphere. I don't respond well to people asking me about my business or gibbering on about the weather. It's Scotland, it rains, right? Where's the fucking story? So all in all, I quickly found myself eschewing the forced camaraderie of the dining room in favour of a coffee shop up by M&S.

I arranged to meet Davie in the bar of the Ubiquitous Chip in the west end of Glasgow. I reasoned that even if I was clocked there, chances were nobody would know Davie, the Chip being a knee-jerk byword for middle-class posturing among his sort, which is another way of saying they were intimidated by any pub where the clients don't have hooves. I brought the drinks over to our table, pint of Furstenberg for him, Chardonnay spritzer for me, what with the waistline and that, and I left my straw in the glass and sipped through it as we talked, just to watch Davie's face.

He told me that yes, he'd had two visits, one from Glasgow CID, the other from Paisley. Glasgow wanted to know about the van, which was registered, as I'd surmised, not in Calum's name, but in that of Gary Moss. Paisley appeared later, a bit tardily Davie thought, perhaps hopeful that Glasgow would pick up the whole tab for the case, bodies and all, not just the van. Davie played it as I'd hoped he would. Big don't-hurt-me-officer eyes and short soft voice that said, 'I poor thick cunt, doomed to die in gutter.' Asked when he'd last seen Moss, David had answered, 'Not since Mrs Waugh's funeral, I think.' The vague qualification would act as a catch-all in the event of any contrary evidence coming to the fore, and the presentation of 'Mrs Waugh', rather than 'Albert's maw', helped stitch Billy's name yet more prominently into the imagined tapestry of events. Hopefully, they'd now let things cool into a let-them-sort-it-out-themselves-we'll-pick-up-the-pieces sort of position. After all if they went after Billy, they'd have to mean it, he knew a lot of polis.

Davie was fretting about the jellies, his allotment hut hardly being, as he pointed wittily out, any Swiss bank strongbox. Heady with potent lager, and warming to his theme, he painted a demented picture of allotment culture, a sort of wild west fellowship, where alleged friends stole each other's topsoil in rustled wheelbarrows, where whole huts, let alone their contents, could be dismantled and borne away in the night, while unsuspecting urban rhubarb farmers slept obliviously on.

I calmed his fears with yet another Fursty and told him how I'd planned to blitz the Glasgow market with an audacious retail offensive within the week. I wanted a quick clearance sale, not a slow drip tickover. I knew it could take up a month for the word to percolate from stinking lane and scabby high-rise landing to chief inspector's desk that naughty jellies were back in town and by then I wanted us to have hit and well and truly run, leaving nothing but a few dead junkies and some gruesome cratered limbs to mark our passing. News reports would show the odd senior plod sphincter twitching on the velvet. They'd regret, publicly, the fact that poor innocent junk fiends had croaked, but privately they'd be thinking, Thank fuck, that's a few more car CD players that can sleep soundly in their dashboards tonight.

I told Davie to put in place a small distribution task force; I preferred 'task force' to 'network' since it's more purposeful in tone and, in my experience, militaristic jargon excited young people and elicited a subliminal attitude of obedience. I told him to hand-pick two people. Those two people were to hand-pick four people and those four people, four more apiece. Of course I was using the term 'people' in a relative sense. By the third outward ripple on humanity's pond you were down to pin cushions on legs but that was okay, if any of them were to be caught and given the desk lamp in the eyes accolade, they could only point at other pin cushions since their knowledge of the personnel involved was, by definition, lateral, rather than vertical. Understand that what I was talking about here were hideous fuzzy-minded smack-heads for whom one craven scam bleeds desperately into another, men and women who'd suck your cock for a pound, a pound of potatoes even, if it could be sold on for a smidgen of anything resembling a consciousness-altering pharmaceutical. In other words, my kind of people. The job of Davie and his two entrusted colleagues was to crack the whip and collect. I told Davie he might have to tap the odd head with a hammer, but if he wanted to fulfil his youthful dreams of hooligan excellence, he'd have to make that leap.

So we flooded Glasgow with emaciated Paisley buddies, and if I tell you that the city opened its arms to us, or its thighs, or buttocks, even, in some cases its prick or neck, in fact anywhere it could find the glimmer of a working vein, then you'll grasp that I'm speaking literally as well as in cosy metaphor. True, trade was sticky for the first couple of days owing to shyness disguised as an outbreak of morals, but I outlined a simple incentive scheme, involving pain, and in no time the cunts were using their heads instead of having them tapped, targeting homeless hostels and rehab units, *Big Issue* vendors and late night Sally Army soup queues, anywhere people looked for cure, there they could be tempted. Sure, a couple of holes down Anderston stiffed us for a dozen but I let it pass as I didn't want to steam in and raise the temperature, maybe have my old man hitting me with his handbag. The fact that Davie and his chosen pair were the only task force members to require payment in cash and not kind speaks of the motley nature of our band. Nevertheless, by their efforts they'd allowed the old Surgeon to raise an axe again in Paisley, so may the scabby fuckers recline peaceably, pining for their methadone, content in the knowledge of a job well done.

Having acquired a wad, I now had the wherewithal to start building a team. I hired a car and went with Davie out to Todholm for the purpose of recruiting some young thugs of potential. I'd heard tell of a burgeoning

Romanian refugee enclave and was keen to explore it. These economic refugees enjoyed a bad reputation, I reasoned, so they'd be free from any inhibiting local allegiances, I mean who'd want to sit watching game shows in Gaelic when there was the chance of some old fashioned pillage and brigandry, just like at home? I outlined this enlightened integration policy to Davie but he explained that it was currently unrealistic as the local hand of friendship hadn't extended much beyond the occasional shite dropped through a letterbox. Kosovans were most socially acceptable, he explained, why didn't we try Kosovans? I made a mulling noise but the trouble was, when I thought Kosovan, I thought victim. I saw some sixty-year-old fucker in a tank top lugging his settee on his back with a wailing cadaver in a headscarf by his side.

I asked Davie about my old team. Yes, he knew some of them, one or two had expressed a mild interest in coming back, we'd meet them in due course, but today was about the new boys. I nodded, but inside I felt affronted by the word 'mild'. For me, mild interest reads, 'Maybe, if I don't receive any better offers.' I mentioned other names, good boys I ran with before my five-year exile. Though still in their twenties, most had succumbed to marriage and the pram in the hall. As I slowed to take a corner, Davie pointed out a paunchy, balding bloke in a St Mirren leisure top standing outside Iceland. I recognized, with a shock, Wee Craigie Wemyss, Mr Quadruple Bypass. He was sucking a fag, his paw tethered by an invisible chain to a pushchair that had some grinning sprog in it.

'You know Craigie, don't you?' said Davie.

'Yes, I do,' I told him, 'I didn't know he had a kid though.'

'He doesn't,' said Davie, 'it's mine.'

I gave him as much of a startled look as safe steering would allow.

'Name's Jasmine,' he said, 'eleven months.'

I left a calculated hole for further elaboration. Being a nice chap, he obliged and fell in. 'My wife and me, we had a trial separation. It was during that time she met Craigie.' He gave a little chuckle as he revealed this and pulled a waggish face. He was hoping to pass himself off as some roistering rogue with a wife grown exhausted by his errant ways. A glib explanation intended to soothe my barbarian mind. Knowing Craigie, my guess was that he was snoking about long before the split. But I didn't say this, of course, out of respect for my boredom threshold.

Davie now lived alone in a one-bedroomed place in Rafferty Street. He showed me into the living room and I asked him who was in the bedroom. 'Nobody,' he said, 'that's next door's telly.' I could hear cursing and swearing. 'So who's in the kitchen then?' He shrugged. 'Not a soul. That's the alkies downstairs hitting the Strongbow.' As I glanced about I could see that Davie was not of a mind to follow suit. The fresh Hoover tracks on the carpet and the hint of primrose air freshner told me that. He went into the small scullery and I could hear him running water into a kettle. 'Tea for me,' I called, 'no sugar.' On the mantelpiece was the type of swirly metal picture frame that cunts from my background are supposed to think artistic. It held a photo of a sullen bint, wearing a party hat with a brat on her lap, Davie's wife and sprog, presumably. It occurred to me that Davie was a man who liked to punish himself. 'What was your wife's name?' I called to him.

'Isobel.'

Of course, I thought, up here, what else? She was pretty, in a domestic kind of way, but had one of those heavy, dairy herd sort of bodies that I find rather repellent, possibly because it reminds me of my own. Anyway, the long and the short of it is, I wouldn't have humped her from the back after a skinful and yet here was young Davie all cut up and bruised for the want of her. Not for the first time I marvelled at the arbitrary Russian roulette nature of love. Davie came in holding two mugs of tea.

'Christmas,' he said, nodding at the picture.

He gave me a mug, then sat down in a dodgy-looking armchair that I personally wouldn't have risked. I could tell from the gingerly way he perched that one of the castors was missing, though he tried to cover this up by being as expansive as chair physics would allow.

'It hasn't been easy,' he said.

I detected a sob story brewing so nipped in quick and made a big play of arranging cushions to support my back. I was on this leatherette settee, I could sense the jammy crusts and furry Maltesers trapped down the sides. I took out my pen and began making squiggles in my notebook to show we'd entered business mode.

I didn't normally approve of holding business meetings in people's houses, there was too much of a temptation, in my experience, to blur the lines. You know, out come the Famous Grouse and the Ritz crackers, next thing cunts start reminiscing and you never get anything done. But where do you hold interviews for a gang? The Freddie Foreman Suite of the Copthorne? Not that there were much in the way of culinary delights at Davie's. As I drank my tea, the stains on the mug looked like age rings round a tree stump. Curious how people attach higher standards of hygiene to cups than they do mugs. To concentrate our minds, I asked Davie to appraise, individually, the boys we were about to interview. I wanted to know his opinions in advance so I could see how they tallied with my own. Which was an oblique way, of course, of developing my opinion of Davie himself. He'd had a hard paperround, I'd decided, and if I could locate enough mettle under his crappy CK T-shirts, I wanted him to help him win. He had arranged the interviews at fifteen-minute intervals, like we were the Patheon Players, auditioning for *Pal Joey* or something.

As luck would have it, the first cunt didn't turn up. To fill the gap, I succumbed to temptation and asked him what had happened between him and his wife.

'You know,' he said, 'she went off with Craigie.'

'I gathered that,' I told him, 'but why did you fall out in the first place?'

He rummaged in his mind for an answer. He looked surprised to find one. 'I think it was this,' he said. 'I think we both felt old before our time, what with Jasmine and that. And I'm not old, am I? I'm young.'

I told him fucking right. I had to, if he was old what did that make me? 'Don't worry,' I reassured him, 'you've plenty of other divorces ahead of you, this one's nothing special. There are stacks of bints out there who'll line up to hate your guts.'

He seemed to respond to this little spot of verbal

rough and tumble. 'You're a cold cunt, Albert,' he said, warmly.

'I try,' I said.

He looked up. 'There's the doorbell,' he said.

I rubbed my hands and clicked my pen rapidly for show. 'On you go then, Davie boy,' I said. 'It's game on now!'

*

That Sunday, to gain parole from the B&B, I planned a drive down to Loch Lomondside in the hired car. I'd intended to surprise my father, by turning up on his doorstep while he was tapping his boiled eggs but it occurred to me, en route, he might not fancy the loch as it probably held unsettling memories for him what with its having been a favoured haunt of Billy. He'd likely insist we took a jaunt down the Ayrshire coast instead and the prospect of sitting in one of those wind swept Prize Bingo booths that crunch wet sand when you close the plastic number covers filled me with hideous gloom. I did a brisk U-turn at the foot of his street, hoping he wouldn't clock me from the corner shop while he was queuing to buy his *Sunday Mirror*. This was a pity, of course, as we were both lonely cunts but whereas I was curious to embrace the ghosts of the past, it was likely he'd be just as keen to avoid them. I took the motorway as far as the city centre, got briefly lost in the one-way system then blundered, by trial and error, onto the long runner carpet of the Great Western Road before recalling, just in time, that sharp, sly right that takes you up by Tarbet and Inverarnan.

It was a typical Scottish spring day, which is to say

anyone over five foot eight got cloud on his head from the big light grey duvet that spread itself over the country till the seasons changed and the big dark grey duvet took over. I could make out the humps of hills, so I put my foot down on the dual carriageway that rimmed the near end of the loch. The sight of water had me thumbing mentally through my book of landscape adjectives for words like 'brooding' and even 'majestic' but maybe that was pushing it a bit. I turned off at a roundabout, where I stood on the little pier admiring the sight of mist and drizzle. Billy had once taken me to this pier to fish. He'd walked off for a pint at a lochside hotel and I'd caught a crab, but I'd become spooked when I reeled it in, not knowing how to kill it without ugliness and mess, so I'd let it drop back into the loch. When Billy came back, I'd lied about not having any luck but a couple of bags in corrective stockings told him about the crab, no doubt hoping I'd get a doing and a stern moral lecture about the value of truth. But Billy didn't do that, he just gave them a look like neither of them were worth using as bait and asked me if I didn't like fishing. I told him I thought the trouble was I was too old for it. Really, it just bored the shit out of me. 'But all boys like fishing,' Billy mumped. I got the impression he'd gleaned this information from pictures of Roger the Dodger out angling with a line on his toe or something. 'Not this boy,' I said. 'It's all foreign to me.' He asked me to give him the rod. When I did, he broke it across the knee and chucked it into the loch. 'Come and have a pint,' he said, 'you're ugly enough, you'll pass.' And that was it, my last tiddler and my first pint. From then on the only fish I ever saw was a kipper at Sunday breakfast.

It goes without saying the kippers were at Billy's. When home had been with the Prick and my mother, all I'd had for breakfast was a piece of toast with maybe a grilled Mars Bar on top, for decadence. My mother had kept sweets in the fruit bowl, along with her kirby grips and the gas bill, though naturally the sweets didn't linger there long, we both being greedy bastards, me and her. My father shunned confectionery, believing our weakness to be evidence of low character. He would point to pictures in magazines of sprouts and carrots and stuff and start gibbering dire warnings about vitamin deficiency, but then again, he turned out a cross-dressing male prostitute, so what the fuck good have carrots done for his morals?

Chapter Six

After her crisis conversation with my father over our debts, my mother had indeed gone to see Billy Waugh. In fact, she went to see him two or three times. The third time, Billy drove her home in his Jag and stayed for a cup of tea. He and my father had a casual chinwag about this and that, after which Billy lead my mother upstairs into the bedroom. I know this, because I was sitting at the dining-room table, pretending to be reading *The Hotspur* when it happened. While they were upstairs, my father sat with the family strongbox, an old shortbread tin, on his lap and began rummaging through invoices and making notes.

While my father did this, I took a stroll outside and had a swatch at Billy's Jag. It was light blue, powder blue I think they called it, and had shiny grey leather seats. It wasn't a Prick's car, as I'd expected, it was a Cunt's car. A Prick's car had little obvious prick embellishments, like a sheepskin coat slung across the back seat, or stickers from foreign climes, to display discretionary income and an expanse of cheesy personality. A Cunt's car, on the other hand, didn't give a fuck, it just sat there, dominant and stark, like Billy's did, showing seats and a wheel, nothing else, as if extraneous contents were an admission of weak humanity. Unless of course you included the small snivelling child sitting in the passenger seat.

This was my first encounter with Mick. I peered in nosily, through the window, watching him sob. I guessed he was three or four years younger than me, nine years old perhaps, with big podgy hands and sticky up hair. He had one of those gargoyle Scottish faces, scared and surly at the same time, that made you want to goad it with a stick for the sport of watching him have a tantrum. On his lap lay a spinning top, half out of its new box. It didn't take much imagination to picture his old man pulling up at the toy shop, leaving the engine running and grabbing the first shiny object he saw before roaring off down to Ralston to give my mother a discreet poke. I knocked, miming for him to lower the window. When he did, I spat in his face, which startled him somewhat.

Thereafter, Billy Waugh called often at our house, usually in the afternoons. Sometimes he brought Mick and sometimes he didn't. Mick always looked a bit tentative following our initial encounter and I imagined he made these trips with reluctance. If Billy required only a quick empty then Mick was left in the car, but if he anticipated an afternoon of languid bliss, then Mick would be fetched in and my Mother would urge me to entertain him while they canoodled. If my father was at home, he'd make us tea, beans with fish fingers usually. Sometimes, on request, he'd take a tray of tea and toast up to Billy; looking back my father was a most agreeable host.

Occasionally, to kill time, Mick and I might tap a ball around in the back garden. Once I asked him about his mother, whether she knew about these visits to Ralston. Mick replied, 'I don't know,' and didn't elaborate. I could tell he wanted to talk but was wary of doing so, no doubt fearful of the hiding he'd get off his old man if he did. Through time, I managed to glean that his mother cried a lot and was prone to throwing things at walls until clumped, at which point she'd desist. She drank and would often sleep in a tarted up stone outhouse at the foot of their garden. When I asked him what she looked like, he said she look a bit like my mother, only older. It started to rain and we went back into the house. Mick was an only child and I was the nearest thing he had to a big brother or confidant. I suppose I abused the position in order to find things out. I could do this so long as the scales were tipped in my favour, if Billy discovered little Mick was telling tales, it'd be him who'd cop the belting, so Mick was reliant upon my discretion. Fine, as I've said, so long as I held the whiphand.

The trouble was, it all changed the moment we walked into the kitchen and caught my father in a pair of women's stockings, applying lipstick while looking into a hand mirror. I was mortified not because it was a novel situation, not for me at least, it was more the fact of worlds colliding; young Mick, an outsider from the Planet Normal, bearing witness to this shabby aberration. At first, my father attempted an amused, defiant air, like he was this bold pioneer, rolling back the frontiers of sexual liberation, but he lacked the balls, so to speak, to carry it off and he slunk past us, like the sad miserable fuck he was, to change back into his boiler suit. I remember feeling numb all over. I made myself turn to Mick. He looked confused, naturally enough, like he was unsure whether to laugh or cry. I showed him a fist and he chose crying. 'If you tell anybody, and I mean anybody,' I said, 'I'll fucking well kill you.' I used the F word to grind it home, and he trembled. Remember, those were innocent times. Even in those days I knew that keeping a secret, to most of us, meant telling only a few people. 'I'll not tell anybody,' he promised. To my knowledge and his credit, I don't believe he ever did. But it did mean the scales of relationship power had been evened up and that henceforth I was compelled to treat the little cunt like a person.

*

'This is where they recovered the limbs.'

An old bloke in a thick overcoat was standing next to me on the pier. 'What limbs?' I asked, a bit non-plussed.

'The limbs,' he repeated, impatiently, like they were clothes pegged on a washing line before our eyes. 'That young man who was killed by the mad homosexual. Police divers located them from this very pier.'

'No,' I said, 'I don't know anything about any limbs.'

But he kept banging on about these fucking limbs. 'But you must remember. Round about Christmas time it was. They found the head on a beach in Ayrshire.'

'No,' I said, 'I haven't been to Ayrshire in years.' He gave me strange sort of look, like I wasn't fulfilling my part of the conversation bargain. 'I'm only up here on business,' I said, a bit limply.

'So was he,' he said.

'Who?'

'The mad homosexual. The world is a horrible place. Mind, this is a nice pier.'

I walked off, leaving him standing peeved, and I kept walking, past the hire car, just in case. Fucking limbs, I thought, you take a quiet drive in the country to get away from work, but still cunts come at you with heads and legs. All the same when I did return to the car after having a Red Bull in the hotel bar, I kept seeing the sheathed yellow muscles on Calum's split shoulders and recalling the great twanging struggle I'd had to sever the slippery veins of his neck. Maybe it was just the cheese toastie I'd had with the Red Bull, perhaps it was a bit dodgy, but I found myself leaning against the passenger door, feeling quite queasy. Don't let anybody ever tell you us nutters get our money for jam. Psychos, mad homosexuals, we earn it, all of us.

I needed a spot of normality following my funny turn on the pier, so on the way back that evening, I stopped off at my father's. I didn't knock on the door, in case I was interrupting anything. Instead, him being on the ground floor, I peeked in through the living-room window. He was Cindy. He was sitting dozing in his armchair, wig askew, legs open in front of the gas fire. The telly was showing *Antiques Roadshow*, but I didn't see him on it. This was quite a prescient sentiment on my part, as it happened, that telly reference, but I'll come to that. Anyway, I didn't go in.

*

My chief concern at that time was how best to further my professional interests. I'd done the laying low stuff and hadn't been questioned over the murders of Calum and Gary Moss so I hoped the polis, though publicly proceeding with their enquiries, were privately adopting the hoped-for attitude of 'good fucking riddance'. David reported to me that Calum's ex had done a spot of paid grieving in what downmarket Scottish-based tabloids like to call 'a downmarket English-based tabloid'. We'd waited nervously for any follow-ups, as grieving loved ones of crims often seem to develop a taste for lurid publicity, but the one splurge seemed to satisfy. It also went without saying that she herself would be under suspicion, as clearly she stood to gain from Calum's demise. So all in all, I felt nicely placed. I'd been off the Scottish scene for five years, more than enough time, in police eyes, for any old scores to have been either settled or forgotten. Additionally, I had the appropriate alibi of the funeral. I mean what kind of nutter is going to go out and murder two people days after his mother's funeral? No, no, Inspector Taggart, this is a turf war and no mistake. You say the van was found in Waugh's street, now what's this you add about an anonymous letter? Calum's ex and . . . who? Darko Lyall? Well, well, time to bring him in then, don't you think? The letter wasn't anonymous to me since I had written it, or to be more accurate, dictated it to Davie. By my inventing the lovely lie of an affair between Darko and Calum's shag, the polis would see a motive for Darko killing him. Therefore, Darko would be enraged. When a holligan's enraged he's not thinking, which was how I wanted him. Yes, prod the Darko beast with my poison pen, a subtle flourish, I thought.

So when I arrived back at the B&B I wasn't entirely surprised to find a brown A4 envelope waiting for me on the hall table. Hand delivered. And battered. A size-eight envelope stuffed through a demure size-four Rennie Macintosh letterbox, so someone didn't want to be remembered. I had a good idea who. Claw Hammill might as well have had me call round for the fucking thing in person, it reeked of sweat and rolling tobacco from where he'd hidden it under his jacket.

I went up to my room before I opened it. I didn't want to be explaining away any unwelcome gifts of turds or dead rats to my fellow guests as they to and froed from the dining room. In the event, I needn't have worried. It was only an *A to Z* of London. A none too subtle hint that perhaps I might care to fuck off and return there. I'd scrunched up the envelope to chuck it in the bin, when I realized there was something else inside. I smoothed the envelope out as best I could, reached in and took out a bullet. I'm no expert, but it looked like a man-sized 9 mm effort to me, and the sight of it gave me a little chill as of course it was supposed to do. Hooligans are fond of making these get-out-of-Dodge-type gestures. They're regarded as a legitimate perk of the job and can often pass into legend if the tale is burnished sufficiently and recycled to enough appreciative ears. I could picture Darko, in a rage, despatching one of his harassed grizzlies round the pubs to buy it. 'And I want a fashionable-sized bullet, not any fucking earring stud, take a mortar shell if you can get one for under a tenner.' I put the bullet in the palm of my hand and tested its cold weight. For morbid drama, I pressed it against my forehead and said, 'bang.'

Of course it was one thing me being all sneeringly metaphysical from the safe haven of the B&B, but I'd no way of knowing whether we were in the land of 'true' or 'bluff', it being well within Darko's violence threshold to blast some fucker. If the polis had pulled him in for questioning he wouldn't be terribly pleased, and a few brief chats round the favoured haunts would no doubt have uncovered the information that I was still skulking about the town and therefore, in all probability, culpable. I began to wonder if my, or to be more accurate Davie's, anonymous letter hadn't proved a goading gesture too far. It wasn't impossible that the polis would disbelieve the information about the affair, but would still leak the information to Darko's wife, Janey, just for badness. Whatever was or wasn't the case, it was obvious that Darko was angry enough to come looking for me, because, well, he'd found me, hadn't he? On the plus side, I needed him angry, didn't I? So I could draw him out into the open, where I could see him. Of course, maybe I was completely wrong and the surprise packet hadn't come from Darko, but Peter and Paul. I doubted this, however, as their presence had become remote to the point where no fucker seemed to know whether they were now international racketeers running an IT criminal empire, or had retired to Prestwick and were sitting on the porch, reading *Captain Corelli's Mandolin*. In either case, what would be the point of their strapping on their armour again to do battle with an unreconstructed hammer-tapping cunt like me? No, all in all, it looked like I was heading for a set-to with Darko, which would have to come sooner or later if I was ever to revitalize my brand name in the bustling local market place. When this happened, I'd be careful not to further antagonize Billy. I had muddied the waters nicely, I felt, over the two murders and, like a good general, was reluctant to fight battles simultaneously on two fronts, No, Billy could wait.

I deemed it appropriate to give Darko a little nip in return. Naturally, the quality and tone of this nip would have to be sensitively judged so as to give the right quality of offence. A touch of scorn, I felt, tinged with contempt would strike the appropriate note. Above all, I didn't want Darko getting the idea I was tense or scared, both of which, of course, I was. I knew he had moved to some ugly custom-built villa at the arse-end of the town, so the first step was to lay hands on his address. The straightforward route for that would have been Claw Hammill but he'd have been straight on the mobile to warn Darko. Much better I found out from an alternative source and with luck, have Darko blame Claw anyway and deal him a justified slap. Naturally, I could have asked Davie, but I didn't get a hard-on when I spoke to him the way I did with Brenda. I called her in the late afternoon and she answered. She began doing girly, I'm-really-startled-by-your-call-type acting, but when you give some cunt your number there's a fifty–fifty shot they're going to use it, wouldn't you say? Then again you've always got to jump through a few hoops with a bint if you've burned her. She settled down after a minute though and I even left her with a little laugh when I described how I'd clocked Cindy by the gas fire. I put the phone down having arranged to take her out for some nosebag the following night.

Darko's house was up beyond the Falside Road, less than a mile from the centre of town. He had the same outlook as Billy when it came to hooliganism and had never lost touch with his roots, eschewing the lure of London or Manchester and the loftier peaks of mayhem. But whereas Billy could enjoy network status as a respected potentate of a major city, Darko, for all his gifts, remained a stunted talent, all head and little light, victim of his own entrenched provincialism, condemned to rage and fulminate over sleights, real or imagined, from the bigger players who, when they tapped on a mobile, spoke to the monarch along the motorway, not the baron in the backwater, rotting in his breeze-block castle.

In this, Darko was akin to some of those dukes of Essex whom I'd met, those bods with quilted muscles and the arms graffitied with naff tattoos, who start off blind to London but then, as they age, grow to resent its mocking presence, since it serves as an Imperial Standard against which their pygmy achievements will, on the day of hooligan judgement, be finally measured. True monarchs were slain singly after weighty deliberations and earnest discussions in dark corners; not in threes, like those Essex boys who ended up like half a six-pack sitting in a Land Rover with holes in their heads. I thought of Old Joe Chisnall, of south Kent and of the Braintree incident. Of squat Ronnie's fat hand on my youthful shoulder after my first estuary tapping. 'Good boy,' he'd said, 'you'll go far.'

It was Young Joe now, of course. Old Joe was a cancer case, long since gone. After Old Joe's demise, legend had it that Young Joe decided to take a bride. In that gooey, disturbing way that some Home Counties hooligans have, he elected to make a romantic proposal. He hired a white horse, a lance and a full suit of armour and turned up at his intended's Barratt semi-detached in Romford. Obviously, he expected this to create a favourable impression. Instead, the intended was mortified and her dad came to the door and told Joe to stick his lance up his kingly arse.

Unfortunately, Young Joe wasn't use to being crossed and took the rejection badly. An argument ensued during which things turned ugly. It culminated with Young Joe walking back to his steed, returning with a mace and attacking the intended's family with it, fracturing the father's skull and breaking the loved one's arm. For good measure, he then ran the lance through the living-room window, avoiding, by a narrow margin, the impaling of an aged relative. Anyone else would have been jailed, but of course no one in Essex would press charges against the Chisnalls.

I had time to let my mind dawdle over such piquant past events as I waited in the bus shelter across the street from Darko's house. Beyond the narrow but long front garden, the lights were on and I could see flickering images from the television set, *Rikki Lake* I thought. Darko's mouth was moving and he was pacing about the room in an agitated manner. I guessed he was talking to his wife and when Janey Lyall's red-tinted nut came into view, I saw this was the case. I was pained to see that Darko now had a goatee too. I decided there must be a new shop up here called Gun, Gut and Goatee, where hooligans of a certain age bought the look as a ready-made ensemble. Darko's face was flushed and, I noted with some satisfaction, they were having a right set-to. They had good reason to do so as, among other treats, I'd had a heart-shaped box of Thorntons Continental couriered to the door with a note saying 'Big Daddy, love and miss you'. I'd followed this up by arranging the Glasgow Ticket Centre to call, confirming two tickets for 'Mr Lyall and friend,' for Bare Naked Ladies at the Armadillo.

A small van pulled up across the street, half on and half off the pavement. A girl in a raincoat got out, hurried up the path and the driver rang the bell. I watched Darko freeze in mid rant, obviously wondering, What the fuck now, and hesitating about whether to open the door. Mrs Darko had no such reservations and I saw her push Darko in the chest before heading for the hallway. The front door opened and yellow light spilled out onto the garden path. This was the cue for the driver to step back and for the girl to open her coat and start singing. She got about halfway through the first line of 'I Get a Kick Out of You' when the door was slammed in her chops. In the living room, Darko was on the phone. He had the receiver gripped like a throat and was shouting into it. I saw him slam it down and turn in time to take an awkward female punch on the temple from his wife. As he grabbed her by the wrists and slapped her fizzer I thought, with some contentment, my work here is done, and I walked out of the bus shelter, and round the corner into the pub car park where I'd left the hire car two hours earlier. It had been a joyous day of boyish pranks but I knew that soon it would be time to unbag my tools once more. Such were the ways of our people.

Chapter Seven

It was strangely comforting to be hated again. At least it reassured me I was still wanted. Half my time in London was spent in an aimless daze, inventing little tasks to keep myself occupied while I waited for creative criminal ideas to seed and flower. Now, in my middle years, it seemed to me sometimes that I'd entered a sort of hooligan no-man's-land. I was too young to slump about on cane chairs chuckling over war crimes with the older crims and too old to be jumping around, hanging out of jeeps and popping pharmaceuticals with the young ones. In my early days in London I'd made the mistake of trying out the club scene, hanging around the bars with these twenty-something oafs from Barking, hoping hooligan chic and a black turtleneck would help me squeeze my gut through the credibility gap. Instead, I'd felt like a vicar at a ping-pong night, and packed it in. Beyond forty the only way you'll feel comfortable in a club is if you either own it or are torching it for a friend. That's why I took the flat in Bayswater; it's a buzzy little area and you get a vicarious feeling of being plugged into life.

'How many does that make?' I asked Davie. We were sitting in Curler's Bar, in the Byres Road, at a corner table away from prying eyes. We were whittling down a further list of interviewees from another session in his flat a couple of days earlier.

'Six,' he said. Davie was excited. I could tell this because for once his mouth appeared to open when he spoke. He looked to me for a show of jubilation but I found myself adopting the pose of Mr Cool Methodical Tactician, the supremo who takes nothing for granted. I knew this was bollocks, as I was just as incompetent as every other flea brain in the criminal community but it was important to damp down any false expectations, when people feel exuberant they blab too much and I didn't want to be providing either information or inspiration to the opposition, something for Darko to mentally pin up on the dressing-room door. So when Davie added, 'With six good boys we could liberate Palestine,' I doused him in sarcasm, pointing out we'd be hard put to attempt a coup on Foxbar with our limited manpower. I didn't, however, necessarily believe that statement. I felt we had tapped the area's resources at a fortuitous time. No one had started up a team in Paisley for some years, not since the wild west atmosphere of half a decade ago. After that, the established, if uneasy hegemony of Darko, P&P, Calum and formerly, myself, had implied a finite market already saturated with daunting hooligan empires. But with Calum gone, and the brothers invisible, the time was ripe for someone, preferably me, to create from their ruin a gleaming and visible new order. Because that's the kind of positive cunt I was. Davie's trust had rejuvenated me and thanks to his grass-roots knowledge we'd now recruited the elite of Paisley's raw and untutored young thugs. Of our chosen candidates, none was over twenty-five, married, or employed. All were from broken homes and each had weaknesses for clothes and drugs.

These last two factors were important, affording, as they did, the possibility that a need for approval might be usefully intertwined with an unfeasible craving for ready cash. I wanted young, damaged men of appetite and despair and I flattered myself I'd found them. Davie slid a bottle of Bud across the damp table, explaining that the lager was off while they changed a keg. I gave him a little rant about how I disapproved of fashionable bottled beers. 'You get half the liquid for twice the price of a pint and they don't even have to wash a fucking glass at the end of it.' Davie nodded, like a man who gives a fuck and I made a mental note to look in the mirror when I got back, to see if I'd turned into Billy. 'Show me the names,' I told him. I ran my eye over a heavily worked sheet of A4. I wondered how I'd ever remember the fuckers, then I had a quirky notion.

'You know what I'm going to do, Davie?'

'What?' asked Davie.

'I'm going to encourage a spirit of healthy competitiveness among these young men. Instead of using surnames we'll adopt names of football teams, English Premiership of course, none of this Scottish sectarian pish. We'll award points for victory and so forth and have them all striving to win the championship or avoid relegation.'

'Where would they go if they got relegated?'

That was the way Davie's mind worked. Not, 'What's the prize for winning the championship?' I ignored his question and paused, smiling, waiting for some spark to kindle into a healthy glow of enthusiasm. Did it fuck. 'What do you think?' I prompted.

'You mean like Gus Chelsea and Tony . . . Tottenham and that?'

'That's it,' I said. I was getting a bit enthused myself now. Then it dawned on me what was wrong. 'You don't want to be in this league, Davie, do you?' I knew by the little pouting shrug he gave me, that I'd hit on it. I did a spot of looking-thoughtful acting then I said, 'You'll be my player–manager. That'll be you, Davie Vialli' He gave a little smile like it was all a silly game. It was, of course, it was a fucking stupid game, but I know how insecure and unloved the average male cunt can feel and since these chaps were a good deal less than average, it followed that any system of rewards and punishments, based on no matter how puerile a premise, could be relied upon to stoke up a spot of creative endeavour. 'Well that's that settled then,' I said, giving Davie a little nudge. To further mollify him, I went up to the bar and brought us each back Buds, doublers apiece, and we toasted the future. Of course, the very next day didn't Chelsea sack Vialli? But by then Davie was stuck with it, so fuck him.

*

The following morning I put on my violence suit, which was a midnight blue Hugo Boss mohair number with reinforced stitching, and set off for an important business meeting with two respected colleagues from the sleaze industry. One of these respected colleagues was a man called John Leask. He owned a club called Salsa One. The use of the numeral implied, grandly, a whole numbered empire of Salsa clubs, but this was a bogus ruse and Salsa One had long been known as Rio until someone with a pulse had pointed out that Duran Duran hadn't had a hit in fifteen years. The other respected colleague was Robin Tierney. He owned a den called Blue. It was nicknamed Black and Blue because of the fights that often took place there.

I met them at the Watermill Hotel and over a pleasant lunch I outlined my future intentions. As these intentions involved, willingly and unwillingly, the use of their establishments, I'd thought it only fair to enlighten Leask and Tierney in advance. I said as much in an above board kind of way. Unfortunately, Robin Tierney, who had the characteristic of impatience, jumped in, misinterpreting my plans.

'You're not getting the doors, Albert,' he heard his mouth say. He was nervous at having dug me up so quickly but obviously he'd come armed with a 'start as you mean to go on' approach and now he was lumbered with it. He looked to John Leask for support. 'Things have changed, haven't they, John?'

Leask had no option but to nod. But it was a faint nod, tinged with fright, a nod to me as well as Robin, a nod that said, 'Let's not provoke confrontation, let's look instead for areas of mutual harmony, lest we get our heads cratered.' All the same, his mouth had taken Tierney's side.

'You're wasting your time, Albert,' said John Leask, with a big magnanimous spread of his thin nervy hands. He mentioned the name of a well-known nationwide security firm that specialized in crowd control. 'I'm like Robin,' he said, 'my doors are contracted for the next two years.' They made resigned, our-hands-are-tied-type of noises.

I let Tierney continue. Hearing no objections from

me, he was starting to gain in confidence. He placed his elbows on the table and he too started using his hands to emphasize his points.

'You see, Albert, Paisley isn't Essex,' he explained, considerately. 'The doors are still a free for all down there, but we've outgrown all that.' I pointed out that doormen down there were obliged to be licensed. Tierney scorned these details with a flick of the wrist. 'And we all know what that's worth, don't we?' He looked to his colleague.

'Gorillas,' agreed John Leask. And they shared an experienced smile, seasoned club pro to seasoned club pro. 'Lots of clubs even have lassies on the doors now, it's true. I mean you can laugh, Albert, but . . .'

I pointed out to Robin Tierney that I wasn't laughing. I agreed it was a useful door policy, not only laudable in terms of equal opportunities but shrewd in its implicit understanding of human relations. No kudos for the average drunken arsehole in threatening a pretty girl; what if she should beat him up? But I also pointed out that this was largely a fashion, an attempt to upgrade the status of a club by pretending yours wasn't the sort of place that needed gladiators on the door since you didn't attract a low-life sort of clientele. Which was, of course, exactly the sort of psychology that would attract a low-life clientele. Once the perfumed air of elitism had permeated the cowsheds, that same scurvy herd would queue at the doors, begging entry; desperate to pay through the snout for its Rolling Rock, eager to congratulate itself that it could afford to drink at a club at which it was ridiculed and despised. I further pointed out to Leask and Tierney that this enlightened door policy wasn't one that was appropriate for every club. Theirs, for instance, as had been apparent when I'd checked up on them the previous night. All prime Scotch beef, silk bomber jackets and headsets.

I outlined my belief that this was a wild town, at the vanguard of mayhem and, God willing, would remain so. I reminded them that people were shooting each other in Paisley when folk in Basildon were still running around with crossbows. Why, even as recently as well, recently, we'd had a prominent crook beheaded. Tierney opened his mouth to speak, but I cut in. Time was ticking on and I still had to buy a new shirt for my dinner date with Brenda. I surprised Leask and Tierney by telling them I didn't want their crummy doors, they could keep their doors, if I wanted doors I'd go to B&Q like every other cunt. I waited while they digested this information over their sticky toffee pudding. I didn't order the sticky toffee pudding myself, or indeed any other pudding, sticky or non-sticky, on account of my dieting regime and the aforesaid dinner date with Brenda. Which is not to say I didn't crave it. I thought about calling for another spoon so we could share, but it's hard to come over all menacingly psychopathic when your front teeth are stalactited with caramel.

It was at this point I informed them of what I required. Which was the sole franchise to deal drugs both in their clubs and within the immediate environs of their clubs. They each did I-am-horrified-by-this-suggestion acting while waiting for the other to speak. So I spoke.

'I know your door persons aren't selling on the doors because they're scared to,' I said. 'And they're scared to because the franchise lies with Darko Lyall.' Hearing no dissent, I continued. 'He sells on the way with his taxi drivers and he sells inside later on when the customers are looking for a top up for their youthful high spirits, then he sells a third fucking time on the way home when they need carry out for their parties. That's three fucking bites at the same cherry,' I said, 'when in fact I don't believe Darko Lyall should have any fucking cherry.' I was throwing in the F word to show that I'd taken the gloves off.

Tierney tried a spot of hedging. 'How do you know Darko's in our clubs?'

Even Leask looked embarrassed by that one. Nevertheless I pointed out with admirable patience, admired by me, if not others, that the only taxis outside Salsa One and Blue were Darko's, even though they weren't licensed to pick up, and that, additionally, his cards were plastered all over the admission counters and payphone in each foyer. When I suggested that a spot of healthy competition wouldn't go amiss, they looked at me like men about to piss their Pampers.

'Sorry, Albert,' said Tierney, 'but I'm not in the suicide business.' He gave a little laugh to cover his cravenness, before adding, cravenly, 'and neither is John.'

Leask gave him an irked look. I could see he wasn't entirely comfortable with this analysis. It revealed, too wretchedly, the true nature of their relationship with Darko. Possibly Leask had been hoping to convince me that Darko was the third side of some caring, sharing, touch-one touch-all triangle, some kind of sleeping partner and Lord Protector, senior and dominant perhaps, but always ready to unsheathe his sword and rush with chivalrous speed to uphold their fair name of mutual self-interest. Now they were revealed as naked victims, with two ugly bastards about to lock horns and fight for the right to rape them. Tierney detected John Leask's displeasure, and the torn hole in the backcloth upon which it was predicated and attempted to regain lost ground. 'We've a business understanding with Darko Lyall,' he said, 'it suits us and it suits him.'

John Leask bent further over his spoon as I said, 'No, it suits you because it suits him.' I leaned back in my chair, at the same time placing my hands on the table like an honest cunt. 'I ask you,' I said, 'what kind of partnership can it be that's based on fear and intimidation?' The answer to that is, of course, 'a normal one' but it sounded manly in the circumstances and in any case I was hoping to drive a little wedge between them. I looked squarely into their troubled faces. Neither of them risked giving me a frying-pan-to-fire look largely because the fight was leaking out of them. The squeeze had long been on them from one direction now here it was, with renewed force, coming from another. No wonder they looked miserable. Leask couldn't even finish his pudding, that's how bad he felt.

'Look, Albert,' he said at last, 'I can't go against Darko, I still value my health, you know what I'm saying?' I did, I knew exactly what he was saying. He was saying a very sensible, nicely judged thing. 'It just isn't in my interests.'

'Nor mine,' said Tierney, hurriedly. He sensed some sort of lifeboat approaching and wanted to jump in.

John Leask continued. 'If we let your server in, and I take it you've got one . . .?'

I hesitated for a moment while I worked out what

the fuck a server was. 'Yes,' I said, 'I've got a server.' He meant supplier. Fucking computer-speak, it's everywhere. 'I've got servers coming out my fucking ears,' I told him, wittily.

John Leask nodded and continued, using an earnest, truthful-sounding tone. 'Basically, the thing is this. If I let you into my club, Darko will be, well, he'll be most aggrieved. And basically, Albert, I don't want to live my life sitting in my living room in a bullet-proof vest with asbestos curtains at my windows, because that's what it would mean for me to go against Darko Lyall. You understand my position?'

'Our position,' said Tierney.

I told them both that I saw their position.

'I can accommodate Darko,' said John Leask, spelling it out, 'or I can accommodate you. But I can't accommodate both.' Realization of his own powerlessness seemed to liberate John Leask and he returned to his pudding with renewed gusto.

'Same here,' said Robert Tierney, but he didn't have any pudding left.

I did a spot of slow nodding, like a man who's grasping the full import. 'Maybe I should discuss the matter with Darko,' I said.

'Maybe you should,' said John Leask, 'that might be a useful first step.'

I looked to Tierney. 'What say you, Robin? You in concurrence?' His sad but brisk nod told me that indeed he was. 'In that case,' I said, 'thank you both for coming. I'll be in touch.' And I rose and strode out in a kingly fashion, leaving them with the bill.

I walked to the hotel foyer and had them order me a

cab. I hadn't taken the car in case I fancied a quick glug at lunch but in the event I was stone cold sober. While I waited, I flicked through an afternoon edition of the *Evening Times*. On page five I was tickled and gratified to read 'Drug Double Killing – Gang Boss Quizzed'. There was a picture of Billy Waugh stepping out of Pitt Street nick looking slightly miffed. I put the paper down and worked on a gravy stain on my shirtfront with a fingernail. It was civilized doing business like this I decided, usually my stains were brains or snot. Perhaps I'd learn a few more steps of the hooligan minuet in future, but in the meanwhile, the tool bag beckoned.

*

I'd gone to a fair bit of effort to make it look like I hadn't made an effort. We'd stopped on Paisley High Street but, looking about, I was assailed by a wave of depression and instructed the driver to take the M8 into Glasgow for my dinner with Brenda. I wanted something dark, but not black, all middle-aged men looked drearily the same in restaurants, I found, cropped hair, rimless specs, black polo sweater and linen jacket, it was a lazy cliché and got you smirked at by the waitresses. I found a rather rakish dark grey number, in a shiny material, at Savoy Tailor's Guild, what used to be Carswell's, in Union Street and decided, after whipping one on and off a few times, that it was a shirt that looked better without a tie. I considered a T-shirt underneath, but eschewed this on grounds of age. Only young men can pull off that bulky effect, with mysterious lumber checks and hoods and stuff that layer down like geological ages to the pale-skinned core, guys over forty just look like they were trying to keep the cold out, which of course, up here, we were. I thought about buying some new trunk-style underwear but dismissed this, not on grounds of decrepitude, since they're built sympathetically to accommodate aged bollocks that swing like a pendulum, but on grounds of superstition; somehow going out with fancy drawers on seemed presumptuous and I felt sure from past experiences that fate was bound to think, Cocky fucker, taking his hole for granted, let's give him a slap. So fancy drawers were there none. Nevertheless, I was in carefree, effervescent mood once more by the time I arrived back at the B&B. Doubtless, this was why I pulled up all the more sharply when I heard my name called out as I put my hand on the gate. I turned to see Mick Waugh stepping out of his old man's ancient two-tone Bentley, the one he'd bought after the pale blue jag.

'Hello there, Albert,' he said.

'Hello, Mick,' I said. 'How did you know where I lived? You been following me?'

Actually, I didn't give a fuck how he knew where I lived, I just wanted him on the back foot. 'You know what this place is, Albert,' he said. 'People talk.'

'Which people? What do they say?' I wanted him to keep active, mentally and verbally, while I fumbled in my pocket for something, anything, I could use for a weapon. I put my Yale key between my middle and index fingers; if it came to it, I'd try and puncture an eye, or ram it into an ear-hole, or better still, open a door with it and run inside. I was all aflutter and filled with unseemly concern, caught, as I was, without tools.

'Wee people,' said Mick, 'feart people, people like you, Albert.'

'That doesn't narrow it down much,' I said. Slanted half bricks marked a border between a patch of lawn and the concrete path. He was a formidable cunt. *Une cunt formidable*. I decided if I lived I'd never step outside again up here without a comforting, luxury-length carving implement upon my person. When it dawned on me he was alone, I relaxed a bit. If he was calling round with a free beating, he'd surely have furnished himself with at least one colleague for restraining and observational duties and the like. Nobody fights his own battles in our industry.

'My dad sent me,' said Mick. 'He'd like a wee word.'

'How about no,' I said, 'is that wee enough?' I said this with a little laugh to try and take the edge off but the bottom line was there was no way I was stepping into that vehicle for one of Billy's magic car rides, you know, start off in the passenger seat, then vanish into the boot. I'd just have to risk being rude to Billy; it was better than ending up a bad smell in a wheely bin. 'I saw the paper,' I said, 'I can imagine Billy's quite pissed off.' I thought I'd try and ingratiate myself with a spot of nervous fear. This was quite subtle and, of course, contemptible, but worse than that it was a waste of personal humiliation as my signals just bounded off the barren planet that was Mick's skull to echo forlornly back to Starship Albert.

'Come on, pal,' he coaxed. 'You've done nothing wrong. Just a chinwag. Billy wants to clear the air.' He gave the Bentley a derisive tap with his foot. 'You don't think I'd take anybody for a run in the woods in this old bin wagon, do you?'

'Why not,' I reminded him, 'I did.' Which was true. I'd killed an accountant chap called Evan Sands in that old bus, for messing up Billy's tax returns. He had cost Billy eighty grand, including VAT, and drawn prurient public scrutiny to his affairs, so he hadn't been best pleased. Six months later, with things smoothed over with the Customs and Excise, 'smoothed over' a casual phrase embodying the further payment of a twenty-five grand liability, I'd taken this Evan for a hurl, tapped his head with a sharp axe, then, with two colleagues, chopped the body into bits and driven it to Stranraer for disposal at sea. Going down south had been a mistake, it cost us five grand to find a silent cunt with a boat. We should have gone up north, to Montrose, where they'd have done it for a bottle of Scotsmac and a bag of chips.

'That was a long time ago,' said Mick, 'times have changed.'

'The car hasn't,' I said. 'What you doing driving the hearse if you don't want to take anybody up the woods?'

'It's getting on,' said Mick, stroking the wing of the Bentley like it was loveable old Ginger, the one-eyed family cat, 'it gets a run out once a month.' He rapped on the windscreen with his knuckles. 'And today's the day.' He gave me a matey smile. 'You know what the old boy's like. Come on.' He was done coaxing, it was an order this time. 'Get in, Albert.'

'No,' I said.

'Albert, get in the fucking car.'

'No thank you,' I said. I was saying no but it was starting to feel like 'Shan't!' And that's the way Mick was looking at me, like I was being an irksome pre-pubescent brat who was spoiling a nice family day out.

'You're being very, very stupid,' he was saying, 'will you please get in the car?'

'No,' I said.

'Go on, I've said please.' I shook my head, to spare me the embarrassment of saying no again. Mick let his shoulders sag. His voice adopted a sighing note of intimate impatience. 'Albert,' he said. I admit, I faltered. I sort of rocked to and fro on my feet before survival prevailed and I came to my senses and shook my head again. I wondered how many men had walked voluntarily to their graves, just to spare themselves a moment of embarrassment on the pavement. Mick gave an exasperated yap and got into the car. He wound down the window. 'Can I tell him you'll phone?'

'Yes,' I said, 'I'll phone him tomorrow.'

'Definitely?'

'Yes.'

'Because it's me that gets it in the neck,' said Mick. He started the engine. 'I'll tell you what though, Albert.'

'What?' Things seemed to have turned normal, and I found myself peeking in through the passenger window.

'It's just as well you didn't get into this car.'

'Why?'

'Because you'd have got in the back of the head.'

I looked at him. 'Are you serious?'

'Work it out for yourself, you spineless cunt,' said Mick. He opened up the glove compartment to let me see. And yes, there was a gun. He gave a little chortle for effect then tried to pull away sharply, like he'd seen film stars do in the pictures, but the useless cunt of a gearbox wouldn't oblige.

'Want a push?' I offered.

'Fuck off,' said Mick. He waited while a bus passed then he pulled out and was gone.

Chapter Eight

Over the next couple of weeks, I worked diligently and in a hands-on fashion with my new young team. They would display the customary recalcitrance of youth if I asked them to embark on the odd spot of housebreakings or car theft, complaining that such offences represented a step down in career-ladder terms and had little to do with the glamorous world of adult hooliganism as they understood the concept. I pointed out that guns, for people like us, came expensive, that they didn't grow on trees and, as it was unlikely we'd qualify for a grant from the Scottish Enterprise Executive, we'd have little choice but to raise the wherewithal ourselves.

Actors playing gangsters get knighthoods and free cocaine on set, whereas actual gangsters get stab wounds and prison sentences for supplying, among others, the knighted actors who play gangsters on set. This galls me. I've committed many heinous acts in my life, but I've never yet stoved a cunt's head in and received well done cards and bouquets of flowers congratulating me on my electrifying fucking performance. I hated trailing round the scrap yards, offering cut-rate stolen DVD players and car radios. Three points for a laptop and two for a car radio helped galvanize efforts through my favoured medium of mindless competition. Fulham now led the premiership race with Arsenal trailing a surprising last, behind Brentford.

I'd thought long and hard over the gun issue before deciding that what our team lacked in numbers it would have to compensate for with an additional threat. Also, having them around just made the chaps plain feel good. 'What's the point being a criminal if you don't get a gun?' being the prevailing opinion. I felt I had no option but to move with the times or lose the respect of my chaps. I met a man in the King's Arms pub in Carntyne, nicknamed the Heroin Arms because of the deals reputed to take place in its toilet cubicles. He sold me a shoebox containing eight firearms. Some scuffed little .22 automatics and a few rickety ex-army revolvers. As a sweetener, he included an assortment of bullets in a freezer bag and the deal was concluded over a large Smirnoff and Red Bull.

To my way of thinking, it didn't matter if we didn't have enough ammunition to fill all the guns, if the appearance of a firearm wasn't enough to bend an intended victim to your will, then firing it would only increase your troubles a hundredfold.

Rationing of bullets, I further reasoned, would help minimize any unnecessary horseplay of the yeeh-hah! variety, and its potentially calamitous social, and interpersonal consequences. Having congratulated myself on my prudence, I was therefore taken aback by the degree of disdain I encountered when I emptied out, with a clatter, the contents of the shoebox and freezer bag onto the shiny pine table in Davie's kitchen. You'd have thought I'd brought the cunts back catapults. Having been weaned on a sumptuous diet of Hollywood gangster flicks and MTV bad mother fucker rap promos, the sight of an ailing ex-army revolver failed to draw the appreciative gasps, applause and spontaneous knicker wetting I'd anticipated.

Tommy 'Charlton' Dolan picked one up sniffly, flicked his collar up and assumed a Croydon whine. 'Let him 'ave it, Derek,' he instructed, to appreciative scorn, aimed at myself.

'Let's scarper, before the rozzers get us,' augmented Kevin 'QPR' Casey, to a heightened guffaw.

I squinted at Davie. He sat gravely, biting his cheek, too mindful of my reputation to giggle.

'Let's not be fitba' teams any more, let's every cunt be a black and white film star,' said Lee, formerly 'Fulham', Fraser. For film stars, of course, read criminals. So it was that the famous old jerseys of London were folded away into the metaphorical hamper as the gates of the prisons and high security units were thrown open wide to embrace new heroes. 'This is Anfield' became 'This is Broadmoor' as new subversive names were scrawled, or etched, according to literacy, over the cherished premiership greats. Ten Rillington Rovers, Hanratty and Hove Albion, and, my favourite, Fred West Ham. I sat with my hands in the pockets of my overcoat, letting it happen, beaming with as much benign grace as I could muster. Okay, I thought, have it your way. But from now on, you young cunts, the gloves are off.

With Mick's visit coming, as it had, on top of the gift from Darko, I'd decided it was time to move out of the B&B. Over my dinner with Brenda I'd told some plausible lies and she'd agreed to let me stay in her flat 'as a friend' pending, of course, Stuart's return from Saudi.

I didn't quibble with this arrangement feeling that, once inside, the parameters of our arrangement could inevitably change. As indeed, it proved. After a day and night of prim decorum and 'after you' bathroom etiquette, a bottle of Fleurie was produced for dinner. This bottle of Fleurie lead, of course, to a second bottle and before long Brenda was sufficiently drunk to excuse herself the betrayal of Stuart on this, their sacred Slumberland. You won't be surprised to learn we fucked with some savagery, what with guilt, the drink and the mutual lack of a poke in some several weeks. I would thoroughly recommend fucking a woman who is experiencing guilt. Women are particularly yielding at this time, owing to a wish to atone through punishment or sluttish behaviour and, of this latter, I was an approving recipient. Just like old times, Brenda strode me, touching herself. 'Feel me,' she would invite. 'Feel me.' And indeed I did, which made my cock swell like an air bag inside her. We stopped, for breath, fags and tea and she took down a picture from her dressing table and made me look at it. 'Stuart's wee grandson. The one in the pram, remember?'

As usual, the sex came with a price tag. Not surprisingly, given our close proximity, some species of gnarled relationship tendril started to sprout its lurid bloom and I found myself engaging with Brenda in various forms of social activity. We'd go to the pictures, a new complex called The Quay, one of those featureless remand-home-with-neon looking gaffs, where you expect to find sixty crop heads marching in close formation on their way to paint the latrines. What did we see? *Billy Elliot* for her, *Charlie's Angels* for me. I'm like a lot of people, I find uplifting films depressing and very often depressing films uplifting, or at least, reassuring. In my view, for every unlikely cunt that escapes a housing estate by becoming a fucking ballerina, there's half a million other flat-footed fuckers who have to lump it and take a job in Greggs serving pies. And these are the fuckers who deserve films made about them.

We went out for meals, Brenda and me, and shopped for food; Marks and Spencer's like the old days. And I never even liked it then. We sloped about, doing middle-aged, comfortable-with-each-other acting, pushing our beast-sized shopping trolley laden with poncy, elaborate ready-prepared meals and melt-in-the-gob over-rich puddings. In fairness, we didn't shovel in as much food as we used to, the reason being that we didn't need to. The richer the food, the poorer the sex – all of them laden trolleys are pure sublimation, in my opinion. And we weren't at that stage, not yet anyway, though that still small voice in my head – who the fuck was that, by the way? – insisted that if I wasn't careful, I might for ever be held, like all those other fat-bellied, roll-necked cunts in the check-out queue, by the puff pastry chains of domestic enslavement.

We took a drive to Potterhill, and parked outside the first, decent-sized house we'd over owned, in Aspen Gardens. Brenda hadn't been keen on the house back then, I remembered, but I'd talked it up at the time mainly because I'd found out that, living fifty yards away in Ardmore was Cissie. She'd married, in that small town way, Leonard from the special needs class. He'd taken over his old man's firm and was a respected player in the world of West of Scotland flange pressings. About a week after we'd moved in, I clocked Cissie at her garden gate, unloading groceries from the boot of her Allegro and I'd given her a toot as I slid past in the soft-top. She'd looked up from the Pek chopped pork and Vesta chow mein packets in time for me to have a good swatch at her coupon. Sweet face, sour look. I could tell at a glance she was demented with boredom and guessed from her sallow colour she was on medication. Leonard didn't look much better. He was already showing a lot of temple and had a sort of clenched look around the eyes. Or maybe that was just the sight of me, a flattering possibility, but I doubted it. I remember thinking, Serves the cow right for trying to be normal. I knew cunts like us weren't made to fit in.

I derived a lot of mean satisfaction during that time from taunting Cissie. I had catalogues for surgical appliances sent to her door, and if I met her and Leonard on the street I'd offer the odd little sachet of coke as a 'pick me up'. Of course, back then coke still had a spot of exotic cachet about it, not like now, which is partly why I stopped indulging, it was like if John Major bought a double-breasted suit you'd know it was time to bring back the single, well, same with coke. It's naff as fuck now, before the decade's out, I fully expect lines to be on sale in M&S food halls, as a piquant accompaniment to their fucking chicken in white wine sauce.

Back then, though, a regular healthy snort would have been of more benefit to Cissie than the fucking Mogadon she was taking, and I believe part of Cissie herself knew this, though that was the part she was taking the Mogadon to suppress.

On the whole, Brenda and I enjoyed a lively reputation in the area at that time, being responsible for many colourful incidents that brightened an otherwise dull, if worthy, landscape. I was a young man back then, making my way in my chosen career and my hours of employment could prove flexible. After one a.m., Brenda would lock and bolt all the doors, back and front, obliging me to shout and swear up at the closed bedroom curtains in an attempt to attract her attention. These heartfelt pleas would fall on only one set of deaf ears, hers, but would awaken every other living being in the street. To gain entry and put an end to the unwanted spectacle, I would have no choice but to lob a brick from the back garden rockery in through the kitchen window. After this we'd have a bawling match, my wife and I, in the course of which some further disturbances, the smashing of crockery, or assaults on the person, or persons, might routinely ensue. These happenings being, as I've said, untypical of the neighbourhood, the police would find themselves summoned by an anonymous hand to restore peace in our home and its environs.

In a spirit of gregarious penitence, we held a house party, I recall, and invited, among others, all our neighbours. Unsurprisingly, few attended. Surprisingly, Cissie did, though not with Leonard. Brenda knew the sacred warped history that existed between Cissie and myself, I having made no secret of it, beyond my original sin of omission. Many local hooligans attended the event and it seemed to me that Cissie, though nervous and unsure of herself, had for the first time since our re-acquaintance, recovered something of the old gleam in her dodgy eye. So much so that Brenda wasn't taking any chances. She took Cissie under her wing and steered her about, introducing her to several handsome, thick and available young nutters. Cissie drank it all in with her Cinzano. This stuff, this was the life she'd lost in living. I told her so, though not in those words, this being an era in which the blessings of a prison library service had yet to be conferred upon me. I remember how, through a fuddled haze, I answered the doorbell and found Leonard, his big temples gleaming under the coach lamp, asking for his wife. I steered him in to join the party. This he did, unwillingly, entering the sitting room and sidling up to Cissie where she stood, having a card trick demonstrated to her by, I think, Kenny Fanshawe. When the trick was done, Leonard whispered something in her ear, then lead Cissie, by the unresisting elbow, out of the room, across the street, into Ardmore and, presumably, the safer delights of *Match of the Day* and *Parkinson*. And that was how I left it with Cissie. No goodbye, nothing. After that, I even stopped taunting her, it hardly seemed like sport any more. Within a few short months, Brenda and I were moving to our first proper villa halfway up Calside. Within a few short years, Cissie was moving to her first proper asylum, Leverndale, near, appropriately enough, Ralston, where to this day, she still receives live-in residential care. What can you say about something like that? Just clichés about 'there but for the grace of violence, go I' and stuff. I can't tell you that Cissie wouldn't have ended up in care if she hadn't married Leonard, what I believe I can safely state is that she'd have had a shitload of a better time en route to the same conclusion if she hadn't. In life, you have to play the cards you're dealt.

There's no point trying to bluff your way to normality if you're a lunatic, that way madness lies. Oh well, weialala leia wallala leialala, as they say.

All in all then, it was a bitter romantic experience, me driving Brenda about our old haunts in the hire car. Once or twice Brenda's voice trembled and her bosom, adequate, never ample, her adequate bosom heaved with the power of memory. I'd roll down the car window and she'd peer at some dowdy rhododendron or some arthritic fingers of climbing ivy like each old address was a cenotaph, and they were wreaths to the fallen. I had to exercise a good deal of cagey tolerance and keep a caring note in my voice, because I knew the lava that lay underneath the heaving black blouse was still boiling hot and liable to erupt into accusation and violence. So I kept a family-size bag of Revels on the go, hoping, by the twin miracles of sucking and chewing, to divest the past of its tang, relegating it, by stealth, to the status of a pleasant diversion like an outing to a museum or a drive-in movie. Some fucking hope. She was quiet on the drive back to Silk Street. But I was hardly in the door before she lunged at me with the old plastic talons bared, berating me for the hurt and pain I'd caused her. I gave her a defensive shove that carried a warning hint of 'fuck off' about it, just in case she got the idea I was some sort of reformed thoughtful cunt because I'd had a book out. I think it's fair to say the exchange left us both shaken as it had both something of the inevitable and the cathartic about it. She'd never been backward at screaming forward, hadn't Brenda, and it had indeed been quite like old times as I stood at the sitting-room mirror dabbing my ragged ear lobes and the rinds of flesh on my neck with Dettol.

When she picked up the phone and started doing this mock, emotional dither over whether to ring Stuart or not, I told her she could do what she fucking wanted and she slammed the receiver down again. She was still simmering but her anger had gone off the boil once she'd drawn blood and it was a matter of making gruff but unthreatening noises now till she cooled enough to stop shouting through her teeth. That's the trouble with passionate women, they're passionate all over the shop, not just in the Slumberland where you want it. Against that, one thing I'd always admired about Brenda was that she'd never been impressed by my reputation. Even when I was one of the most feared cunts in Scotland, I'd still return home to find my dinner on the ceiling if I'd been detained unexpectedly on mayhem business. Unable to understand men, Brenda solved the problem by adjudging us the enemy and declared outright war whenever the tiniest clause in the marriage vows was threatened with violation.

Felice was different from Brenda. I compared the two in my mind and kept my reflections, for survival reasons, to myself. Felice was a younger woman and bore the distinctive brand, I recognized, of middle-class female subtlety. She valued in a relationship what she described as 'honesty' which is to say she was keen for me to place all my cards on a table of her choosing, while she kept the odd fly ace up her sleeve for prudence. I was sneaky enough to go along with this policy of honesty, though imprudent enough when in drink or in a rage to flourish the odd attempted trump which would then be deemed 'hurtful' and stowed away to justify a sulk, spending spree, or, if 'hurtful' enough, revenge affair.

If you asked me now, in the quiet cunting autumn of my mellow fucking years, what lesson I'd learned from love, I'd say the trick was not to let it last longer than your erection. I'd hoisted one fat-arsed white goddess after another onto my tawdry pedestal and not one of them was worth the hire of the block and tackle.

I sat irked, thinking these heated thoughts, as Brenda wept into a cushion on the settee. Barbra Streisand was singing on the hi-fi. 'Cunts that need cunts are the unluckiest cunts in the world,' she was crooning, just for us. I went to the kitchen and made us both a cup of coffee, Brenda and me, Barbra could make her own. As I sipped the coffee, I felt better because my ears were starting to crust and I savoured the calming benefit of the Martell bolster. I asked Brenda what was really wrong and she told me.

'What's this about, Albert?' she asked, her eyes hot looking and inflamed. 'This is fucking crazyland, I shouldn't even be talking to you let alone sleeping with you, you hurtful bastard. How do you think I felt when you left?'

I pointed out I'd had to leave. 'Things were hairy,' I said, 'remember the Braveheart incident?'

'Of course I do,' she said, vaguely soothed by memories of shared mayhem, 'who could forget the Braveheart incident?'

'And the letter bomb?' I prompted.

It was true, we'd received a letter bomb, only the

freelance killing industry being the shambolic mess it was, this cold-eyed assassin chap had shown an over optimistic reliance on the reverential handling of the postal service. The results of this was that some sorting office workers had chucked a weighty parcel into a bag, ripping the envelope containing the said device, so that the resulting explosion had shattered some pigeon-holed shelving, buckling the conveyor belt and blowing off the workperson's ear. Now why my assailant, who obviously knew where I lived, had elected to send this potent missive on a perilous journey through the intestines of the postal delivery service when he could just have dropped it through my letterbox on his way to work, only he could answer. The interesting thing about this ear, though, was that although the police launched a search for it in the sorting office, it couldn't be found. It was only when an innocent householder, taking possession of a Freeman's catalogue on her front step in Cardenden, made what's fondly called 'A Horror Find' and discovered some spattered remnants on the underside of the plastic covering, that the mystery of the workperson's ear could be conclusively solved. As for the embarrassing Braveheart incident, well, coming hard on the heels of the ear, this was the moment when I finally knew I'd taken a step too far for the good of my own sanity and that my life was careering out of control.

A publican, name of Lonnie Tannahill of the Clifton Arms, a popular and unpretentious drinking pit near Elderslie, had defaulted on a payment he owed a colleague of mine for the installation of a widescreen television set on his premises. As is often the way with these things, a dispute had arisen over the quality of the equipment provided and the competence of the installation, but my colleague protested that these were mere quibbles and a cover for payment fatigue and he'd sought my assistance. Now, ordinarily, I wouldn't have involved myself directly in such matters, I'd simply have telephoned this Lonnie Tannahill and requested that he adhere to the agreed arrangement. Normally this act of contact in itself would have provided a sufficiently veiled hint that common sense had better prevail. However, I'd been bunkered up in my own house for so long following the letter bomb fiasco and that, hitched to both a nervous disorder and a heavy cold, had made me somewhat stir crazy. When I say stir crazy, the fact was I'd been going out of my box on a deadly cocktail of drink, drugs and, of course, Night Nurse for the heavy cold. These factors, combined with boredom, had conspired to impair my judgement so that instead of taking recourse to the safe and simple expedient of the telephone, I'd liberated a horse from stables across the field from my house and ridden the cunt up Paisley High Street, beyond the old Regal Cinema, onward past Feegie Park and forward into Elderslie, reputed birthplace of Sir William Wallace, iconic freedom fighter and nobleman. To this day, I do not know what was in my head, which is to say I know exactly what was in my head, since it's obvious I wished to be William Fucking Wallace. I told you it was embarrassing, didn't I? On arrival at the Clifton Arms, I was later informed by a sober witness, more sober than me anyway, that I'd produced an impressive, red-tipped, fireman-type axe and brandished it. Can I really have tethered my horse, well, somebody's horse, outside H. Baxter and Son while I first selected and then purchased this implement? We may never know. What we do appear to know is that, after swishing the axe around my head, thereby scattering all the customers and shattering two small wall lights, I'd demanded satisfaction from this Tannahill chap. Satisfaction, apparently, being the word I'd used.

What is it about the criminal mind and horses? Young Joe Chisnall, me. Taking to the streets on a quadruped appears to mark the imaginative apex of the febrile hooligan mind shortly before it wobbles, then bowls over down the other side into enforced monastic sobriety, or self-destruction. Young Joe cleaned up at a Sussex health farm, rumour had it, following his spree with lance and mace, while I fled to a Bayswater basement and healed my howling psyche by allowing it to masturbate into a book. The troubling factor for me concerning the Clifton Arms incident, apart of course from not remembering it, is that I appear to have taken some sort of fit on that occasion, scaring casual drinkers with my spasmodic shudderings and dripping foamy mucus onto the carpet tiles, though that, I like to think, was due to the effects of the head cold. Tannahill himself, incidentally, failed to appear, though he did telephone my colleague and let him know that their prior arrangement would, after all, be satisfactory. I have no idea how I arrived home following the Braveheart incident, nor, for that matter, if the horse achieved the same feat. I only remember coming to on my front lawn, shivering from the bones outward, minus, for some reason, my tie and shoes. The dawn, or thereabouts, was breaking and I could hear various birds making their morning racket as

I sat in a huddle, too stiff to complete the task of standing upright, feeling like the last man in Europe. The fireman's axe lay at my feet, lighting a dim pilot under the gas of memory. When I saw where I was, I started to feel somewhat afraid, both for my body and for my mind. I had made many enemies, both locally and at large, enemies whom only my carefully manicured reputation kept at bay. Now, people were taking the trouble to send me letter bombs. Why bother, I thought, as I got to my feet, which appeared to be attached to the ends of my Bendi toy legs, all they have to do is step into my garden and they can prune me to fucking death. For what would be the last time, I found myself shouting up at the bedroom window. As I did so, I thought of many things. I considered the future. I wondered why my suit trousers ponged of dung. Then I remembered the horse. Was it still tethered to a bike rail outside H. Baxter's? Or sitting in Clifton's with its legs crossed, waiting to be bought a pint? If so, was it over eighteen? Who was this H. Baxter anyway, and where was his son when I needed him most?

I poured forth to Brenda, as we sat in the living room, me trying to transform these and other events from crazed and mindless hooligan excesses, which they were, to troubled cries from a mind spiralling helplessly out of control, which they also were. The trouble is that women are territorial about pain, judging that theirs is always a purer, keener strain than anyone else's, especially a man's, more especially a husband's. So the upshot of my naked need to talk was that I'd to run the engine of my personal pain idly at the barrier, so to speak, till Brenda felt ready to vacate the space and allow me to park my angst. Even then, she wouldn't listen. The cunt had never listened.

If only she'd listened back then, five long years previously, I might not have acted the way I subsequently did and taken off for London. Now here we were again, teetering on the brink of another momentous conversation. Only this time it was my job to listen. Well, fuck it, I thought, come ahead, you wounded cunt, talk to me, I can take it. The trouble with talking, of course, even to Brenda, was that at some point she might blunder into an area of clear logical thinking. There were dangers inherent in that. For instance, it was bound to dawn, had already surely dawned, that me having fucked her over once meant I might in all probability do it again. Stuart would be home soon and she'd be forced to choose, him or me. Then again she might be thinking, What if I choose Albert but Albert doesn't choose me? In that event she might well lose not only me, but Stuart too, since nobody wants to play second best, which is often the way it goes with these love triangle efforts.

These and other thoughts would be darting through her cunning womanly head. I knew this, because they had already darted, at a leisurely pace, through my own cunning, manly head although, being me, I'd consigned them to the attic of my mind, pending further, by which I mean no further, rumination. Speaking personally, my own favoured option was the one I'd favoured down the years with women, the wait-till-it-all-blows-up-in-my-face option. The reason I leant towards this solution was simple, I felt I could absorb the blast and still win. In my view, no matter how old, or rational, people don't venture very far from the school playground. I knew I was a bigger noise than Stuart who, from what I could gather, wasn't any kind of noise at all, large or small. Knowing how partial Brenda was to noises, metaphorically and, as I've described, literally, it seemed to me that so long as I hovered, so to speak, in her eyeline, her attentions would remain diverted by my impressive howls and barks and her relationship with Stuart would be for ever gratifyingly compromised. In short, I wanted the option of Brenda for as long as it suited me. Now, it might suite me for the next thirty years, or the next thirty minutes, but whatever the time scale I was prepared to do whatever was necessary to service my interests. That was the sort of rational, or, if you prefer, shallow, selfish, insecure, small-minded cunt I was, but then again, you'll have gathered that by now.

'But Albert,' some of you might protest, 'how could you even think of putting your poor ex-wife through such pain again, considering how badly you hurt her the first time?' May I provide you with a rustic answer to that? There's an old Spanish proverb I've just made up. It goes like this: 'A woman, she is a field. A man's job, it is to plough her. Once he's ploughed her, he may plant anything he wishes on her at any time, that's his right. If she didn't want to be ploughed, she should have offered the man only stones and dust, not rich red loam for the parting, uh, my friend?' It's a bit long, I admit, by proverb standards, but fuck it. So what I'm saying is, I felt innately assured that no matter whatever was said when this Stuart cunt reappeared on the scene, Brenda was still my woman, deep down, and she'd part her loam at my request. Naturally, I didn't put it that way to Brenda. She wanted rationality, not reality, and I was happy to oblige. These daunting truths should remain quietly unnoticed, in my opinion, to be used only in an emergency, like fire extinguishers.

*

One night, perched in awkward truce on the sofa, like two guardsmen at ease in sentry boxes, a *Frontline Scotland* documentary appeared on television. I heard the words 'jelly' and 'tragedy' and allowed my ears to prick, imperceptibly, up. Without either of us having moved a muscle, that queer couply tension sat down, making itself comfortable in the empty space between us. If I'd had the remote to hand, I'd have turned it off, but it was on the tea tray by Brenda and I didn't want to appear evasive by making an issue of anything. So I just sat there and appeared evasive by not making an issue of anything. The girl reporter was walking through an area I recognized at once to be Clydebank. And yes, as they cut to the riverside I can report that I, Albert, callous, brutish git that I am, felt my stomach flip effortlessly over. They knew where the stuff was arriving and they knew where it was being distributed. This wasn't difficult to divine as now we cut to Anderston bus station, where an emaciated-looking young hole, you knew she was young because she looked that certain kind of old, stood by the corner of Wellington Street, relating her tale of woe. She spoke, in a whiney voice, about her brother, an honest to goodness, decent, clean-living young junk fiend who'd never harmed no cunt, who was now sadly croaked, owing to a batch of illegal jellies that had recently flooded in to the area. 'There have been four other similar deaths in the last six weeks,' said the girl reporter. I confess, I don't know how I kept my hand steady as I lifted my glazed tea mug out of my lap and put it to my lips for a swig.

I could sense Brenda eyeing me as I watched. A simple-looking smack-head appeared on screen showing his cratered leg. I pulled a brief 'how awful' expression, for show. We'd cut back to the corner of Wellington Street and the hole winding up the eulogy to her useless cunt of a brother when a dreadful thing happened; a hideous crone loomed into the back of shot, looking like some ghastly extra from Paisley Players' production of *Cabaret*. Now Brenda could have focussed on any number of things about the lurid events we were watching, any one of which might have elicited an unconvincing response from me. As it happened, she said, 'Isn't that your father in the background?'

I leaned forward theatrically, doing what-surely-not acting, anything to keep Brenda on the relatively safe ground of paternal transvestite prostitution. I knelt in front of the set and gave a shaken and alarmed you-know-I-do-believe-it-is performance, which was in truth only half a performance, or, to be more accurate, a performance for the benefit of an audience of one, namely Brenda, the larger part, the Big Picture performance being no performance at all as I was, indeed, shaken and alarmed, not only by the simple cunts waving their horrible legs about, but by the ghastly spectacle of my father displaying his gender confusion for the curiosity and probable amusement of the ordinary television-watching public. By which of course I meant, other hooligans. If word got generally out that my old man looked like Dame Thora Hird in a split skirt, I'd be hard pressed to raise my hammer in public ever again.

I looked at Brenda and gave a sort of limp shrug, affecting what I hoped to be a look of sad but plucky vulnerability. 'I keep telling him,' I said resignedly, 'but you know what he's like.' The implication of intimate complicity wrung a squeeze of the hand from Brenda and I felt the tension ease as we cut to Pitt Street nick and heard a senior cop mouth the expected platitudes about drugs being 'a worldwide scourge' and how 'new initiatives' would mean a 'vigorous assault on the perpetrators of misery'. I took this to mean, 'We'll lift a couple of dealers from the schemes to keep the press off our backs, then return to fiddling our overtime and filing our claims for stress payments.' What interested and heartened me most was the police expert's insistence that, despite testimony to the contrary, the deaths hadn't been due to any mix of jellies and heroin but to a 'shipment of heroin of unusually high purity'. This high-purity heroin had presumably proved too potent for the delicate systems of Glasgow's well-bred young smack addicts to digest.

Now I don't know about you, but 'too much' I can comprehend, but 'too pure' makes no economic sense whatsoever. Bear in mind, cunts were killing and selling each other and themselves for this stuff, yet those principled zealots who worked in the drug import and distribution trade had gone and erred on the side of perfection in their laudable attempts to bring nothing but the best to their valued customers. I ask you, it's like going into the newsagents, paying for twenty fags and him insisting on giving you sixty for the same price. Now possibly this was some subtle constabulary trap, calculated to tempt marauding bears like me back out into the open but experience suggests this unlikely. What experience does suggest is that the polis can be just as reassuringly stupid, or lazy, as us criminals. And good thing too, say I. Else how would any cunt ever get any work done?

Chapter Nine

So all in all then, it was with a grateful spring in my morning step that I tucked the old axe into its overcoat pouch and, liberated briefly from the debilitating demands of female tenderness, set off for my daily shift at the coal face of wholesome criminality. Fred West Ham, Kevin Casey, sat proudly at the top of the Ouzi Premiership, above Rillington Rovers, Lee Fraser, and Charlton Athletic, Tommy Dolan, for whom, disappointingly, we couldn't find a convenient mass murderer to provide a waggish pun.

We'd started touching the odd pub and bookie for security money in order to keep the chaps occupied and match fit, pending our big fixture against Darko Lyall which, if not imminent, wasn't far away. I stuck only to the free houses and few remaining independent bookies as I didn't want to ruffle any sizeable corporate feathers and risk unwanted publicity for activities that were merely secondary to my aims. I didn't trust the chaps in public with firearms and kept them in a biscuit tin up the chimney behind Davie's gas fire. Naturally, young men being what they are, this didn't endear me to the collective bosom, and I came in for fair amount of testy comment, most of it of a jocular nature, but some of it, noticeably, not.

I pointed out, reasonably enough I felt, that if, as

self-respecting and ambitious young hooligans, they were unable to impose authority through a cool head and force of personality alone, they'd be unlikely to ascend any of the more daunting rungs they'd encounter on the criminal ladder. This was, of course, bollocks. A six-year-old could point a gun at the chief of the SAS and guess which one would be looking worried? No, the simple truth was I didn't want half a dozen fresh-faced young yahoos playing Billy the Kid in Marks and Spencer in Paisley High Street. Apart from anything else, I shopped there.

Working with these unruly but effervescent young people had given me a first hand look at how attitudes towards the venerable elders of crime had changed.

One day, Tommy Dolan had asked me if I'd known the Krays. When I admitted, with what I hoped was an undetectable inward swagger that I'd not only known but worked with the said brothers, Tommy Dolan's impulse was not, as I'd expected, to touch the hem of my raiment but to point out, to some merriment, that I must be 'fucking ancient'. I told him that I was now fifty-one and had just turned eighteen when I'd first killed a man; name of Desmond Elkins. I explained that while we'd been working in south Kent, the actual demise had occurred in Braintree. 'Braintree in Essex?' enquired Tommy. 'In Essex, yes, that Braintree. Why, can you think of another, Tommy, you illiterate cunt?'

Tommy bested me, to my keen annoyance, by asking me to write down 'illiterate,' claiming an inability to penetrate my Anglo-Scottish accent, a veiled local insult, implying affectation. Tommy was one of those lads who appear to have a half smile playing permanently about their lips, the nature of which is never sunny and always sneering and infuriating. Lee Fraser asked if I'd ever worked with the Richardson brothers. I told him no. This drew an all-round 'aww' of what seemed like genuine disappointment. The Richardsons were regarded as more credible than the Krays, seemingly because they'd resisted the temptation to turn themselves into 'legends', with all the attendant WWF-type pantomime villain naffness that invariably fuelled such illusions. As a result of resisting the temptation to be legends, the Richardsons were now, inevitably, legends. Privately, I had a good deal of ambivalence towards the Richardson approach. After all, I myself was the fucking Surgeon, wasn't I? If I didn't consolidate my achievements with the odd volume of moustachio-twirling memoirs, who the fuck would? What I couldn't tolerate, however, was having my authority threatened by any veiled sleights to my reputation. After all, I'd worked hard to obtain a certain status within our community, and whatever these young Turks might go on and achieve in the future, they hadn't achieved it yet, so a spot of 'Well Done, Albert', wouldn't have gone amiss.

Their attitude grated with me. To them, being under thirty was somehow a talent in itself. Cunts like me, with our mohair suits, slipped discs and home-made jacuzzis with the bad plumbing, we were the fucking establishment, the Kremlin generals in our great coats and medals, ready to topple over with the first stiff breeze. Well fuck off, you cunts, my name is Albert and I'm still climbing, so get off my fucking ladder before I crater your insolent, youthful heads. Thoughts like those coursed through me, as I sat there, watching them take the piss. I smiled benignly, after all that's what piss is for. But underneath I wasn't smiling. I was smarting. I suppose it was at that point that I decided to 'get' Tommy Dolan. I judged it would set a healthy example to all. Though as I sat, watching him smirk, I decided I wouldn't in this case, be writing the word down for him, he'd just have to see it coming for himself.

I calculated when it'd be best to pursue our plans. I didn't want to act just yet because there was too much attention, what with TV documentaries and Pitt Street under pressure, so I was biding my time, keeping my head down till I felt confident and ready. Meanwhile, my problem was keeping my Reeboked jackals off my back and in a pack so we could act as one. The thing was, there could only be one leader of any pack and I had to be vigilant that the undercurrent of disrespect didn't escalate into some form of anarchy or coup. I found myself biting my tongue a good deal, even when, on one occasion, Tommy Dolan produced a copy of my memoirs he'd picked up for a pound in Bargain Books. Passages were read aloud by him and Kevin Casey, with Lee Fraser calling for more. I forced myself to smile along, controlling my feelings by telling myself this is how it is with the generations, and after all, I didn't need any MA in irony to remind me that this was akin to what I'd dished out to Billy all those years ago in Duck Bay. The difference between then and now, however, as any secondary school teacher will tell you, was that whereas in my day you'd usually find only one big mouth per class, nowadays every lippy fucker is at it. Also, more importantly, Billy commanded a respect bordering on awe through the innate authority of his royal office, whereas, as these young scamps could clearly see, I was just another foot soldier with blood on his hammer, craning his neck to see the king pass in his Big Chair. Fulfilment of potential, which is to say destiny, remained for me a state I yearned to achieve.

I was discussing this matter of discipline with Davie as we walked to the corner minimart for milk and tea bags. He felt he could vouch for his chaps and that the problem wasn't simply lack of activity, it was also excitement over actually being wanted. I was, he pointed out, a possible usher to a better life for these neglected young men, and once they'd passed the showing off stage, Davie felt, they'd prove themselves to be talented young hooligans. We passed through a narrow lane that looked onto the back yards of a double row of those tarted up co-operatively run flats. Trim little lawns with well-tended shrubs chafed against abandoned settees and mangled bike frames. The occasional burnt out flat acted, appropriately enough, like a firebreak along the huddled way. Sometimes, less benignly, they presented targets for squalls of pre-school brats, who chucked stones and thrilled to the dunk of brick on corrugated iron over what used to be windows. It was a quiet miracle to me how anyone could keep anything as demanding and complicated as a family together in this seething grotto with its dismal bustle.

Davie pointed to an open kitchen door with a dining-room chair outside. A brat in a pushchair bawled on the scrub lawn. As we passed, a young, and I use the term advisedly, couple appeared. A cyst on legs that I took to be the father shushed the kid with one of those sugary dummies I remembered from my own brathood. The father had baggy jeans and a straggly beard, nothing ever grew on those cunts except spots, and the mother, well, put it this way, she was about nineteen, slim, but I wouldn't have ridden it for fear of contracting contagious depression. I said as much to Davie.

He was relieved. 'Glad to hear it,' he said, 'that's my sister.' Davie pointed to the empty dining chair. 'That's Granny Bab's place. She sits in that chair all day doing tenner wraps.'

Because it was his family, I nodded in a grave, regal, something-must-be-done sort of way, but Davie just gave an off-hand wave to his sister and kept walking.

'I blame that fucker,' he said, meaning the fucker with the spots as opposed to the absent fuckeress Granny Babs. 'Louise was off the shite entirely till she took up with him.'

I asked about Granny Babs, wasn't she taking a big chance dealing openly, from the rolling vistas of her own back yard?

Davie smiled and shook his head. 'No more than anybody else,' he said. 'There are four more dealers in that wee lane alone. They keep grassing each other up to the *Daily Record* 'shop a dealer' hotline, but it makes fuck all difference. It's business as usual the following week. Anyway,' he said, 'junkies prefer Babs because you get a cup of tea and a caramel wafer.'

I gave a little cackle of surprised mirth. 'A caramel wafer, you say?' In an odd way, I could see the attraction. In a lot of these dealers' flats there's nothing but floor-boards, a spy hole and a smiling host in a crusty sleeping bag to greet you. Everyone responds to a spot of human comfort, even people who've stopped being human.

Things have changed in five years, Albert,' said Davie. There was an odd note of purring revelry in his voice, like he was proud to be showing off these latest hot new developments in human degradation. Not for the first time, I found Davie's wry defeatism bringing out the evangelist in me. We performed an inelegant little trot down a steep grassy bank onto a quiet street and I spoke to him in brisk terms. 'Look here,' I said, employing my favoured affectation, 'it's not just the others that have potential, Kevin Casey and Dolan and that, it's you too, Davie. I want you to get out of this.' I made an imperial dismissive gesture of the hand, 'but it's up to you.' He shrugged, giving me his shy smile as I slapped him about with the wet verbal towel, but I could tell he was absorbing attention like a half-dead geranium takes water. 'I can only point the way, Davie,' I said, 'I can't move your fucking feet along the path for you.' He kept saying, 'I know' and 'You're right' in a kind of abject way till eventually I ran out of steam and began repeating myself and realized I'd better stop. I hated cunts lecturing me myself, but we'd had this little orgy of contact, me and Davie, the subtext of which was, 'I like you, you young cunt, that's why I'm slagging you off,' with him responding under his wan smiles and shrugs and that with, 'I know you do and I like being liked.' Anyway, I felt mildly disgusted yet exhilarated at the same time, as if we'd made, through the miracle of verbal abuse, an unspoken understanding that neither of us understood. Davie said, 'The shop's just up there,' and we resumed walking, accompanied by one of those slightly awkward, bewildered silences, like we were two people who'd just stepped out of mild trance which, no doubt, we had.

Anyway, this was just as well, this awkward silence I mean, else we might never have been conscious of the scooter that passed us on the opposite side of the street, its mosquito-engine noise first fading, then swelling as it turned and, at our backs, headed again towards us. I was expecting to see some baggy-kneed insurance salesman in a pacamac pull up just ahead of us, take off his helmet and ask directions, it had that kind of feel to it, but the wee putter and gargle of the engine seemed steady and overpowering like the bike was keeping apace just behind our shoulders. I turned. When I did I saw a helmeted figure in a puffa jacket doing that motorbike driver ski walk thing they do when they're going slow. With a free hand he was fumbling inside the chest of his jacket. I remember saying 'Fuck.' There was a yank on my arm that took flesh as well as overcoat and I realized Davie had reacted first. There were two, perhaps three, cracks from a gun, though one may have been an echo, anyhow something chipped a breeze-block wall close by us as we ran. Over a wooden fence I vaulted, bad back following behind, into a communal bin area, then out of the communal bin area, along the corridor of a close and into a quadrangle of weedy asphalt and chained-up plastic swings. We stood half-crazed, panicking and gasping and in a sort of fearful frenzy that the scooter cunt would come careering out of some pedestrian alley to try his luck again.

Davie started to gibber some words but I told him to shut the fuck up and listen. Once he did that, we could hear the wee sewing machine of the engine roaring off up the road and from its tone you could tell the driver wasn't in the mood for slowing.

'Fuck me,' said Davie.

'And me,' I said.

We were looking at each other, incredulously, like two men who'd been shot at and are now looking to each other for confirmation that they were two men who'd been shot at.

'Fuck me twice,' Davie said.

'And me,' I repeated.

Davie tugged a packet from his jeans, and offered me one. 'Only if it's fucking Valium,' I said.

Davie lit up a Lambert and Butler with excited hands. I shivered and we both laughed.

'I've never been honoured by a drive-by shooting before, have you?' I said.

Davie admitted that no, he hadn't.

'No, nor me,' I said, all bemused and aquiver from events. 'Maybe I'm not so old after all,' I said.

'Well,' said Davie, 'shall we?'

'Yes,' I said, getting to my feet and stretching, 'let's get the tea bags.' And we did.

*

The incident started me thinking about the differences between down there and up here. In London, you can be ignored to the point where you doubt your own visibility, up here though, it's different. In Scotland they're warm, which means that no matter how lonely or down on your luck you may be, you'll always find some cunt who hates you. A bump of the shoulder here, a stare in the pub there, opportunities for human contact abound, thanks to the wonderful Caledonian gift for blind aggression. Why are Scots aggressive? Because we live in a boring, damp, vicious and repressed little culture where only booze, drugs and emigration keep mass suicide at bay. We are one big unhappy family. Saying this, I know, will not make me popular in my homeland. But being unpopular is what gives me the liberty to speak my mind. A few short years ago, Albert Blaney wrote a book. Lots of crims write books, it's an accepted, though some might argue gnarled and ugly, branch of the literary tree. In England, which is to say London, such books, no matter how vulgar, vain, or badly written, are tolerated. Crim authors from the ludicrous Dave Courtney to the perceptive if self-preening John McVicar are regarded at worst, as quack showmen, at best as lurid and entertaining chroniclers of the sewers, the Gustave Doré of the Christmas hardback. That's because England is, relatively speaking, a big country. Big, that is, relative to Scotland. Scotland is smaller than small. It's tiny. And vicious. And poisonous. As tiny things, worse than small, often are. So when a Scottish crim of any standing, even of small or tiny standing, writes a book, a frisson runs round the family dinner table. A crim is a threat to the satus quo, sitting as he does, with his cutlery in his hand, next to the First Minister, and the Lord Provost and the rabble-rousing MSP. In Scotland, you got the feeling that any man of mettle is only a dinner party and a few armed nutters away from a total *coup d'état*.

I keep these thoughts in my head in order to fuel my sense of grievance and to justify my standing, small or tiny, in the land of my birth. In Scotland, smaller-than-small, tiny, vicious Scotland, to be hated is to be loved. If I can take the Big Chair, I can take anything. I can stand on the Big Chair and help myself. If a thing is possible, it will probably, someday, to someone, happen. I have a dream. I have seen the promised land. It is full of tiny vicious cunts, fiddling their expenses and arguing about the Barnett Formula. If William Wallace were alive today, he'd turn on Scotland, not England. He'd have a sunbed tan and a Hugo Boss suit and be photographed in the *Daily Record*, helping some cunt out of a coma, or into one, with his powerful rhetoric, while his army of scumballs huddled in the housing schemes, watching Rikki Lake and fondling their Glocks, waiting for the call.

These ravings poured through my head as I stood in Brenda's kitchen, making her a cup of tea. I hated this country therefore, by my own logic, I must love it. As it, no doubt, loved me. And others. Its prodigal sons, who felt no need of forgiveness, only vengeance. Fuck the Pope. And the moderator of the general assembly of the Church of Scotland. Fuck Ibrox, Parkhead, that pathetic fucking Parliament and while we were at it, fuck Princes Street and John Smith's memory too. Oh, and did I mention Billy Waugh? And my father? Oh yes, for fuck's sake, some cunt fuck my father. If only out of kindness. I'd pay.

Brenda asked me why I was tense, but I didn't mention the gunshots. We sat watching *Changing Rooms* and she told me about her headaches, she'd started having these headaches which, in her martyred way, she blamed me for by insisting I was not to blame. Oddly, they didn't interfere with the sex, which had yet to settle down to the domestic. If I'm honest, though I've been married and almost continuously partnered, I've never wanted to live with a woman. When I see her every day, brushing her teeth, lounging in her pyjamas, or Hoovering under the settee, a woman becomes as humdrum to me as I do to myself and I lose interest and patience. Let's face it, all life is a flight from boredom, isn't it? Crime, rocket science, cures for cancer, everything is an adrenalin fix to lift the weary mind from the stale bed and the plates in the sink. Throw loneliness in there too, a flight from loneliness.

I realised, as I steadied my mug on my knee and waited for Handy Andy Kane to drill a hole in something, with any luck Laurence Llewellyn Bowen's skull, that this was why I was prevaricating about stoking up my affair with Brenda any further. It was the boredom factor. She knew that, she detected I was uneasy about stepping down into the relationship pit and let's face it, it wasn't as if I could play the well-why-don't-we-see-how-we-go contingency plan card, we were married for fifteen fucking years, we know exactly how we do, or do not, go. But the question wasn't how, of course, but where? Where do we go, exactly? The uncertainty was what was worrying Brenda, and what was causing the headaches was the resultant guilt and fear of being hurt. The fact was she had not been returning Stuart's calls as promptly as before and now he was sitting in the desert with his roller brush, having a good think to himself. The upshot of this, as Brenda had now revealed, was that she'd admitted to him I was back on the scene. Naturally I'd recommended she do the honourable thing and lie, but Brenda pointed out, with undeniable justification, that Paisley was a small, not to say minuscule place, and she'd sooner Stuart heard it first from her and not some helpful stranger. Such forthright logic I couldn't argue with, even though it was shot through with deviousness and self-interest. Basically, Brenda now got to look like Miss Honourable-Above-Board-I-Cannot-Live-a-Lie, while the effect of all this honour was to force the issue between me and Stuart. We were now, effectively, in competition for this walking, talking trophy called Brenda and must tilt our lances to win the prize of her favours. Brenda was covering her bases and at her time of life, I couldn't blame her. She'd told Stuart she could have me and told me she was torn between myself and Stuart. Naturally, as I've already mentioned, I didn't, in my heart of hearts, believe there was any competition. Given the choice between a good, gentle, considerate loving man and a selfish criminal bastard, most women would, of course, choose the bastard. Mr Rights grow on trees, but it's not every day a girl woos and wins the Mr Wrong of her choice. Basically, they want to be shaken to the core by the cruel seductive hand of his indifference. It gives their lives a sense of drama that sees them through the dead hours spent queuing in Asda or talking into headsets at work trying to soothe awkward customers.

So in order to hoodwink Brenda, I told the truth. I apologized for my recent inattentiveness and confided that I'd been under a spot of pressure lately. Knowing as she did, something of the nature of my former business activities, Brenda was astute enough to equate the term 'pressure' with 'potentially injurious to health'. I was glad I'd treated her fairly over the divorce settlement, it meant I could now draw on the credit accrued from our jointly invested capital of goodwill. I explained how I was hoping to start up a new venture in the area but this would involve, inevitably, treading on and possibly severing, the odd unwilling set of toes. I didn't have to mince my words with Brenda, she knew Darko and how slap happy he could be when threatened.

The main purpose of these confidings was, of course, to plant a seed of hope within my ex-wife. I wanted her on my team, and quiescent, supporting me devotedly through loyalty and self-interest, secure(ish) in the knowledge that if my venture succeeded I'd be all the more likely to stay and formalize, or rather reformalize, our union. This was the way I chose to play it, naked, I always feel, being the best disguise. When she asked about Calum, I did, I admit, reach for the mincer and feed in my lying tongue. It had been such a lurid, almost hysterical form of execution. I found myself wishing to ascribe authorship to some anonymous source through sheer embarrassment. This is where, in my opinion, the supple multi-faceted mind of the schizo holds the edge over we mundane, common or garden, psychos: the former inhabits his various strands of personality whole-heartedly, shaping and altering the signature of his violence with a dastardly disguised flourish. The latter, me and mine, are mere plodding clock-punchers of mayhem, workies, condemned to thump and gouge our way through years of fixed, hammer-swinging soul-destroying routine. The killing of Calum confirmed to me an unflattering portrait of myself. Looking back, I'd made such a botch of it. I'd aspired towards the sinister, a professional, cold-eyed, sadistic-looking execution and instead what I'd achieved was dog-in-a-butcher's-shop. The problem was, I'd overreached myself. I hadn't been match fit, so to speak, but had been so keen to create a favourably appalling impression that I'd hoped the power of aspiration might suck achievement along in its slipstream. Not so. When I'd got to Glasgow Airport, I'd found a length of neck vein sticking to the shin of my trouser, that's how professional I'd been. Anyway, the long and short of it is, I lied to Brenda about killing, or rather not killing Calum and Brenda lied about believing me. Or so I believe.

When, after a spot of theatrical agonizing on my behalf, I ventured details of the Darko-inspired drive-by incident, Brenda said a curious thing. She said, 'How do you know it was Darko?' This pulled me up short, convinced as I was in my blinkered way that Darko, appraised of my desire to replace him in the clubs of John Leask and Robin Tierney – and of course Darko would be appraised since, I'd no doubt, both Leask and Tierney would have done the appraising – would have taken vigorous and aggressive steps to dissuade me. In truth though, as my dear ex-wife had reminded me, I was, popularly speaking, unpopular, and there were other, perhaps many other, persons in Scotland and indeed elsewhere, and let's not forget elsewhere, who might be harbouring sufficient reason, in their eyes, for wishing my demise. If indeed, it was I who was the intended victim.

Two shots, at least, had been fired. One each? Or two for me, none for Davie? No, share and share alike. Here, Davie, have one, I insist.

Lying in bed, later, after an expedient and elaborately loving poke, from me that is, the poker, unto Brenda, the pokee, I drafted in my mind, a list of possible persons who might wish me dead. I stopped when I reached fifty-one, my age. The curious thing was that the longer the litany of names grew, the greater the sense of peace that descended upon me. When you know one person is out to kill you, the tendency is to become obsessive, to start seeing the face and handiwork of your enemy at every turn, in fact, to demonize him. When there is a small army of such persons, all baying for your blood, control is impossible and the burden of personal survival is surrendered to chance or fate, which may or may not be the same thing, anyway the effect is to invoke an attitude of humility and supplication in the soul of the intended victim, thereby allowing him, which is to say me, the prospect of a decent kip. In this way cruel despots and megalomaniacal overlords may proceed about their daily business. Bonaparte, Amin, Waugh. I guarantee they've all lain awake in the small hours, counting their enemies, and felt comforted by the anonymous hand of the mob.

Chapter Ten

In my beginning is my end. And not only my end, the end of others. I'd a spot of killing to do. The Paisley sky, a puffy cotton wad from a billion discarded anti-depressant bottles, covered the sun, inviting fears of ill omen. I was putting the last cleaver in my holdall and the zipped holdall into the privacy of my suitcase when Brenda shuffled into the kitchen, bleary eyed, dressing-gowned, reaching for the kettle. 'Tea?'

'Coffee please,' I told her, deciding it'd blend better with the aftertaste of the brandy. She filled the kettle, flicked it on, spotted the quarter bottle flask on the worktop.

'Well,' she said. She eyed the suitcase, raised a slippered foot and gave it a small shove. Over it went onto its side, in a dull crescendo of rattling weaponry. 'Well,' she said again, looking at me. 'Just like old times.'

I kept working the silver polish from the quick of my nails with the kitchen roll. 'If I polish my tools, I will not die,' said the voice of superstition, reasonably. It's as good a superstition as any and it must work because, well, I'm still here, aren't I?

I struggled for an even tone as I spoke. 'What are you doing today?' is what my voice said.

Brenda gave a little yap of doleful glee at the

incongruity of the question. This humdrum couple, going about their wholesome daily business.

'I'm minding Stuart's wee grandwean,' she said pointedly, dunking her tea bag. She could've used the grandwean's name, which I'd forgotten, but she wanted the opportunity to say 'Stuart,' for the thrill of the reaction.

'That's nice,' I said, as off-handedly as I could muster. There, you bitch, try coming in your pants to that.

She pressed on, ambushing me with domestic details. 'Her mummy's got a doctor's appointment, a problem with her ankle. She thinks it might be the start of arthritis.'

'What's that got to do with it,' I told her, seizing the opportunity to discharge a spot of bitterness. 'It will be arthritis. Every fucker rusts up here. You, me, Stuart, every fucker.'

'Don't start,' said Brenda, 'I know what you're doing.' I asked her what I was doing. 'What you always did before a fight,' she said. 'You're having a go at me to get your maddy up.' I refuted this notion, dismissing it with the contempt it deserved. Even though it was true. Brenda binned her tea bag and took a sip from her mug. 'You're getting too old for this game, Albert, you know that, don't you?' I didn't like the smugness of her tone. She was all cosy with herself, now she'd had a chance to drag her comfy world of Stuartness into the kitchen where I could see it, floating about among my clanking tools.

The contest for Brenda's heart was crisply polarized. In the white corner, all the way from House of Fraser's soft furnishings department, the heavyweight champion of Niceland, mature family man and all round touchy feely sensitive chap, please will you welcome, Stuart Slumberland. And in the black corner, from the dark state of paranoia, the senile psycho, Albert 'The Cunt' Blaney.

Child-bearing had always been a thorny issue, so to speak, between me and Brenda. I'd been convinced, from an early age, I wonder why, that I never wanted to devote my life to anything that would grow up expecting me to pay for the privilege of having it despise me.

Impressed by my vehemence on the subject, Brenda had respected my feelings, no doubt because she thought herself capable of changing them, but throughout the years of our marriage I'd remained, like the Boys' Brigade, sure and steadfast. Now that Brenda's fertile years had come and gone with, as they say, barren yield, I sensed how glad was her heart at this late-flowering miracle of child-rearing by proxy. The price for Stuart's grandkid being, of course, Stuart. With a few utterances along these lines, I was able to puncture the protective bubble of Brenda's smugness, and I took uplift from the realization that I'd probably ruined her day, if not life. Poor bitch, she hadn't known what a crim looked like till she met me. Then neither had I till I met Billy Waugh. So it goes, brats or no brats, we can't help passing down the poison spores of our seed. I took a sip from my coffee mug and came over all mellow from the brandy glow in my belly.

'On Sunday,' I said, 'let's go visit my da, I've been meaning to.' Brenda raised a pleased eyebrow. 'Yes,' I went on, 'we'll go for brunch at Princes Square then take him shopping for lingerie at Debenhams. It'll be nice to do something normal.'

*

Wednesday night in Paisley and it was pissing with rain. My back hurt, my suit was torn and there were rasping marks on my cheek from eye to neck. Nevertheless I had the plastic bag at my feet and that was all that mattered. I was sitting in the car with Lee Fraser and Craig Picken, a bony late addition we'd recruited from Kirklandneuk. The rain battered off the roof and though I had the heater on to dry the condensation, it was all we could do to make out the splodgy neon lights of Blue across the street. What had become clear was that the professed relaxed and stylish door policy involving pretty bints with headsets had been permanently scrapped in favour of the more traditional approach. Lumps of meat again sheltered under the awning. Davie phoned me on the mobile to say that Salsa One was just the same. There were three bears on the door. Nevertheless he'd gone in there with Kevin Casey and Tommy Dolan, our best chaps and I was waiting for him to ring me with the upshot. I had intended to hit both clubs at once but opted for caution, lest Davie ran into difficulties and required assistance. Needless to say, I'd be deeply disappointed, not to say disturbed, if Davie did ring for help, since Salsa One and John Leask were the easier option and if three men with guns could't take a piss pot like that then we might as well all have stayed home and watched *Paddington Green*. The growlers on the door of Blue looked like local labour since they had no headsets and only an approximation of uniform, trousers that didn't match and T-shirts of what appeared to be multiple shades of blue. I was pleased about this as I was nervous of waving guns in the faces of people who worked for large security organizations with directors and lawyers, who had harmonious relationships with police and local press. I reasoned from the odd sidelong exchange with the queuing clientele that they were dealing on the doors. Being local, and therefore both desperate and expendable, they'd take a chance with this, despite the presence of an official house dealer, or as John Leask vomitingly put it, 'server', working inside. This meant they might well be put out by any additional competition from, say, the likes of us. So all in all I'd probably have to be at my persuasive best in order to have them see reason and allow us to enter.

To be truthful, I could have done without this. I'd wrenched my back preparing a neck that hadn't wish to be cleavered and now I was raking in the glove compartment for the Co-Proximal. I should have swallowed them earlier as they'd take around two hours to work. Craig Picken offered me some sort of upper but I demured. I watched him place a pinch of coke on the U-bend of his thumb and forefinger, hoover it up his phlegmy snout and felt depressed. I knew he was only doing it because he'd seen some Liverpool hooligans in a drama-doc do it that way the other night on Channel Four. I knew this because I had seen the programme myself, and even though those involved were the dreariest, over-muscled set of endangered simpletons you'd ever clap eyes on without recourse to a Serengeti tour guide, they'd now been elevated and blessed by its Holiness the Camera, so that up and down the country like-minded arseholes would be at this moment waving pistols they scarcely knew how to load let alone aim and snorting 'beak' like they were cheery, rosy cheeked Dickensian uncles hitting the snuff, only of course, without the rosy-cheeks or the cheeriness.

I felt a tackiness on the soles of my shoes and, fearful that the bag might be oozing, called over my shoulder for a black bin liner from my tool-bag. Even a half turn caused me pain and this expressed itself in short temper. Picken catching the worst as he revolted me more than Fraser.

They'd been for the most part silent, apart from Picken's snorting of course, on the return trip from the woods, and I took this not as an expression of awed wonder so much as wary disapproval. I'd even, on the drive here, stopped the car tetchily on the hard shoulder of the M8 and invited them to speak or shut up. Which was a mistake, of course, as they'd chosen the latter option and had gone from sullen monosyllables to fuck all. It was also a headstrong and risky action given the nature of our cargo, but their moodiness grated on my skin like a pox until, through pain and tension, I'd snapped. It had only been the uncharacteristically impassioned nature of Lee Fraser's pleas that had prompted me to put the axe down and leave Craig Picken's nose alone.

Now we'd all cooled down and I was more concerned about having been clocked on CCTV than by any injury to his sensibilities. However, as the altercation had taken place within the car, and therefore out of camera shot, I felt fairly sure it had passed unremarked. Now, as a consolation, Picken got to snort and as a punishment, we'd had to listen to him do it. As well as making me depressed, this sniffing also made me uneasy since we had more work to do once Davie gave the signal through the inane medium of the mobile phone jingle. To be fair, my higher self reflected, Picken wasn't the first hooligan, and he certainly wouldn't be the last, to toke himself up, one way or another, before a fight. Hadn't I tippled a few brandies myself through the day since waving Brenda ta-ta this morning?

So where was my moral high ground, or indeed low ground for berating Picken? Did I in fact, have any grounds at all, other than disgust? No, indeed I did not.

*

It had taken six attempts over three days before we'd found an opportunity to seize Darko Lyall. The fucker never seemed to stroll to the paper shop in the morning, the bookie's in the afternoon, nor any of the myriad little tasks that propel you and me out of our own front door, unaccompanied, to engage with the world. His small empire appeared to work, these days, from his home office, administered by diligent accountants instead of hooligans, with Darko's silent fingers occasionally glimpsed as he paused to lift coffee mug to desk-lamped profile. On the third day, impatient and exasperated, I'd joined the hunt myself, having entrusted the capture of the great beast, thus far, to my minions, my plan having been to reveal myself to him at the height of the third act, so to speak, in good time for the coda. We'd put our heads together and devised a dastardly yet simple, some might say embarrassingly simple, plan. The nub of it was this; if Darko wouldn't come out, then we, or at least some of us, would have to go in. All we had to do was tempt him to answer the door. In a hurry. Without thinking to arm himself with a gun.

To this end, we fell back, once again, on the pranks of youth. We bought Lee Fraser and Craig Picken a plastic football. We also provided them with cans of Tennent's Special. Then we had them step into Darko's garden, shouting and doing drunken yob acting. Lee threw the ball at the upstairs window. Tucked across the street, I saw Darko's big red fizzer duly appear, take in the scene, mutter something inaudible, then disappear. The question now was, is he going to come out? The supplementary then being, if he does come out, what'll he be holding? Assuming it won't be a butler's tray with afternoon tea and Ferrero Rochers. Anyway, Lee Fraser and Picken stood quaking, still performing, though less convincingly, their we-don't-give-a-fuck shouting antics when the door opened. Darko appeared on the step and yes, he was holding something. Luckily, it was not a Magnum or a Glock, as we'd feared, instead it was a Le Creuset, possibly the most powerful omelette pan in the world. He shouted a get-to-fuck greeting and was about to step off the doormat onto the lawn when Kevin Casey and Tommy Dolan, as instructed, appeared from both sides and placed their pistols behind each of his ears. This didn't have the effect of ending Darko's rant, he was still blasting away about his marigolds or some fucking thing and gesturing angrily with the pan. The boys were nonplussed by this unexpected reaction and were glancing at each other in a this-isn't-in-the-hooligan-manual kind of way. For a moment it looked like four of Scotland's top young tearaways were about to be bested by a middle-aged man with a plastic kneecap and an unloaded omelette pan.

I shouted advice from inside the car and though Lee Fraser was looking, I knew all he could see was my screaming skull in an overcoat, mouthing silent obscenities. I watched Darko clunk Tommy Dolan with the pan before Darko turned to stone, frozen in a stately, almost Olympian, pose, the discus of his pan poised, immobile, behind his raised shoulder. Kevin Casey had taken up a new position. He was standing in front of Darko now and Darko wasn't arguing any more. Not now that the barrel of Kevin Casey's pistol was jammed in Darko's open mouth. Now Darko had calmed down. Darko was, in fact, doing as he was told. They steered Darko back into his house, the gun still jammed in the mouth. That gun was now assisted by the other gun, Tommy Dolan's, which was stuck well inside Darko's ear. They all clustered carefully inside, all five of them, and once inside, I saw Lee Fraser's hand push the front door shut.

Darko's house had a windowed porch affair that was built as a corridor adjoining house to garage, so that, presumably, Mr and Mrs Darko could step from kitchen to car with minimal intrusion en route from external Paisley reality. I watched the strange party shuffle along the corridor towards the garage. As a concession to the elements, Darko had been permitted to don a dark baseball cap. He still had the gun in his mouth. And the other at his ear. When the steel door of the garage opened, Craig Picken drove Darko out, in his own car, to a pre-arranged spot in the Johnstone woods. Once the deed was done, Davie would pick up Darko's car and drive it to a different pre-arranged spot, a homely street corner in Springburn near Billy Waugh's house. Predictably, Tommy Dolan was unhappy with this plan, doubtless on the grounds that it wasn't his, grumbling that it meant a traipse through the woods to my own car, parked half a mile away. I'd apologized for this inconvenience and promised that next time we went on a job I'd rent not a Mondeo but a Chieftain fucking tank. I disliked Dolan, the fucker, but he was hungry and I believed from the glint in his little glittery eyes, he'd love to shoot some fucker in the mouth, just to see what it felt like. From the placid manner of his acquiescence, it looked like Darko thought so too. Naturally, like the prudent general I was, I kept myself aloof from further petty skirmishes, feeling, as I've said, that my own contributions should herald the culmination of events, not their inception. Basically, I wanted Darko rattled, scared, and a long way from home before I confronted him. As I say, I'm not a believer in fair play until the odds are stacked heavily in my favour. Davie who, up until now, had shown dangerous signs of intelligence, asked why we had to dispose of Darko, couldn't we just operate a bloodless *coup d'état*, seizing his interests, after all he wouldn't argue with six thrusting young hooligans with guns, would he? The fact, I pointed out, was that he would.

Darko, when bested intellectually, had been known to bite off noses, ears and chunks of cheeks in lieu of a cogent response. I'd been personally present, I informed Davie, when Darko had confronted a business colleague on the golf course, wrestling the colleague down on the twelfth hole at Elderslie and ramming the blade of a six iron into his ear. It had taken three of us, myself and the

Grady brothers to restrain him, Nick Faldo checks flapping in the breeze, he'd had to be hauled away to his trolley and soothed by the calm of the putting green. The colleague, it goes without saying, was badly shaken and could only halve the hole. Ah yes, Darko, myself, Calum, the Grady brothers, we ran the town, don't you know? 'Yes,' said Davie, 'we do know.' At which point, I shut up. And with that, we ran Darko Lyall to the woods.

I can't pretend there wasn't a sexual element to all this violence caper my sort of person went in for. Any hooligan who tells you differently just isn't in touch with his feminine side. I've killed men and women both, but on balance, I prefer men. For killing, that is. As well as friendship. I liked to kill powerful men, more powerful than me at any rate, the bigger the better. The *Daily Mail* psychologists among you will no doubt put this down to the fact that I'm a short cunt, physically at least, but that's only relative, at five foot eight I tower over most of the population of Scotland, so height, or rather the lack of it, has never been so to speak, a big issue with me. I haven't got any sort of dwarf complex so it wasn't that which made me do it. Could it then be connected to the fact that my father is called Cindy? Well, without a doubt there's room for exploration there, but the fact is I was well beyond my formative years before I had any inkling of his proclivities, so that in itself is unlikely to provide the key, if key there is to the jumble of nerves and grudges that form the unwanted gift we like to call personality.

If I was short, I was short on achievement, I hadn't yet reached where I wanted to be. But does anyone, ever? For a hooligan, anything short of 'Verily, thou art the light and the way' is to be damned by faint praise. Ah, so you crave reassurance then, eh, Albert? Well protect my eyes from the dazzle of that piercing insight! I mean, who the fuck doesn't need reassurance? No, in the end, we, I, did it because I liked it. Simple as. I must have done, mustn't I? Else why wasn't I a village postman or a rather tall jockey? I liked the gratification of the job, the reward, the short working hours, the sense of tawdry celebrity that hung in the air like cheap scent. I liked psychologists and Colin Wilson trying to explain us, I enjoyed lurid prose and stern judgements and smart women who hated themselves for wanting to fuck banal cunts like me just because we'd cratered a few heads. I mean, what an extraordinary stupid reason for wanting to hump someone, what hooligans do isn't even a talent. Any cunt who could whack his own thumb with a hammer hanging a picture could have done my job, probably better, because a head's a bigger target than a thumb. So you see, luckily, there's no justice. I mean, I admire jugglers myself, but how many bints dream of humping a guy because he's handy with a few bean bags? Not even jugglers' wives dream of fucking jugglers. Whereas nothing seems to put women off murderers, not even murderers who kill women. If anything, this adds a little extra sheer to the already fine edge of risk. I pity those bints. I mean, how jaded must the female sexual palate be if they'll risk a shallow grave under a hedgerow in return for a fucking orgasm?

As I've said, we bundled the fucker into his own car, a pair of socks stuffed into his gob in view of the dangerous impracticality of a gun barrel, blindfolded him, and took him round the back road, through Barrhead, passing sentimentally close to where Calum used to live, en route to our rendezvous in a quiet lay-by about a mile off the Lugton Road. Hands bound, shoes off, socks in gob, we propelled the beast at a brisk pace out of the car, along the marshy verge, down the grassy slope through the tall, cutting ferns and into the comfort of the dark trees. As we trotted, Darko's face turned purple, obliging us to remove the socks. We stood around while he bent forward, steaming, taking in great glugs of air. He was a strong man, but not a fit man, like many beasts he was built for the sprint and not the marathon. At one point he asked, 'Where are we going?' And Lee Fraser whacked him hard with a stick, as per instruction. Beasts have to know you'll use the rod, else they'll test you and take advantage. And we couldn't afford that, not with this big cunt. Once you grab a thing like Darko, you're in up to the eyes, you've got to finish him, it's tiger by the tail time and there's no going back. So we hit him with our sticks and drove him on, further into the woods, away from the dog walkers and the tinker vans. Big sweat patches started to appear on Darko's blue shirt, showing up the rippling six-pack of his muscled torso. Except that nobody has a rippling six-pack on their back, so I gestured for Casey to unbutton Darko's shirt and there it was, a bullet-proof vest. It was one of those shortie models, dark blue in colour, possibly chosen by Mrs Darko to offer a nice contrast with the shirt. No wonder the poor fucker had a job running. I mean, they call these things vests, but that's purely sales pitch. If the fucker's supposed to stop bullets, it's got to be a tad sturdy, hasn't it? It didn't look very bullet proof to me, but I assumed Darko knew what he was buying. Anyway, we would soon be testing its quality in the hurly burly of the market place, so to speak, so Darko could judge whether he'd bought wisely. We sat the big chap down on a tree stump and ordered him to shut up, which was a tad superfluous, since he hadn't opened his yap for fear of more welts. I suppose what we actually meant rather than 'shut up' was 'don't listen', as the nature of the discussion was bound to spook him involving, as it did, his demise.

'What happens now?' asked Lee Fraser.

To which I foolishly replied 'Shut up, Lee.'

Foolishly, because Darko then asked 'Is that you, Albert?'

'Yes,' I said. 'Hello, Darko.'

'Long time no see,' said Darko. Which was quite droll, I felt, for a man in a blindfold. He went on. 'What's it all about, Albert? This the big bid for glory? Glory doesn't suit you, it goes to that fat head of yours. Look at the way you arsed things up five years ago.'

'Do you want the socks?' asked Lee Fraser. I nodded.

'You're like St Mirren, Albert. You should stay second division, promotion just makes you unhappy. You're not built for it.' He was trying to get me rattled. I wasn't sure why. Nor, to tell the truth, did I very much care.

'These boys know that, Darko, I said, 'they realize I never had all your gifts.'

This drew a brief snigger from the chaps, irony lovers all. I reached over, a bit gingerly, and removed the blindfold. He blinked a bit and our eyes met. Our eyes said, 'How strange it is to meet you again, my old psychotic friend, and how bittersweet is this journey we make through the years of our lives.' And our eyes were right. But our mouths carried the day, speaking, as they did, for the moment.

'Open your gob,' I ordered.

'Fuck off,' said Darko.

I grabbed a springy stick and whacked him across the shoulder. The recoil caught me on the ear, drawing blood from my healing scab, darkening my temper. 'Open your mouth,' I said again, like a man who means business.

This time Darko did as he was told. He licked his lips a bit, swallowed, opened. I plugged the gaping hole with the socks. 'There, you see,' I said, 'you thought you were going to get shot then, didn't you?' He didn't reply, what with having the socks in, but even if he'd been sockless, I feel sure he'd have still remained silent, he had that sort of look about him. I suppose it was hearing me clanking around in the holdall that did it, gave him that look I mean. I took out a cleaver, still shiny and smelling of metal polish and swished it through the air a couple of times, for effect. I was showboating, it's true, but not for my benefit, for someone else's. I tossed the cleaver from left hand to right, then back again, watching the boys watching me.

Finally, Tommy Dolan, tiring of my tawdry gamesmanship, held up his pistol and said, 'What's with the fucking cleaver, why don't we just shoot the cunt?' Which was the kind of impetuous outburst I'd been rather hoping he'd make.

'We are going to shoot him,' I said 'but then we're going to chop his head off. Hence,' I said, giving it a twirl, 'the cleaver.' I looked at Darko, expecting to see his eyes widen, like they do in horror films when gagged actors hear alarming news. But they didn't flicker. Maybe his shoulders sagged a bit, maybe I just imagined it, but an air of resignation seemed to exude from him, not unlike the look those big wildebeest efforts get in their eye when they're lying in the grubber with a pack of little jackals at their throat and joints.

Tommy Dolan looked at me. 'What do you mean? What's the point in chopping his head off when we've already shot him?' He was trying to sound like it was an issue of practicality, but the tightening of his voice in his throat told me, and more importantly, the others, including for that matter, Darko, that he just wasn't up for the task. They knew I was up for the task though, and Darko knew too.

I tugged out the sock plug from his gob. 'All right, Darko,' I said. 'That seat comfortable enough for you?'

Give him credit, he told me to fuck off. 'Fuck off, Albert,' he said, 'don't you think I'm going to shit my pants for you, you second-division useless cunt.'

He was about to add to this summation but I replugged his gob using the heel of my hand, I suspect damaging his dental plate through excess force. I then requested of Darko that he stand up. When he did so, I turned to Tommy Dolan.

'Go on then, Tommy,' I urged, 'shoot him.'

Dolan stepped forward, his swagger now back in place. Nearly a foot shorter than Darko and on uneven ground, he looked awkward trying to rest the barrel behind Darko's right ear. If he shot from there, he was going to get soaked. 'Tell him to sit back down,' said Dolan, looking at me.

Darko was breathing hard and moaning through his socks. Lee Fraser and Kevin Casey stood shivering with pocketed hands, though I felt warm myself, kicking at the clumps of leaves.

'I think he should sit down,' said Tommy again.

'No,' I said, 'it wouldn't be a good idea for him to sit down.'

Hearing this, Darko gave a cry, startlingly clear for a man with a pair of socks in his mouth. 'Don't, don't,' he was saying, from behind the M&S wool/nylon mix.

But I did. Taking Tommy's outstretched arm by the wrist, I redirected it, jamming it into place through Darko's trousers, into his sphincter, and together we pulled the trigger. The body gave what Stanley Unwin used to call a 'fallollop', meaning one of those floppy judderings, like a puppet with snipped strings, and fell forward onto the face. I made Fraser and Casey roll it over in order to get them implicated. They did this willingly, out of fear but with a certain trepidation about what they might see. But they needn't have worried. The bullet hadn't exited from the head, as you might expect it would when shot through the arse, but rather, having ricocheted off a rib perhaps, had burst out of the chest, through tissue, vein, shirt, lightweight shorty-style bullet-proof vest and all, thereby confirming my earlier impression that Darko's vest couldn't have stopped a cheque if it had managed a fucking bank. Everyone, including me, was nervous of the crack the shot had made and everyone, except me, started to pick the corpse up, straining with unruly arms and legs, ready to lug it the couple of hundred yards back to Darko's car.

'Where are you going?' I asked them all. Tommy looked at me with a sort of 'not now, Albert' nervous impatience. 'We haven't done the head yet,' I said.

'We don't need to do the head, the head's unnecessary,' said Tommy.

'Oh no it isn't,' I said, 'how else are Leask and Tierney going to believe we've killed him?'

They all looked at each other, clutching and struggling with those big Darko arms and feet and stuff.

'We could show them his wallet,' suggested Lee Fraser.'

'And his wedding ring,' threw in Craig Picken.

'So what?' I said. 'Any cunt can steal a wallet and who the fuck apart from him and his fucking wife would recognize his wedding ring, say something sensible or shut it, you pair of cunts.'

'Cut his hands off then,' said Casey, eager to be gone. 'He's got a swallow tattoo above the thumb, they'd recognize that.'

I shook my head. 'So have half the cunts in young offenders,' I told him. 'No,' I said, 'if we take them the head, they'll believe us, anything else is open to doubt and misinterpretation.'

They were all sagging under the weight of Darko. 'With his head cut off he'll be a lighter load,' I told them. 'His face is him, we take his face for identification, they say thank you, that'll do nicely, here are the keys to our empire, do enjoy. That's how it works,' I said. Despite these reasonable explanations, nobody wanted to proceed with the head, not even to watch it being done, you could see by all the shuffling they just wanted to get out.

'Is that why you shot him up the arse, so's not to damage the head?' asked Fraser.

'Yes,' I told him, which wasn't true. The truth was I'd shot him up the arse because that's how Billy's chaps did it, it avoided those fucking vests and gave a nice final touch of ludicrous humiliation to the send off. It was Billy's signature, so to speak, but Fraser's explanation was simpler so I went along with it.

I could tell Lee and Casey were starting to resign themselves to the head, if not exactly to warm to the prospect. 'Why do you have to do it here, you could be seen?' Lee asked.

I gave them one of my smiling-assassin-type looks. 'Where would you suggest,' I said, 'on Davie's dinner table?' I knew this incident was on its way to becoming a legend and I was naturally keen to show myself off to best advantage. 'We do it here,' I said, 'we do it now, we do it quickly.'

Lee glanced at Dolan for support. 'Go on then,' he said, 'you'd better get on with it.'

I put my foot on Darko's chest for show. I was relieved Davie was a good hundred yards off, keeping watch, else I'd have felt him cramp my style. 'Not me,' I said, and I proffered the cleaver to Dolan. 'You.'

He looked a bit bemused. 'What do you mean?'

'You,' I said again. 'Big mouth. You do it.'

I made a thrusting gesture towards him with the cleaver, forcing him to take it. He took it briefly, then dropped it, hitting Darko on the ankle. It looked a sore one and everybody winced, except of course Darko, who was making his way up to heaven, to sit alongside God in one of his corporate hospitality boxes. Who knows, maybe they'd watch St Mirren together, with maybe St Mirren himself.

'You're fucking off it, Albert,' said Tommy Dolan, calling me Albert as a sweetener to his refusal.

I picked up the cleaver. 'Roll him over onto his front,' I ordered, and they did. I bent down, picked up a few clogged sheaves of leaves and piled them over Darko's shoulders, neck and head, so that to all purposes, if not intents, the head was slightly buried. Then I made brisk chopping motions. Not big chopping motions like say, a masked executioner in a period drama, just short, firm ones, more like a butcher routinely cutting a few lamb chops. Except mine were mutton. When you've done one head you learn that the art of cranial severance lies not so much in heat, as in light. It doesn't require huge expenditures of energy, once you learn to let the body roll this way and that, letting gravity assist, a bit like natural childbirth if you will, only in this case you're removing a head, rather than teasing one out. The clumps of leaves, as you'll have surmised, were there to douse down the effects of any big squirts of blood from the neck arteries, as these can be both alarming and nauseating. When I'd dealt with the last of anything resembling a bone or piece of highly resistant gristle, I dug out a moss-covered stone from the ground with the cleaver, then slid it into position under the lolling head. With metal against stone. I was now able to sever the tendons and springy neck veins that had offered such stubborn resistance in my encounter with Calum. As I say, light, not heat.

I picked up the head, not by the hair, in an odd way

it seemed disrespectful, but with both hands, around the base of the jaw, and placed it carefully on top of the tree stump, leaning it against the mossy stone to stop it rolling off. I told Lee Fraser and Craig Picken to lift the body but they wouldn't, neither being willing to take the meaty end. Tommy Dolan, to save face, so to speak, offered to take the ragged end but only if it were sealed off so he wouldn't get his denim jacket gunged up. What he meant, I suspected, was that he didn't want to look at it. I had some bin liners in my tool bag and fortunately there was enough neck left on the main body of the, well, body, so that I was able to wrap the red meaty end with the bin liner and seal it tight with the belt we'd used for tying up Darko's hands. Actually, it's as hard to staunch a severed neck with a belt as it is to tie a set of hands with one, the buckle ends get in the way, unless you're in movies, which, apparently, we weren't. So there it was. Tommy Dolan, his big mouth temporarily smaller, lifted Darko by the armpits, with Casey and Fraser on a leg apiece, and Darko, his white hairy legs visible where the trousers had ridden up, revealing not his socks, of course, but, touchingly, the marks from where his socks had been, headed off, never to be troubled by his plastic knee again.

I squated, watching, wiping my hands clean on the dirty leaves, preferring grime to blood, feeling both satisfied at a job well done and oddly, a slight sense of shame at having done it. Why? Well I'm not talking religious epiphany or any other pious bollocks but some deeds, it seems to me, go beyond morality. It goes against the spirit of nature to kill a great strong beast like Darko, it's an unseemly perversion of nature's intent. Admittedly, it was one that suited me very well, but you see my point? I felt a tinge of sorrow that nature's favourite had been struck down by an inferior cunt, meaning me, who brought nothing but trouble in his wake. This headless man they were loading into the boot of his own car, he'd been to dinner at my house, more than once. He liked Brenda's gravy, I recalled, complimented her on her gravy. From any other man, I'd have taken that as a challenge, but Darko, give him his due, he didn't play those games. If he liked your juices, he'd just come right out front and tell you so. He brought flowers, roses, probably hand-picked from his own garden. Oh well. Fie, fie and thrice fie as they say, it was done now, so fuck it. I stretched and arched my back. I checked my flannels for stray entrails and finding none this time, I followed my staggering partners in crime back out from the comfort of the dark trees, through the tall, cutting ferns, up the grassy slope, along the marshy verge, towards the waiting car.

*

Now, sitting outside of Blue, we were all getting twitchy, waiting for Davie to ring. I took another Co-Proximal, more to pass the time than anything else. Admittedly, Davie was having a busy evening, what with taking over the driving of Darko's car and, given his burgeoning knowledge of the Springburn area, dumping it, once again, on the same corner outside Billy's house where he had, weeks ago, left Calum's jelly van. Davie would have parked the car a yard from the pavement, so as to attract wanted attention and Darko's headless, sphincterless body would, in accordance with ancient hooligan tradition, be consigned to the boot, along with his golf umbrella and a ladies' two-piece suit in ultramarine, evidently destined for the dry cleaner. Of course, if I'd been thinking properly, I'd have dressed Darko up in it, but pranks like that can often be a subliminal giveaway, especially with sexy Cindy hanging around the street corners, barely two miles down the road.

The windows of our car were steamed up with condensation and Lee and Craig, ace professionals both, were playing noughts and crosses on every available scrap of breathed up misted window they could find. I mean, here's a cunt, Craig Picken, who'd gone out robbing to put fifty quid of coke up his nose, and to what ecstatic end? So he could play noughts and crosses on a rainy night on a car windscreen. I mean the fucker was losing to Lee who'd had nothing stronger than a packet of Wrigley's spearmint. So all I'm saying is, if there's an afterlife, I pray that I never come back as a septum in Paisley, that's all. Then the mobile sang its daft wee song, putting us out of our misery. It was Davie. And it was okay.

'Here we go,' I said to the boys and I lifted the bag and we were away across the street, not stopping to think, with our hands already reaching inside our coats, just like proper hooligans. Which was all my boys ever wanted. And all I ever wanted to avoid, involving, as it did, a face-to-face confrontation with large men. Nevertheless I adopted my firm-but-tactful-underpinned-by-an-air-of-menace voice and explained to a tall shaven-headed gentleman that we'd come to visit Mr Tierney. Or 'Robin' as I called him. 'Rockin' Robin', judging by the noise from downstairs. Or even 'Robin bastard' as I glanced at his admission charges. Six quid on a week night in Paisley, erring on the slide of plunder, in my opinion.

Tall Shaven Gentleman was regretful, explaining that Mr Tierney 'is no' a-fucking-bout, right?' He suggested our time might be better spent by going away and taking a quiet fuck to ourselves. I, equally regretful, explained that Tierney was indeed 'a-fucking-bout' being as how I'd seen him enter an hour earlier from my vantage point across the street. A broad man, with a light talcum dust of fair stubble on his head where people used to keep hair, joined Tall Gentleman and enquired whether everything was, 'Sound.'

'Cool, cool,' said Tall Gentleman, and we continued a polite circular discussion on the theme of Robin, or Mr Tierney, and about how he was, or wasn't, according to personal taste, in. Or indeed out. And as we did so, I became aware of that same sticky sensation from earlier, the tackiness I'd experienced inside the car, and I glanced down and noticed that my shoes were dribbled on and the soles gummy on the blue neon-stained pavement where we clustered, my chaps and I, having our carefully restrained discussion at the door with Mr Broad and Mr Long. A discussion that swung our way when I showed them a cleaver and they found themselves paying extra close attention not only to me but to a trio of small, nippy-looking gun barrels that had suddenly manifested their support beside me. Davie and Kevin Casey had emerged from their car, with John Leask between them, looking an odd mix of grumpy and terrified, and now we were all standing on the pavement, waiting for the doormen to decide, as they surely must, whether they'd prefer to be injured, possibly killed, protecting their employer's craven arse, or whether to step inside safely, out of harm's way, and lead us downstairs to Robin Tierney's office. Happily, common sense prevailed so that I was able to sheath my cleaver and the boys to pocket their little pistols.

We followed through the gaudy foyer, beyond the doors marked 'Private', past the staff lavvies and the stacked up beer crates, and turned right to pile, like breathless demented fuckers in a Marx Brothers movie, all adrenalin and severed body parts, straight into Tierney's office. He was at his desk, talking to a dark-haired man who'd had it cut to look like the stupid one in *Friends*. There was money on the desk in bundles of tens and twenties, as well as a big mass of change which Tierney and Stupid had obviously been counting. It dawned on me that Stupid was probably Bryan Bennett, the server for Tierney's establishment. He backed off to the wall when he saw us, or more specifically our cleavers and guns, and waited for Tierney, as owner, to take control of the situation. This Tierney attempted to do by remaining calm and, in a headmastery voice, instructing us to wait outside. We didn't wait outside, however, and instead I instructed Tierney to shut his fucking yap, before I cut him an extra smile for his two faces, the weaselly cunt.

In truth, this was unfair of me, two-faced, in fact, as I'd wanted all along for Tierney to enrage Darko by slinking off to tell him of my earlier approach at the Watermill. Which, of course, he'd duly done. So, as I've said, I'd worked up an entirely unjustified head of steam, but the trouble was I needed the head of steam more than I needed the justification as I always find it hard to dominate a room with my temper, so to speak, in neutral. All the same, I thought it was a little uncalled for when Tommy Dolan, who else, held up his little pistol by the barrel and gave Tierney's nose a cuff, making it bleed. I didn't protest as I knew where this aggression was coming from, he'd lost face over the head incident and was anxious to retrieve his status as a remorseless up-and-coming sadist. Also, I didn't think it did any harm to warm the room with the odd slap, it ensured that the threat of violence was explicit and actual, not just some abstract possibility. Perhaps with luck, someone would mess themselves, which was always a nice enhancement to an evening's violent theatre.

So as not to be outdone by Dolan, I pinned Bryan Bennett against the wall and went through his pockets. He had some phials of amyl nitrate and a large quantity of pills, marked with an E, which, being acquainted with the alphabet, I knew to be Ecstasy. Nice clean drugs, for wholesome people, with jobs and stuff. Not my sort of public at all. Anyway I relieved him of these items. I gave four tablets each to Mr Broad and Mr Long and told them to please go away, they were finished for the night. Bryan Bennett asked me who the fuck I thought I was and I told him I was the Surgeon. I felt like being the Surgeon again instead of just Albert because, as I've said, my blood was up, and so I gave this Bryan Bennett a little draw across the cheek with the sharp edge of the cleaver, which made him cry out, as indeed it does most people.

Robin Tierney, to my surprise, told me that not only was there no need for such behaviour but that I shouldn't have done it as Bryan was pally with 'formidable' people.

I took this to mean he thought I was 'unformidable' and I went on, at some length, asking him which sort of formidable people Bennett was pally with. I pointed to pictures on the walls with my cleaver, saying, 'Is that one?', 'How about him, is he formidable?' I had to string out the verbals more than I'd have liked while I struggled to free the head from the bin liner, where it had become trapped in its own stickiness. Frustrated, I took Darko by the hair and shook him a bit in the faces of Robin Tierney, Bryan Bennett and John Leask and I can't say his presence passed unnoticed. Which is, of course, to say his lack of presence, as the rest of him was tucked up safe and sound in his car boot outside Billy Waugh's.

It's fair to say that all three, Tierney, Bennett, Leask, looked a bit ashen. But then, so did Darko. White, bloodless, twigs and mud adhering to his stunted neck and trim goatee, not dead, only mulching. I was quite sorry I'd closed the eyes, this being a Moment and no mistake; one of those longed-for instances of memorably banal horror that could sprout wings and fly off into the everlasting sunset of eternal hooligan memory. I put the head down on Tierney's desk, upsetting neat prissy piles of five and ten pences and attempted to open, for show, the eyes. But eyes, as you may know, or one day discover, have a will of their own. Darko's eyes, on the point of death, had been unwilling to close. Now, faced with the glamorous gift of resurrection, they were equally unwilling to open. Or at least to stay open. No matter how much I thumbed and flicked and cursed their lack of dramatic flair, those lids stayed down like roller blinds on a pawnshop at closing time. 'Open you cunts,' I tried shouting at the eyes. But the eyes weren't listening. So

I tried the ears, bawling, then pleading for a response. But the ears weren't listening either. At least not to me, though maybe they were listening to the eyes, perhaps having engineered some sort of private agreement. You listen out for me and I'll watch your back, sort of thing. Yes, that was it, I decided, as I looked Darko in the full face, eyes and all, telling him in no uncertain terms, just what I thought of his fucking eyes and ears and why couldn't he train them, the recalcitrant fuckers, to obey a few simple commands?

And what did Darko say? Not a dicky bird. Just sat on the desk, eyes closed, ears shut, corners of the mouth turned down, quietly mulching. So I gave the head a little slap out of frustration and it rolled across the desk and onto Tierney's lap just as he tried to unfreeze himself in time to rise. So the head hit the floor with, what else, a meaty dunk, as Tierney stood, wringing his hands and uttering in a sonorous voice that may or may not have been his, 'Oh my God, oh my good God.' Tierney gave Darko a startled flick with his shoe that sent him, Darko, rolling unevenly under the desk and out, once again, to rest at my feet. John Leask watched, hand over mouth, as I picked Darko up, mindful of my delicate back, and mimed a rugby pass to Bryan Bennett. Bennett had his hands locked deep in his pockets and his mouth pursed tight as a drawstring, as though Darko's head were a bomb that might go off at any moment. So there was no point chucking Darko to him, he couldn't have played the game. So, when he flinched, I wheeled and threw Darko to Kevin Casey, who, facing two alternatives, drop it and look like an arse or catch and feel sick, chose the latter. As I laughed, big bellied, Zorba-the-Greek style, Casey flicked on a smile and tried to pass the head to Craig Picken who turned away and was sick in a corner. Kevin, growing bolder, took the head by the hair and tried to hand it to Lee who also turned a bit green as he shook his own, attached, head, in refusal. 'Any takers?' asked Kevin laughing. 'Any takers?'

The only man in the room willing to take up the challenge was, I noticed, Davie. He alone seemed possessed of the questing human spirit of enquiry. I mean, who wouldn't want to handle a human head, just to you say you'd done it? Davie tapped Kevin on the arm and wiped his hands on his jeans. He held Darko by the cheeks, staring intently into the frozen mask of the features, now raising it aloft, slowly, over his own head, like it was a triumph, the Scottish Cup of Heads. 'We got the bastard,' said Davie, all the more loudly for its being quiet. 'Old cunts nil, young cunts one,' he shouted. And they all, all the young cunts, responded as one. 'Hullo!' they cheered. 'Hullo!'

I applauded, sportingly, taking in the scene and smiling. But more taking it in than smiling or applauding. I was an old cunt myself, remember, a month older than Darko had been. Or would ever be. I would have to watch my portly, elderly step, I told myself, as I took Darko's head from Davie and swaddled it again in its snug bin liner hat. 'Now you see him,' I said to the room in general, 'now you don't.'

I was aware of a tug at my elbow. Davie had located something. I opened up the bin liner and let him drop Darko's dental plate into it. 'Thanks, Davie,' I said, 'I'm going to wear that on a neck chain.'

And we adjourned, as they say.

Chapter Eleven

Once again, I disappeared back to Bayswater. At least that's how it felt to me, 'disappearing'. In London, hardly anybody knew, far less cared, about me and I found that the geographical distance from events gave me a commensurate emotional detachment. It pays to remove yourself at such turbulent times, away from the eye of the storm, so to speak, otherwise you risk being consumed. Down here I wouldn't be dazzled by any blaring headlines, or be on red alert against a guilty runaway tongue, or have to avoid acquaintances, old or new, lest the subject of Darko and his sad demise came up and I appeared shifty or evasive. Both of which, of course, I was.

I bought a *Daily Record* from my regular shop in Queensway then slipped into Starbucks for a grande latte and a keen peruse. Better my hands should shake down here than 400 miles up the road, in the shadow of Pitt Street nick. Darko's killing made the front page with a big 'Second Hoodlum Horror Slaying' headline. Inside, taken from a cunning angle was a picture of some cops, standing by the taped-off car with, I noted with satisfaction, a glimpse of Billy Waugh's disgusting mansion in the background. There was an inset photo of Darko's head, an old photo, since the head was still on his shoulders, alongside an arrow that helpfully pointed out

Billy's house, lest anyone should miss the connection. Even though there wasn't one. A further picture of an irate Billy, in braces, reading glasses on forehead, being restrained on his doorstep by Mick, finished off this satisfying tableau. I perused the prose quickly but thoroughly, checking for references to myself, but found only a single oblique mention, furnished in a doorstep quote from Billy to the effect that the police were arseholes and that their enquiries should be made 'not in this fucking town but the one next door'.

Arseholes, yes, I think that was Billy's term. Once I'd filled in the asterisks, it seemed to fit.

The next couple of days followed in similar vein. 'Was Lyall a Death Dealer?' Meaning did he sell drugs. You could tell the papers didn't have much because soon afterwards they started squeezing out the juice on Darko's love life, portraying him to be this glamorous underworld figure who enjoyed the affections of top-quality bints. To support this doubtful contention there were old pictures of Darko with an air hostess, a barmaid and a former Miss Paisley. Obviously Janey Lyall had provided the photos, though there wasn't one of her, perhaps, smart woman, she'd traded off the past in order to control the present. Then I turned the page and realized I was mistaken. 'The Mobster I Loved' read the headline. I recognized the living room, it was the same one where a few weeks ago she'd been trying to scratch his eyes out. Now she sat looking pensive, done up to the nines, blue gown, pearls, the lot, with their wedding picture on her fat lap. 'Derek loved this dress,' ran the quote, 'now I'm wondering if I'll ever get the chance to wear it again.' She was saying this even though she was wearing the dress again, then. If you see what I mean. Basically it was just a come-and-get-me call to any sweaty accountant or jaded lawyer who fancied a bit of lurid in return for helping out with the finer points of Darko's will. Sometimes I despair of women. They don't want you, Mr Unique, they just want a Husband. As long as you've enough dosh and don't dribble or fall over the furniture, just flash the diamond and you're on. At least until a heart attack, or in Darko's case, head attack, does you in, then they're on with the backless dress and the winsome look and off down the meat market with the old chapped elbows flailing.

One of the few women I ever came across who scorned that tribal law was Cindy, my father. Cindy dressed not so much to attract men as to repel women. Or rather, a woman, my mother. By the time I was fifteen I was more or less living at Billy's. This was tough on my old man. He'd come back from a hard day's hitting metal with a hammer, or whatever the fuck it was he did when he walked out that door of a morning, and returned to a cold room and no noise but the ticking clock. I'd be up at Billy's playing pool with Mick, or out on Billy's speedboat on Loch Lomond, glowering at the girls in Duck Bay Marina. The first Mrs Billy had just about served her time by then and, following a series of calculated rows, calculated by Billy that is, she'd been relagated to living full time in the stone cottage near the big house, pending clear out and divorce. Naturally, break-ups being what break-ups are, this meant an overlap between my mother moving into the marital bed and Mrs Billy moving out.

I don't know how my mother squared that situation

in her head. Maybe, yes, she was just a selfish, callous cow, which I'm prepared to believe. After all, people want what they want. On the other hand, love being viewed in those days as some sort of cleansing gift from God, rather than the simple act of chemical greed which we now know it to be, she'd have been full of that coy, simpering self-congratulation that likes to dress itself up as concern: 'I do hope she'll be all right', 'Are we doing the right thing?' All that guff. To the winners love's a game, to losers, a tragedy. Mrs Billy in her stone outhouse, Cindy, on his burst settee, watching *Softly, Softly*, and hugging the biscuit barrel, where was the justice? There isn't any, there's just appetite and its consequences. And appetite isn't love. And when appetite runs out, that's when love's losers can take their revenge. Passive gloating at the least, cold rebuttal if the fates are truly kind. As they were to Cindy, later, when my mother needed him most. Ah me, how the Cindys of the fathers are visited upon the sons. Looking back, I should have married Cissie. There I've said it. We'd have lived happily ever after. For a while. She'd have gone picturesquely doolally at a convenient early age, allowing me to play Rochester to her Grace Poole, back lit against the intriguing glow of madness. No guilt. Not my fault. It's in the genes, you see. Too good for this world. The genes that is, not me. Me bad man.

Back home, I feared the loneliness of London. I wanted to be anonymous but not invisible. Why hadn't I made my mark down here when I had the chance? Spot of scuffing, bit of networking, I'd have been gliding up the ladder to a nice pensionable position as enforcer with a family firm, at worst a freelance psycho for hire.

Which, come to think of it, was what I was now. Unfortunately, I lacked the social skills, the easy laugh at a crap joke, that cloying love of children, pints, and dogs. Criminals bored me. It was Sunday. We never made that trip to Cindy's, me and Brenda.

*

I walked up the steps into Craven Gardens. It was only eleven a.m., yet the traffic was end to end, the cafés choked with foreign bodies, brats and fag fug. Too much, too early. I walked up, onto Bayswater Road, then down, towards Notting Hill. And on, down the sorrowful, dandified slope of Holland Park Avenue. In Tootsies, I could connect nothing with nothing. I had the *Sunday Mail*, the Scottish one, open on my lap. Flicking through, I hoped to meet a blaring headline that would greet me like a friend. Or enemy. It's all the same to me. Any shallow in-depth feature would do, so long as it alluded, safely, to me and reminded me that I existed. I, Albert, newly crowned King of Paisley. For I was exiled from my kingdom and was all sadness. Save for sentimental yearning, a pull of the heart, or cock, or both. Last night I dreamed of the past and I woke up measuring the present.

There was no headline about heads, past or present. No follow-up feature of lurid gang history. That day, we hooligans were ousted for tales of weight loss and marches against drugs. 'Join our Campaign'. I'd join, that minute, if it paraded down Holland Park Avenue. I'd carry a banner and weep for poor teenies dead from E. And why not? You take comfort, in this life, where you find it. And I didn't find it today, under the glum pavement parasols or in the cool moneyed murmur of the Halcyon. It was this fucking dream, you see, more portent than reality, this sense of loss, that's always been with me.

Felice. Who did I want, the real or phantom her? She came to me when my guard was down. What did she want? More to the point, what did I want, since it was me who conjured her? I moved one café up, a gesture of defiance, against myself, since if she was not there to see me do it, what was the point? I thumbed through the *Mail* again, looking for signs of me. But I was not there; Mistah Paisley, he dead. So the Ruthless Psycho read the football, charted the progress of the Hoops, waiting for the dream dust to settle. And when it did, he realized the prosaic truth, dull as his empty coffee cup; which was that what he wanted of women was still to want them but not necessarily to have them, since that was when the dream dust turned to ashes. This king prefered to long for rather than possess, because longing implied ideal, and possession only disappointment. What a complex king he was. What's that you say, a wanker? Yes, a wanker too, but an honest wanker, I prithee. The King of Paisley was a romantic. His queen, Brenda, existed in flesh and blood and was therefore unworthy of his ardour. Similarly, if the great goddess Felice were to sit opposite this King of Paisley, wantonly caressing his sugar packets, he'd still be gazing over her shoulder towards the beguiling twilight world beyond the espresso machine. This king knew not what he wanted; only what he did not. Therefore did he seek refuge from self through the way of action. This king was an arsehole, in accord with his subjects. All hail Arsehole, King of Paisley. The king paid his bill, leaving a small tip, and walked on towards the roundabout beyond the Hilton, where he veered right into Shepherd's Bush. I suppose I wanted a neighbourhood that suited my mood, or maybe I just wanted to be somewhere that gave me the feeling of Paisley, and of home.

I shared a crumbling bench on the green with a young tramp who was stowing a sleeping bag. I'd have struck up a conversation but he'd have assumed me a poof, so I kept schtum and sat there aching a bit inside, which at least was a vague improvement on the nothingness I knew and detested. The mobile tinkled, startling and rescuing me. It was Davie, asking if I'd seen a particular Scottish broadsheet. They'd been doing one of those lists the Sundays love so much, this time on Scotland's top thirty hooligans, though they called them gangsters, well, they would, wouldn't they? Apparently, I made the lower reaches of the top twenty, some way behind Paul Ferris but ahead of Hugh Collins, which doesn't say much since he's been retired for a decade to my certain knowledge. The article was written in a tongue-in-cheek way to lighten the possibility of litigation, though most hooligans I knew would have been more aggrieved by their alleged position in the hierarchy than by the job description. Billy, no doubt thanks to his recent profile, was firmly installed at number one. This wouldn't have pleased him, as he'd much sooner have been, like all the other real top criminals, off the list and practising a life of genial terror in the privacy of his own fiefdom. In his photo, they'd dubbed on an Al Capone light-coloured fedora. I was holding, apparently, a violin case, as indeed I often did when on my way to a gangland massacre. Davie asked when I'd be back. Even as I heard my mouth say, 'Not for a bit,' I knew I'd be obeying the itch I'd had since morning to head for the airport. Yes, a flight this time, fuck superstition, and cost come to that, the sooner I was back in the fray the better. Too much action and contact had eroded my capacity for solitude, let alone, I realized, for thinking and writing.

I shared a spot of is-it-raining-up-there-fuck-sake-it's-beautiful-down-here-type banter with Davie before pocketing the phone. When I did, I realized I had a smile back on my face. Fuck me, I thought, I'm turning into a human being, pals, grinning, the lot.

*

I caught a cab back to the flat, a focussed man, no longer becalmed by the siren song of whimsy, to find a message on my answering machine, but the message was full of the siren song of whimsy, being, as it was, from Felice. Yes, that Felice. Oddly, I wasn't surprised; it seemed, in a strange way, inevitable. There's a rhythm between a couple, even when they're no longer a couple. I whisked around the flat, stuffing the cleanest of my dirty clothes into my trolley holdall, ready for departure. When I had the task down to socks, I pressed play again, just as I'd promised myself I wouldn't do, for the sheer glow and torment of gnawing out the nuances in her voice. That distant intimate voice. Cultured. Middle class. Fragrant of quim. 'Albie, it's Flick. Are you in . . . ?' I'd forgotten I was Albie. Though to me, to my private self, she'll always be Flick. 'Wondered how you were. Are you in London? Be lovely to see you.'

Well, of course, given all that had gone before, you'd have imagined I'd have been beside myself with glee to receive this oral missive from my true love. You'd have imagined my first impulse would have been to pick up that phone with a song in my heart. But that wouldn't be taking account of the splendidly fucked-up psyche of the average human animal, would it? So I didn't pick up the phone. Because that wasn't my first impulse. It was my second. My first impulse was to think, in a smugly beatific sort of way, Ah got her! She's still on side. I can let her ride. I was upbeat and effervescent because I was off up north to further my aims. If I'd have picked up that phone, I'd have gone back to being Sunday-afternoon Albert, long of chin and round of shoulder, the national expression of weekend relaxation. And I was better than average. Didn't I have a fucking kingdom to prove it? So I packed my bag and put Flick's call, mentally, in my holdall. I had no time for love games, was the love game I was playing. I was a working monarch with a country to run. All the same, as the king minicabbed it to the airport there was still a fucking song in his battered old heart. Though I flattered myself that this time I was singing for myself. Oh yes, and of course, my people. Our people.

If only some cunt had reminded me I was tone deaf.

*

They say in life there are only six degrees of separation between every fucker on the planet. Except in Glasgow, where there's two. There's your mother and every other cunt. I'm saying this is a small community. I'm saying if you tell something to anyone, it will get around like a pox. This is the sort of community where, if you cut off a couple of heads, they're missed.

I knew it was a mistake to come back so quickly the moment I stepped off the plane. Because of recent events, hooligans were in vogue again. Hence the lists in the Sundays. Hence Billy's agitation. Hence the looks of recognition as I slurped my latte in Costa. Hence the cool reception from Brenda when I phoned to say I was on my way. I made up my mind there and then I'd never do another head. I'd got away with the first one but doing a second was a vulgar mistake, based on insecurity and a desire to show off. An artist, even a hammer tapper like me, should never repeat himself. As a result, the old clichés were being dusted off by the papers and the Scottish branch of the industry was finding itself in the spotlight. Take a tip, if you're going to commit a murder, make it as dull as possible, it avoids unseemly attention.

Brenda opened the door and headed for the living room without giving me as much as a smile let alone a welcoming squeeze of her tits. I followed her in, lugging my trolley over the doorstep and before I'd even taken my coat off, we were straight down to the familiar heated recriminations. These went along the lines of, 'You bastard, how dare you involve me in something like this.' And, 'You shit, you've treated me like an idiot.' Like most men, I don't mind being called a bastard, but I balk at shit. The first step was to find out how much she knew. So I mollified her with a cup of tea and we each had one from the box of Thorntons I'd bought at the airport. She'd seen the papers, of course, and was 'appalled' by these 'horrible things'. Calum's murder she'd accepted, she said, it being well known that since his missus had left him, he'd been 'into sleazy sex with dirty people'. But Darko's murder, that was different. Darko was a loyal upstanding pillar of the criminal community, if they'd malky Darko, as well as Calum, then it could only mean one thing – 'There's a coup going on.' She gave me a hard stare as she said this. But I knew Brenda well enough to know that this hard stare didn't mean, 'Albert, I'm deeply torn and suspicious. Is it or isn't it you who's behind all this tragic mayhem?' No, this was a new stare, prudently adopted in case of High Court Witness Box Emergency, one selected to fit our new status as fleeting lovers rather than stable marriage diehards. This stare said, 'Don't you dare tell me anything, you fucking cunt. If the shit hits the fan I want to come out of this looking betrayed, deceived and stoic.'

Let's face it, Brenda knew how I made my money. She'd helped me spend it for enough years. I couldn't blame her for trying to distance herself and play innocent. After all, she was innocent. Technically. As long as I didn't tell her anything, she could continue to play the love-is-blind card. As I've said, I didn't blame her for doing this, but it saddened me. It was a reflection of how our relationship had changed. The old Brenda would have stood by me through thick and thin and protected me without being asked. But women are principled; they'll only lie for you if you marry them. I intuited that bastard tactics would only exacerbate the situation, so I'd no alternative but to enter shit mode, which, after all, is what she thought of me anyway. The problem was that this situation had been thrust upon me too suddenly, I hadn't decided what I wanted to do about Brenda but I knew that, for now, I wanted to keep her on side. So I did bull-by-the-horns-let's-get-to-the-bottom-of-this, straight-guy acting and demanded to know what, exactly, she was accusing me of. Then before she could answer, I lied through my teeth, denying all implication in, if not knowledge of, what I referred to as 'a couple of tit for tat trade murders'. Brenda asked what I meant by 'tit for tat'. I told her I was only going on what I'd heard. And what I'd heard was that it was Darko who'd had Calum done and that some mate of Calum's, Danny Wooler possibly – after all if you're talking 'sleazy sex with dirty people' then his name was first out of the knicker drawer – had chivalrously avenged his slain companion. I mean that's what I heard. Didn't know for sure. Already said too much by telling her. Blah blah.

'And it wasn't you that done Darko?'

I raised my eyebrows. 'What, for Danny Wooler?'

I did do-me-a-favour acting with my eyes. Even if she didn't believe me, it was what she wanted to hear.

'So you're telling me it's just coincidence? You're up here and suddenly two of Paisley's top established gangsters are malkied?'

I ran my hands through my hair, sighed, and did okay-you've-asked-for-it-so-here-it-is acting. I took a deep breath and told her openly, with shocking frankness, 'I knew it was going to happen.' Brenda looked at me for more. 'There'd been rumours. So I came up on the sniff. I knew there'd be openings in the market once they'd been popped.' I shrugged, doing all-right-so-I'm-not-proud-of-myself stuff.

Brenda blinked and was silent while she took this in. She made nervous, bird-like movements with her neck, which were, I estimated, only half false. Basically,

I think she was having difficulty sorting out my lies from her own. She nodded to herself and glanced up at me, attempting to give her eyes that hopeful yet distrustful look, like a woman who's being asked to learn to love again. I played with it, being a cad, or shit, take your pick, and informed her with equal sincerity that, 'Whatever I've been doing has been to try, God knows, to give us a future.' I find it helps chucking in the creator's name when telling an outright lie, people still have a vestigial respect for a brand name, however waning. At the same time, like all the best cowards and liars, I lied to myself about believing my own lies. This is entirely reprehensible but the point is, she bought it. Or seemed to. It was a game of cards, right? And like all the best lady gamblers, Brenda kept a Derringer down her cleavage. Its name, which I'd forgotten, was Stuart. And when I tried to wrestle her onto the couch for a fumble, she reached down her chest and flashed it.

Her: 'Don't.'

Me: 'Why not?'

Her: 'Can't you guess?'

Me: 'What, you still having periods at your age? You little show off.'

Her: 'No, it's not that. Stuart's coming home tomorrow.'

Me: silence; stunned.

'You fucking picked you're moment with that one, didn't you?' I told her, no longer silent, or stunned, but fucking annoyed.

'I wasn't expecting you back, was I,' she said, and lit up a Consulate. I stood, at a loss for a moment, trying to work out how I'd gone from high elation at being back to edgy paranoia in no time flat.

I forced myself back to basics. 'Where's he staying?'

'Here,' said Brenda, 'this is his home, isn't it?' I asked if he owned it. 'No,' she said.

'Then it's not his fucking home then, is it? The fucker stays here at your discretion.'

'I suppose,' she said. She didn't shrug when she said that, as people would ordinarily, which told me, as no doubt it was meant to, that she was coolly weighing things up. To my surprise I found myself, well, fuming at this coolness. Hot breath was coming down my nose, I could feel its heat on my upper lip. One more word and I'd be pawing the ground and ramming her with my head.

'You mean you actually bought this shithole gaff?' I gave a scornful glance about, for effect. 'Where's the rest of the money you got from the sale of the house?'

'In a distribution bond,' she said, puffing out a lazy blast of smoke, 'for my old age.'

I had that sensation of the ground shifting under my feet. It only dawns on a person they're a control freak when something happens they can't control. I couldn't decide how much of this new found empowerment stuff was real on Brenda's part and how much of it was acting out a role, like she was Ms Haughty Independent Woman from a Renault Clio ad. There was one way to find out. 'So if that fucker's living here and so am I, who are you going to sleep with?'

She gave me a look. I picked up the penny a little after it dropped. Brenda gave me a smile to go with the look. 'I don't know,' she said. 'Maybe you and Stuart had better put your heads together.'

I don't object to bints tooling themselves up with power, but I bristle when they come over all smug about it. It crossed my mind to climb in the sack with Stuart, when he turned up, just to spite her. 'We will,' I said.

'How will I know when you two have come to a decision?'

I helped myself to a handful of the Thorntons, choosing caramels I could get my teeth into. 'You'll know,' I told her.

Chapter Twelve

It was good to see the boys again. We'd come through our first assignment with cheerful aplomb and already the chaps were chafing at the bit for another. Already history was being rewritten to accommodate the brave endeavours of the various players.

We met in Davie's flat and as he made tea there was much excited reflection about the business of the head. I reclined modestly in Davie's shoogly armchair and waited for the praise that was my due. Instead, I'd to make do with my cup of tea. The talk was of the surprising weight of the thing, who had held it and by which means, hair or ears, and the ecstasy of tension that had preceded the assault. My own contribution, I noted, had been recorded by implication only. 'When I was slung the head I . . .', 'When it rolled under the desk and I . . .' No mention of who it was that had instigated the said slinging or rolling nor who, for that matter, had cut the fucking thing off in the first place. It reminded me of the strange displaced feeling I'd had when a one-act adaptation of my book had been performed at the Orange Tree in Richmond. All the after-show talk was of the director and of the innate menace of the cunting leading actor. It seemed to me that being a writer was like being God, you created everything yet your existence was constantly questioned. Needless to say, after that,

I'd taken every tawdry interview and local radio chinwag going.

This case was different, of course, and when I appealed to my higher self, the Wise Old Cunt, he told me to rejoice and be exceedingly glad, for everybody in the room was a witness to each other's implication in the event, and here they all were not only acknowledging that event, but exaggerating the degree of their personal involvement. I knew that soon enough, human reality being what it was, these piquant and humorous tales would take root in each mind, creating seductive pictures and supplanting the more humdrum reality. I mean the truth is that no matter how much a hooligan may froth at the gob and flash his menacing credentials, a severed head is only that, nothing more, it wasn't as if Darko's was singing 'Mad Dogs and Englishmen' or doing anything remarkable, the fact is we've all seen far worse, or better, at the Odeon. Which only confirms my long-held opinion that what we see isn't reality, because what we see, on its own, isn't eloquent enough to convey meaning, what we feel about what we see is the crux. And if what we see isn't unique enough to leave its emotional imprint then we prefer to superimpose our own more satisfying images.

The only gratifying element of the gathering was that Tommy Dolan was now more subdued. I could tell this because he was making more noise than usual, shouting and laughing, his jokes not quite hitting their accustomed mark, he and I both aware that while he hadn't funked the head, he'd nonetheless had to force himself against his own nature to handle it, and that maybe he wasn't quite the fearless and versatile young villain he'd fancied himself previously to be. No, the one who'd really caught my admiration was Davie. He had the gift. With the same quiet grace and fellow feeling, he could offer up your steaming heart on a plate or hand you a Jammy Dodger. If he were to wield a hammer with as much enthusiasm as he did a Hoover, he might afford himself some better armchairs.

Kevin Casey put his feet up on the coffee table and I could see Davie looking uncomfortable so I made him take them off again. When Kevin obeyed with minimal backchat, it struck me that perhaps my forceful performance under the russet mantle of the trees hadn't passed so blithely unremarked after all. I kept forgetting that in Scotland, silence was a good review. Picken asked when we might see action again and I told him he wouldn't, if he didn't sort out his disgusting nasal habit.

'You mean the coke?'

'No,' I told him, 'I mean your breathing, it's gruesome.'

Breathing was a simple in and out task, I explained, performed with the nose, it didn't require the monstrous oral trills and curlicues he embellished it with. This rebuke drew parodied oral trills from all, so it was obvious my new respect remained sadly conditional. Not that I minded cutting the chaps some slack, I wanted them laughing, even a little at me, if it kept them in good fettle for the next stage of the battle. Which was, of course, consolidation. Though Tommy Dolan didn't see it like that.

'Never mind all that, when do we make some fucking money, Bert?'

'When we consolidate,' I told him. 'And don't ever call me Bert to my face. Save it for behind my back, you weaselly little cunt.'

I shouldn't have called him a name. At least not in front of everyone. It was a challenge for him to confront me or back off. Characteristically, Tommy confronted me, by pretending to back off. 'Awright, awright, no more Bert. If you don't like Bert, I'll not call you Bert any more. Fuck me. What's the matter with Bert anyhow, Albert?'

I felt my hand close around the handle of the hammer in my coat pocket. In years gone by I wouldn't have thought twice about standing up, trotting a pace or two forward and braining him with it. Even now, it wasn't the braining him that was the problem, it was the standing up and trotting that made me pause for reflective thought. To perform a successful maniacal attack, the movement has to be swift, smooth and carried out with the minimum of fuss. I couldn't risk my back locking as I hurtled, red in tooth and claw, at my opponent: He'd have time not only to relieve the hammer from my grasp but to mend the broken castor on Davie's easy chair with it before biffing me himself. I mean, clobbered with your own hammer, what road back to industry respect would that leave? It would undo the work of a lifetime. So what I'm saying is I sat there and took it, rather than run that risk. True, I did cold-menacing-stare acting but people in my profession do that when they're buying a packet of crisps, it's a tactic, which, unless accompanied by action, carries little threat to a tormentor. Basically, the net result was that Tommy Dolan got to keep his brains in his head rather than on

David's living-room carpet because I'd neglected to support my lower back with a cushion.

'There won't be any money,' I pointed out, 'until we make them clubs our own.' I gave Dolan what I hoped passed for a benignly amused, but condescending sneer. 'Consolidation,' I said again, sounding like some sort of Paisley Dr Phibes. Any more arch and I'd be a listed fucking building.

The enforced restraint hadn't improved my mood any and by the time the meeting broke up I was feeling tetchy and mildly paranoid. Sensing this, Davie asked if I fancied a drink at the Anchor but I resisted the temptation, since I couldn't have trusted myself not to bad mouth Tommy Dolan in a wet wick, cissy way. All in all then, as I rang the doorbell of Brenda's flat, I was of a mind to give some fucker a bad half-hour.

'Albert, this is Stuart,' said Brenda and indicated a pale-skinned red-haired cunt sitting on the settee, holding my favourite mug between his knees. He didn't give me anything resembling a welcoming smile and neither, admittedly, did I he, but he did stand up to shake hands, presumably to let me see he was taller and less lardy than me.

'Hello, Albert,' he said, 'I've heard a lot about you.'

I wasn't having any disrespectful familiarity pish, so I reached my hand out and, instead of shaking, swiped the mug from his loose, complacent left paw. 'That's my cup,' I told him. 'Have you heard that about me?' He looked a bit startled by this petulant, rather childish outburst and a little smile started to play about his lips. Then he remembered stuff about me and binned the smile.

'That's actually Stuart's mug,' said Brenda, 'I was with him when he bought it in a craft shop in Jedburgh.'

'Shut up,' I told her. 'Go and wait in the bedroom.'

'What for?'

'Developments,' I told her.

I looked at Stuart and pointed again to the mug. 'My cup,' I said. Then I jerked my thumb at Brenda's receding arse. 'My woman. You remember that,' I said, 'and we'll get along lovely.' I left a little pause to see what he'd do. But he didn't do anything. He just looked at me blankly, wondering why I'd left a little pause. I decided, as it were, to consolidate. 'And will you remember?' I asked him. His cheeks went slightly red and a wretched look appeared in his eyes. 'Will you?' I said again. I wanted this conversation to conclude with a full stop and not just three fucking dots. He waited till the bedroom door clicked shut then gave me a brief, almost imperceptible nod. 'Good,' I said. I thrust the mug at him. 'Now go and make us all a nice cup of tea.'

I'd like to report that he did just that. But he didn't He just stood, with his present from Jedburgh in his hand, looking stricken. For a moment though, before he pulled himself together, I'm convinced he thought about it.

*

I've never liked clubs. I've always felt like a misfit, standing in the wrong clothes, drenched in blue light, shouting intimate things at the top of my voice into the ear of some unknown woman who doesn't fancy me. I can't cold sell myself in those sort of situations, I prefer the warm stroke and pummel of the social massage, the party at a friend's house, or a gathering of business colleagues where I can be skilfully back lit by the seductive allure of fabled achievement. 'You see him over there with the Kenzo suit and the head in the carrier bag, you know who that is, don't you?'

I'm exaggerating, of course, but you get the point. The first club I ever went to was the Maryland, in Glasgow. I was sixteen and it was the sixties, it should have been a marriage made in heaven but it wasn't. I liked the music, loved the music, the Ethiopians, Ben E. King, Otis Redding. I mean to this day I've never bought Wilson Pickett's 'In the Midnight Hour' because I don't want the brass section in the middle to turn ordinary. But the trouble was, every cunt who went there was obsessed with looking cool and in my opinion there's nothing more conformist than an excess of cool. The dress code was ferocious. Unless you wore a suit with the requisite length of vent, sleeveless pullover, brogue shoes, white shirt, button-down only, no tab or pin collars, recognized tie with some sort of establishment motif, preferably the Royal Artillery or Coldstream Guards, or some such pish, then you stood out like Grampa Joad at the Viper Room. Bear in mind, this was the generation that elsewhere was burning its draft cards. So the point is, I couldn't hack it in a club. A sixteen-year-old, with access to a speedboat, who couldn't get his hole. Mind you, I might've done if I could have carried the fucker in on my back and ferried some bint home in it via the Forth and Clyde canal.

'Ah, the follies of youth, Albert,' I hear you empathize, 'but you're a mature man now, with a divorce and the blood of many dead cunts on your hands, what is the relevance of your stroll, delightful though it is, through the blue-remembered holes of youth?' Well, basically, from being a chap who didn't like clubs, I now found myself the owner of a pair of the cunts. Of course, I use the term 'owner' in a loose-fitting criminal sense. John Leask and Robin Tierney were still sole proprietors of Salsa One and Blue respectively. I was happy with that. Didn't have a problem with that. Respected their right to do so. So why then, after they employed and paid me as a 'consultant' did both clubs head for the drain like a fag end in the gents trough on a Friday night? Well, first up, I suggested some changes might be made. I dispensed with the current crop of doormen and put in my own chaps. Needless to say, I charged for this service. I also dispensed with Bryan Bennett and his equivalent over at Salsa One, a part-time DJ name of Tugg. From now on, my chaps would supply and serve the needs of both clubs and their patrons. Tugg took this blow without complaint and steamed off into the sunset, but Bennett made a nuisance of himself, threatening reprisals from his 'formidable' friends. I was compelled to warn him that if he spoke to these friends about any of the club's private business, up to and including the use and abuse of heads, he wouldn't need to spend any more money on his fucking stupid haircuts. He appeared to take this threat seriously, which relieved me, as I truly wasn't keen to put it into practice, being all too aware that another violent incident might be pushing my luck over the edge. Some people though, wouldn't take a telling.

Another significant change I made was the slashing of admission charges at each club. Six quid a shot was, in my view, prohibitive and, while the patrons might tolerate it on a weekend, it would still impact upon the sales of the commodities within the establishment and do little to encourage visitors during the lean nights from Monday to Thursday. So I cut admission to a pound on a weeknight and four on Friday and Saturday. Naturally enough, this drastic reduction had the effect of altering the class of clientele to which the clubs played host. Both clubs, though on occasion rowdy, were nevertheless regarded as upper-end establishments. Meaning, in a Paisley sense, that people with jobs brought their girlfriends in and wore their new clothes to go there. Within a month these well-feds had moved on, panicked, like a herd of nervous gazelles, to the safer pastures of Glasgow and the coast. The rat faces had moved in, with their pimply skin and ersatz labels, their home-made tats and low-grade, ravenous tastes. I now sold Buckfast and Thunderbird in addition to JD and Barcardi and, through the thoughtful innovation of a confectionery counter, was able to accommodate those clients with blood sugar requirements who might otherwise have felt the pull of the all-night garage too strong to resist. We operated a strict policy on drugs. All clients were frisked and any mind-altering substances removed and confiscated, which is to say consumed or sold on by the frisker. Small-time dealers had to check in their goods in a special room, off the door, like gunslingers in a Western, though in this case their property wasn't returned when they left, but counted and a 50 per cent levy placed on all sales. If the terms of this arrangement proved unsatisfactory, they were invited to deal, free of charge, from the comfort of a street corner or midden, at any point no less than a one-mile radius from either club. This policy was robustly enforced and when Tommy Dolan was compelled to take a brick to the hands of an offender following an infringement, the lesson was not lost on any potential transgressor.

So it was that a tablet of E became viewed as a hallmark of celebration, the Bollinger of drugs, while wee mini wraps of brown in the toilets gave a wryly amusing slant to the familiar television slogan 'Ready, Steady, Cook'. Davie's sister and her wispy-haired man enjoyed house jellies in my office on her birthday and Granny Babs called to complain about Tommy, it having been her nephew he'd bricked. In short, I was running the clubs into the ground. Both Leask and Tierney, powerless to stop me, grew keen to conclude a change of ownership deal before word spread to the licensing authorities and their names were for ever blackened. So within a further month, I held the controlling interest in both premises and could look forward to restoring them to the elegant grandeur they had formerly enjoyed before heathen hands, namely my own, had defiled them in such a brutal manner. Naturally, a makeover was in order so that the unpleasant memories of the recent past might be visibly expunged. I had the exteriors painted gleaming white, with stylized black graffiti strategically emblazoned as a wind-from-sails gesture to budding local scriveners. As an afterthought I changed the club names. I fancied something crisp that might catch the eye. After brief consideration the answer presented itself. I called one club Calum's, and the other Darko's in tribute to my sadly departed colleagues. I felt sure that somewhere, on high, they were looking down at me and nodding.

The following morning, I received a call on the

mobile that startled me. A weak, phlegmy voice said, 'Hello, son, it's your da.'

'Well hello stranger,' I said, 'how's it going?'

There was a bit of breathless wheezing then he said, 'Not so good, I've been mugged.'

He left a pause and it dawned on me I was expected to play the dutiful son. I told him not to move, I'd be right over. But of course I didn't go right over. I was scrambling some eggs with one hand, at the time, while moving fingers about inside Brenda with the other and I was keen to slake both appetites before confronting some whiney old man in torn stockings. Because I was feeling beneficent, I gave Stuart a shout in the spare room and handed him in some tea. It doesn't do to behave in an over-villainous fashion with people you live in close contact with, they've too many opportunities to catch you off guard and do you in. I once knew a wronged wife who poured a pan of boiling water over the head of her armed robber husband while he sat in his recliner watching *Through the Keyhole*. Fourteen skin grafts later he was the only criminal in London who had to wear a stocking over his head even when he wasn't working. The thing is, women are more vicious at retribution than men, and as devious as fiends. When I put this argument to Felice once, she agreed that it was true, but only because retribution was an aggressive act and therefore came from the masculine side of the female character.

In other words men were to blame for the faults of women. You can't buy low cunning like that, can you? On the other hand, if it were true, the reverse might also be the case. If this Stuart started to feel emasculated or whatever, then he might want to assert his manliness by behaving like some vicious woman. In truth, he didn't look the sort, he seemed a bit milk and water in my opinion, but then, fuck me, if Cindy could pick up a client who cared enough to mug him, then anything was possible. Either way, I made the cunt a cup of tea, ate my eggs, poked Brenda from behind in the kitchen, then puttered off round to see Cindy.

'They got my pension book, but they didn't get my purse, it was under my bacon. My bacon saved me.'

'What bacon?'

He was sitting on his settee. He had a mouth on him like a couple of burst plums and an Elephant-man lump on his forehead.

'The bacon in my handbag. It was for my supper after I got back from my shift.'

His shift. He still talked like he sweated eight hours a day in the steel foundry. 'How many of them were there?'

He looked at me tetchily, like I hadn't been listening. 'One, I told you.'

'But you said they.'

'I always say they,' he said, 'if you'd listen more, you'd notice.'

So it was my fault he talked in meaningless plurals. There was more of the woman about this old cunt than a few corns and a FraserCard after all. 'And he didn't get your money?'

'No,' he said, 'even if he'd got my purse, he wouldn't have got my money. I keep my money somewhere else.'

'Where else?'

He hesitated before answering, the old fucker, like he was working out whether to trust me. 'In my shoe,' he muttered through his plums. 'Keep it to yourself. You don't know what they're like round here.'

'Nothing like you, I'll bet,' I said. I gazed, lazily, around the room. There was a photo of me on the mantelpiece.

'Do you want me to take you up the A & E for an X-ray?'

'I've been for an X-ray. The polis drove me to the Southern after it happened. They were magnificent.'

I smirked, I admit, at 'magnificent'.

'Aye, smirk,' chided Cindy, 'but next time you're burgled, try calling a criminal. Anyway, the young doctor took one look at my injuries and I was saw right away.'

'Why didn't you ring me? I'd have taken you in.'

'Three o'clock in the morning, what good would you have been?'

'What good am I now?'

He didn't answer this. He didn't want to admit he just wanted company and a good bleat. He gave a wee irritable sigh.

'The town drag's changing, Albert. It's not the place it used to be. Rough boys, in motors, pummelling folk's bodies for a laugh.'

'You've changed too,' I told him. 'You'd never have called it the drag before. The papers never called it that till a few holes got murdered.' Which was true. Poker-up-the-arse demi-perm columnists had taken to calling those few shitty fly-blown streets, 'the drag'. It made them feel sassy and smart, like they were all female Joe Fridays with their collars up, stalking the Big Bad City in the small hours, instead of the cosy fuckers they really were, who whined about their expenses and measured social progress by the size of their conservatories. If a hole moved in next door, they'd be the first cunts to have the Residents Association thumbing through Yellow Pages for a hit man.

'That's not what I mean,' said Cindy. 'Habits are changing. The lasses are still out there but the clients aren't. The clients are feart of being lifted by the polis. The murders have drove the clients off the streets and into the flats. You can get a Kosovan hole up Blackhill for a tenner a poke! It's crazy money! Decent, ordinary, Scottish holes can't compete. If you ask me it's them that's committing the murders to stimulate business.'

'The Kosovan holes?'

'No. Him.'

'Who him?'

'That Danny Wooler.'

And it was right then I realized what the next tentacle of my criminal empire should be. And what my next step should be. Ecstasy is the new Ecstasy. But Cindy had one more surprise for me.

'One good thing,' he said, taking a squint at himself in his hand mirror, 'at least it happened after rather than before.'

I was already on my feet and heading to the bog for a pre well-must-be-off-now piss. 'Before and after what?' I shouted back to him.

'My television appearance.'

I swear my arc froze halfway to the bowl. I clumped back into the living room, forgetting to flush. 'What television appearance?'

'My appearance. On television. I'm to be in a documentary about girls on the drag.'

'You're not a girl, you stupid cunt. You've a cock and balls sweating under them tights.'

'I'm on the drag though.'

'And stop calling it the fucking drag. You're the only drag up there. And who'd want to beef you, it'd be like riding fucking Widow Twanky.' If I'd been disturbed by his last television appearance, I was bricking it over this one. I stopped shouting and sat down calmly, so as not to rile him. I didn't want him joining the fucking Tiller Girls out of spite. 'How did this come about?' I asked him, as evenly as I could.

He sat back in his armchair like it was a throne, enjoying the attention. 'They did a programme a couple of months ago about drugs on the street.'

Yes,' I said, I saw it.'

'They interviewed a few of my fellow rides. One or two of the television people noticed me.' He couldn't keep the little flicker of preening pride from his lips as he said this. I'll bet they did, I thought, I'll bet they noticed you. I felt my heart sink, as I remembered the *Frontline Scotland* special I'd watched with Brenda, and of the horror I'd experienced on seeing the hideous apparition of Cindy, slinking into the back of the shot. 'Anyway,' he went on, 'recently one of the lasses was found folded, in a skip, wrapped in a roll of carpet.' He flicked back some imaginary lock of hair from his eyes. 'So they obviously thought it would be a nice time to do a programme devoted to our work and, well, my name came up.'

I heard the alarm bells clang, fit to burst my eardrums.

Firemen slid down the poles of my nerve ends. 'Your name?' I said slowly. 'What name did you give them?'

'Cindy,' he said.

I relaxed.

'Cindy Blaney.'

I tensed. There's no cunt like an old cunt. 'What did they get you to talk about?'

'Relax,' he said. 'I kept your name out of it.'

'My name's Blaney,' I said. 'It's in it.'

He gripped the arms of his chair and fidgeted. He was silent for a moment, but I could hear a sort of gastric thunder of words rumbling about in his ancient guts. Finally he shat them out. 'Well it's my life, isn't it? I'm entitled to my own experience! It doesn't belong to you!' I wanted to hit him, or hug him, but preferably hit him. Unfortunately, some young roustabout had beaten me to it and I didn't want anybody's sloppy seconds. I ran my hand up and down the velveteen arm of the settee. 'Don't do that,' he said mechanically, 'you'll take the pile off.'

How could I blame him? What sort of life did he have? He was an old man, living on an estate where there was so much crime you could pay the muggers by direct debit. He'd gone from being ignored for his entire working life to invisible once he'd retired, how could he fail to melt like an ice cube on a radiator when those nice friendly telly people had courted him? There should be an offenders' register for current affairs producers, they should be named and shamed on billboards like drunk drivers in Texas. When you boiled it down, what Cindy had done wasn't much removed from my own efforts at self-expression. I had written a book, he'd confided to a camera. The difference was I wrote from solitude, he blabbed from loneliness. The former was empowering, the latter pathetic; though it's true the two might, on occasion, overlap. I resented them for using him less than I despised him for being used.

'So what did you tell them?'

He looked at me a bit pleadingly. 'Nothing,' he said, 'hardly anything.' He looked anxious, eager to please. 'They talked to two or three other lasses as well, you know, not just me.' When he said that, I entertained thoughts of escape, that maybe Cindy might be smuggled through on the arms of others, like some grotesque dummy in a British prisoner of war film. If he were recognized, I'd find myself in the tabloid limelight, if he wasn't, I could skulk around in the shadows, where it was safe. Of course as soon as I'd thought that, he opened up his blundering yap again and jumped right in.

'Mostly, they just filmed me.'

'Where?' I asked him. 'Where did they film you?'

'Here,' he said, 'where you're sitting now.' I found myself springing up and staring intently at the dented cushion. 'They filmed me relaxing at home, then going out in the evening, to queue for my bus, on my way to work. Only I was just pretending to go to work, to save them paying overtime rates to their crew.'

As I looked around the room, I could imagine the hollow voiceover of one of those crap Scottish actors; he'd be biting his cheek and thinking about his dead granny or some crap rival cunt who'd got the part of tough-talking Dr McGregor ahead of him in *Casualty*, anything to keep the giggle out of his voice as he watched

Cindy pottering about the kitchen in his fishnets, stuffing corned beef into a bap for his tea break between the rides. If he ever got any rides, which, as I've intimated, I doubted.

'No,' said Cindy, 'rest assured I played it cagey. All I said to them was . . .'

As his mouth moved, I heard a poncy voice in my head say, 'A spry and vivacious pensioner, Cindy is the oldest of the city's working girls. But this isn't her chief distinction. Oh no, she also has an Adam's apple and is the only one of Glasgow's street girls to have undergone a vasectomy. For by day, Cindy is retired labourer . . .'

I looked at Spry Vivacious as he droned. This cunt wouldn't need to open his yap. They say a picture is worth a thousand words, probably ten thousand if they're as tediously crap as the stuff he babbles; but let's face it, if I saw Cindy on the telly in that fucking tea cosy wig, not only on the pull, but expecting to be paid for it, I'd be having a right good guffaw to myself with my mates later on in the local. If I had mates. Or a local. Cindy was one of life's top-value, low-rent, economy-sized geeks. Fair dos. But I, spawn of his ambivalent loins, was a hard man. Over decades, I'd built up, diligently, a reputation for thuggish violence that was rarely equalled and never surpassed. If I was in the clown business, fair enough. 'Ha ha,' I'd chortle, 'let's all ho ho at Cindy.' But I wasn't in the clown business. My life depended on Front. Meaning it not only depended on my actions, but on the wary anticipation in others of what those actions might be. It's not only boastful but true to say I was a feared man. The Surgeon, remember? Crossed hatchets, cold eyes, all that pish, right? Then along trots my father in a silk thong and Jane Norman skirt to trash the image. And yes, he'd bought them specially for the show because he, what else, 'wanted to look my best'.

I had choices, of course, I could've killed him: symbolically, perhaps poetically, with one of his own chiffon scarves; just wrapped it round a cleaver and battered the cunt for a while. Patricide didn't bother me, I'd watched this fucker die before, remember, the day Cindy was born, once more wouldn't make any difference. But, to be honest, the timing was bad. With the programme coming out, his appearance, or more to the point his disappearance, would be noted for a change, and there'd be every likelihood of some great big hoo-ha if yet another cunt known to me was to take unexpectedly dead in the Paisley vicinity. Also, I'd no idea who'd seen me enter his flat and I'd have no control over who saw me leave. So all in all, I'd no alternative but to leave my father's head where it belonged; atop his sequinned shoulders and below that scratchy monstrosity he thought made him look like Doris Day. Fucking Robin Day more like, and I'd sooner have dug Robin up and shagged him dead than Cindy live.

*

When I got back, I'd tried talking the matter over with Brenda, but she wasn't much interested. Notice I didn't say, 'got home'. The fact was, that after my last foreshortened visit to Bayswater, I now considered my London flat even less of a 'home' than before but that didn't mean I'd chucked any extra unfulfilled domestic longings in Brenda's direction. The problem was that the

Stuart situation had turned, predictably, difficult. Not from my point of view, I hasten to add, but from his. And, if I'm honest, hers.

After three nights, he'd moved out. After three more, he moved back in again. He was 'in turmoil', he explained, 'all this' was tearing him apart. We'd sat at the kitchen table, all three of us, and I'd rummaged around in the pit of my being for some sort of caring tone to use and urged him to talk. I was gleefully hoping he'd dig his own grave, women having little sympathy for men they feel sympathetic towards. But while there was the occasional quaver in his clumsy workie voice as he staggered over hurdles like 'respect for your feelings' and 'nurturing relationship' he didn't dissolve into the satisfying spectacle of blubbering wretchedness I'd hoped to witness. In fact, he came over as sincere and dignified, the cunt. It made me wonder whether it was the times or Brenda that had changed. In the old days she'd never have been amenable to any signs of weakness in a man. But then, in the old days, she'd been young. Anyway, the upshot was that things settled down after that into some sort of uneasy peace. All the same, I detected a change. And, as usual, it was in bed that it made itself most manifest. At first, following Stuart's tipping of his agony basket onto the kitchen table, I'd got Brenda tanked up on M&S food-hall claret before bed. With that, and a subtle application of weasel words, I'd been able to convince her that the close presence of this pale-skinned Dulux of Arabia through the wall was actually a salty enhancement to sex rather than a constraining factor. She'd gone along with this warped titillation in that dopey, confused way that women do, before an accidental bout of sobriety had brought her, unexpectedly, to her senses during intercourse.

'What's up?' I asked her.

'Nothing.'

Her eyes were wide open and I got the impression they'd been so for some time while I'd been pumping merrily away. One of those chill couply silences was filled by the sound of Stuart's coughing, not in the room, but through the wall. It was a quiet cough, thoughtful almost, scarcely a cough at all, but it dawned on me that it wasn't so much him clearing his throat as sending a message to her, his heart's desire. Through the magical love language of phlegm, he was saying to Brenda, 'I'm still here for you.' I couldn't work out from her look, in the dim light, whether this missive was welcome or unwelcome but, women being women, I surmised it was probably both. Either way, there was more than enough light for me to read the warning signs.

I didn't confront him directly, next day at breakfast. I mean, how could I? 'Have you been coughing at my woman, you bastard?' How paranoid would that sound? But what I did do was place a bottle of Sudafed, you know, that stuff for dry ticklish coughs, in his cornflake bowl where he couldn't miss it. Of course, the real test would be if she started coughing back at him, dueting, so to speak, like a couple of bronchial Paisley operatics. I'd have to part them with a sneeze, like a wicked uncle.

Chapter Thirteen

Running a bunch of hooligans is like running a government, you have to keep your cabinet focussed on targets or complacency sets in. We lost Lee Fraser to an actual bodily harm charge following an affray near the abbey. He'd been going to the aid of Picken, who'd been mouthing at some Rangers fans as they went by on their supporters' bus and when the bus stopped at lights, about half a herd of these fans got out and went for him. A knife was used, a leg was stabbed and Fraser who, to my knowledge, never carried a knife, took the blame. The net result of this was that we lost both chaps; Picken drifting off in a pouting huff after being cold-shouldered by the others for his stupidity. Luckily, a timely diversion appeared that raised morale and should have prevented any further outbreaks of internecine bickering.

'Talk about laugh,' said Dolan, 'I've seen that old fucker up at Woolies, buying pic 'n' mix. Nobody would touch the plastic shovel after it.'

It was a wet Wednesday afternoon. We were in my office at Darko's. I was standing, leaning on my desk, trying to appear indulgent and superior.

'Me too,' sniggered Casey. 'I watched it going up an escalator at the Braehead Centre. It was peeking at itself in the mirror and sucking in its cheeks. It thinks it's fucking beautiful!'

'Escalator, eh? Bet you hung around at the bottom for a swatch up his kilt.'

'Aye, man, unbelievable. I thought he was carrying onions in a string bag till I realized it was his bollocks.'

I flew at Casey and pinned him to the door by his throat. I said something like 'Shut the fuck up, you fucker,' something erudite along those lines. I was incensed. I couldn't stand back and let them take the name of the Prick in vain. That was my privilege. Like I say, laughing at the ludicrous cunt who was my father should have mopped up any potential for bickering among the infantry. But it didn't. I, Field Marshal Albert, DEDC, Donkey's Ears and Dunce Cap, had seen to that. Dolan separated us and Davie pulled me off, in his Davie way, gently, by the elbow. After the usual microsecond of exploding sincerity, I'd rotted down into performance. By the time I'd allowed myself to be sat down on my typist's chair and calmed with a nip of malt, I was well into character as Me. I did seething-and-glaring acting and made some jerky don't-patronize-me-I-can-erupt-at-any-moment body movements.

'Why are you so het up?' said Dolan. 'Anybody would think he was laughing at you.' He turned to Casey, 'You weren't, were you, Kev?'

Casey looked flushed and was rubbing his throat. Neither by word nor gesture did he confirm or deny Dolan's proposition. I knew this was because he was turning over in his mind whether or not he could take me. If truth be told, there is no doubt he could. But he didn't have the will. If he took me that would put him in charge. And he wasn't born to be that sort of animal. So that was one of the reasons he didn't punch my lights out. The other was I'd by now visibly demonstrated that of which I was capable. At my feet was a waste-paper basket where a head once rolled. He'd have to finish what he started or wear an iron turtleneck for the rest of his life, just in case. Grudgingly, Casey grunted out the words, 'Just a joke,' and I realized that would have to suffice by way of fulsome apology. I feigned an equally grudging forget it gesture and the ice in the room began to drip a little. In actual fact I was only too happy to accept an apology, however constipated, and was mightily relieved that Kevin hadn't turned on his dainty heel and flounced off, like Picken. On the desk, under the glass of Talisker in my fist was a *Daily Mirror*, open at page seven. If I mention that the headline read 'Telly Slapper Cindy is Top Gangster's Pop', you'll grasp the import. The page number matters, I always prefer an even number for an unflattering story, because that means it'll be on a left-hand page. It's well known that people pay less attention to the left-hand stuff, so things can sometimes slink by unnoticed. But no, page seven it was. The Prick at the bus stop. Scratchy wig. Tesco bag. White denim jacket, the lot. And me. Or rather a recent shot of me at the Cuntess's funeral, one I hadn't even realized they'd taken. In the holligan game, there was always someone looking at you.

'It's not like you to be so touchy,' said Dolan. He'd pulled up a chair and was sitting with his hands outstretched on the desk, irking me, so that I had to resist another eruption. I took out a cleaver from a drawer and threw it against the wall opposite. It didn't stick though, when your luck's out, it's out, instead it clunked with an unseemingly clatter to the floor. Dolan didn't flicker. 'Keep your head, Albert,' he said. He had his little smile on. But I chose to interpret it as benign. The programme had gone out the previous night. I'd hoped to sit and watch it with Brenda, have a good rant, then allow her to console me with womanly assurances that, as usual, I'd got it all out of proportion and that it wasn't nearly as bad as I thought. I mean that's what molls are for, isn't it, mollifying? Only she wasn't available, was she? Stuart had played the grandkid card, and she'd gone over to visit her, with him. So I'd been left to sit and stew, to absorb the affront on my own.

The telephone rang. As I answered I watched Davie pick up the cleaver. Being Davie, he took a crumpled paper hanky from his pocket and gave the edge a little thoughtful rub. It occurred to me that the next fucker to take a tap from that cleaver would be in more peril from tetanus than the wound itself.

'Darko's,' I said into the phone.

A voice hesitated, then spoke back to me. 'Is that you, Albert?'

I had a sensation of smelling stale rolling tobacco from down the line. 'Yes, Claw. Long time no see.'

He gave a grateful little chuckle, relieved not to be on the receiving end of any oaths, or vows of vengeance for weaselly sins he most likely couldn't even remember committing. 'We spend a lot of time saying that, you and me, eh, Albert?'

Chumminess from Hammill made me feel uncomfortable, like when the local scabby cat rubs up against your bare leg on holiday. 'A lot's changed since the last time we said it,' I reminded him. It wasn't a tester. I knew he most likely knew everything. I kept silent to let the greasy cunt get on with his sympathy. He didn't.

'I was up Harvie's last night, Albert.'

'Oh yes?'

'Bryan Bennett was in. You know him, don't you?'

I told Claw we'd met. 'What about him?'

Dolan was peeling back Sellotape from a trussed-up carrier bag. It made a rasping sound that spooked Claw. 'Who's that with you?'

'My tiny nephews, home from their Ladybird Group,' I told him. 'What about Bennett?'

'He was pissed. He was telling anybody who'd listen about, you know, you and your tiny nephews and that. And, uh, Darko.'

'So what, it's just talk. Vicious rumour from a man with a grudge.'

'What is?'

'Everything he said.' It occurred to me that Claw didn't know the whole story after all. 'Just what did he say anyway?' I pulled myself up. I was annoyed for allowing my mouth to become exercised through guilt. It was the prospect of this sort of behaviour that had made me slip prudently back to London. And now imprudently back up again. I listened to Claw but was watching Dolan as he fished his hand around inside the carrier bag. Claw was telling me that Bennett had made an arrangement to meet the polis the following night. He mentioned a pub in the Broomielaw where polis go. He suggested that I might like to speak to Bennett before he spoke to the polis. 'Hold on a minute, Claw,'

I covered the mouthpiece and looked at Dolan. 'What's that?' I said.

He laid out two guns on my desk. 'Astra .357. They're Spanish.'

'I know they're fucking Spanish,' I said. Though I didn't. 'What the fuck are you doing with them?'

'Three hundred sheets apiece,' said Kevin.

'We've been saving from our paper round, Uncle Albert,' said Dolan.

Claw was still gibbering down the phone, even though I'd told him to shut it. 'We'll discuss this in a minute,' I told Dolan and Casey.

'We can get AK 47 Kalashnikov rifles for well under a grand,' said Casey.

'In a fucking minute!' I shouted again. It was like the cunts were talking about Pokemon cards. I realized how mothers must feel when they're trying to deal with brats and hold a sensible conversation at the same time. 'Where will I find Bennett?' I asked Claw. I could sense his nerves and picture him standing in a corner of some bookie's all fetid, and squeezing his cock in a pincer movement for comfort. 'You never heard it from me, okay?' he said.

'Just tell me fucking where!'

He named a brothel at an address in the south side of Glasgow, up near Maxwell Road.

'Oh, yes?' I said.

He sounded surprised. 'You know it?'

'Not as well as you, maybe.'

'There's no need for that,' said Claw. 'I'm doing you a big favour here.'

'You're doing yourself a favour,' I told him, 'there's no Calum or Darko now, who the fuck else is going to bother their arse with you?'

'You, hopefully,' said Claw. I had to chuckle. I didn't want to but I had to. I was the King of Paisley now and Claw had just, in his roundabout Scottish way, acknowledged that fact. 'By the way, Albert, sorry about your dad.'

'Fuck off.'

I hung up. Davie had removed the guns and was working, with a damp finger, at a scratch on my leather desktop. Tommy and Kevin were standing shoulder to shoulder, resolutely bracing themselves for an argument. I cranked myself up to oblige. 'Fucking guns,' I said, glaring at Kevin. 'Remind me what you paid for them?'

'I'll tell you,' said Tommy, 'if you remind us what you paid for them scuzzy wee two twos and revolvers.'

I cranked myself down again. I could see Davie, still rubbing diligently, biting his cheek against mirth. 'What the fuck are you smirking at?'

'Nothing.'

'There's no point buying you a gun,' I told Davie, 'I'll just give you a tin of Pledge, you can polish cunts to death.'

'It's not as if we're charging them to the company nor nothing,' said Kevin, 'it's out of our own pockets.'

'Bloody right it is,' I said. I was still grumbling, as a sort of rearguard action, even though I knew I was, in this instance, fucked.

'That mean we can keep them then?' asked Kevin.

'Not my money is it?' I said. Tommy started putting the Astras away into a big bag, along with the little automatics and elderly revolvers. We'd started keeping firearms in the safe, since taking over the club, in case Davie had a break in. 'What'd you think you're doing with those?'

Tommy frowned at me, puzzled. 'How'd you mean?'

'You're going to be needing them fuckers.' I said.

And I remember how they looked at each other, all grins and excitement.

*

Brenda came home late from the grandkid visiting, which didn't surprise me. I knew she'd want to keep me on a rope and, if possible, twisting, hoping that tension would force some sort of conclusive showdown with Stuart. I'd had my seven-day free trial offer, now it was, 'Pay up or I pack away my suitcase full of top-quality quim samples.' Basically, it was another wedding ring or nothing, I knew that. So when I heard the door slam and Brenda's voice on the stairs, I howked the bottle of Cordon Rouge out the fridge. I'd set the table for two and by the time they stepped into the room, I'd managed, with a mighty effort from my purpling thumbs, to be pouring and smiling, suavely. 'Nice time?' I asked, all glidey and Jeeves-like.

'Uh-huh,' said Brenda, slowly. She was taking off her coat and looking at the little buffet of chicken drumsticks and cold ham on the table. 'What's all this?'

I didn't answer, just handed her a glass. Then I handed Stuart a glass. Then I picked up my own glass and raised it. 'To the future,' I said.

'The future,' said Stuart, a bit bemused. But he drank anyway.

'What's all this?' asked Brenda again. Only now she wasn't talking about the cheesy nibbles. Looking back, I flatter myself she looked a bit pale, but that may be just the rosy afterglow of spiteful memory. I ignored her question, preferring to let matters dawn on her by unspoken instalments. I put on my coat and drained my glass. Then I went into the bedroom and reappeared, holding my suitcase. Brenda realized she was clutching a glass and put it down in an irritated way on the table.

'Where'd you think you're going?'

'Easy, Brend,' said Stuart.

'Fucking shut it,' she shouted. 'What the fuck's going on?'

'Don't, Brend, that's what he wants.'

And it was, it was what I wanted. It wasn't what Brenda wanted though. She pined for pistols at dawn. It wasn't in the script that I should concede defeat. Which is to say, walk out on her again. And like this, in public; cowardice masquerading as a generous heart. My lover was silent; she did shut the fuck up; for it occurred to her that she could say little, do less, with Stuart around as witness to her emotions. I was spared the tantrums, the facial weals, the screeching threats delivered with and without knives, or saucepans. In short, the passion. Or perhaps, as I've said, I flatter myself. We'll never, she and I, know.

Stuart stood behind Brenda, and held her by the arms, gingerly, just in case. But she made no disapproving move. And nor did I. 'It's for the best,' I said and picked up my suitcase.

'I think so,' said Stuart. 'Have you somewhere lined up?'

'Let's see,' I told him, 'how should I put this? I hope to be living above the shop for a while.' I was doing perky-barrow-boy acting, even though I'm not a boy and I've never run a barrow. No matter how empowered we feel in a break up there's always some bit of us that's cowering in a corner, snivelling. I watched Brenda lay a gentle, discreetly indiscreet hand upon Stuart's; reassurance to him, get-it-up-you to me. To his credit, and mine, Stuart said, 'Well, good luck, Albert.'

I jiggled my suitcase in hand. 'Well, cheerio, Brenda,' I said. She didn't say anything. She was already engaged in the panicky struggle to tug her emotions out of me and transplant them into Stuart. I rummaged around for something suitably memorable to say.

'At least we'll always have Potterhill,' I told her. And I was gone.

But so was she.

*

That night I closed up Darko's on my own. I dismissed the chaps and sent them over to Calum's without inviting them to linger, as usual, for a nightcap in my office. I made an excuse of our important task with Bennett the following day, but really I just wanted to be left in peace to ruminate. I made up a sort of bed with coats and dust sheets on the floor, but when I heard scratching in the dark, I realized we had rodents, so I moved myself onto the desktop; as if a fucking mouse couldn't run up a table leg. Of sleep, of course, there was none. My back ached if I lay on it, my hip if I turned side-on, and my feet were fucking freezing no matter which way I folded myself. I should have had the prudence to book myself into a hotel before making my spontaneous farewell gesture but I wanted somewhere familiar to curl up in, and Darko's was as close to the fond idea of home as I could muster.

I supposed the Cuntess had felt the same thing that time she turned up from nowhere, out of the night, at Ralston. She had a black eye, I remembered, and her nose was runny with dark blood. The Prick was upstairs, so I'd answered the door. I was irked, because I'd been watching *Miss World* and warming up my cock for the swimsuit round. She sat on the settee, all snotty and smelling of fresh air, like she'd walked all the way there. I didn't know what to say. 'Where's your father? I phoned to tell him I was coming.'

'He's upstairs,' I said. 'What happened?'

'Take a wild guess.' She lit up a Kensitas. 'Anyway, how've you been?'

'I've been here,' I said.

'The man's an animal.' It was a voice that made us both look up. 'But then, you knew that.'

And there stood Cindy. And I recalled the faintest of slaps as the Cuntess's jaw hit her chest, followed by a rumble as the drawbridge to Castle Ralston thudded shut against her. There was a rear shot of the contestants in swimsuits. Miss Paraguay favoured us with a wedge of her arse cheek, thereby giving a welcome enhancement to my dismal routine of bed and sleep.

'In the name of God!' exclaimed my mother, putting her hand to her puffy mouth.

You could tell she didn't know whether to laugh or cry. When he was Cindy, he had that effect on a lot of people; though not, for some time past, me. Cindy stood, defiant and proud, savouring his moment. He'd dreamed of this; of besting his wife in his manly way, by turning woman. *Once I had a Secret Love*, had been their favourite record. Cindy's secret love was himself. Healed at last, he had neither room nor need for any other. Whip-crack-away and my mother was gone, horrified. And in a way, so too, was my father. Long live, the Prick and the Cuntess.

Soon afterwards, she and Billy summoned me to the Big House and I went to see it out of curiosity. I never went back much to Ralston after that. Not even for Father's Day. Or Mother's Day, whatever.

Chapter Fourteen

I saw the cunt first and shouted, 'There he is!' but too loudly. Bryan Bennett was standing at the entrance to the tenement close talking into his mobile, then his eyes met mine and whoosheroony, he was on his heel and off. We'd catch him though, Tommy and Kevin were fast as fuck though Davie wasn't, which at least took the bad look off Uncle Albert. We reached the close in time to hear his feet on the stairs, so we knew he hadn't fucked off out the other end, even though the back door was only half a door with one buckled rusty hinge. Tommy and Kevin were already on the upstairs landing by the time me and Davie had hit the first step and we could hear the sharp, echoey shouts of all and sundry as Kevin tried to stop the door from slamming with whatever body part had been closest to Bennett before he'd jumped into the lobby of the flat that was Danny Wooler's brothel.

'Hold him, Tommy!' Davie was shouting, I suppose in lieu of contributing something useful.

As I galloped up the stairs, I could hear Kevin yelling, 'Aya, my heid, my fucking heid!' which at least answered the question of what he was using for a doorstop.

'Leave it ya prick, we've got fucking guns!' I arrived in time to see Tommy trying to stick the barrel of his lovely new Astra into the gap of the door and at that point Bennett must have decided to let go because Tommy and Kevin both fell arse over tit into the lobby. I heard an interior door slam as they were picking themselves up and I remember shouting, 'Which door, which door?' Tommy was pointing the gun vaguely ahead but he didn't shoot it, which pleased me, because apart from anything else a gunshot in a tenement flat makes a helluva racket. There were a lot of doors in this flat, a typical DSS-looking gaff, with rooms on both sides of a long corridor and a honk of sweat that caught you at the back of your throat. A dark skinny lassie in a bra and thong ran out, squealed and ran back in again. It was like a fucking saloon scene from *Carry on Cowboy*. I ran in after her waving a cleaver, but there was only a bare-naked fat cunt on a bed who started to hide his face as if I was part of a documentary film crew. I turned and ran into the room opposite, following Davie, but he was coming out as I was coming in, so we hit each other and I got a fleeting glimpse of two more bints standing shivering in a corner, shielding their fannies. Mind, if they were working in this pit, they were about a thousand rides too late. It must've been then I heard feet on the stairwell outside, hitting the stone stairs hard, and jumping, several at a time, a man in flight. The door across the corridor was at an adjacent angle and three-quarters open and I ran in expecting to see Davie. But I didn't see Davie. I think I even shouted, 'Davie?' And I realized then who the running man was and I was thankful he'd got away, even if I hadn't. Or Tommy. Or Kevin.

'Hello, cunt,' said Mick.

'King Cunt, isn't it, Albert?' asked Danny Wooler.

They both had guns, though it was Mick's which caught my eye since it was an old army Bren gun. He saw me looking, tilted it, and said, 'Lovely old piece, isn't it? A grand. Same cunt you bought yours from.'

'All the youngsters are wearing them,' said Danny Wooler.

'Quiet, Dan,' said Mick.

I looked around the room, my senses calming to take in the detail. Though why anything inside me should have calmed, I've no solid idea. There were four other men with guns. I vaguely recognized one, a ginge called Corcoran who used to run a bingo hall in Pollok. Bennett had his head in a sink and was running his crimson face under a cold tap. Kevin should have been with him since he was bleeding from the gums and holding his jaw in place with his hand. I guessed he'd taken the end of the Bren in the mouth and when I looked there were teeth among the spunk stains on the carpet. Tommy was up against the wall, in body-search position, with feet and hands splayed. His legs were trembling and when he came down off his tiptoes some cunt would hit him in the ribs with the flat of a hammer. Someone, somewhere had been watching interrogation videos, or else visiting the Tricycle Theatre during its 'angry phase'. Either way, some cunt in the criminal world had finally got something right, and here we all were, victims and vanquished, scratching our heads and wondering how.

'You've been suckered, Albert.'

'You don't say.'

I took a fist in the face from Mick for my insolence and I must say I wasn't only hurt but shocked. Not to mention alarmed. In all the years I'd known him, Mick and I had never lain a finger on each other, so long as you discounted, that is, the time as kids when I'd spat in his face. Obviously my recent pranks had stoked up a deal of resentment. On the instant, I damped my insolence way down. I was deeply worried that Mick, having torn up the book of taboos, would now think, Fuck it, and be unable to restrain himself from further, perhaps greater, violent outbursts. That's how it worked with me, anyhow. So I remained still and silent, hoping not to further excite him. Like I've said, I've always been aware of the sharp edges that lie between hitting and getting hit. There, then, at that moment, I'd have done anything not to be badly hurt.

'Look at you,' said Mick, 'you'll do anything not to get dunted, won't you, Albert?' I glanced at him but didn't answer, being unsure quite what he required to hear. 'I know you, you soft cunt. Oh aye, I know you fine well.' He took the hammer from the guy who'd been tapping Tommy's ribs, then walked behind me and stopped. He let me hear the hammer's soft beating smack as he tapped out a clock rhythm on the meat of his palm. 'What would you do not to be dunted, Albert?' he asked.

'Let's get their cocks out!' shouted Danny Wooler.

'Quiet, Dan,' said Mick. He leaned in closer to me, his breath on my ear, comforting, human. 'Go on, Albert. What would you do?'

My mouth was a bit dry and I'd to fight the flutter in my voice in order to say it. But fair dos, and I can't tell a lie, I did hear myself say, 'What would you want me to do?'

And yes, hands up, I did it.

I'm not proud though.

'You can pick up these efforts through European agents, like footballers,' said Danny Wooler. He was explaining how a refugee was a blue-chip investment. 'A lot safer than drugs, or Marks and Spencer. Look at what's happened to M&S, just shows you.' We were standing by the open door while the men with guns worked between us. One had shooed away the fat cunt and Mick was ushering all the girls into a single room at the opposite end of the corridor. As they passed, Danny Wooler said, 'Albert, wait till you hear this, it's the best laugh.' He stopped a hurrying girl who was wearing a pair of tights, a pair of manky trainers and nothing else. I noticed she had a nipple missing. Just a neat round hole, like it had dropped out and rolled down a drain like a runaway coin. 'Say "fish and chips".'

'Fesh ang chees,' said the girl, and Danny haw-hawed, all tickled. 'Two grand,' he said to me, 'and I'll make fifty off her. Honest to God, sixteen hours a day, works through her bad week, flu epidemics, the lot. These lasses are grafters, Albert, I won't hear a word against refugees.' She looked early twenties; nervous, vulnerable, and out of her depth. Normally this would have stimulated me, but what with the nipple thing and the manky trainers, I felt no impulse connecting eye to dick. Anyway, I had a job to do.

Loud music from down the corridor became muffled music as Mick shut and locked the door of the room where the girls were. 'Right, that's us,' he said, pocketing the keys. He shouted to me as he walked back up the corridor. 'You ready, Albert?'

I nodded.

'I'm not making any promises, right?' warned Mick.

'I know,' I said, risking speech. 'We'll wait and see what Billy says.'

'That's right,' said Mick. He was starting to sound like a leader of men. Now I felt nervous, vulnerable and out of my depth. Mick gave a cursory squint around the room before nodding his approval 'Okay, in you go,' he said.

They had lain out a warehouseman's brown coat over a chair and spread fresh newspapers on the floor for the blood, and any shite or pish. I put on the coat and buttoned it up. Then I picked up the hammer. Kevin came in, naked, hooded with his own underpants and gagged with his own socks; hands tied behind his back with that old-fashioned, fibrous electrical flex. Kevin made to kneel, and I surprised his head with heavy pummels, not allowing him to settle, hoping to spare myself, and him, but chiefly myself, any fruitless, if muffled, pleading. After several minutes, when he'd stopped crawling, howling and twitching, I slid his carcass with my foot, like a clubbed seal pup, towards the far wall and the dingy screen of the window blind. I ran the cold tap in the sink and took a drink of water. Then I edged around the walls, opened the door quietly and nodded.

'The Surgeon will see you now,' said Wooler. Which was a cunt of a thing to do, as it didn't make my role, or Tommy Dolan's, any easier. I could smell Tommy's body heat as he passed me in the doorway; a faint warm whiff of underarm deodorant. His hot bare feet, I noticed, left dull, matt imprints on the shiny border of the lino. I say 'noticed' but of course I was looking, with a sort of detached inner glee, for little mental keepsakes of that order. He knelt and I let him kneel. I shouldn't have spoken, but seeing him there, pliable, so to speak, and at my disposal, I couldn't resist it.

'How are you feeling, Tommy?' I said. I unsocked his mouth to let him speak.

'Better than you, you scabby cunt. You're a fucking disgrace, Blaney.'

'Fair comment,' I said.

And I hit him.

When I was all finished I called out but nobody came in. I could hear a voice behind the door and then there was a big eruption of laughter. The door half opened and Mick looked in, his face all flushed and smiley and I realized he'd been telling, or listening to, a funny story. I pointed to the pulp by the window and he said, 'Fuck me. Very well done, Albert. You'll go far.' He said something else I couldn't hear and then the men with guns came in, only now they were without guns and holding big, stained dust sheets and cleaning stuff. It was all a bit perfunctory for my liking. I stood among them dripping sweat and blood, like Donald Wolfit after giving them his Lear, while the cunts just shuffled around me with squeegees and plastic buckets. Finally, Mick favoured me with a hand on the shoulder and said, 'Albert, there's a young man here who's been dying to meet you.' A tall, good-looking young blond chap, not unlike our own present and much-loved Prince William, stuck his hand out for me to shake. 'This is Jez,' said Mick, 'short for Jeremy.'

'Oh yes?' I said. I looked at Jez, short for Jeremy's hand, then at my bloodied own. 'Best not,' I said, and we all three shared a chuckle.

'Jez is up from Essex,' explained Mick, 'he's seen the cathedral and the Kelvingrove Art Gallery, now he wants to see a fucking good murder, eh, Jez?' He treated Jez to one of his big beefy smiles. If Mick was going out of his usual surly way to dispense social charm, I reasoned that this chap must be some sort of VIP, so strove to adapt my demeanour accordingly. After all, I was still, technically speaking, bargaining for my life.

'Essex?' I said. 'You'll know Young Joe Chisnall then, eh, Jez?'

'I work for Joe Chisnall,' said Jez, 'though he's not so young now, Albert.'

'Which of us is, sadly,' I said, 'eh, Mick?' I still wasn't sure what sort of note to wear for the occasion, and thought I'd risk a loose-fitting Loyal Family Retainer number.

'He's a great admirer of your work though.'

'And I was a great admirer of his father's work,' I said. 'God rest him.' This came out sounding bogus and craven, so I accelerated smoothly into another dewy reflection. 'Mind you, I haven't seen Young Joe in years.'

'Well now's your chance,' said Mick. 'He's sitting having tea and cake in Billy's.'

And I took off my coat and scrubbed my hands. Then we all walked downstairs around the corner to fetch the car. Which, as it happened, was the Bentley.

'Time of the month, Mick?' I said.

But Mick didn't engage. He just said, 'Get in the car, Albert.'

And this time I did.

We drove onto Maxwell Road, with its Bollywood video shops and crash repair centres, then right towards the city centre. A stain of sun appeared in the grey cloud fabric, momentarily warming my grateful knees and heart. Jez, short for Jeremy, sat next to me on the back seat. He didn't look so young with the daylight on his fizzer, early thirties maybe, and his fair hair had a lank look as though he spent too much time in loud and smoky Essex pubs. Nice suit though. 'Gieves and Hawkes?' I asked. He gave me a manic, uncomprehending look as he rummaged in his mind for a connection. I nodded at his suit.

'Oh,' he said, 'Principles. They had a closing-down sale.'

The sad, wise cunt that lives inside my head felt oddly touched by this reply while the shell outside, the Surgeon, he who craters heads and attempts to topple criminal empires, felt jaded and corrupt. A perversely satisfying sensation, as it happens. This boy was raw young talent done up in his good suit for an away day jolly, it couldn't help but take me back. After asking Mick's permission, I lit up a Marlboro Light and felt the bracing choke fill my lungs. Outside in the street, poor cunts were doing poor cunt things, walking about with loaves under their arms, looking vacant, or scowling. I turned to Jez. 'Not exactly an Essex name, is it?'

'What, Jeremy? My mum's idea. She was a big fan of Jeremy Hawk, you remember Jeremy Hawk?'

'*Criss Cross Quiz?*'

'That's it.' Jez looked pleased. I felt gleeful that he looked pleased. 'My mum liked him because he was posh. They're all the fucking same, aren't they, mums?'

'Yes,' I said, 'different.' I couldn't imagine calling any cunt mum, least of all my mother. I was glad when Jez had said fucking though, it showed he'd responded to my jovial good nature and felt relaxed; I wanted us all at a nice, comfortable, emotional room temperature prior to seeing Billy. Jez asked Mick if he could open a window for the smoke. Mick being Mick, he had to turn it into an issue.

'Smoke?' he said.

'Yes, is that a problem?' asked Jez.

'I cannae let the smoke out without letting air in. I don't like air in a car. Albert?'

'Yes?'

'Put that fucking fag out.'

I put that fucking fag out.

'My dad, he hated it,' said Jez.

'Smoking or Jeremy?'

'Jeremy. He couldn't stand it. So he called me Jez.'

'What does your dad do?'

'Not much. He's been dead since I was three. He used to do a spot of work for old Joe though.'

'Oh yes?' I said. 'What was his name?'

'Elkins,' said Jez, 'Desmond Elkins.'

All at once, I came over rather chilled.

'They called him Des,' said Jez.

'Yes,' I said. 'I know.'

'You must have good ears, Albert,' said Mick, without turning.

'Why's that?'

'To hear a penny dropping after thirty fucking years.' He laughed.

But I didn't laugh. 'Des and Jez,' I said.

'That's right,' said Jez, 'like a double act.'

Mick laboured at the ancient wheel, making it spin.

After a bit of cursing he found reverse and backed the old Bentley, crunching, onto a driveway. I wiped the steamy window with my arm and looked out. 'This is us,' said Mick.

And so it was. We were at Billy Waugh's house.

I rarely talk about the Braintree incident. Young Joe doesn't live in Braintree anymore, he lives in Tiptree, about half a mile from the jam factory, but in those days the Chisnalls lived in Braintree, it was the family seat. You only went there when you were summoned.

Sometimes, if you were lucky, you came back out again. You knew where you were with Old Joe, even if it was oblivion. I got summoned twice, at the end of the sixties. On the second occasion, he showed me the basement. 'This is the basement, Albert,' he said, and he had a look on him that made me know he wasn't asking me to put in a damp course. I'd just done a task for the Krays in the south Kent, a kneecapping with a hammer, and they'd admired the aplomb with which I'd desported myself. That's when Ronnie had said to me, 'You'll go far.' I was happy to start with knees but was keen to work my way up to heads and felt sure I'd done enough to merit another outing. Strictly speaking, I'd been farmed out to the Chisnalls; ostensibly to learn my trade but really because I'd been aggravating Billy. I disliked Essex, finding it a louder Paisley, but had always been attracted by the dark mythology of the East End. To an impressionable young man from the north, Whitechapel was Macondo. I wanted to be on cackling terms with Queenie Watts, to get the breeze up, whatever the fuck that was, drink pints of mild, then be called away on hooligan business, leaving the pretty wenches of Plaistow pining for my return. So I'd written a letter to a well-placed minor hooligan of the day and he'd effected an introduction to Ronnie Kray. This suited Old Joe quite well, since it was obvious my abilities were restricted to hitting people with hammers and around Braintree people carried hammers like Edwardian dandies did walking canes. In short, I seemed set fair, in my mind at least, for a productive career and I'd returned to Old Joe's fold ready to work with a will pending my triumphant return to the capital.

Which is when the incident occurred that changed everything.

To this day the matter is etched clearly in my mind though the details are murky. As usual, it commenced with the sound of a dropping bollock. We'd gone to a pub in Romford to have words with some local rivals and a rumpus had broken out, in the course of which an off-duty detective had become embroiled. We subsequently learned, to our dismay, that our timing had been awry and we'd actually interrupted a discreet gesture of financial gratitude these rivals had been making to the detective at the time. This would have proved little more than embarrassment all round were it not for the fact that some fingers, belonging to the detective, had been later handed in to Joe. When confronted, I remember telling Joe, 'I don't know anything about any fingers,' but he was having none of it. It was easier to blame me, an outsider, than to blame Young Joe, his beloved son who, I believed, was the true culprit. I say 'believed' but of course I'd been swallowed up in the heat of the fighting moment, as had we all, so who among us could truly say? In any event, people were nervous about these fingers and immature things started to happen. Joe was concerned that this was the excuse the local polis needed to barge in and have a right good rummage about his property.

Nowadays folk take it as read that guys like Joe were hand in glove with the polis but that's just romantic cynicism. It was never as easy as that. You could bribe some of the polis all of the time but you couldn't bribe all the polis all the time. They'd be on side so long as things were quiet, but as soon as some new Divisional Commander stepped in with a hymn book in his hand and a poker up his arse and started spearheading another corruption crackdown, it was a case of self-interest rules and every cunt for himself. Fair enough, a year down the track it was business as usual, but in the meantime people were walking on eggshells. Which was why Joe lead us down to the basement and kept banging on about these fucking fingers.

They were on a napkin and he was waving them about like they were a portion of chips and screaming, 'I'm a businessman, not a fucking hooligan, I can't be having chunks of people lying about my home, it's unprofessional! I didn't contradict, even though I knew he was talking bollocks. Only the previous week I'd taken possession of a set of ears at his behest. Joe was what might be described as thorough but lazy. He wanted proof that his instructions had been carried out without the inconvenience of getting up off his arse and visiting the location. Unlike his boy. Young Joe seemed to relish the involvement; a real coats off, sleeves up, let's-get-our-hands-dirty sort of thug; never happier than when he was up to his elbows in gore.

Anyway, Old Joe went to me, 'Now what about these digits, Albert? I think you owe me an explanation.' I knew I was in an awkward spot. Old Joe had accepted me down from Glasgow to learn violence at his knee and I hadn't been what you might call a popular addition to the squad. There'd been a bit of that tedious mumping about foreigners stealing our jobs and denying local talent a chance, all that minging, small-town crud. So anyway, the gang was all there, Joe's slinging me the beady and I was trying to appear calm and keep the flutter out of my voice. There was fear all over that basement and I didn't want it coming to rest in me, so I was doing my best to pass the parcel. I was taking these very shallow deep breaths as I spoke. I was trying to keep my heart rate steady and my mind was going like the clappers. I knew there was a spot of stimulation coming. Joe wanted his feed of mince, and I needed that parcel passed.

'I did a face, Joe, I'll own up to a face,' I heard my mouth say, 'knees and heads, certainly. That's my territory, but hands, you know me, Joe, they're just not my province.' He didn't know me, of course. Which was why I was carrying the can.

'A face you say? And did you make him a corporal?'

'A sergeant. Three stripes.'

And everybody chuckled a bit and the tension eased slightly. All except this one prick, who was a bit slow and was looking a bit puzzled. And my mouth was smiling and we were all having a bit of a guffaw which I knew wouldn't last, and I was looking genial and fresh faced but underneath I was honing in on this prick and thinking, You'll do. And Joe was enjoying himself because there was a dynamic in the room which he was controlling and he strapped on this look of concern and asked me more about the face. I steered him back onto the fingers because, truth to tell, there wasn't any face, I'd made that up. And to buy time I bowled him a googly by saying, 'How do we know they're actual policeman's fingers?'

Joe said, 'Why, should they have tenners sticking to them?'

I said 'No, but what if these fingers were intended to stir up unrest?' I could see he was at a bit of a loss, so I pressed on. 'I believe they've been dumped on us by someone in this room.'

A bit of what might be described as a frisson went around the basement. Joe looked a bit incredulous. He glanced about the place. He had relatives present. He looked at me and said, 'Who?'

I said, 'Somebody.'

He said, 'Do you have conclusive proof?'

I said, 'Very conclusive.'

He said, 'Well what are you going to do about it then?'

I said, 'Well I thought I might do this.'

And I shot out my arm and struck Mr Puzzled Prick in the chest with a boning knife. He went on one knee, looking a bit surprised. His mouth fell open, giving me an impression of impending speech, so I stopped and prodded a quick supplementary to his throat. I didn't want him holding any conversations at that particular juncture. We all stood around, watching him gurgle.

Old Joe said, 'How are you settling in at that boarding house?'

I explained that it was a little formal and unfriendly, with the other guests a good deal older than myself. I told him I intended to share a flat with friends, once I'd found a flat and some friends. But Old Joe said, 'Oh, don't do that, living with friends. You start getting under each other's feet. Next thing you know they're not your friends any more, they're your enemies. And who needs more enemies?'

'Not me,' I said.

'Nor me,' said Old Joe. 'But you've got some now.' He gave the body a little jab with his toecap to check for pain or death or whatever then he said, 'Better pack your bag and go home, Albert.'

'What, home to the boarding house?'

'No,' he said, 'home to Scotland.'

And that was that, my first murder, The Braintree Incident.

That's how I killed Desmond Elkins.

Well after that, the phone didn't ring, did it? I'd created an incident that had unruly consequences and though the polis grudgingly accepted the apparent tit for tat justice that had been dispensed, the friends of Desmond Elkins didn't, and I was henceforth viewed as a liability to any prospective southern employer. Including, sadly, the Krays.

Even back in Glasgow, the reverberations affected me and I was never wholly forgiven by Billy for sullying his reputation with his estuary peers. All the same we'd rumbled on in a grudging sort of way for about a decade and a half before my outburst at Loch Lomondside made inevitable a parting of the ways. But I'm starting to repeat myself.

'You blundering cunt, Albert!'

Billy was standing with his slippers on, legs astride for added manliness, an empty glass in his hand. With a shock, I registered Old Joe Chisnall sitting on the sofa, balancing a teacup on his lap. He'd worn well for a corpse of fifteen years. 'You'll remember, Mr Chisnall,' said Mick, 'Young Joe?' Mick made an if-I-may-be-so-bold acknowledgement in the direction of the sofa.

'Hello, Joe,' I said, 'it's been a long time.'

I took a step forward, with my hand extended. I'd hoped for a spot of buddy punching, some joshing remarks about past misdemeanours, maybe even a canter through our mutual horsy tales, but no. Not-so-young Joe didn't even uncross his legs, nor pay me the respect of fiddling with his teacup out of awkwardness. The cunt just sat there, immobile, with a sort of vacant benign grin on his face, letting me know the lie of the land. Two men sat by the window with guns on their knees, like they were waiting to be interviewed for some position, possibly as men-with-guns-on-their-knees. I recognized them from Maxwell Road. Finally, when he was good and ready and I had egg all over my flushed Scottish fizzer, not-so-young Joe deigned to speak.

'Hello, Albert,' he said, 'you're looking well. Glad to see you've resisted temptation.'

'What temptation?'

'A goatee. The trade's gone goatee mad.'

'I've got an agreement with the goats,' I said, 'I don't wear their beards, they don't borrow my suits.'

'What's a goatee?' asked Billy Waugh.

'He's just fucking well told you,' said Mick, 'it's a beard.'

'Oh,' said Billy simply; a reaction that was all the more interesting for being an uncharacteristic under-reaction. 'Well we're not here to talk about fucking beards, are we?'

'Aren't we?' said Joe, puzzled. 'Oh dear, I thought I was here for the Facial Hair Conference, I'll just go.'

Mick laughed as Joe made to rise. Billy sort of tottered, looking more awkward than I felt. He was trying to hold centre stage but it was like trying to pick up the soap in a shower.

'Why don't we all get beards?' suggested Mick.

'Yes,' said Joe, 'let's all send out for beards, it'll be a fucking laugh!' And since he and Mick laughed like drains, I suppose it must indeed have been a fucking laugh, even without any actual sending out for beards. The cunts were hitting it off, Mick and Joe. With a single guffawing bound, Mick was forging the kind of rapport with a top estuary hooligan it had taken old Billy a lifetime of greetings-from-my-country politeness and gifts of wee kilted pipers to achieve. Billy then did a thing I'd never have thought him capable of, and I'd have thought him capable of most things, provided they were unpleasant. He played the sympathy card. He pitched forward, grabbing his knees and wheezing.

'You all right, Billy?'

'All right, Joe, I've not been well though. I've got cancer.'

'You haven't got fucking cancer,' said Mick.

'There's something growing in my lungs.'

'That's the mould from your fucking teeth, you've been told to get new ones.'

'Maybe,' said Billy, grudgingly, 'but I've definitely got fucking heart trouble.'

'Angina,' explained Mick. 'But he doesn't like it called that.'

'Angina's a wumman's disease,' said Billy, 'I've got heart trouble.' He waved his empty glass vaguely in my direction. 'And this fucker here, he's the cunt responsible!'

It only then occurred to me that everyone in the room was either toked up or pissed. They all looked at me.

'You've been a right arsehole, Albert,' said Mick.

'A blundering arsehole,' refined Billy. 'Running about chopping folk's heids off, it's fucking medieval! Who'd the cunt think he is, Henry the fucking Eighth?'

'Henry the Eighth invented the pole vault,' said Joe. 'Can you imagine?'

'He didn't.'

'He did.'

There was a brief hysterical pause while Mick and Joe imagined Henry the Eighth doing the pole vault. I'd have enjoyed imagining too, under other circumstances.

'You've gave me a lot of aggravation, Albert. You've ruined my fucking health.'

'The drink ruined your health, Billy, years ago.' I said.

Billy made a growling noise and, jerking forward, struck the glass in my face. Luckily it didn't shatter, being one of the good heavy lead-crystal glasses, for guests, and not the cheap wee fuckers with the pictures of Highland dancers that he normally used. I did hurt-dignity acting as I blotted blood from my gum with a crumpled Handy Andy. I was hoping he'd feel shame faced and back off but he didn't. His stiff finger jabbed me in the chest. 'I promised that fucking tart of a mother of yours I'd see you all right and haven't I been as good as my word?'

'Yes,' I said.

'There's many's a time I could have gave you a sore face with the greatest of pleasure, but I never raised my hand to you. Did I ever raise my hand to you?'

'Not till today, no,' I agreed.

'This is nothing, Albert,' said Billy Waugh. He was gleaming now, like the other Billy Waugh, he of the old habits that had kept him young for so long. I noticed Mick and Joe weren't laughing.

'Jumping about with that team of wee boys. Look at the fucking age of you. What happened to the wee boys?' He looked at Mick.

'Albert obliged us with his hammer,' said Mick.

'Young lives, tragically wasted,' clucked Billy. 'And all for your fucking vanity, ya blundering cunt. You gave me the fucking boak. You've always gied me the boak. Look at Braintree.'

He glared fiercely at Joe and I could tell he was looking at Braintree. In fact they both were. He'd been feeding Joe his cue. He took it.

'You know how it is, Albert,' he said. 'Sometimes debts go away with time and sometimes they don't. I'm sorry to say this one hasn't.'

'How'd you mean?'

'I'm retiring,' said Billy, cutting in. 'Blithering cunt here's taking over the show. He wants to start with a clean slate.'

Mick shrugged. 'There's no choice, Albert,' he said.

'The business is expanding. These blood feud efforts, they get in the way.'

Joe nodded. 'If it was up to us, Albert, we'd just give you a goatee and send you on your way.'

'But it's not up to us,' said Mick, hardy professional, biting his cheek against mirth. 'And there's a young man downstairs, who's waiting for his pound of flesh.'

'Downstairs,' I said, 'what downstairs?'

'Oh, we've got a basement now,' said Mick. 'Joe persuaded me to put one in.'

'Yes, every house should have a basement,' Joe said. 'I've had one in all my homes.'

I looked in a sort of blind panic towards Billy. But there was no Billy, just the empty space where Billy had been. From the kitchen I could hear the sound of sloshing glasses in the soapsuds. Joe was on his feet now and standing before me. He was very tall. He put out one of his great big hands. 'I'll shake your hand now, Albert,' he said. So I gave him my tiny little hand to shake, and we shook. I looked, in a sort of plaintive way, to Mick, who was now standing next to Joe.

'Mick,' I said.

But Mick didn't speak. He cleared his tubes with a snort and spat it into my face.

'I've waited a long time to do that, Albert,' he said.

It was then I felt my body stiffen with resistance as all the men in the room took me by my arms. 'Mick,' I heard my voice say, 'please.'

'Shut up, Albert,' said Mick.

'Let's go down,' said Joe.

And we did, we all went down to the basement.

Except it wasn't yet a working basement, as people

in my profession would understand the term. It had been a sort of granny flat for the Cuntess; one she'd been banished to after Billy had grown tired of poking her, the way he had with Mrs Billy One. Her furniture and kit were still packed in bin bags in the corner, pending a good clear out. Her picture was still on this old granny sideboard, a snap from years ago, with her looking what passed in them days for radiant. I asked for, and was granted, permission to turn it face down before they started.

'You know who I am,' said Jez, 'you know what I'm here for.'

'Yes,' I said. Though it wouldn't have mattered what I'd said. He'd been rehearsing these lines into his bedroom mirror since he was five and he wasn't going to rush them now.

'I'm here for my dad. You remember my dad?'

'Yes,' I said.

'Well,' said Jez Elkins, 'this is to make sure you don't forget him.'

And half a second later he'd given me a stripe; across the face; from cheek to chin; which, in over thirty years of professional mayhem, was something I'd always managed to avoid. And I sort of gasped, then crumpled, from the shock of it all. Next thing I was lying there taking the boot, trying to hold my face together and taking the boot, great thumping footwear, from an assortment of angles, I lay there taking it and holding on to my flapping face like it was a security blanket. And apart from the shock, which I've mentioned, and the pain, which goes without saying, I was sort of, well, mystified and startled to find myself in this position, me, a man who's paid to dish it out and who is having to lie there and just take it. And all of this was swirling around my head; the pain and the shock and the mystification, and it was all starting to get too much, trying to take the pain, those fucking boots and the face, which is flapping, and I started to hear a word coming out of my lips, a word I wouldn't ordinarily use, and neither probably would you, yet it bubbled up from somewhere inside me and I was saying it over and over again. 'Mercy,' I was saying, 'Mercy.'

I ask you, fucking mercy. I mean get a grip.

When they stopped booting, they took a break and lit up fags while they got their breath back. I watched them from the floor with what eyesight I had left. It was only when Jez Elkins put his fag down and picked up a cleaver that I started to, what's the word, whimper. I thought I knew what was coming. And I just hoped he was more of a surgeon than me.

*

I paint a bit now. Flowers and birds and that. It's something I started at the therapy class, to attune the hands. I find I'm more patient with wildlife than I used to be, in the old days I couldn't see the point of nature, just grow the animals in tins, save us all them fields, that was my attitude. Jez sent me my fingers in a jiffy bag about three weeks later. They'd gone past the stage of being black and shrivelled, instead they were white and shrivelled, too late for the medics to get stuck in with the microsurgery, but he knew that, it was just a spot of cruel theatre, meant to keep me in tears. I threw them in the wheely bin on my way to Whiteley's coffee bar for tea. I've been left a thumb and forefinger on each hand and the rest are just stumps cut off above the knuckles. My hammer-wielding days are over. I can't achieve a proper purchase on anything substantial, so my lifting powers are limited to delicate instruments, like say, a paintbrush, or a pencil or, luckily, a cock. Not just any cock, of course, my own dear, special, personal cock. Billy wouldn't permit me to be beheaded, on account of the sacred promise he'd made to my mother, the Cuntess. So I was humanely maimed by Jez Elkins. Since honour was satisfied all round, I suppose it was a victory for common sense.

All the same, I can't sit here and tell you I'm not a changed man. I am changed. It's that 'mercy' business. For the life of me, I can't work out what it meant. I can sit up till all hours having a good think, wondering where that word came from, though I suppose, since I said the fucker, it must have come from me. The Prick comes to stay with me now and then. He takes a Virgin Megadeal down from Glasgow Central and sleeps on the couch. He's in his element and hangs around Sussex Gardens by night. It tickles him that he can take off his wig on a hot day and yet nobody turns a hair. It was him who told me I should ring Felice. So I did. She wanted to meet for lunch but I couldn't face that, what with the stumps, and we made do with a long talk on the phone. She'd left her property developer boyfriend and married a wealthy fucker with a private zoo who bred lions from captivity. I worked out later she must have been betwixt and between on that Sunday she'd phoned me, so I suppose that was my window of opportunity if I'd wanted to win her back. But I'm not bothered. Which is to say I am bothered, but some things you've just got to live with, haven't you? Anyway, let her wealthy fucker have her, he's better equipped, he's used to holding tigers by the tail.

I got a get well card from Peter and Paul. Brenda had passed them my address. Turned out they'd been living a mellow Californian lifestyle in an apartment near Brighton Pier. I was disappointed by this, but they enclosed a gift of gloves, which at least reassured me there's still life somewhere, deep down, in those dark old dogs. They say they'll try and punt my paintings and stuff on the Internet, if I can learn to be a silver surfer. And Davie, he phoned a while ago. I asked him how he was getting on and he told me he was back with his wife and kiddy. When I asked him what happened to Craigie Wemyss, at first he wouldn't tell me. But I can coax Davie, what with me being me and him being him, and finally he said, 'I hit him with a hammer.'

'What, seriously?'

'Yes. You'll not tell anybody, will you, Albert?'

'Of course not,' I said.

And do you know what? My addled old heart felt a glow of quiet pride.

Things finish, but they don't end.

When all's said and done I've dreamed the Impossible Dream. Though I've ruined many lives, I've fulfilled myself.

That's entertainment.